Pity

Pity

J A M E S
B U X T O N

ORION

The right of James Buxton to be identified as the author of
this work has been asserted by him in accordance with the
Copyright, Designs and Patents Act 1988.

This edition first published
in 1997 by
Orion Books Ltd
Orion House, 5 Upper St Martin's Lane
London WC2H 9EA

A CIP catalogue record for this book is available
from the British Library

ISBN: 0 75280 471 5

Printed and bound in Great Britain by
Clays Ltd, St Ives plc

My thanks to Caroline Oakley for her close attention to my characters' characters; Sara Fisher for her enthusiasm throughout the writing of the story; Liane Jones for her support and Alix for intelligent questions and good advice.

1

This is my story. I lay it before you.

When I was nine my mother and father died and I was sent to live with my grandparents in Lincolnshire. When I was eleven my grandmother died, the year after that my grandfather, and I was put into an orphanage, supported in part by a small amount of capital.

At the orphanage I showed an aptitude for drawing and was apprenticed to a technical draughtsman in Nottingham and learnt that trade.

An illustrated history of art introduced me to the line, and first in pencil, then in ink, I copied diligently copies of the great masters. At the age of fourteen I saw my first oil painting – an imperfect copy of a Hogarth. I was almost physically excited by it.

At the age of fifteen I could turn out a competent pencil portrait, from sight and from memory. I copied pictures of nudes, changed their expressions and sold them to my friends.

At the age of sixteen I was spending every free waking hour at my canvas. All that limited me was the cost of materials and hours in the day.

At the age of eighteen I was asked by a local factory owner to paint his daughter.

I made the mistake of inviting her to adjust her dress, she told her father and misunderstandings followed. I was beaten badly by the factory owner, who had social pretensions, and by the technical draughtsman, my master, and cast out into the world. Like so many before me, I made my way to London.

All my life long a cold wind has been blowing. All I ever wanted was shelter. This is what happened to me. This is my story. Pity me.

2

I went to the meeting because I was cold and I was hungry and I was desperate. If I had not gone to the meeting, I would not have met Giles. If I had not met Giles, I would not have met Pity. If I had not met Pity, no one would have died. Perhaps I had better explain.

It was a political meeting arranged by an overprivileged socialist called Formby whose father owned a piano factory and let his son play poor man's friend. Formby had chosen to live in a flat above a Jewish rag man's shop in Clerkenwell, and liked to have artistic types, as he called them, in attendance to listen to his friends drivel on in their high-pitched, faked-up cockney whines. The meeting was on the subject *Whither Now The Workers?* For all that crowd knew, the workers could have been up their arses and they would still have been none the wiser, so it wasn't for truth or enlightenment that I was going. Nor did I want to meet other artists, for I hated other artists and the way they talked of the sublime, while all the time trying to steal a look at your canvas in order to judge whether you were important enough to despise or sufficiently insignificant to ignore.

No, I went to the meeting for three reasons: Formby would have coal and I could get warm there, he might have food so I might eat there, and there was the slimmest of chances that he might have dredged up a dealer who might in turn be prepared to see the work of an unknown artist.

There were two ways of succeeding as an artist: being accepted by the Royal Academy, or being taken up by a dealer. As far as I could see, neither way was possible for me.

I was twenty-two and destitute, my savings having already run out, and the Royal Academy Summer Exhibition, where if I were lucky I might be selected, and even luckier noticed, and luckier still bought, was still a number of months away. In the meantime I had more pressing worries, like how not to starve or freeze.

I had long since given up coffee, and tea, and tobacco, and any sort of drink. I could buy a bowl of stew for tuppence, and two stale baps for a farthing. Rushlight cost a penny farthing, but we still had some candles. I was almost out of paint, my brushes were worn, my jacket had cost sixpence from a flying dustman, and anyone in the whole wide world was happier and better off than me: the mush-faker, the pure finder, the bone picker and rag gatherers, the street orderlies and Ethiopian serenaders, the cat meat dealer, the cess pit and sewer men; even the Night Soil Thief of Camberwell, who according to the papers, was caught red-handed stealing suburban shit for 'his personal usage', was better off than me. At least he had been happy for a time.

That was the state I was in when I pushed open the door to Formby's lodgings and climbed the narrow stairs to his rooms.

I was enveloped by the smell of indoors on a cold day: camphor, wet tweed, smoking coal, sweat. Dark patterns on the wallpaper crawled to the cornice and there was a stain in the corner by the window which looked like a joint of meat. The crowd of faces, London grey, which is a base of porridge, an icing of black dust and a glaze of a sweat, and the tight, jostling press of bodies, did not oppress me so much as squeeze in on me from all sides, evenly, so that I felt like a bladder under water. Hunger made me light-headed. I thought I might faint, that the press would shoot my soul from my body like an apple pip between the fingers. I fought my way to a window where a thin draught of cold air trickled in and let it bathe my face.

Someone was saying that once those engaged in production exercised their right to control it, milk and honey would flow.

I listened; my heart sank. I thought of milk in cool, glazed earthenware jars, its surface yellow and heavy with cream. I thought of honey comb on a plate, the cells dripping with sticky, ochre nectar. I thought too long and my stomach groaned so loudly that I thought people must hear. All the faces around me were looking at the speaker, but on the other side of the room a man was looking at me.

He was tall, well-knit I would say, and easily the best dressed man there with a fine, black cut-away coat and a waistcoat of damask silk that was red like blood and a silk cravat that was white like milk. He made me feel my state all the more keenly: dirty, small, odoriferous. And even hungrier.

If he noticed this, he did not let it register. He merely raised his eyebrows and tipped his head dismissively at the speaker. I had the impression that he had probably tried to catch everyone's eye in that room; he had that air of bored, arrogant insouciance, and a desire in me to ape his superiority and seem worldly and wise made me shrug and roll my eyes in a derogatory sort of manner, all the time trying to think what it was about him that made him stand out, apart from his clothes, his whiskers, and his size. Then I realised. Looking at him was pleasant. I felt the sort of relief a man might feel on seeing a tree in the desert, or a ship in a featureless expanse of ocean, or a child playing contentedly in an empty street. He was a man who was happy in his skin.

He began to push his way through the crowd towards me. I was suddenly embarrassed, all the more so when he said, slightly too loudly: 'I'm as bored as sin, and I think you are too.'

His breath smelled of violets. I was disturbed by his attentions, by the way he leaned close to me. I found it hard to look at him at first. I smiled tightly and tried to move away. He held my arm.

'Come on,' he said. 'I've been watching you. You've got the mark on you.'

My heart began to beat more strongly.

'What do you mean?'

5

'You couldn't give a damn about all this. People like us – '

He stopped when a young man with a bulging forehead and centre-parted hair announced that he, too, had fellow feeling for the common man.

'Oh, for pity's sake!' my new companion said, loudly enough to be heard.

The man-of-feeling looked sharply in our direction. His eye wavered between the two of us. I could somehow *feel* my companion challenge him. His eye finally settled on me, as the weaker of the duo.

'You doubt my sincerity?' he said nastily.

I felt myself flush and answered: 'I said nothing,' then feeling myself belittled, added: 'Though in fact I do.'

'What? Do what?'

'Doubt your sincerity, or the use to which you put it. Words are cheap. I could tell you that I had feeling for the Lord of Araby, but what good does that do for him or me? Can he feel my feeling? And can you?'

A whisper, a sort of nervous flurry, went round the room, like a breeze passing over a field. I heard a couple of people mutter my name, as if in answer. The voice in my ear said: 'Bravo.' A devil on my shoulder.

'You would accept,' the man-of-feeling said, his voice a superior whine, face swinging round to exhort approval from the crowd, 'you would accept that actions proceed from feeling? And if that is the case, one's feelings, whether for the Lord of Araby or the Sultan of Timbuktoo, or more pragmatically for the oppressed, the downtrodden, the spat-upon of our own nation – ' his voice rose in a harsh bray, his face reddened ' – have a real bearing on one's actions?'

'I – ' But my confidence had suddenly waned. Words stuck in my throat. Then my companion said: 'I don't know about any of that but I'll accept that you bore like a weevil and bet that everyone else here thinks so too.'

Murmurs of 'Shame' and 'Far from it'.

He said: 'Insects, the lot of you.' Then I found myself being hustled out of the room and into the street, where the man began to laugh.

'Oh, come on,' he said. 'Cheer up.'

'But you can't just – '

'You can. You just did. You can do anything you like, Auguste Coffey.'

'How do you know my name?' I said sharply.

'Oh, I've been watching you. Asked people who you were. As I said, I know you're different, even if you don't. And what's more, with me by your side, you can eat.'

So we ate, or rather I ate. Giles knew a pub nearby which served what he called a creditable pie. Giles watched, fed me beer, heard me tell of my circumstances, prompted me to drink my beer, eat my mutton pie, take another plate. He was charming, solicitous, generous. He said he would visit me. I couldn't refuse.

At the end of the meal, at the moment of nervousness before he had paid, I asked him what he had meant when he said that I had the mark on me.

He answered me with another question: 'What are you after in your paintings?'

'Truth,' I said. It was a lie. Truth had been replaced by the exigencies of hunger. I would have done anything to eat.

'That is the mark,' he said.

3

It was cold that winter in London, and spring came late, and the cold stayed forever and nearly broke me.

Ice greased the smug ranks of cobble stones so they gleamed, and fog hugged us day in, day out, and along with the cold killed a lot of old people and young people. You heard them coughing, then raving, then coughing, then the coughing stopping and the dying starting. Dying never properly stops because when you are dead, you are dead forever. I felt I was dying from the inside out.

I was almost always cold, even in bed. I could not afford a fire and my conscience, such as it was, stopped me from burning the coal bought by Paul Frederic, who shared my meagre lodgings, unless he was in. I stole a chair from an unoccupied room downstairs, and burned it, but the sight of the flames going out depressed me more than the brief warmth had cheered me. I like a fire.

I had been so close on so many occasions – so close to painting the picture I knew I could, to attracting the dealer I knew I needed. But each time my poverty-stricken condition had intruded: pictures spoiled through poorly prepared canvases and bad paint; weeks of work lost through ill health brought on by living in wretched surroundings; a miraculous opportunity to meet a man who liked my work enough to seek out my address – lost when one knee of my trousers disintegrated with a faint sigh as I knelt at his front door to brush the dust off my shoes. Too ashamed to be seen in rags, I ran back to my lodgings where I wrote a hasty, lying note about a sudden illness in the family and, expressing my intense regret at my unavoidable absence, begged for another meeting at the same time on Thursday. No answer. No more chances. Just a steadily worsening struggle as my strength gave out.

It was made worse by the way I had come to resent the close proximity of Paul, even though I could be warm only when he was present. Due to him, I felt that my days were no longer truly my own, and at the same time I was being sliced apart by bad memories, fragments like shards of broken mirror, each one carrying a shameful scene on its false, slick surface, each one bearing its sharp little cargo of cold.

So I was in the habit of going wherever I could to keep warm.

A list of places to keep warm in London for free.

One: on the back of a cess-pit wagon.

Two: behind the bakery in Wardrobe Court.

Three: in a public house or coffee house before being caught sponging and kicked out.

Four: the stables behind the Old Cock Inn of Ludgate Circus where I knew the lad.

Five: the National Gallery.

Six: the new underground stations, if you could bear the smoke, and the thought that the heat was caused merely by the press of bodies and held by the earth.

I once tried the Rotherhithe tunnel to get out of the wind, but when I walked down the great, circular, clanking stairway it was colder down there than on top, a terrible sort of cold, and frightening with the mighty river so heavy and mobile a few feet above my head, and some of it sliding down the walls.

There's a painting, you may have seen it, of a great banquet held in the tunnel the day it was opened, just twenty-five years ago. Today the arches and alcoves shelter whores and robbers. The place stinks of dirt and piss and damp and gas lamps. In other words, it has been Londonised. I ran from it because in it I saw my own future.

9

4

Our lodgings overlooked the river. They were low-ceilinged and dismal, the attic of what once had been a factory for making naval blocks. But the business had gone bankrupt and the building had been partitioned into rooms. You paid extra for a window. In our case we had a window but not much roof, the two factors cancelling each other out. A wide, unstable leaded window stretched almost the width and height of the room we called our studio. The uncovered floor was of bare thin boards that gave as you walked on them. It was freezing in winter, sweltering in summer. Six storeys below us the Fleet ditch carried half of London's filth into the deeper filth of the Thames. From the window the river resembled iridescent, soiled jelly. It crawled to the sea and crawled back again. It looked like old meat and stank of far worse.

At that stage in my life, had you asked me, I would have said that I saw myself in two ways: earner and artist. Pressed further, I would have admitted that the artist I saw as a sort of heroic figure; the earner as a base, worn, sluggish and squalid figure, crawling in the muddy gutter with hand outstretched, biting the shoes of those who tossed him pennies.

How did I earn? The wage slave turned out engravings of popular paintings, as often as not taken from other engravings, for a printer called Batty, who specialised in occasional cards. He had spotted a rare talent in me: I would do almost anything for money. The wage slave had copied Holman Hunt's *Light of the World* and John Everett Millais's *Order of Release*. He had copied Bellini Madonnas, and portrait after portrait of Victoria and Albert. He was sometimes asked to compose his own scenes: fir trees with snow were proving popular around Christmas time, following the German custom of bringing a whole tree into the house. His darkest hour had been when Mr Batty, on hearing somehow that he was a *real* artist, had asked him to compose something moving and sensitive for the 'bereaved' market. He had drawn a depressed dog lying at the foot of a cot and had captioned the picture:

YEA! E'EN THE LITTLE DOGGY WEEPETH
NOW HIS TINY MASTER SLEEPETH

Mr Batty had been delighted and had asked for more like it. Now the wage slave had almost finished adapting a Landseer spaniel (better than the original, in his opinion), to be incorporated into another death scene:

ALONE AND SAD THE HOUND AWAKETH
LO! DEATH HIS MASTER'S SOUL NOW TAKETH

The engraving tools, handles buffed to a soft gleam by use, were laid out on the table top. I would not be paid until I had finished, but I could not bring myself to finish.

Auguste Coffey, artist, had two pieces of work in progress. One he painted by day, the other by night. For the Pre-Raphaelite Brotherhood had said that the painter should only paint what he saw, and if a night scene were attempted, the artist had to render the colours of night *by* night. It was the way to truth, the only way to start. There was something moral in the crusade. Yes, Auguste the Artist thought that he was moral.

His night-time painting was called *The Vigil*. It showed a page boy kneeling in a chapel, the whole scene lit by moonlight entering through a broken lancet window (background, high, left), and two altar candles (centre, left and right of page's head). The perspective had gone wrong at an early stage but he had just discovered that by shading under the page's knees, he could produce the effect of the boy hovering. He realised that Dante

Gabriel Rossetti, who had never grasped the basics of perspective, had stumbled on the same effect in his *Annunciation*.

It was a narrative picture. A woman's tearful face at the vestry door, the ruined castle glimpsed through the broken window, the flowers tied with a violet ribbon (for constancy, he thought, but would have to check) lying crushed beneath his armoured knee – all these showed how devotion to a higher cause bore with it a high price. That was the idea anyway. The painting was a vehicle to show off his technical mastery. Sometimes he thought it too derivative; sometimes not derivative enough.

His day-time picture was called *Pandora's Box*. It was simpler and showed the influence of Rossetti even more clearly than the flagstones of *The Vigil*. Pandora, heavy-lidded, raven-tressed, with interesting, curved lips, looks straight at the viewer. In her hands is an elaborately carved box which is open a crack. Light, streaming up from the box, fans her hair into raven wings. Her expression is poised between horror and delight. She knows that what she has done is wrong, but cannot stop herself. Behind her a rural landscape can be glimpsed through a window, where a shepherdess watches her sheep, unaware that a ruffian is moving stealthily across the fields towards her. I was too poor to afford a model and had based the face on my own. My face is striking, although most do not notice it; poverty has a way of making people invisible in this world. I am small – stunted, some would say – although I am well proportioned. People think me younger than I am.

I turned to my work. I had set up an altar at the other end of the room for *The Vigil*. I lit the stubs of the candles, and stood back, examining the play of shadows on the folds of the cloth, the fraying at the ends of it, admiring my own treatment of it. I looked at my brushes, pathetic, worn down almost to the ferrule, cheap to begin with and used beyond their meagre life span. Every time I used them I was aware that I was speeding the day when I could not use them any longer. I was like a man on a spent horse, desperate to reach his destination. Does he go fast, tire his horse sooner by having covered more ground? Or does he go slow, tire his horse later, but make less distance? Or does it make absolutely no difference whatsoever? Should we just give the horse its head and let fate do the rest?

Fate is a luxury for people who can pay the rent. Sometimes I would dream of new brushes. A sable filbert; a sable round; a new bristle flat; a sable flat. Two of each! Half a dozen of each! And as for the paints, even the words excited me: carmine, madder, umber, barium, peach black, Davy's grey, cobalt blue, litharge, alizarin crimson, verdigris, cerulean, ultramarine. I could chant myself into an ecstatic trance, given the time, although I knew the risks. As soon as the daydream ended, the sick panic would rise in my throat and I would regret that I had ever tempted myself with the promise of so much.

I looked at my palette, at the cracked and withered tubes. I looked at my rag, a scrap of one of my landlady's sheets which I had begun to use when I started *The Vigil*. It was now a stiffening, irresolute mess. That was the way of all life, of all colour: to return to earth, a muddied brown, with all brightness, all goodness, and all promise gone.

'Oh, Auguste, you're back.'

On cue, Paul. With my back to my friend, I closed my eyes and made a face. I clenched my fist around the haft of my brush and tried to make it hurt. I didn't want to turn around and see him standing there like a wary but eager schoolchild in his nightshirt and with his fair, thinning hair sticking up in an oily cockscomb, ready, now that he had dragged himself from his warm bed and dashed cold water on his face, to start one of his interminable conversations with me while I sweated over my work. I didn't want to talk. I didn't want to. Didn't want to!

Paul had been the model for the knight, when I started, when I could look at him without wincing. Since he had stopped posing for it, night after night on his knees with the damp, cold Thames air sending his white skin into goose pimples, I had little by little changed every feature: thickening the hair, turning the button nose thin and aquiline, widening

13

the mouth. How had we talked so much? How had I seen in his ineffectual ways and his puppy-like devotion a model for innocence and loyalty? We had talked, but we hadn't talked. We had been as children, one mimicking the other, or, if we disagreed on some incredibly abstruse point of aesthetics, sulking like babies for a day, two days, until one would clumsily concede the point, or bring a gift, or make a gesture of reconciliation, each sucking the nipple of the other's weakness.

'I didn't wake you. I thought you might have wanted to sleep,' I said.

Paul blushed. 'I wanted your advice, I seem to have painted myself into a corner.'

The same joke he had made two weeks before: his easel stood in the opposite corner of the room. I walked across the floor, letting my irritation show – legitimately, for if he had asked me if I was angry, I could have pointedly said that I was preparing to work. At the same time I was happy to demonstrate my own superiority.

Paul too was painting a medieval scene by candlelight: *The Death of Arthur*. The dying king looked like melting marzipan; Sir Bedivere was out of proportion and anyway looked like a costermonger; Excalibur had developed an odd kink halfway down the blade; the chapel walls were a virulent orange – Paul's notion of candlelight – and the lake a messy splurge of greeny-grey. The painting was an irredeemable mess and Paul could not accept it.

'It's the play of light on the blade, Gussie. I just can't seem to *see* it.'

I touched the paint with a finger nail. It was dry. Paul could not have worked on the picture for days. On the window sill lay a long, blunt flensing knife that he used for Excalibur's model.

'I see nothing wrong,' I said.

'You must. The moonlight . . .'

'Ah, yes, the moonlight.'

'As we discussed, you must remember? The moon is pouring

14

her beams through the gaping roof of the lonely chapel. Her light is playing in fractured glints on the sombre surface of the lake. It flickers on the notched edge of the dying king's weapon.'

Did he have to talk like that? Dear God, I supposed I did too.

'We were going to learn from each other, weren't we?' I continued.

'Why, yes,' Paul said.

'My candlelight, your moonlight.'

I very pointedly looked out of the window, at the black fog. Somewhere on the river a lighterman's bell tolled three times. Stopped. Started again. A voice shouted hoarsely.

'Oh, hang it,' Paul said. 'Am I a fool? No wonder the effect was going wrong. Only paint from nature.'

'And when the moon does shine, we'll lay a knife out on the ledge, study it, and then see who'll be able to bring off the effect.'

I felt my stomach turn as I talked, the lie bitter within me. Why couldn't I say that his painting was terrible?

'I shall watch you paint,' he said happily. 'Shall I read to you?'

I badly wanted to paint but the thought of Paul reading Tennyson to me in his parson's voice put me off. 'I was thinking I should finish the spaniel,' I said.

'How is it going?'

I tilted the metal plate at him and smiled bitterly.

'I feel so bad about this,' he said.

'What? What do you have to feel bad about?'

'I feel bad that you have to do such demeaning work. I feel that I should be able to – '

'Paul, for the love of God, I am not a child. I don't need supporting. I'll pay my way – fifty-fifty, as we agreed.'

He raised an eyebrow. I was already regretting my outburst. My gratitude – my manufactured gratitude – was all he had. But I could not bring myself to utter the customary words of thanks, because I could not bear Paul's simpering reply: that he considered me an investment. I was stupid to have unleashed my frustrations.

'Oh,' he said consideringly. 'Fifty-fifty. Well, I've paid another month's rent, so that's – '

'I haven't got it, and you know it.'

'Well, I'll leave you to your work then so you can earn it. Oh, by the way, where were you this evening?'

'Not spending money,' I said. 'I went to a meeting in that oaf Formby's rooms. Why weren't you there?'

'You said we were to meet at the National Gallery beforehand and then go on.'

I remembered; he was right. I frowned and said: 'Really, I don't remember saying that. Well, if that really were the case, I'm sorry but in all honesty it's the first I've heard of it. What did you do?'

'Tim waited with me some of the time, then had to go. So I waited until closing, and then waited outside, and then came back here.'

Tim Brownlow was Paul's other friend and a better one than I. He was a predictable, priggish journalist, and an even more predictable and priggish art reviewer. He treated me with disdain and I hated him. I was determined not to give Paul another hook on which to hang his reproach. 'Well, at least that's given Brownlow even more cause to dislike me! Seriously, though, you should have come on to the meeting,' I said airily. 'You would have seen me thrown out.'

'Thrown out?' He was genuinely shocked.

'Yes, some pompous little fool started mouthing on about his feeling for the proletariat and I let him know what I thought.'

'And you were thrown out for that?'

'Not exactly. Another fellow joined in. Interesting chap. We put the wind up that lot, I can tell you.'

'That lot happen to be my friends.' Paul's voice was sullen and petulant. 'This doesn't sound like you talking.' He walked

16

to his canvas and squinted at it. 'Who was this new man you were thrown out with, by the way?'

'A surgeon, as a matter of fact. Giles Bouverie.'

'Bouverie, a surgeon? He's a beast and a wastrel who lives off his father's money.'

'Rich, is he?'

'Bouverie's Moonlight Soap,' Paul said, with all the disdain of a pauper. 'Soap money.' He turned to his painting again, then with a loud sniff went back to bed.

5

It was a strange, dry, mild day, a brief foretaste of spring, when Giles Bouverie came to see me for the first time.

Paul was out, working on a watercolour of London from Hampstead Heath. Giles walked in without knocking, grinned, tapped the ceiling with his fingers (his head almost scraped the plaster), and said delightedly: 'By God, a real artist in a real garret. I must have read about you in a book. But what's this' He had picked up *Pandora's Box* and was studying it. 'This yours?'

'Yes, but – '

'I like this.'

'It's nothing. Just a sort of dream. This, on the other hand – '

'It's very striking. Who's the model?'

'It's me, as a matter of fact.'

'You? Well, well. What's this other one?'

I stood back and showed him *The Vigil*. He was polite, but non-committal.

Then he spotted Paul's painting. He grimaced.

'That's not you, is it?' he said.

'No.'

'It's awful.'

'It's not. It represents a year's hard work. If you only – '

He pulled such a comic face at me that I laughed, although I tried not to for Paul's sake.

'If your life depended on it, is it good?' he asked.

I was still laughing, although I did not fully understand why. 'No,' I said.

'Your life still depends on it. How bad is it?'

'It's awful.'

'Is it truly awful?'

'It is truly awful. Awful.'

Relief, pure relief, blessed relief, washed through me. Betraying Paul had carried me across the bridge and taken me to Goshen. Giles dotted his tears of laughter with a handkerchief and pulled another terrible face: 'Is it as bad as this?'

'Worse!'

I was bent double with mirth.

'As this?'

'Worse.'

And so it went on. No real reason for our laughter, nothing we said was truly funny. We were not laughing out of cruelty – that was incidental. We laughed because we had started laughing, and once we had started, it felt fine, and so fine that we wanted to laugh some more. As I say, there was nothing cruel about it, it was just that Paul happened to be in the way.

The sheer joy engendered by this new friendship overtook me like a storm. We seemed to leap over the normal, halting formalities of social intercourse. Our talk escalated like a fire, an edifice of flame: a flickering architecture of intellect and passion that was both ephemeral and solid, and consuming, and brilliant, and warming, and exhilarating. Such talk burned up time, discomfort, self-consciousness, and old ideas. It engendered, from the heat, a constant phoenix stream of new ideas, passions, everything.

We talked of what we knew and much we didn't: of art, of nature, of aestheticism and morality, of John Ruskin whom I revered and Giles thought mad, of empires, and soldiers, of passions and fears, of Keats and Coleridge.

Giles suggested we go out to look for a place to eat. We linked arms, quite instinctively, and such physical intimacy, and his ease with it, only seemed to affirm his self-confidence and manliness. We walked parallel to the river down the narrow streets that squeezed between the high, blind warehouse walls.

To our left alleyways sloped down to the river, where the masts of the shipping made a stark black cross-hatch of angles against the usual smoky, blood-red-and-orange London evening sky.

'Art is mostly a matter of persistence,' I said. 'People talk about urges and impulses and the muse. But it's persistence that drives us on – persistence that makes the baby cry for milk, or the fox gnaw off its leg to escape a trap. That was what stopped me from staying a clerk to a technical draughtsman for the rest of my life. That was why I begged and wheedled the fine arts tutor to accept me into his school. That was why I drew nothing but plaster casts of plaster casts of plaster casts of broken Grecian statues for three years. But perhaps you'd have to be an artist – a practical, practising artist – to know that.'

'Surgeons – ' Giles began.

'Surgeons! What chance do you have to turn your experience into anything?' I rejoined. 'You are trained, then you perform. There is no chance to create. Any deviation from the rule would spell disaster.'

'And truth? Where does that come in?'

'I follow the Pre-Raphaelites,' I said. 'To paint truthfully, one must paint what one sees. One must cast aside convention and search for something good, and true, and faithful. In truth, one must copy nature, not other artists.'

'The Pre-Raphaelite brotherhood?' Giles was all mock incredulity. 'Prigs, cocksmen, coxcombs and self-publicists! Millais wanted to further his career, Hunt joined up because no one else would have him, and Rossetti was after the girls and thought it sounded better to be part of a brotherhood than a greasy-haired foreigner who wanted to roger his models. The initials PRB . . . you know they signed their early work like that? In Rossetti's case it stood for "Penis Rather Better".'

He was roaring with laughter, one arm slung over my shoulder. I twisted away from under it, feeling sick.

'That's not – '

'Oh, dear,' Giles said. 'Oh, dear. Don't say you didn't know?

Oh, you didn't. Well, you shouldn't have tried that dig at surgeons. We're artists too, you know.'

'So you were just getting even with me?'

'If you want, Auguste, if you want.' But there was an edge to his voice. 'So here's a dilemma,' he continued, his voice calmer. 'Which one of your two paintings is the most true: *The Vigil* or *Pandora's Box*?'

'I would say *The Vigil*. It has more observation.'

'And I would say *Pandora's Box*. It has more honesty.'

'But *The Vigil* is a painting about beauty,' I said, 'and morality, and how both spring from sacrifice and self-denial. Perhaps not things that someone like you would know about.' I was nettled by what I saw as his arrogance.

'Denial? You think I do not know about self-denial?' He took a step towards me; he seemed to loom, grown suddenly taller and wider than before.

Something had changed. Cobbled streets; the sound of coughing in a doorway; the smell of piss and rotting fruit and horse dung; darkness creeping through alleys like a thief's shadow; the vastness of the city out of sight. But instead of being mere backdrop, I felt it engage with Giles, with me, as if we were in a melodrama and the music swelling to a crescendo. I was unaccountably frightened, not so much by any sense of physical danger but more because I was seeing how things could suddenly change, and in that change grow worse.

'Giles, step back. You're scaring me.'

'Am I? And is that any reason for me to stop?'

'Yes. What are you doing?'

He placed a hand on my chest. It seemed to cover it. He pressed me against a wall.

'Truth, Auguste. What is my nature?'

'Your nature?'

'Is that not something that interests you? Or am I just a means to an end for you?'

'What end?'

'A meal here and there. A little light diversion from your miserable life.'

'No, Giles.'

His face was close to mine. I could smell mutton fat on his breath.

'So how far will you allow me to know you?'

'No, Giles. No. This was so . . .' I searched for a word. 'It was so easy. It was so right. And now you're spoiling it.'

'What do you want? What do you want from me?' he asked.

'Your friendship. Not your meals, not your . . . money.'

'Nothing else. Not excitement? Not new experiences? Are you really content – ?'

It was too much for me. I ducked, and twisted out of his grasp. I heard him swear. I ran. Behind me I heard him call: 'Auguste, come back. I'm sorry. Sorry . . . Come back!'

But I was gone.

I crashed into our attic, sweating like a horse. Paul, who had been lying on the sofa, rose.

I stood still, suddenly aghast at what I had done. I saw Paul, his face red with relief. I saw the awful squalor of our rooms. I was so shocked that breath refused to come, and Paul, mistaking my emotion, rose, and took me in his arms, and tried to comfort me.

6

I woke the next morning feeling scoured; sore, but clean and empty, and my mind working in a way I had not anticipated. Truth. How could I say I was a seeker after truth if, when confronted with it, I ran? I had been so confident in my little world, so sure that my hunger, my sacrifice, would somehow communicate themselves through my painting and consequently elevate it. Now, confronted with it, I had run without even finding out truly what Giles had meant.

Within two days my old life with Paul settled down to the same mean placidity with one difference: I now had something to compare it to. But while in the past Paul had seemed merely irksome at times, now he was insupportable. Or perhaps I have placed the emphasis wrongly. In the past I had been able to stand him for most of the time; but now I could not stand him at all. I had changed, he had not.

How boring my life was, how smug! How certain I'd been that I was right to live the way I did. But suppose I was wrong? Suppose a lifetime of abstinence and discipline was not the right way to creative heaven? Suppose I needed to live, to be burned by a cold sun, numbed by burning winds. I looked at *Pandora's Box* with new eyes. Was *this* the way? Was it possible now to go back to my old, cramped routine? Might I need excitement in my life?

Then there were other questions, other doubts. Did Paul know he had no talent? No. Had I ever told him? No. So how could I be sure that *I* had talent? Because people told me? Suppose they had lied as I had lied? What then? To die unknown, unfulfilled, miserable, never having lived at all? To die never having known excitement?

Paul sensed a struggle going on in me and wisely said nothing, but even that silence seemed pregnant with restraint. At meals he talked bravely of people *he* had seen, *his* work, *his* dreams, while I ground my teeth and tried to avoid his eyes. I made an effort. I tried, and when I really tried I could see how decent he was, how upright, how clean and untainted, but it was always an effort. I was spoiled. I needed more than this.

And then Giles came.

The first I knew of it was Paul's voice in the doorway, quavering.

'I don't think we want you here. You are not welcome. I said, you are not – '

But by then Giles was past him, and I had turned, and he had spread his hands and said: 'What can I say but that I am sorry?'

And I had no more dissimulation left. I had lied so much to Paul that my heart was sick of it. I looked at Giles and said: 'And so you should be.' But in my heart, I added: *But I am glad to see you*, and let it show in my eyes.

I felt the attention of both men on me, and it was as if I was caught in two beams of light. Where they crossed, there was I. It was the strongest sensation of being I had ever had in my life. Neither of them knew what was in my heart; no one knew but me. And that knowledge gave me pleasure.

'I want you to come and live with me.'

I stopped dead. Time froze and congealed. I saw that we were in a small square. Droplets of fog on my eyebrows; droplets of fog on Giles's cashmere scarf. I took my bearings. The taste of smoke on my tongue; the cold; the flare and hiss of gas lamps; the way our footsteps sounded both sharp and muffled; a fur of moisture on black assegai railings; lights between curtains, in areas, glinting faintly on wide front doors like deep and distant memories.

'Auguste? Are you all right?'

'Yes.'

'I would like you to come and live with me. I would like to be – of help to you. I think you need a patron. I think then your talent would blossom.'

I was so startled that I could not reply.

'It wouldn't be – Damn it, why don't you answer me?'

Shock followed the excitement, a sort of counter reaction. Canniness overcame me, a desire to play a dead bat, not to appear too excited. But underpinning it all that sense that if he really meant it, my life would change and I might be transformed into the creature I'd always thought I was.

'Why should I trust you?' I asked.

'What, after I frightened you? Auguste, you were scared to find yourself wanting something else. You live a life of such meanness that the thought of its opening up terrifies you. I can understand that, but you must too. You allowed me into your life, admit it, in order to learn, in order to expand your own miserable horizons. Come on. It is the truth.'

I was silent.

'Well, you do not deny it at any rate.'

'And you?'

'I'm your friend, Auguste,' he said energetically. 'I wouldn't do anything to hurt you or your career.'

We walked on.

'It would involve a place to stay,' he said. 'And a studio. It would be conditional on your accepting that. There. It's hardly conventional, but that shouldn't bother an artist. I could – I mean, I should be happy to offer you financial support as well.'

Time measured in the tap of our heels on the pavement, in the thud of a distant engine, in the warm slap of my heart in my chest.

'Come on,' Giles said. 'Yes or no. All I want is a simple answer.'

'Then yes,' I said. And I knew it was right because it was as if a skylight had been opened and I was flooded with sunshine.

25

We passed out of the square, which was oddly silent, through an empty, darkened back street and on to a wide, busy thoroughfare where crowds were pouring out of a theatre, standing on the pavement in groups, spilling into the crowded road that seemed blocked by cabs, horses steaming in the cold. It was better lit here. There was lamplight from open shops; a harsher light from the theatre. As we walked, people came at us in flurries – people like us, ambling through the night. A child whore, ten years old with the eyes of a crippled soldier, pouted at me, whispered something in my ear that I missed, then turned her attention to Giles. He bent, listened, threw back his head and laughed, then cuffed it away. The crowd tried to flow between us, and he took my arm.

'I was thinking about a commission. Of course, you'll have to see the room but I thought a mural would look fine in there: something suitable. *The Canterbury Tales* perhaps. Did you know the pilgrims started from Bermondsey?'

'Bermondsey?' I said in some surprise. The place was notorious. After all the badness in London had been strained through the rookeries of the west end and east end, the residue settled in a rancid mass in Bermondsey.

'Near St Thomas's and Guy's, the teaching hospitals,' he said. 'Just over London Bridge. Of course, Keats trained as a surgeon there. Perhaps – '

'Don't say *The Eve of St Agnes*,' I said. 'It's been done to death.' Then, suddenly remembering, 'Of course, if you want . . .'

'No, no, whatever you . . .' Giles said, almost embarrassed. Then, more decisively: 'The theme is your choice. Think on it. Give it some time.'

And I did think on it, but not in the way that he meant. And I did realise that this was the first time our respective positions had affected our relationship. It seemed a riddle why it should, and like all riddles it had the simplest answer, but it was not until later that I discovered it.

'There is a problem,' I said.

'What is that?'

'Paul. This will hurt him.'

'Hurt him? You vain thing!'

'It's not that. It's – '

'Paul's big enough to look after himself.'

'I know, it's just – '

'Do you have an agreement?'

'Not as such,' I said, knowing the answer to be much more complicated. I had lived off Paul's generosity for the past eight months, and within his narrow limits, he had never stinted. His father, a greengrocer from Hertfordshire, a mild, misty little man, tremulously proud of his son's talent yet terrified lest he lose him to art, paid him an allowance. Paul had given himself three years to succeed. If by the end of that period he had received no encouragement, he would join his father's business.

'He helps me,' I said. 'If I were not there, he would be much better off.'

Giles squeezed my arm. 'Exactly,' he said. 'Frederic is a decent fellow, even if his greens are grey and reds brown. I like him. But I think your friendship with him must stand the separation, or be no friendship.' He lowered his voice. 'To tell you the truth, I don't think you've been the best influence on poor Freddy. He's got no future in painting. There's no spark there. You are the influence dragging him on, as the moon drags the sea, but you must see that his work is going nowhere, whereas yours . . . I'll be frank. I've heard people compare you to Millais. I know I have said some dismissive things about artists, but not where you are concerned.'

I flinched, flushed. I felt oppressed by the preposterousness of the statement even as it strummed my vanity like a harp. Millais was the greatest artist of the day. Before he had run off with Ruskin's wife, the famous critic had called him 'the greatest Englishman since Turner'.

We walked on, through Trafalgar Square, not saying much.

27

All that had happened between us that night made the last hour or so of our time together uncomfortable. We parted when Giles hailed a cab. I walked back to my rooms in Blackfriars. And to Paul.

7

Paul was still awake. He had banked up a fire in the grate and was warming some milk in a pan over it.

He looked up, the firelight making his face glow.

'Thank you,' he said. 'Thank you for taking that dreadful man out of our home.'

I said nothing, but squatted in front of the fire and extended my hands.

'He had to come, didn't he? Had to come and try and twist the knife. He's a . . . a blackguard. He's the worst kind of man. Tim says he's nearly been thrown out of the medical school on countless occasions for his insolence and laziness. Not only that, Tim's found out that he lives alone attended by a housekeeper who is too young for it to be respectable. If you had not taken him away, I don't know what I would have done.'

I looked around the garret: at the crumbling walls, at the gaps between the boards loosely tacked under the roof slates. A month ago I had woken up with snow on my blankets.

'Brownlow's been busy,' I said. 'He probably thinks Giles and I are well matched. As a matter of fact, Giles has made me an offer.'

'Trying to buy your affection now? It's too easy for him, isn't it? He'll never know what it's like to struggle through. For a painting, was it? For *Pandora's Box*? No? *The Vigil*? I didn't think he had the taste. You know how much I admire it. Not that I don't think that *Pandora's Box* is good. It's just – I'm forgetting. Did you accept?'

His voice was just broken noise. It made me confused.

'What?' I asked.

'The offer. *The Vigil*. Can we drink to your first major sale?'

He'd had a bottle that he had been saving for a moment such as this, a good claret. I knew it was good because I had drunk it one evening when I was bored and yearning for company. Paul had said nothing at the time. My mind cleared. In that moment I was resolute.

'Actually it's a broader offer than that.' I picked my words with care.

'A commission?' Paul's voice was hesitant. 'God knows, no one deserves it more than you. No one is happier than I that you have won the race. Of course, it shouldn't come from Bouverie, but that's the artist's lot, our discipline.'

'It involves the possibility – Giles has a spacious house, I believe, and a studio. The studio has northern light and is thirty feet long.'

'Is he talking of an exhibition?'

Then, as soon as the words were out of his mouth, he knew it could not be so.

'The arrangement. That is . . .'

There was a pause. I managed one look at Paul's face and knew that he understood. One look showed me a mask of sorrow and reproach and hurt. If only I could imagine him hurting me like this, I thought, not out of a sense of kindness but just to assuage my guilt.

'I understand perfectly,' he said coldly. 'Of course. It was stupid of me, perfectly idiotic.' His head sank between his hunched shoulders and he began to lose control. 'Oh, but how can you trust him? He is a beast! He will spoil you . . .'

I put my hand on his shoulder. He knocked it away.

'He will spoil you . . . spoil you! Stay with me, Auguste. Stay, for your own sake.'

'Oh, for God's sake, stop being such a choir boy.' I had meant to show him nothing but patience and forbearance but found that I could tolerate him no longer.

'I thought you were my friend,' he said.

30

'As I am. I am your friend.'

'Not if you go with him.'

'But I'll still be your friend. You can see me whenever – '

'Don't pity me!' he howled, and kept his mouth open to draw in air.

'Well, what can I do?' I asked. 'If you behave so – I cannot stay.'

'Don't spare me, I beg you,' he sneered. 'Mr High and Mighty. One whiff of a wallet and you're off! What have I to offer?' He stood in front of me and spread his arms. He was a pitiful sight, his nose red and eyes tearful. 'Look at me. What do you see? What can I, someone like me, possibly offer a great man like you? Tell me, what do you see? Don't spare me. I need to know.'

'All right. I see nothing but a jealous … brat,' I said, 'unwilling to share in another's good fortune.'

Paul stopped howling and stared at me, aghast. 'Unwilling to share? *You* accuse *me* of being unwilling to share? Oh, I know that you despise me but – what have I been doing these past six months but sharing what little I have with you? And in return for what? Something I thought was friendship but see now was scorn. Who has paid the rent? Who buys the candles and the food? Unwilling to share … Who talks? Who tries to inspire? Who has sacrificed? You can't do it!' he screamed.

'And you can't paint! Not only that, you smother me with your neediness. I can't even breathe with you around. It's like having a baby round my ankles.'

'A baby? Me the baby? You can't even keep yourself! How can you say that I've smothered you when I've been supporting you these last six months?'

'Don't bleat on about sacrifice when it was freely given. Support? How can you have been supporting me when the need was all yours? You *wanted* this. You *wanted* to support me. You all but begged me, and in the end your pitiful self-abasement has come to revolt me. The need was all yours and I'll prove it by going. Then we'll see who needs whom.'

He stared at me, standing quite still, as if he had not believed that so much hurt could exist in all the world. Then he shook his head and began again.

'I won't let you leave.'

'What?'

'You owe me too much. You haven't paid me back. I won't let you suck me dry and just pass on.'

'How can you stop me?' I asked.

'Like this!'

He threw himself at my feet, wrapping his arms around my legs. Taken by surprise, I lost my balance and fell. Paul crawled on top of me and started pummelling me.

'You must stay,' he cried.

'You can't stop me leaving,' I shouted back.

'Stay!'

'You cannot stop me.'

We were fighting weakly in front of the fire, spent before we started. He reached behind him for the poker. That shifted his weight from my shoulders and I wriggled out from under him, and found my feet. He stayed on his knees, as if I were still between them, then began to hit the floorboards with the poker as if I were still there. Even in his rage he was pathetic.

'You cannot stop me leaving,' I said.

He looked up at me, his face dull with tears and blurred with snot. I kicked him and kicked him, and as I kicked him the words made a rhythm in my head: You cannot stop me leaving. You cannot stop me leaving. You cannot stop me leaving.

I tired quickly: I was weak. Paul was still. I carried him to his bed and laid him on it, then went to mine and shivered myself to sleep.

8

Mild air. An almost spring-like day. Looking at the garret through sleep-blurred eyes, listening for Paul, hearing nothing and hoping he had gone out, then the sudden heart-bursting gush of happiness. Free! Sleep sluicing from me in a sudden, shocking torrent; a new world emerging from its shell. Colours brighter. Air softer. My body miraculously lighter. My mind blessedly clearer. The past is back there, a tangled and barren landscape, while in front the future stretches along a wide, noble avenue.

I tiptoed to Paul's corner of the garret and peered around the curtain. In the gloom I could see his empty bed, the coverlet rumpled and creased, half pulled off. He must have recovered and gone out.

My packing. A duffel bag of clothes; my paintings bound together, and the rope looped to go over my shoulders. Easel and paints. My engraving tools. I left the garret bowed like a Chinese tinker, my heart singing like a lark's.

I crossed the river by Blackfriars Bridge and walked east along Southwark Street. Off the thoroughfare streets like gullies cut between black warehouses to the river; off these wound little alleys in no discernible pattern except the random one of progress. The address that Giles had given me was number seven Crucifix Lane. It was, he had said, just south-east of London Bridge, an area of tanneries, slaughterhouses, small factories and every nefarious activity known to God – and some of which he had no idea. Giles's house was close to the docks, but cut off now from the immediate riverside areas by the massive arched piles of the new South Eastern railway that stamped through tenements, squares and alleys, cutting in half streets, terraces, buildings. They had shored up some of the buildings with wooden buttresses, but some they just left, sliced down the middle, rooms exposed, lathes fingering the air, walls leaning sleepily towards the arches like tramps dozing.

Near the Borough Market the streets began to fill with costermongers and their carts. The Borough High Street, with its large stores, hop warehouses and quaint courtyard inns, looked every inch the busy centre of a prosperous market town. Only if you looked closer did you see signs of decay, the wear and tear of progress. Buildings were filthy and ill-maintained; the choking traffic on the streets like a blockage in an old man's throat. The old coaching inns, fallen on hard times since the railway opened, had become penny spikes and doss houses, their courtyards full of washing, children, rubbish.

I walked east, always east, past the great hospitals, and wondered where Giles was at this moment. Was he watching a surgeon cut? Poring over a heavy volume in the library? Comforting the sick? I knew I must be close to his home. He'd said St Thomas's was barely five minutes from his front door.

But the streets had narrowed, lost their meaning. I found myself stumbling down an alley where the cobbles were slippery, the gutter down the middle running with dark, streaked liquid and the stench so strong that I was almost drinking it. From over a high wall I heard the bellowing of cattle; an open gate showed holding pens, a courtyard of crimson-black, blotted with blood, and a gloomy, cavernous hall, empty now but for a lanky youth sluicing away grey gobbets with a bucket of water. I hailed him and asked the way to Crucifix Lane. He answered in the curiously rustic accent which was that of the Borough, as this corner of Bermondsey was known.

Tired now, with the straps of my pack cutting into my shoulders and hands blistered from gripping the easel, I found my way to Crucifix Lane, and thence to Giles's house.

My heart lifted. At first sight the house looked no more than fifty or sixty years old. Built of dark brick, it showed a single window on the ground floor to the left of the front door, while on the right double wooden gates closed off a passageway through to the back. The first floor had three tall windows, the middle one set in an elegant, jutting bow. Above that three more, and topmost of all, in place of a roof, a clapboard penthouse which I imagined would be my studio. An ugly house all in all, but a solid one, and my imagination was teased by that elegant first-floor bow window – an improvement perhaps, added by the grandfather to celebrate a good year of selling soap.

The factory had long ago moved from Crucifix Lane to the southern suburbs of London, and under Giles's father had become one of the leading manufacturers of soap in the country. Nowhere, it seemed, was safe from the eye of the Bouverie Soap Wizard – a tall, mysterious figure who gazed from vast advertising hoardings all over the capital, promising in one picture to remove dirt with the Bright White Magic of Bouverie's Moonlight Soap; in another threatening that his all-seeing wizard's eye would spy out housekeepers who failed to buy Moonlight Soap, the Clean Winner.

As I stood there, a strange and unpleasant feeling began to overtake me. I say overtake deliberately; as soon as I had identified it, I realised the sensation had been creeping up on me for a number of minutes. I felt exposed, not at risk but very alien; detached, but not so detached that I was invulnerable. On the contrary, I felt naked, like a snail without a shell.

I had not made any attempt to ascertain that Giles knew I was coming. In fact, I could be certain he did not know that I was. Nor did I know how his servants might treat me. I knocked on the door. Once, twice. And stood back.

The house was still.

Suppose Giles had gone away? Suppose he had not meant it at all? In the weak sunlight I felt a prickle of sweat break out, and the beginnings of fear – a nameless, formless, misty fear, not linked to anything specific but rather the primal terror of being homeless, rootless, roofless. It was a fear that mounted as I stood there. It clouded my bright future, blanketing it in dirty London fog. Then I saw myself as others might: sweaty, dirty, dressed in near rags, one of those pedlars who are so destitute they are forced to sell their only means of sustaining life and limb. The knife-grinder selling his whetstone, the fiddler his fiddle. Yes, I could be trying to palm off my easel, my bag of withered paint tubes, my worn-out brushes, for one last meal before I crawled off to a hole in the wall and died, or cast myself into the poisonous soup of the river as a penny's worth of business on the end of a riverman's gaff.

How quickly these black thoughts possessed me, and how quickly they were dispelled, or replaced by another sort of anxiety when I realised that I was being watched. I had been staring blankly at the house. Out of the corner of my eye, out of the range of clear vision but within my general perception, I saw a still figure in a pose of deep concentration and alertness. More than that I could not discern. I turned. There was, although I could have imagined it, a cat's tail's twist of movement, as someone or something whipped back into a doorway. This was some distance away, fifty or so feet down the road. More immediately, however, I had attracted the attention of another.

A boy. Legs short, thin, bowed, bare. Body barrel-shaped, peaked at the breast like a rowing boat's bow. Hair dusty black spikes. Eyes of an ancient blue. One withered arm that ended in a pink, glossy claw; the other gripping a bucket of what looked like turds.

He approached me as I pretended to study a cart piled high with cow hides that was grinding past.

The child spoke. 'That's the soap factory. You going in?' His voice was high and hoarse. He spoke as if his tongue belonged to a smaller mouth. I felt revulsion and confusion, but the child was there, and so was I, and I had to accept that. Rather in the spirit of knowing my enemy, I turned to him and looked, and gave a stiff smile, and looked again, and found that my gaze, instead of sliding off him, was actually attracted to him, so absolute was his awfulness. His ruined hand was the colour of raw rabbit breast. Shaped like a cloven paddle, in the wedges that made up the two halves, one could see tiny finger nails set into the taut skin. His nose was snub, little more than a smear of gristle, his mouth wide, and full of teeth and gum and tongue, his neck slightly crooked, set on narrow sloping shoulders.

He shifted from foot to foot. The bucket fell, spilling its contents on to the pavement. He gave a cry, bent and began to pick them up with his good hand. I must have winced, for he looked up, his face reproachful.

'For the tanneries, sir. It's only dog waste. You really going in?'

'Of course.'

'I wouldn't.'

'You weren't asked.' I smiled, to soften my rather tart rejoinder. I was torn between a desire to laugh at the contrast between his appearance, his attempt at gentility, and that misplaced compassion.

'Do they pay you?' I nodded at the bucket.

'Yup.'

'Enough to live?'

'She helps me.'

'Who?'

'She helps.' He looked confused. 'She.' His face suddenly lit up, and he began to jab his dirty finger at a point behind me. I turned, quickly, and so was able to see a person, whom I think was otherwise about to move hurriedly away. A girl of twelve or thirteen – quite tall and thin, and dressed in an array of adult finery. A hat which hid her face, a long full dress of red velvet, rather tattered, a shawl, thrown over her shoulders and gathered over the low breast of the dress. The hands, I noticed this particularly, were gloved, and her skin was very clean.

'There you are,' she said. 'Not bothering the gentleman?'

The boy shook his head.

Another level of understanding. I had heard resonances of her voice in his. Her gloves were too big for her; it looked as if she had dressed in her big sister's clothes. There was nothing brazen about her. Just something self-conscious in the way she held herself that engaged my attention. I wanted to see her face.

I said: 'We were just talking, the lad and I. Is he weak in the head?'

'He's been told he is so often, he believes it. Sir.'

Anger sheathed in mockery. She lifted her head. I looked more closely at her. A thin face with the sort of skin you only ever see in redheads, and then rarely: skin so pale that the blood beneath gives it a mysterious blue tone. A face that narrowed to a delicate chin; large, heavy-lidded eyes and a thin nose. Not a beautiful face, but an arresting one. The hair had been pulled back under the hat. It made the face seem vulnerable.

'It's for the tanneries.'

She turned her gaze to me and gave a small smile.

'I taught him to say that, sir. Unless people know, you see . . .'

'Yes.'

Her eyes were green, and dominated her face. There was a vein apparent, running from the gap between her eyebrows, across her forehead and into her hairline.

'Come on. Off.' She said it gently. The boy nodded slowly.

'You look after him?'

'Yes, sir.'

'But you're only a child yourself.'

Then the boy ran across the road. She looked at me once more and nodded. I nodded back. She crossed after him, then paused. She frowned, touched her head as if something were amiss, fiddled the hat free, tipped back her head and, with a single gentle shake of the head, let her hair loose. It made a thick wing of copper, gold, yellow and red and moved in a single mass, as glossy and liquid as mercury. When she tilted back her head, I could feel its weight.

She tried to gather it, a glossy living column, so thick it seemed that her little hand could hardly grasp it. She let it fall again before finally holding it, twisting and taming its glory into a loose knot.

It was not until she had gone that I realised two things.

She had displayed herself for me, and I had to paint her. I made as if to follow her but at that moment heard someone call my name.

9

Suddenly Giles was there, slightly out of breath, as if he had been running.

'Auguste! I saw you. I hardly expected – You've hurt yourself.'

I touched the side of my head, finding it sore. Paul must have caught me when we were struggling the night before.

'It's nothing, or rather it was my own fault. Paul and I argued. He made it clear I would not be welcome back in the garret. He took it badly – the news that I'd be coming to you. He'd thought that whatever one did, the other would too.'

Giles looked amazed. 'Well, he caught you a good one over the eye. It's always the same with those quiet types – underneath they're seething. I hope you gave as good as you got? Did you thrash him?'

He was fussing with a key and pushing open the door.

Had I thrashed him? Yes, I had kicked him senseless. 'Honour was satisfied,' I said.

Giles opened the door. 'I hardly knew the man and he made it quite clear what he thought of me. Looked like a cat staring at a dish of sour milk.'

'It wasn't you, it was me. I think he wanted rather more from me . . .'

'Jealous? But he's not a child. Surely he understands the need to take up whatever opportunities present themselves?'

'As I said, he felt that perhaps I owed him more, that I had been exploiting him.'

'You, exploiting him? But how?'

'Oh, I don't know,' I said. 'That was what he thought. That's what he said to me.'

'Then he should be glad to be shot of you. The jealous little puppy! Now, cheer up,' Giles said. 'You have come to stay? Say yes.'

He hardly heard me answer as he bustled me in through the front door.

I had a confused impression of a dark hallway hung with prints, narrow stairs leading off and doubling back, a growing sense of light and space, and then we were in the bay-windowed room I had seen from the street. A Turkey rug lying on dark, polished boards glowed in the sunlight. The furniture was elegant and fine – a table of pale wood, two wing-backed chairs set to either side of a small grate. There was a smell of cigar smoke and beeswax, and then Giles was thrusting a tumbler of brandy into my hand and saying I needed a drink.

The heat of the brandy, the instant rush of sensation, steadied me. But I realised that behind it, and my sense of disorientation, something was disturbing me.

I looked around. A sight? A smell?

'Better?' Giles asked.

'I think so.'

'Good. You looked like a worried old woman. No, bring your drink. Oh, all right, finish it if you will. Now for the studio.'

'The ground-floor rooms were all offices,' he told me. 'Great-grandfather, Grandfather and Father all sat in this room and planned their empire of soap. I remember my grandfather sitting me on this desk and telling me the name of everyone who walked past the window, and having me guess their business.'

'There was a very striking girl I met outside just now,' I said. 'Seemed to be looking after a crippled child who collects dog waste.'

'Striking? In what way?'

'Not her face. But she looked . . .' I searched for a word '. . . different. Her hair, though – it was like molten metal.'

'And you . . .?'

'I would like to paint her,' I said.

'Find her. Make her an offer. We can come to some sort of arrangement. She'll be your Lizzie Siddal or your Annie Millar. No, I'm serious. I know you don't get many respectable girls to strip for a painter, but round here they'll do anything for a penny or two.'

Miss Siddal had been Rossetti's model and mistress for years; Annie Millar, though the affair was not so well known, was the object of Holman Hunt's baffled passion. Rumour had it that he would not sleep with her until they married, and could not marry her until she had learned to read, write and carry herself like a gentlewoman. Other people had it that Miss Millar, while happy to service almost any of Hunt's friends, would not pleasure him until he made a firm offer of marriage, by letter. He took a subtle revenge. That's her you see, rising from the man's lap in his painting *The Awakening Conscience.* That expression of dawning ecstasy, as she realises the error of her ways, is new, painted over the original expression on the request of the patron who said he could not live with the original terror-stricken, horror-haunted visage another minute. It always struck me as in dubious taste, to say the least, to portray the woman you want to marry, or say you want to marry, as a whore staring into the abyss. But that's thwarted passion for you. Rossetti once drew Lizzie Siddal on her death bed being tended by his various mistresses, and once as Saint Catherine being broken on the wheel.

We passed by the kitchen, then a brick extension jutting from the back of the house.

'Servants' quarters, and before that something to do with soap.'

I peered in through a dirty window. Between bars I could see a vast copper, a stack of square tin baths, rows of basins.

'Of course, this place hasn't been the main factory for years. Grandfather used it for his experiments and trials. Even then we used to have a fair number of people working here.'

'What sort of trials?' I asked.

'Oh, you know. Scents, ingredients, chemical processes. They use palm oil now but before that we used anything we could – or tried to. Whale blubber, mutton and cow fat. The place used to stink. That's why Great-grandfather wanted to be near the slaughterhouses. He thought he could refine animal fat sufficiently, but the soap always smelled funny.'

'I had no idea,' I said.

'Oh, soap's simple enough,' Giles said. 'It's just oil and ash. It's when you start trying to manufacture and sell it that things get complicated. But come on, I can tell you all you want to know about the factory later. What do you think of the court? Mother had it paved.'

'Very fine.'

From the front, you would never have guessed that the courtyard existed. A yard ran the full width of the property and was paved in fine stone. A fountain, dry and full of leaves and graced by lichenous *putti*, was set into the left-hand wall. A slim bare tree overhung it.

'And there's your studio.'

At the back of the yard was a long hall. It was raised on a row of squat pillars. Above each pillar, a graceful pointed window. Wide stone steps led up to a small door set to one side. It was built of stone; the roof steeply pitched.

I would like to say that I could not believe it, but in fact, at first sight, my heart and soul went out to embrace it and I accepted it in one rapturous, sweeping glance. My studio. I loved it.

I stood in the doorway and looked into the long hall. The air was still and cold, and smelled faintly of fat and rose petals. The high windows were shuttered. A floor of wide, bare boards. Empty. Waiting. A narrow beam of sunshine sliced through the air. Dust wandered through it.

'I had the place cleaned out,' Giles said. 'A while back. It's been waiting ever since.' I loved the way he no longer sounded insouciant; his voice was trembling. At the far end of the hall, taking up almost the whole wall, was a massive, stone-hooded fireplace. No ceiling, only massive chamfered cross-beams, and above that the pitched roof.

'We used to slide the cold soap blocks over there for cutting and swing them out through the end window on to the carts. The monks built it originally,' he said. 'They owned most of the land hereabouts. I think it was the order of Greyfriars. The developers knocked everything down apart from the refectory, which is what this was. What do you think?'

I walked to the centre of the room. I thought it strange that an empty room could carry such an air of mystery: the almost tangible absence of things no longer there.

Happiness welled up inside me so strongly that for a minute I felt suffocated.

'Poky. Cramped. Where would I sit an easel? Where could I place a model?' I pretended to find fault.

Giles was silent. Then he burst out laughing, and I burst out laughing and he went to a window and threw back the shutters. Cold, clear light flooded the hall: northern light, reflected light, spent light. He approached me, hand extended. I grasped it, met his eyes, and could hardly bear the pleasure I saw in them.

He embraced me. I felt the pressure of his arms on my shoulders, his shoulder beneath my face, the length of his body. He pressed into me, loins against my body. I looked up at him, pleadingly, but his eyes were closed and his breath coming thickly. I twisted sideways, he grasped me more firmly and put his hand on my shoulder so he could turn me either way. I looked at his hand and gave a cry. Giles saw what I was looking at. He grimaced and swore. Under his finger nails were sickles of dried blood, and his cuffs were stiff with it. Giles, the trainee surgeon, smelled ever so slightly of death.

44

'I'm sorry, Auguste,' he said. 'I should have washed, but I was so pleased to see you. I won't let it happen again.'

In the doorway he paused.

'I won't force you,' he said. 'I will never force you. But you must have known that.'

10

Later, my easel was set up, a camp bed brought for me from the house (for I would not sleep anywhere else), together with a basket of wood. Giles came also, bringing with him a decanter of brandy. I had not realised before how much he drank.

He picked up *Pandora's Box* and began to scrutinise it. Suddenly I did not like the way he did it. I tried to read his face and to my surprise saw that his expression was proud.

I took the painting from him, feeling oddly vulnerable, and began to gabble nervously: 'Pandora sits in full sunlight, but I was anxious to include two forms of light. The warm, benign rays of the sun, signifying paternal authority, strike her hair. The cold light from the box, moonlight in fact – '

' – signifies femininity?'

'Exactly.'

'What women have you known?' he asked.

'None, really,' I replied.

'Mother?'

'Dead.'

'Sister?'

I shrugged.

Giles raised an eyebrow. 'You've caught something in the face. There's understanding there – I mean, your understanding of her. She knows what she is doing is wrong, can see somehow the horrors she is unleashing, but for all that, you understand and embrace her. I'd like to buy it. I thought so the first time I saw it. Now I am certain. How much will you take for it?'

'I can't.'

'Can't?'

I found it hard to explain the peculiar reluctance I felt. In theory I should have been delighted: a studio, a patron, a sale. Was that the problem? The selling?

'You've been so generous,' I said. 'I could not sell it to you. I could not take your money. You must have it.' But I could not say what I was thinking.

He gave a sudden, joyous laugh.

'Auguste, if only you could see your face!'

'What? I don't know what you mean.'

'You're transparent, I know what you're thinking.' He gestured to the great hall. 'Is all this worth it? Auguste, you should never, ever take a step into the unknown without first calculating the risk.'

'Is there one?' I asked, my voice sounding weak and distant.

He ignored my question.

'Well, I cannot accept the picture as a gift. It would skew things between us, so that, I suppose, makes it no one's. Look, we'll talk about this later. You unpack and I'll meet you for lunch.'

When he had gone, I picked up the picture and looked at it. Suddenly I put it down. I could bear to look at it no longer.

I had used no model for *Pandora's Box*. I could not afford one. It was, in effect, a self-portrait, and it was this that made it so hard to part from it. Selling it to Giles would have been like selling myself, while a gift, I thought, might have been accepted in token of some other sacrifice.

11

I supposed I was drunk. The room looked golden. I held the brandy glass up to the window. Light broke on the clear base, swam through the liquid and shivered in a million tiny points of burning white, gold, emerald.

Colour showed because the pigment in the medium absorbed into it all the other shades of the spectrum. The drink was tawny but held in it every other colour under the sun.

'And does it really?'

'What?'

'You said it holds every other colour under the sun.'

'It does. That's a scientific – a fact.'

'We're drinking colour.'

I raised my glass.

'What colours does blood absorb?'

'All apart from red, which it reflects.'

'I saw blood today. Cut open a woman. Took off her breast. Scraped her rib cage clean of a tumour. Watched. Took it well. Couldn't drug her – said she was more frightened of chloroform than the knife. Said Queen Victoria used chloroform. Said she didn't care. I held her left arm. Endured with fortitude. Her man was there, going mad. She kept calm under the knife. While her breast was dropped in a bucket on the floor, she kept calm to keep her man calm. Could see her watching him. What a woman! Thanked us, then passed out.'

'Will she live?'

'Not if we've got anything to do with it. Freeman was the surgeon. Sepsis ... Heard of sepsis? It's Greek. *Septikos*.

Putrefaction. Post-operative sepsis kills them all. The hospital kills them. They come there, they die. But I know something. A secret . . .'

'What secret?' I asked. The room was beginning to spin. I could slow it by concentrating hard on a corner of the ceiling, but as soon as I looked away, it would start again, stealthily, then with gathering momentum.

'Aha! Shall I tell you?'

'If you want to.'

'No. If you want to. Enough. We trade. The game. We play the game.'

'Don't want to play a game.'

'But you want to know the secret. Everyone wants to know the secret. Freeman, he wants to know the secret. I know the secret and it's in this house.'

'All right. I want to know the secret.'

'Then we must play the game.'

'What game?'

He leant forward in his chair. 'Truth or Dare.'

I burst out laughing. 'That's what babbies play.'

'Babbies know a lot. Come on, choose. Truth or dare?'

'I don't know what to ask,' I said.

'Ask anything. Go on. What do you want to know?'

'All right,' I said. For a minute my mind was blank. More out of desperation than interest, I said: 'What's your secret?'

'Soap!' he yelled. 'It's soap and no one knows.'

'What do you mean?'

'I mean, that's the answer. That's the secret.'

'Soap? But that doesn't mean anything to me.'

'Then you didn't ask the right question.'

'All right: what's the right question?'

'Too late. You've used up your turn. My turn. Truth or dare?'

'Dare,' I said, without really thinking. I giggled stupidly. 'No, truth.'

'Truth?'

'Definitely truth.'

'All right,' said Giles. 'What do you think I really want from you?'

I repeated the sentence twice but could not follow it to its end. The room began to spin faster than I could bear, and it all blurred, and grew darker, and now Giles appeared to be further away, then nearer, and all around him blurred in what, I remember thinking, was true Academy style. I felt so weak I tried to lean forwards, then overbalanced and fell on the floor. I think I remember Giles carrying me across the courtyard and into the studio. I remembered his practised fingers unbuttoning my shirt and trousers, and I realised with the dreadful lucidity of a drunk that I had allowed myself to get to this state so that if he were to have his way with me, I would have the excuse of insensibility.

He left me.

I wept and fell asleep weeping, ashamed of having betrayed myself, and shamed by Giles's honesty.

12

I woke up in the night feeling no better than I deserved. When I moved a cannonball ground and rolled inside my skull; when I sat a mad dwarf perched on my shoulder smashed the back of my head with a mallet. I was thirsty and needed to make water and wanted to wash my face. I thought I might have been sick. There was no water in the studio but I remembered a pump at the back of the house.

I walked into the night. It was cold and the stars were painfully clear. Inky light; grey stones; the joins between the flags very black.

I pissed in the little fountain. My water crackling on the leaves sounded too loud. I glanced up at the black windows of the back of the house while the building wheeled against the sky. There was a faint light in one of the top-floor windows – a candle behind a half-closed door.

The pump worked. The cold killed the water's slight staleness. I drank, washed, drank again, aware of the noise: the creak of the handle, the rush of the water.

Have you noticed how crowds are always noisy at night, and individuals silent? The man alone dares not wake the sleeping terror; the crowd flaunts its silly strength. Halfway across the courtyard, I turned. My blood froze.

A shadow moved across the glass of the upstairs window and something white pressed against the glass. A body in a night-dress; a woman's face, staring past me at the studio. My heart bolted; my body froze. It wasn't so much the spectral apparition itself, so much as the expression on her face: abject terror mixed with misery, the blackest brew. And as one shrinks from a horrid injury, so I shrank from that awful sight. I backed into the shadows, grateful that I was still wearing my dark day clothes. Then the whole face seemed to change.

From abstracted misery, the expression shrank to a concentrated point of loathing, recrimination, and bitter grief. I saw what happened next as if in a dumb show. Her head turned. She saw something behind her, pressed herself against the glass, and a hand stretching out of the darkness behind her clamped itself over her mouth and dragged her back and away from the window. That was enough for me. I ran up the stone steps, bolted the great door behind me, then cautiously looked out of one of the high pointed windows. Glazed darkness was all I saw in the house.

I tried to think my way through the horror. Who was the woman? Whose the hand? Whence those emotions? And why were they directed at the studio where I had to stay?

I could speculate: the hand was Giles's, the woman his housekeeper. But who treated their housekeeper like that? Did he have a mistress? A prisoner? A slave? He was training to be a surgeon – thoughts of the resurrectionists, the body snatchers, filled my head. And yet, and yet . . . he had had the chance to kill me tonight. Perhaps he was saving me; perhaps the studio was his store, his larder. I kept on telling myself that thoughts like this were ridiculous, but in truth there had been nothing ridiculous about the woman, and her face, and the significance of that hand. And then, when at last the horror of that had faded, I remembered Giles's last question to me: *What do you think I really want from you?*

The more I thought of it, the more I hated it. What did I think he wanted from me? Asking the question seemed to mutate the answer. On one level, the answer seemed simple. He wanted me. But on another level, I sensed a deeper motivation. Giles had wanted to gauge the depth or shallowness of my understanding of him. He had suspected that I was ignorant, naive and stupid, and I had shown him that I was. It seemed demonic at that hour, another strand to the lash which all drunks apply to themselves, but I applied the lash with a will, and then lay down, quite shriven.

Eventually I slept, although I had not meant to. The terror pursued me even in my dreams.

An ocean built inside me with waves and foam, white and green, and bitter, bitter cold. The red-haired girl swam up to me from the bottom of the sea. Her skin was green, her wet hair a cruder, bloodier red, and her body was smooth, marble smooth – as smooth as a body sliced clean by the surgeon's knife – and slick with white foam. She said: 'The secret is soap,' and then her hair turned to snakes. They crawled down her back and her front and joined in a harness between her legs. I could pull her by the harness, but when she began to sink, I found that she could pull me. I was drowning, and it was good, apart from the pressure which built in my skull and the headache which woke me.

So my first picture in Crucifix Lane was a charcoal sketch of the dream. It was my first work not drawn from life. It never had a proper name but I always called it *The Mermaid*, and drew it in the clear dawn light and shivering cold of my studio.

And somehow, the drawing of it rooted me there. I was like a cat that finds butter on its paws. The drawing was good, and as the light gathered, and the room lightened, I felt my soul expand into that great, clean, empty space. I put off thoughts of leaving and resolved to seek an explanation from Giles.

13

It was the middle of the morning before I stopped work and started feeling hungry. That, combined with curiosity, took me across the courtyard and in through the back door. I had heard the sound of pans clashing. Now there was a chance to meet the housekeeper.

I opened the door. The woman stood at the sink, her back to me, and I caught her in the act of stretching, back arched, hands on her hips, fingers pressing into the small of her back. I cleared my throat. She became quite still, then let her hands drop to her sides as she turned. She was in early middle age, with very dark hair parted at the centre and pulled tightly back into a bun. Her eyes were very brown and her skin very pale, in spite of a faint olive tone. She also had an air of composure. She stared at me without insolence but without any trace of deference either, and precious little curiosity.

'I am an artist,' I said. 'I live across the courtyard, and I am hungry.'

Not a flicker from those dark eyes.

'Are you the housekeeper?'

'I am – Mrs Tully is my name – and today I am cook as well.'

'I didn't see you yesterday, when I arrived.'

'I was not here yesterday, when you arrived.'

'Might I ask if there is any chance of breakfast?'

'No.'

'Lunch then?'

'Yes, when Mr Bouverie comes back. He has said he will be eating with you.'

I felt a spurt of irritation. This woman only seemed to regard Giles's orders.

'Should I talk to you about my arrangements?' I asked. 'Water and so forth. I woke up in the night and needed water. I had to use the pump outside and was worried that the noise might waken someone.'

'I'd be more worried about your health if you drank that water! It's not fit for animals. Seepage from an old graveyard has spoiled almost all the local wells. I'll see what we can do about your,' she paused, 'arrangements. If you would like a bun, there is a baker's down the road. The key hanging from the back of the door is for your use.'

She passed through the doorway, paying me so little attention that I might have been a ghost. As it was I had to step quickly out of her path. I had a penny or two left. I spent it on a good fresh currant bun and a canister of coffee that I drank in the courtyard, sitting on the edge of the fountain.

I was impressed, but then I am impressionable. She was the woman of the night before, but my feelings about that mystery had changed. Her glacial manner repelled any further curiosity on my part, while her composure confounded any thoughts I might have entertained of effecting a chivalrous rescue. She had buried the mystery in her manner and frozen it stone dead.

Giles came home in high spirits.

'It would have died had I not been there, the little scrap! Cord round its neck and midwife too drunk by that stage to count her own fingers, let alone spot a strangulation. Yes, I saved it, and yes, I also observed a phenomenon I had heard about but never yet observed.'

He had set a trestle table out in the courtyard to make the most of the sun. He drank straight from a jug of beer, lower lip cupping the spout.

'It looked like it was going to be a heavy labour. The head had dropped but the cervix would not dilate. Add to that the poor girl was having contractions that would have squeezed the

Bank of England, and I was seriously worried she'd be too tired to push at the right time. Then the midwife, looking like a witch and a half, extended her filthy forefinger, stuck it on the birthing mother, and stimulated the poor girl's clitoris: to help the little bastard out, in her immortal phrase. And help him she did! The neck of the womb dilated – another never-before-observed phenomenon, I would wager – and the stimulation, without actually pleasuring the mother, probably diverted her attention from the primary source of pain. Anyway, she didn't howl as much as they usually do, the baby came out quick and slick, and everyone was well pleased. What do you think of that?'

'Apart from barely understanding a word of it,' I said, 'I think I get the gist. You saved a life, and observed a new phenomenon, which has put you in high spirits.'

'Three in one go. I'll teach you the medical terms some other time.'

'It's almost fantastic,' I said. 'I mean, what for you is routine is so far from my normal daily round that I can hardly take it in.'

'Me too,' said Giles, and burst out laughing. 'Now eat this mutton and chew this bread and tell me how you spent your morning?'

Later I showed him my drawing. 'A new departure?' he said. 'A freedom of execution I have not seen before.'

'Then the fact that it is not drawn from life . . .' I began.

'Draw from life, by all means,' he said. 'Find a child, lay her out on a rock, then find a fish, draw its tail and join them together. Auguste, do this and you will have done more than any surgeon. Oh, to be able to transform brute experience as you do, to take it, turn it . . . You are right. I just hack.'

And he looked so sullen and forlorn that I was startled to see his mood swing so fast.

'But you just saved a life,' I said. 'You came in and were elated. The child would have died had you not been there.'

'The chances are that the child will die anyway. What use then my intervention? It will be given Thames water to drink that half the world has shat in. It will be given food that would kill a dog, and the breast it feeds on is dirtier than a navvy's breeches.'

'By the same token,' I said, 'what good do any of us achieve?'

'Doing good is not the point,' he said angrily. 'What good do you do? Less than a knife grinder. Achievement – that is the key. Achievement, the respect of your peers, and when you have gone, some kind of memorial. If only they did not die! Surgery is like life: the deeper you go, the more you achieve but the greater the risk. Have you ever been to an operation?'

'No. The sight of blood – '

'Don't say it. Don't disappoint me. The sight of blood is beautiful – there is no colour like it. You should learn to appreciate it. Never be ordinary, Auguste.'

'Yes, but cutting into the living body . . . It cannot be right,' I said. I wanted to make a point, defend my squeamishness somehow.

'Why not?'

'The body must be complete for a reason. I mean, it must be made this way for a reason, so it resents intrusion and becomes – what is the word? Septic?'

'Ah, but why does it become septic in some cases and not in others?'

'Is this another of your riddles? How would I know that, any more than you would know how to foreshorten a body in space?'

'Don't say a saw bones can't foreshorten a limb! Listen, I'm assisting at an operation tomorrow. Freeman's cutting. Want to come? It's an opportunity not many have. I'll square it with the porter. You can sneak in the back way.'

'What will I see?' I asked.

'I don't know, but you will be present at history in the making.'

The spring had died that day, killed by a bitter, winter wind.

The women's wing of St Thomas's Hospital was a stern, grey building set in the angle between Borough High Street and St

Thomas's Street. The operating theatre had originally been next to one of the wards but the screaming had so horrified the patients that operating theatre and herb garret had later been installed in the roof of a next-door church.

The back entrance to the theatre was at the bottom of the church tower. I wrestled the door shut behind me. The air was suddenly still and my breath hung in a cloud around my mouth. In the church someone was practising the organ and sheets of rich, drifting sound enveloped me. I would have stayed to listen but a porter in a wooden booth gave me a bleary look, then deliberately disappeared behind his counter. On my left was a stone spiral staircase.

I was to see history in the making, Giles had said. I climbed the stairs slowly, pausing at window apertures to look at a shifting view of grey slate roofs and grimly concentrated pattern of streets and alleys. That was history, I thought, a slow, uneven accretion making up a random grid. History just happened, no one person made it, and life was a matter of finding a way through the maze before you died. Giles had said I would see history made. Working in the roof of a church must have given him delusions of grandeur.

The theatre was due for closure. It was painfully small: five narrow, curved steps ranged in a tight horseshoe around the head of the surgeon's bench. A skylight had been cut into the roof above it. Simple gas lights hung from the sloping roof. The furniture was homely. Two wooden chairs with amputated legs were placed at the foot of the bench. At the open end of the theatre the surgeons' coats hung on hooks by a plain jug and ewer. A comforting coal fire glowed in a grate. The only formal note was an inscription in Latin painted on the wall: *Miseratione Non Mercede.*

The theatre had been built on a raised floor, the space packed with sawdust to stop the blood from the operations seeping through to the nave of the church below. The students ambled in, chatting. I was expertly nudged from my good position at the front of the little amphitheatre, to the back row where all I could see were heads. The operation due to take place was a suspected cyst in the ovaries of a thirty-year-old woman. Giles had made the diagnosis, and as a reward was being permitted to assist in the operation.

He was the first to come in. He looked pale but determined, shy rather than nervous. The surgeon, Mr Freeman, came next, and was in turn followed by two porters assisting a thin, drawn woman, bent almost double. They stood to either side of her while the surgeon described the procedure. She would be chloroformed, an incision made above the pubic bone, the ovaries exposed and the cyst excised. One of the students asked if this would involve the removal of the ovaries themselves; the surgeon answered that he would make the decision once she was open, but as the benefits of this procedure had been well rehearsed, and as she had already borne five children, it was likely. The woman, growing greyer as the discussion continued, suddenly collapsed and was led to the bench. The surgeon sniffed, and called for anaesthetic. It was administered by dropping the chemical on to a gauze pad held above her nose by a metal mask.

The room went quiet. 'She's gone,' the anaesthetist said. I could smell the drug.

The surgeon lifted his arms, one after the other, and a porter helped him into the heavy, black frock coat he used for cutting. It was made as stiff as armour by dried blood. Each movement he made contributed to the heavy sense of imminence.

The patient's nightgown was lifted above her belly and the students crowded forwards.

'Has everyone felt this?' the surgeon called.

There was a general murmur of assent.

'In that case, I will make the first incision. Mr Bouverie will assist me.'

There was a pause. I could not see what was happening. The students were craning their necks. Someone called: 'Heads!'

'I will make the first incision,' he repeated.

Something was going wrong. I tried to peer through the crowd to see Giles but everyone was doing the same.

'It's Bouverie,' I heard someone say. 'He's only gone and dunked Freeman's knives.'

I found I could raise the level of my head by balancing with one knee on the railing in front of me, while resting my hand on a ledge.

Giles had moved the table with the pitcher and ewer to the foot of the bench and replaced the ewer with a shallow tray. The cutting tools were soaking in a pale yellow liquid. Giles's face grew paler as he took a knife from the liquid and handed it to Freeman.

The surgeon looked down at it, lifted it to his nose and sniffed it theatrically.

He said in a quiet voice: 'Remove this man from the theatre.'

Giles said: 'You cannot – ' but his words were drowned out by a sarcastic groan from the students. A man in front of me remarked generally: 'He's gone too far. He's out this time.' A Scottish voice called: 'Giles the Soap!' and there was laughter until the surgeon shouted: 'Silence!'

Giles was being pulled back by the porters. I heard him call out: 'You must try it. You must – ' before he disappeared from sight.

When the room was silent again, the surgeon very deliber-ately took the shining implements from the bowl, placed them on a wooden table, and emptied the liquid into a bucket. He spat on each blade and wiped them dry on his blood-caked coat. He sniffed his fingers and rubbed the blade against the ball of his thumb. He muttered: 'At least it's sharp,' then in a clearer voice said: 'We will proceed.'

I heard, or perhaps imagined I heard, the whisper of the blade as it passed through the woman's belly. Then I slid from my perch and went to find Giles.

14

We were walking into Rotherhithe. The sky was burning out in a smutty, violet haze, the buildings thinning into silhouettes. Our feet crunched on cold dry grit.

Giles was carrying his black doctor's bag like a passport. He led me down an alley by the side of a pub. Jutting balconies, stuck desperately on to house fronts to enlarge rooms within, almost roofed the alley. Above, thin as a ruler, the last of the sky. Instead of lighting our way, it sucked out the light.

I could hear people but could not see them and did not want to. We were wrapped in something more than darkness. I felt my shoulders touch a wall, but once when I put out my fingers to steady myself, I touched skin and heard soft laughter.

'We're safely here,' Giles announced. He called: 'Doctor to see Mrs Reeves.' Then added more quietly: 'She was married to a fence.' In other circumstances his words might have produced a curt laugh at the absurdity of the notion.

A fence? Here a woman might marry a fence like Caligula might marry a horse? What else could happen? I began to feel panicked by Giles's fast stride. In the darkness behind, I thought I could hear the soft pad of footsteps in pursuit. Once I swung round and the sounds stopped.

'Notice,' Giles said, 'no one is begging. There is no one from whom to beg.'

'What are you trying to prove?' I asked.

He stopped. 'I am going to prove that ass Freeman to be

little more than a murderer. I am going to prove that I can make a difference. But first I am going to prove to you that if this is hell, doctors can make a hell within a hell.'

Poverty had taken on an outward shape. Crazy houses with bulging walls, rotting balconies, blind windows hung with scraps of withering cloth, had raised themselves, coral-like, slowly forming from layers of dirt, rubbish and despair.

But nothing I can tell you can express the terrible sense of pressure building up on all sides in such a place. It threatens to pop out your soul like a pea from a pod. Everyone here was mere shell.

Gas hadn't reached this part of Rotherhithe though a gasometer hunched like a travesty of a castle at the end of the street. Candles set in some windows emphasised the gloom, but for the most part people sat on the pavement or steps outside their houses. Their voices delivered a soft commentary on our passing.

We passed into a slightly wider, lighter street. Two-storey houses built on half basements were sinking into the mud. The pavements were laid out with carefully arranged rubbish: piles of boots, bags of rags, more boots, petticoats, dirty handkerchiefs, aprons. There were bags of dirty clothing hanging like fruits from lamp posts, and people fingering them – dying fruit pickers in the devil's orchard. I had the feeling we were being both watched and ignored, curiosity immediately smothered by the heavy pall of squalor. Giles stopped in front of a door, knocked, then opened it.

Inside the room an old woman had a crying baby pressed down in her lap. The room was furnished with a table and two hard chairs. There was a cracked beaker on the mantelpiece above the fire.

The woman was trying to stuff the swollen finger of an old leather glove into the wet pout of a baby's mouth. The glove leaked grey liquid. The baby itself was red and grey. It broke off crying to cough, and each time it coughed it convulsed, shooting its tiny limbs out like a frog, then sucking down air in a hoarse whoop.

Giles walked past with his eyes lowered and made for the stairs. I stopped. I wanted to fix in my mind the way in which such sparse possessions could produce such squalor. A tall, thin man stopped by the open doorway and peered in before moving languidly on. I heard voices upstairs. Two rooms led off the narrow landing. Giles suddenly filled the doorway to one. He held out a candle to me.

'Light this from the one on the table.'

Back in that terrible room the baby was silent, but suddenly began to cry again on an odd intake of breath. The old woman looked down at it and clucked. I was sure she had been trying to suffocate it. Renewed screams followed me upstairs.

Giles hunched over a pile of rags in a room that smelled both sweet and bitter. He was talking to the rags. The smell bore in on me like noise.

'Stand between me and the wall.' He spoke over his shoulder. I moved into the gap. He was talking to a head that was layered with wet dirt like a recently pulled turnip. The lips were drawn back over large blackened teeth. Giles lifted the head, holding it tenderly between both hands. I was too frightened to faint, or even feel sick. A body followed: mostly naked, filthy like the head. The smell grew worse when it moved. It had been half buried in rags. That was the reason I had not seen it.

Now I wanted air but there was no window. The room was just a box of sickness. I looked up. A hole in the ceiling; above that tiles. Through the tiles the evening air. I managed to hold on to the memory of it.

'Hold that candle steady!'

I leaned against the wall to steady myself and forced myself to look.

I saw thin thighs that closed in a little nest of dark hair, a belly that had fallen in and was folded like wet linen, ribs that stood out like the edge of an old bonnet. The left arm was gone.

Giles was looking at the stump. A filthy, bandaged bundle

63

was held in place with a rough harness of cloth strips passing across the breast and under the arm. I shut my eyes, my throat beginning to close.

'It's no bloody use your being here if you faint! You nearly burnt my collar off.'

I opened my eyes. The woman had rolled up her eyes at me. She said something inaudible.

'What's she saying?'

'Sorry. And Gin. Are you both ready?'

Without waiting, he pulled the pad off the stump with a noise like a knife going through pie crust. The smell streamed out again. I saw a rough mass of yellow and black and red, and something white that moved in the middle of it. The skin across the shoulder was as taut and red as a ripe tomato. Giles inhaled deliberately, then looked away in disgust.

He opened his bag and took out a fresh pad of cloth and pressed it to the wound, then bound it with the harness. The cloth smelled of creosote.

'What's that?' I asked.

'My own invention. A pad impregnated with liquid soap concentrate.'

I thought of the raw stump.

'Won't that hurt?'

'Like hell, but without it she's dead. I'm hoping it'll burn the gangrene off.'

'Burn it off?'

'The bone is out, the skin putrid. They should have left a larger flap. What there was has shrunk and is rotting.'

'Who are "they"?'

'The butchers at the hospital.'

The woman began to writhe; her stump twitched like a fledgling's wing.

'That's the carbolic getting through,' Giles said.

'Help her.'

The woman began to scream, a high, monotonous sound.

Giles reached into his bag, brought out a bottle and spoon.

'Support her back.'

I placed the candle on the floor, knelt and put my hand against the woman's back. My cheek was near the stump and I had to hold my breath. I could feel the heat coming off it. I forced myself to look at her face and saw that it was quite young. Dark eyes, a fine, high-bridged nose. Sitting up, her breasts seemed fuller. Her back was bowed with pain.

'Straighter.'

I moved my hand further round her back and gripped her firmly, but I had slid my hand so high I was holding one breast. I felt a thrill of revulsion. She didn't react, and Giles did not notice. Then I grew ashamed and disgusted with myself and let her go. Giles gave her four spoonfuls of medicine and left the bottle. I think it was laudanum. As we passed the old woman at the table, he put down some coins in front of her. The baby was in a rough cot in the corner; it was panting and the sound filled the room. The old woman put a finger to her lips, but too late. Giles's heavy tread woke the child and it began to cry again. The old woman looked close to tears herself.

On the way back, I thought I heard the footsteps again. I saw no one following us but turning suddenly in mid-step, I caught a quick, certain dart of movement that was different from the aimless eddying of the crowd. I mentioned this to Giles. 'Someone who doesn't know who I am,' he said. His self-importance struck an odd note. We found a cab on Jamaica Road and clattered home.

The night was so clear that a few stars glittered above London. It was so cold that the cab's windows carried thin fossil patterns of ice.

'Her arm had been crushed,' Giles said suddenly. 'A cart ran over it and bone fragments pierced the skin. You can't get away from gangrene like that. So the operation was justified.'

'But?'

'Having removed one source of rot, we replace it with another. Half the patients in the wards die from it.'

'Why?'

65

'Some people think it's something in the air – miasmic effluvia, they call it.'

He rammed his feet against the front of the cab. He was trying to sound nonchalant.

'What do you think it is?'

'Remember how we played that drunken game, the first night you were here?' he asked. 'Remember me saying that my secret was soap?'

'Yes, and you used soap on the dressing.'

'Listen. There is more in this world that we don't understand than we do. Sometimes our observation is flawed. At some point the ancients started wondering where wind came from. The natural state of things is stillness, so why does the air move? They looked at the trees waving their great branches in the air, they flapped their hands in front of their faces and said: "That's it."'

'What?' I asked.

'They mistook cause for effect. They thought that by waving their branches, the trees made the wind blow.'

'That's ridiculous,' I said.

'It's not. It's very obvious. It's just wrong. So sometimes theories work and sometimes they don't. Soap, we know, is made by mixing potash and fat. Why that should emulsify under certain conditions, why that emulsion should, when rubbed, produce froth, and why it lifts dirt, is beyond us. But we know that if we do this and we do that, something is made that produces a certain effect. Are you with me?'

'What has this to do with that woman?'

'Because cutting makes for putrefaction, and putrefaction is somehow linked to septicaemia. Septicaemia is the bane of surgeons. Something happens when the skin is broken. Many theories have been advanced. One is that the body is a complete, water-tight, air-tight sack, which once ruptured reacts like a chemical to a catalyst when a foreign body is introduced. Another is that the air is filled with humours that

66

enter the body and act on the blood. Another is that puncturing speeds up the natural aging process. I have another theory.'

'Which is?'

'What would you say if a place existed where none of this happened?'

'I would say that you had danced through the looking glass.'

'Perhaps I have. But listen. If I told you that in a hospital, after surgery, seven out of ten patients die of septicaemia after the operation that was initiated to cure them, you would be impressed to hear of a place where cuts produced none of these bad effects?'

'I would.'

'Well. You are living in it.'

'What? The house?'

'Yes.'

'But people are cut in every house with no ill effects. It is no – '

'That's a normal house. You forget, our house was once a factory . . .'

'. . . for making soap.'

'A process which involves cutting and burning. Making wood ash caustic by boiling it in lime, burning the kelp for the soda, boiling the oil for saponification – even cutting the soap into bars – all these operations carry their own risks, but the answer to septicaemia was here, in front of us. The phenomenon was first noticed by my great-grandfather who kept a record of injuries and recoveries. In cases where men, burned or cut, were injured in the factory and kept there for healing, sepsis occurred in fewer than one in fifty cases.'

'Something in the air?' I said.

'Try again. Air is common to all places, and in all places sepsis occurs.'

'Different air?'

'No, try not to think of what is common – rather what is uncommon,' Giles said patiently. My brain felt oddly slow.

Suddenly I saw it so clearly that I laughed.

'Soap?'

'Soap,' he replied. 'Soap is the secret. Perhaps its base of ash and fat corresponds somehow with the natural warmth in flesh, which is made up partly of fat, and thus reinvigorates the tissue, allowing it to grow. Perhaps the pain observed when raw soap is applied to an open wound is part of an important process that involves melting the flesh so that it co-joins, like . . . like . . .' He flicked his fingers.

'Like candle wax?' I ventured.

'Exactly. I have been – ' But here he broke off.

'You have been what?'

'Oh, nothing. I have been boring you, that is all, with my talk of soap. Honestly, I don't know. You must stop me. One man's enthusiasm is another man's purgatory.'

'But there was nothing dull in what you were saying. I was fascinated.'

'No, no. My lips are sealed from henceforth. Stuff a soap bar in my mouth if I so much as breathe another word of it.'

'If this is a secret, Giles, and you think I might give it away, I can assure you that – '

'No, no. No secrets. You've seen the reaction of the greatest minds in medicine to my secret. No, it is as I said, too dull to bear.'

But I was puzzled. Giles was acting exactly as if there were a secret, but the why or the wherefore of it was a mystery to me.

15

Under the vast canopy of dirty glass crowds massed and rushed and drifted. Trains ground and wheezed, pumped busy plumes of smoke into the air, leaked excess from weird arrays of polished valves as if the power in them could barely be contained, only to expire in vast, slack, gushing exhalations. The air was a haze of steam and smoke, and the sun, baffled by a million million specks of dust, gilded the whole show in light.

And yet, if you stayed long enough, if you looked hard enough, patterns showed. There was a pattern in the way the passengers disembarking would move in a solid black phalanx to the ticket barrier; a logic to the way travellers scurried down a near-empty platform as a train got ready to leave. There was knowledge and experience in the way the porters hovered; in the way the pedlars of matches and trinkets and cakes and drinks darted in and out of the purposeful crowd, calling up to windows in monotonous barks, or yowling at each other like cats on the street. Back against the end wall lounged a few more sinister characters, their eyes darting over the passengers as they came through the barriers, or fixing on a bag dumped carelessly too far from the hand as a traveller looked up at the destination boards.

Selection. There was too much going on. I would have to choose what I wanted to show. A crowd of sportsmen dressed in dirty bright clothes, drinking at a stall? A pickpocket, hunched like a vulture? A matchgirl? A sweetmeat seller?

I set up my stool and bent over my board. A crowd gathered,

as crowds always did, always changing, always standing a few feet back, commenting in mutters.

I concentrated on the arches, the perspective, the lines of the roof, the section of daylight beyond.

Concentration made me absent-minded. I saw the red-haired girl I had met outside Giles's house twice before I realised who she was. As is always the case in second meetings, I was initially disappointed. But then my fascination was rekindled. She was with another girl and the contrast between them revealed her otherness. The redhead was thin and supple; tall for her age, barely developed around the bust. Her face was thin, gaunt even, but having seen it close up, I knew how clear her skin was. Her hair was up again today, bundled into a hat. The two of them were walking arm in arm down the platform towards me. The platform was otherwise empty. A train would be drawing in soon. I dithered, and as I hesitated a train approached the platform. They turned and walked quickly to the other end.

I stood and watched the surging crowd as it squeezed its way through the barrier. There – there was the red-haired girl's companion, hanging on the arm of a middle-aged man. She was talking to him earnestly; he was staring downwards, the rim of his hat pulled over his face.

They're meeting people off this train, I thought, and felt a stab of disappointment. But as I watched the crowd squeeze itself through the bottleneck, there was no sign of the redhead.

A station official came up to me then and said I was causing an obstruction. I wasn't, and was getting ready to argue when I saw her pass through the gates, hand over a platform ticket and walk slowly in my direction.

I picked up my stool, tucked my board under my arm and shouted: 'Hey!'

She looked up, saw me, and looked through me.

'It's me,' I shouted stupidly.

She looked away, annoyed, then around her.

I grimaced and pointed straight at her. She walked towards me, her eyes narrowing questioningly.

'What do you want?'

'We met,' I said. 'In Crucifix Lane.'

'Did we?'

'I was talking to the pure finder boy. The one with the crippled hand. In the street. You took him away.'

'Oh, yes.' It could have meant anything. It certainly did not suggest I had made an impression.

'I'm an artist,' I said.

'A what?'

'A painter.'

'What do you paint?'

She stood uneasily in front of me, looking around, hovering between curiosity and awkwardness.

'I'll show you.'

I put down the stool and laid the sketch on it.

'It's only a scribble,' she said.

'First you lay it out in pencil. Then, if it's right, you transfer to canvas.'

She shrugged.

'Look,' I said. 'This is another sketch.' I unpinned the station study. Under it was one of a girl, a country girl. 'She's getting off the train.' Her interest quickened. 'And frightened by all the noise and hubbub around her. The pickpockets, the – '

'And that?'

She was pointing to a sketch under that one.

'You'll like that,' I said. 'It's the boy in the street. The pure finder.'

'I call him dog boy. Oh, my Lord! That's him. To the life. But this hand!'

She was looking at the picture, her hand in front of her mouth.

'His hand? Oh, I redrew it,' I said.

'He'd like that,' she said. 'He'd like to see it.'

71

'You should bring him to me.'

'Could he have it?'

'What, the picture?'

'Of course.'

'No, it's mine.'

'But it's him.'

'But not his. Tell you what, why don't you bring him round to the studio to see it?'

'Oh, yes.'

'I could draw him again. And you maybe.'

'Me? Draw me?'

'Why not? In fact, I was thinking of using you as the model for the country girl.'

'Use me? As the model for a girl?'

'This girl.' I pointed to the study. 'I'd dress you as I wanted her to look, then draw you stepping down.'

She looked at me blankly.

'You could come to the studio. I'd pay you.'

'You don't want me.'

She said it politely and firmly, but I wasn't going to give up.

'Oh, come on,' I insisted. I was trying to gauge her age but found it hard. 'A pretty girl like you. Surely you'd like to be painted?'

She put her hand in front of her mouth.

'You're making a mistake, sir,' she said.

'I'm not. Truly. Ever since I saw you in the street, I've been looking out for you. You've got . . . something. I truly want you to sit for me.'

She backed away from me.

'What is it?' I asked.

But at that moment the station official saw me again.

'I told you to clear off,' he said. 'I mean it.'

In the blink of an eye, she was gone. I saw her head, then her slim body through a gap in the crowd. There was no way I could have caught her. I was left feeling rejected, and because rejected, intrigued.

16

Giles had been readmitted to medical school. At a hearing it was decided that Mr Freeman's words had been misinterpreted and that Giles's actions, while putting the patient at risk, had not endangered her life. His punishment was a two-week suspension and the medical school received a fellowship, courtesy of Giles's father.

It was evening. I had lit a great fire, and was preparing to clean my brushes and begin work in earnest on my new work, when Giles put his head round the door and said: 'We need to cheer ourselves up now.'

I gestured to the canvas. He wagged his finger. 'Won't take no for an answer. Need company. Well, what are you waiting for? Change. Wash. We're going out.'

Half an hour later the cab was rattling westward. The streets were dark and the rows of houses, offices and factories had dwindled into dark stage flats. We passed the new Prudential Building, a baby-beetroot, black-roofed, Gothic nonsense. The pavements became more populated as we approached the Tottenham Court Road. As we passed down the long straight track of Oxford Street, Giles began to peer out of the window. We turned left down New Bond Street then stopped.

'Tonight, the German Gallery in New Bond Street is showing Holman Hunt's new work. It is a private view. I'm going to show you what your Pre-Raphaelites are all about. Come on, I thought you'd be thrilled?'

'I am. It's just that – no, it's embarrassing.'

'Come on.'

'It's just that Paul and I – we used to go to shows like this. I mean, not get in, we were never invited. We just used to stand and look at the people going in and talk about the day when we had our exhibitions and all the fine and fashionable turned up at our shows.'

In my discomfiture I imagined myself as two beings: one sweeping into the show, the other a watching shadow-self.

It was true that Paul and I had always gone to private views together, partly to get out of our lodgings, partly for the simple thrill of seeing the great men walk past, partly to spur ourselves on. By the end I was sick of it – sick of being outside when I wanted to be in, sick of the condescending waves of acknowledgement, sick of the hunger, sick of the waiting. Sick, sick, sick. But Paul had never tired of it. He was happy to watch and wait – I think it gave him pleasure. And perhaps that was why I was where I was and he was still where he had always been. I was terrified of seeing him again.

'The gallery owner, Thomas Gruber, like all successful dealers, has worked out the thing behind the thing. Ask nine-tenths of the world what he sells, and they would say: "He's a dealer, he sells paintings, you soft-headed dolt!" But *they're* the dolts,' Giles told me earnestly. 'Gruber and men like him do not just sell paintings, they sell promises.'

'Of what?' I asked obediently.

'Respectability, acceptability. Ask any of the poor bloody middle classes what they want, and they will say independence and financial security, even as they bankrupt themselves in their relentless quest to be like everyone else. That's Gruber's trick. "Come to me," he says, "and that picture on the wall can be your ticket to acceptability. You may be just a soap seller's wife, but hang that picture on the wall, *mein Liebchen*, and number yourself among the great and good of this proud isle."'

I was shocked by the bitterness with which he spoke. 'So it's through your parents you know him?' I said.

He allowed himself a smile. 'Indeed it is. I once calculated that my father had to sell five million bars of Bouverie's Moonlight Soap to get himself invited to these private views.'

The cab stopped for the last time. We were pressed a little, jostled by the small crowd. I kept my eyes down, but near the door had to raise them. Paul was not there. I turned and scanned the faces. No sign of him. Of course, if he had seen me first he might have hidden, but I was suddenly gripped by the sure knowledge that *he was not there*.

Then I saw Brownlow. He was standing by the door noting who was going in. His jaw dropped as I passed by him. He recovered and raised an arm. I thought he was going to try and grab me. He looked furious, determined. I pushed my way through the crowd and crossed the threshold.

17

The painting was hanging at the other end of the room and all people were talking about was money.

It was the most ever paid for a contemporary English picture by a dealer. Hunt had gone to Dickens himself and asked him how much he should sell it for, and the great man had asked him how much *he* thought it should get, and Hunt, never lacking in confidence, had said three thousand guineas, and Dickens, who conducted all his own business but was killing himself through overwork, told him to charge another two and a half thousand guineas for the copyright. Which he did. And Gruber paid up!

My head was dizzy with the numbers. It was an unimaginable amount. Giles barged through the crowd with me in tow, introduced me to Gruber, and someone whom I think was Holman Hunt, and another whom I think was Rossetti, allowed me to look at the picture, hanging in state at the far end of the room, all the walls around it bare. (Indeed it had the whole gallery to itself and Gruber made the money back, purchase and copyright, within a year by charging the public a shilling a head to see it.) Then Giles said, 'Ah,' and pulled me to the far wall where a tall, heavily built man with whiskers and a woman with a fine-boned, slightly hawkish face were standing. He tugged me in front of them and drawled: 'Hello, Mother. Hello, Father. Meet my artist. He's the one I wrote to you about.'

The first thing I noticed was that they glowed: he with a reddish fiery light, she with a paler candle glow.

The effect was immediate, and gained impact from closer observation, when you saw how everyone around them seemed dull by comparison.

Then it struck me: they were clean beyond imagining. Not just washed, but clean. There was no trace of grime or dirt on their pores, just scrubbed, glowing skin, set off in each case by collars that were startlingly white. They were walking advertisements for soap, and as I drew closer I began to smell a sort of fatty rosiness in the air, mingled with cologne. The mother managed to look at, over and through me in one quick glance. The father, without smiling, inclined his head. He took my hand and folded his around it, gently, as if he were afraid of crushing it — a curiously awkward gesture.

'What did you think of the work, Father?' Giles asked.

'It's far too expensive. I cannot imagine what Gruber thinks he is doing.' While he talked, he watched me.

'We cannot think,' his mother intoned. 'And where do you exhibit?' she asked me. She was watching me too, as if she were trying to understand something.

'Nowhere yet, but he will.' This from Giles. 'I was going to ask you to come and see his work. He's in the monks' hall. Lives there like a hermit. Isn't that so, Auguste? Just today, he completed a sketch. Been up all night — these artists, you know. When the muse is with them they can't stop. Must paint.'

His tone annoyed me. I felt I had only been brought to be shown off, like a new toy.

'Is this true?' the father cut across Giles to ask me directly. 'Is this true, because I have always through they were quite ordinary fellows. I mean, look at Hunt.'

'I'm afraid we are more ordinary than Giles would have it. In my opinion it is he — '

'Ordinary, eh? It is as I thought. What are your hours?'

'Normally I rise at seven, start work at eight, and after that it is up to the light. Six hours, eight, twelve.'

'I'll wager it's just hard work that's got you where you are today, young man. Hard work and application.'

'That comes into it. Of course, inspiration – '

'And where does the inspiration come from?' he interrupted.

'I don't know.'

'In business we have an idea: a new process, a new idea for selling, a new market or a new way of reaching that market. We have the idea, but that's the easy bit. The hard part is making it work. That's something Giles has never understood.'

'He's never applied himself,' the mother said. 'He tried to paint. Oh, dear, gave it up. No talent, you see. Won't even look at the business – too squalid for him no doubt. So what does he want to be instead? A butcher. No more. No less.'

'I cannot believe that to be true,' I said. Giles's face was a mask.

'To return to my theme,' Mr Bouverie said imperturbably. 'Seven hours' concentrated mind-work is all a man can manage. A woman less, of course. More than that on any regular basis and you risk mental exhaustion. Isn't that so, Gruber?' The dealer himself had joined our group. 'This young fellow will knock himself silly painting twelve hours a day like a clerk. A friend of my son's. He might be good. I'd thank you to see his work.'

Gruber inclined his head, first to Mr Bouverie, then to me, just enough to show that he had registered the request. He smiled at Giles, and I thought I detected real warmth in his face.

'He should write to me to arrange a time to visit.'

'None of that! You go to him. Well, why not?' Mr Bouverie popped his eyes at us all. 'Giles would have us wait hand and foot on you, I suppose.'

I was seriously alarmed by this and assured Messrs Bouverie and Gruber that I would be only too pleased to visit the gallery. Bouverie raised an eyebrow, Gruber acknowledged my deference. He said, more to Giles than anyone: 'Indeed? You are confident about it?'

Giles nodded. Gruber said to me: 'You will write to me, yes?' Then he moved away from us and joined another group.

'There. Managed that,' the father said. 'Now, let's see if I can't introduce you to someone else . . .'

At that point I saw a painter called Watkins whom I thought Paul had known and worked my way towards him. After he had disguised his disappointment at my being there, he said that he had not seen Paul for a while but there was nothing strange in that. What was odd was that Brownlow had just asked him the same question. Watkins was too busy cultivating his own air of hauteur to ask me why I had not gone there, but the question was implicit in his raised eyebrow.

'I am worried about Paul,' I said to Giles. 'He is not here, and has not been seen for weeks.'

'Well, what are you going to do about it?' he asked.

'Go to my old rooms and see if he is there.'

Giles raised his eyes to the ceiling and laughed.

'I need to square things with him.'

'But you left on bad terms.'

'Largely my fault. If you want to know the truth, I left owing him money. These past weeks I've been half expecting a letter from him, demanding repayment. Now I think he may be ill or something. I want to get there before Brownlow does. I think his seeing me tonight has reawakened his concern for Paul.'

'And you're worried because he hasn't written to you?'

'I want to see that he is all right.'

'A guilty conscience is often a sign of exaggerated self-importance,' Giles said. 'We'll get there and find him toasting his toes by a roaring fire while he leaches the energy from another man more talented than himself.'

'That's unfair!'

'We'll see.'

By the old factory the air was wet and foul. I looked up to the top floor. No light in the window, but then candlelight does not travel.

'Take my hand,' I said to Giles, 'or you will fall.'

We climbed the four flights to the attic in pitch darkness. On the landings we heard sounds of life from the other rooms – low conversation; the clatter of a pan; coughing. Outside Paul's door, nothing.

I knocked. No answer. I knocked again. The silence infected me like a fever. I began to shiver.

'What now?' whispered Giles. He too had been infected by apprehension. 'Perhaps he's drunk, unconscious with a floozy by his side.'

'Quiet,' I said, and knocked again.

'Can you get in?'

'Easily.'

The door was loose on its hinges, and one could always open it by lifting it up, and sideways. The emptiness behind was a vacuum, pulling me across the threshold.

Giles sniffed.

'Odd,' he said. This smell was new and indecipherable.

Inside, the oblongs of the windows showed paler than the inky blackness of the room. I could just make out the black bulk of the table. I touched it, struck by how cold it felt. A small window above it was open a crack – it always blew ajar in the slightest wind. I went to close it automatically but could not. The sill and frame were thickened by a hard rime of frost and ice. It must have stood open for days.

Behind me a match flared. Darkness fled to the corners then danced back in shy shadows. Giles swore and dropped the match.

'Light another,' I ordered.

On the table was a plate and knife. On the floor a poker. Ash spilled from the grate on to the hearth.

'Nothing's changed,' I said.

'Of course it hasn't.'

'No, I don't mean that. Nothing at all has changed since the morning I left. The place is exactly as it was then. That knife. That poker. The fireplace.'

'Is there a candle?'

'There should be.'

I walked to the other end of the room. There was the old stub of candle by my mattress.

'Paul must have cleared off,' I said.

'Without taking anything?'

'Just packed up his personal belongings and scarpered.'

'I suppose so.'

Giles sniffed again. 'There's some food somewhere going off. I know that smell.'

'We hadn't had meat for days,' I said. 'It must be the river.'

'Perhaps he – '

A sort of scratching flurry came from the end of the room where Paul had slept. Having thought the place unoccupied, the fact that he might still be here froze my blood.

'Rats, if you want my opinion,' Giles said. 'Big ones.'

'We should look to see what he took.'

The floorboards shifted beneath our feet; the darkness curled around us. We stayed close together. The curtain to Paul's sleeping area was closed.

I yanked it open.

Darkness and a foul smell.

'Lift that candle,' Giles said.

The bed was unmade, and I swear it was exactly as it had been on the morning I had sneaked away, except now the rumpled sheets were covered in tarry droppings.

Then, imperceptibly, I saw a blanket begin to move. It was lying across the bed, falling off it on the far side as if it had been pulled. On the back of my neck I felt the short hairs rise against my collar.

'Did you see that?' Giles's voice.

I was relieved he had seen it too.

'Frederic,' he called.

No human answer, just an agitated flurry behind the bed.

'Rats,' Giles said, in a loud, clear, normal voice. 'I'll show them.'

He yanked the blanket, frowned as it caught on something, yanked again.

The blanket flew free. Something that had caught in its folds thumped at my feet.

I jumped back, then looked down. It wasn't a rat. When I bent and moved the candle to it, I screamed and fell backwards. The candle went out. Giles swore. I scurried across the floor.

My first reaction had been instinctive. It was not until I was pressed against the wall that I properly realised what I had seen. Then fear came over me and I began to shake.

Giles lit another match.

'For God's sake, what's the matter?' he asked. 'Some rats have made a nest in your friend's old bedding, that's all. Can't you speak?'

I held out the candle and pointed behind him to the floor.

He snatched it from me and drew back the curtain. I heard him exclaim and he bent to examine the thing on the floor, then gingerly peered over the bed.

He started, drew back, then deliberately looked more closely. When he came out again, his face was tighter and older.

'What was Paul wearing when you saw him last?' he asked.

'A jacket over a nightgown.'

'That's him, then, behind the bed.'

'What did I see?'

'His jaw, I'm afraid. The cold's preserved him but he's been with the rats a month. That and the cold have kept the smell down. They've eaten most of his insides.'

Without warning I was sick. Once finished I staggered to a chair and began to shiver. I was bathed in cold sweat.

'What happened?' Giles said.

'He must have died in the night.'

'I know that. I'm asking you what happened?'

'We fought. He came at me with the poker. You saw the bruises. I beat him off and he became unconscious. I carried him to bed. That's all I know. In the morning I looked in quickly but there was no sign of him. I just left. I thought he must have gone out. I just thought he must have gone out. I didn't realise . . . he was dead.'

'He might not have been. He probably had a seizure in the night brought on by something like a blood clot – I've seen it happen – then rolled off the bed and passed out again. He may never even have woken up.'

'He wouldn't have woken up. He couldn't have woken up,' I was chanting monotonously. Giles said: 'Shut up.' In the silence we heard the stairs creak.

Panic rose in me.

Giles sped across the floor. I could see his face, very white in the candlelight. He closed the door silently, and put his shoulder to it. He was mouthing something at me.

I couldn't hear and tiptoed across to him, but even though I was smaller and lighter, I made the boards creak.

'The candle!' Giles looked furious and exasperated. I tiptoed back as the sound of footsteps grew louder. I blew out the candle and curled myself up on the floor. My heart raced, the footsteps stopped. A knock. Then Brownlow's voice, hissing: 'Paul. Paul!' He knocked louder. He paused. Giles was still in position, his hand on the latch, pushing downwards.

Brownlow knocked again. 'Paul. It's me. I must see you. I'm sorry.'

Another pause.

Then the door began to move. I saw Giles adjust his grip. The door shook.

'I can't get in, Paul. I beg you, if you're in there. Please.'

A pause.

'Please. Someone's in there, I know.'

A pause. I could hear him shift his weight. I could hear him breathe.

'I'm going away, Paul. I'm going.'

I heard footsteps. I uncurled. Then the door boomed in the frame, once, twice, three times. Brownlow started to sob, then slid down the wall and began to cry properly. He stayed there forever. When he eventually left, Giles groaned: 'I'm cramping, Auguste, help me.'

He was bent like a crab from having to exert constant pressure on the latch in that freezing cold without moving.

He lay face down on my old bed while I rubbed his neck and his shoulders, even his calves. After a while he said: 'Can you think straight?'

I nodded.

'How did you pay the rent?'

'Paul did,' I said stupidly. 'He did all that kind of thing.'

'How often? With what frequency?'

'Monthly.'

'And you've been with me, how long?'

'A month.'

'So in a day or so, your landlady comes knocking.'

'Yes.'

'And what does she find?'

'Paul,' I said through clenched teeth.

'We were just lucky with Brownlow. It's my belief he did not know you had left, but thought Paul was a fool for putting up with you and so they argued. It's not hard to imagine the scene. Paul loves you; Brownlow loves Paul. I feel almost sorry for the fellow. Still, back to our little problem. The landlady finds Paul dead and you gone. What does she think?'

'I don't know. Oh God, I don't know.'

'That fight you had . . .'

'I kicked him. Just kicked him.'

'Well, none of that would show but people may have heard. Two men fight. One man runs. One man found dead. Even the peelers could work that out.'

'I can hide. I can hide with you!'

'For the rest of your life? Think clearly.'

'Then we must hide him.'

'Exactly.'

'Tip him out of the window?'

84

Giles went across to look out of it.

'Tide's out,' he said. 'No, we'll have to hide him somewhere else.'

'But how?'

Giles thought. 'Leave it to me,' he said.

He was gone. The candle burned low, and then high as it guttered. Unless I wanted to be left in the dark I would have to get a new one, and the only new one would be in the drawer of the table by Paul's bed. We had to keep candles in a drawer or the rats ate them. At first I could not move. I was engulfed by remorse, drowned in it. I remembered Paul as he had been when we first met at an open day of the Royal Academy's Summer Exhibition, less than a year ago. How we had both been standing in front of Millais's latest opus, how we had both first professed admiration for it, then agreed that while Millais was blessed with the most talent, only Holman Hunt seemed true to the Pre-Raphaelite cause: truth, honesty, beauty, light. When we each said those words we knew what the other meant, and understood each other perfectly. He had heard of a garret going cheap in Blackfriars, and though it was beyond his means to rent it alone, together we might . . .

I had met his parents. His father had embraced and kissed me like a son and said I was to be a brother to Paul. And now I had killed him. I had killed all that. All the hope, fear, promise, courage, optimism, stupidity, all that, and every impression he had ever made on anyone, and would have been capable of making, I had stopped. Like that.

I found I had clicked my fingers. The thought, examined afresh, seemed weird and clear. Enormous. I found that I had risen to my feet and had walked to Paul's end of the room. I found I had twitched back the curtain. I found I had lit another candle, had peered at Paul, and in my mind was drawing him, in order to comprehend.

I drew the empty eyes and the way the shadows ran into the scratch marks like ink into wrinkles; the terrible absence of his jaw and the ragged shred of tongue; the corrugated gristle of his wind pipe; the casual elegance of his upraised arm, bent at the wrist, a gnawed finger pointing to heaven like a Quattrocento saint's; the dark hole of his belly where the rats had dug deepest, and then the pathos of the protective inward twist of his feet. In my mind only I drew Paul as he really had been. Then I crammed his painting gear into a suitcase and gathered up his clothes and rolled them in a sheet. Whatever we did with him, we would have to leave the room as if he had upped and offed.

When Giles arrived back he looked triumphant.

'It's perfect,' he said. 'There's a mudlark's hole not fifty yards away. The tide's on the turn so he won't be there much longer. We'll wait for him to finish, bury the body, weigh it down and the tide will fill the hole with mud.'

Mudlarks dug for coins in the soft ooze of the Thames's foreshore when the tide was out. What Giles said made sense. The holes filled up in two tides. The foreshore was parcelled into fiercely defended territories and no mudlark would dig the same hole twice. By the time Paul was discovered, if he ever was, he would have decomposed beyond recognition.

We wrapped him in a sheet and carried him down the stairs. I ran back up for his clothes and suitcase, locked the door behind me with the very key I had left on the table by the door, then slid it back underneath. We carried the body like a rolled carpet the ten yards down the alley to the river. Giles scouted ahead, came back to say that the mudlark had gone but we had better hurry. We pushed Paul over the embankment wall, slid down an iron ladder, dragged him across the mud to the hole, folded him and dropped him in, followed by his clothes. The foreshore was scattered with lumps of undressed stone. I dropped three or four on top of him, and from the digging kicked in as much mud as I could.

We climbed the wall: Giles first. As I reached the top he gripped me firmly by the forearm. For a second I was uncomfortable. He could have pulled me from the ladder and pushed me back. I lifted my eyes to his. A deep, almost unfathomable communication passed between us. In his eyes I saw excitement and approval. In mine, I suspect, fear turned to relief. We began to walk, quickly, then trot. By the time we reached Southwark Bridge we were running, but it was not the flight of panic; it was the flight of gods or schoolboys, frightened, but elated by fear so that every breath seemed to dispel the weightiness of earth.

We reached Crucifix Lane when the night was darkest and the cold worst.

As Giles started up the stairs to his room, he turned.

'We do well together, don't we?' he said, then carried on up to his bed.

18

I now owed even more to Giles. He had saved me. Without him, Paul's body would have been found, my former landlady would have identified me, and I would have been a face on a poster on every street corner from Notting Hill Gate to Whitechapel, Hampstead Heath to Dulwich Common.

All the next day I watched Giles, and the next. He hardly came near me, but I felt him watching and waiting too. I knew I should thank him – I should go down on my hands and knees and thank him – but I was terrified as to how he might react, what he might demand. So I kept quiet and tried to make myself invisible, and one day Giles came up to me in the studio, looked at me, shook his head in amazement as I stared steadfastly at my canvas, then turned on his heel and walked away.

But something had been born inside me and was growing in my breast. I did not know what it was, except that it made me restless and at times I felt the confines of the studio and the house, and my position within them, were intolerable.

To escape the feeling I took to wandering. I explored my neighbourhood from the docks to the Old Kent Road, from Borough High Street to the Rotherhithe peninsula. Perhaps 'scoured' would be a better word. I was looking for something as elusive as the vanishing point. In a picture you can touch it. In reality you can never reach it. It is the end of the rainbow; it is the fruit of Tantalus. It is the ever-receding dot, the narrowing funnel that traps the wasps in the jam jar; the hook in the flesh that draws you on.

I gave my wanderings a motive. I was looking for the

crippled boy so he could take me to the red-haired girl. I was looking for the red-haired girl because she had touched me in some way. When I questioned myself about how she had touched me, I was left with a shifting mystery. There were girls more beautiful; there were girls more refined; but the red-haired girl had me smitten. And burying Paul had given me the courage to explore, to do things that would previously have been beyond me.

Crucifix Lane was a busy street intersected by yards, some of which housed factories, some tenements. There were two pubs on the street, The Wheatsheaf and The Valentine and Orson, and any number round about: The Skinner's Arms, The Whitesmith's Arms, The George, The Prince of Wales, The Marigold in Hand, The Grapes, Simon the Tanner. My poverty kept me out of them, but even if my scruples had allowed me to sell *Pandora's Box* to Giles and thus give myself some money, I think my restlessness would have kept me away.

It was a cold, clear afternoon when I found myself staring into The Horns on Druid Street, long enough for my eyes to accustom themselves to the gloom, long enough to see a line of dirty deal tables and benches, a long bar, a few men sitting hunched at the tables, a couple of women who looked drugged, and a tall thin man who made me start.

I looked at him closely. I thought I had seen him before, but the question was where? Then he saw me staring at him and beckoned. It struck me that he had been waiting for me to spot him. I pointed stupidly at myself and shrugged. He nodded once, then more urgently, and smiled at the barman as if to say: The noodle's frightened of something. He had a long, frightening face with a jaw like a ladle and eyes the colour of beer, but a pleasant smile which he was using on me. He was dressed like an undertaker in an arrangement of black tubes: for each leg, for the trunk, for the arms; clothes so tight I could not see how he got in or out of them. He kept on a bowler hat. He had a red ribbon tied around the crown, like some sort of trophy.

I stepped inside. My reaction to him had been immediate. Now, as he peeled himself away from the bar, I remembered. I had not seen him so much as sensed him. He was the odd movement in the street I had seen on two occasions: once the first day I arrived in Crucifix Lane, the other the night we had been to the sick woman in Rotherhithe.

'Aha,' he said. 'You've smoked me. I knew you were a clever one the moment I saw you, standing outside the old Soap House so boldly. "Who's he?" I asked myself. "Will we see the chimney smoking, my deario?" I think not.'

He held up two fingers to the barman who poured us glasses of gin. The man pushed a glass to me. His manner was easy but his eyes belied him. They were sliding up and down, trying to piece me together, trying to make me fit in somewhere. All the time he was watching me, probing me with his eyes to see what effect his words had.

'The woman,' he added. 'Annie Reeves, poor dear.' His voice was as cold and as smooth as a wet pebble.

'You were following us that day?'

'Following? Watching more like. Mr Giles should keep an eye on his back, but failing that, I will. For those of us who rely on him, who service him,' and he gave me a smile of complicity, 'his health is a prime concern.'

'And the woman?' I asked.

He rolled his eyes heavenward. 'Died,' he said. 'Though no doubt Mr Giles and yourself made her passing easier.'

'I had no hand in it,' I said.

'No, no,' he corrected himself hastily. His eyes were paler than beer, I thought, and rough, like London brick.

'And the day I arrived here?' I asked. 'Were you watching my back then?'

'You saw me? You have quick eyes.'

'You seem to make a habit of being near Mr Bouverie,' I said.

'Or vice versa,' the man said, then realising he had shown

side, added in a more fawning tone: 'And you would be his assistant?'

'I'm a painter,' I said.

He raised his eyebrows and shot a meaningful glance at the barman. 'Well, well,' he said. 'I've always fancied having a crack at that myself. Painting. But, of course, that explains the eyes, does it not? Painters must have good eyes. Like a detective, eh? Tell me, whom or what do you paint?'

'Scenes,' I said.

'And do you use models?'

'I have used models.'

'Ah. Life drawing with models. That is the vogue, I hear. One thing. When we see a picture and in it there is a clothed lady, do she start off clothed, or do she start off naked? Do you paint her nude and dress her, or simply paint her dressed? You see, I heard two painters talk in a drinking establishment up West. "Ah, yes," one said, "I always strips mine whether they're to be painted dressed or not." "Is that better to understand their form?" says the other. "You might say that," says the first – leaving me wondering what exactly they mean when they talk of form?'

'I know what I mean,' the barman said.

'But artists is different. I've heard tell you get twenty or thirty of them in a room together, and sitting in the middle of them a young, naked girl. All staring at her, they are, and she with nothing on to hide her shame. Have you done that, sir? Stared at a naked lady?'

His manner was designed to make me angry, and he almost succeeded. I pushed the gin away. He said: 'Don't be proud.' Menace ran through the words like a metal shim. 'No, I've upset you now, haven't I? Drink your drink. I'm all talk. I'm a friend of yours in a manner of speaking, or a friend of a friend, which makes us sort of friends once removed.'

I took a sip of the gin. It tasted of warm oil.

'That's better. By the way, you can tell Mr Giles that I'm still looking.'

'For what?' I asked.

'You tell him that,' he said.

He turned his back on me then, hunching his thin shoulders. I left. It was colder in the pub than on the street.

'I dropped into a public today,' I said. 'The Horns on Druid Street. Met an interesting fellow there. Tall man with a yellow face.'

'Oh, yes?'

We were eating a cold dinner by candlelight. Giles held a glass of red wine up to the candle. The flame was caught and broken in the angles of the stem and lived in the wine.

'We chatted – '

'How very . . . Auguste, I do believe you're fishing. Fishing for information, being curious without wishing to admit it, is very common. Now, listen to me, and in future do as I do.' He roughened his voice and lightened it in what I took to be an imitation of my own. '"Giles. Who the hell is that long streak of dirt and piss I met in a pub?" That's the way to my heart, Auguste. By the way, did he say that he knew me?'

A sudden flash of his eyes indicated the doorway behind me where Mrs Tully was on the point of leaving. I heard the rustle of her skirts stop, then start again, as if she had signalled something back.

'As a matter of fact, he did,' I said, cautiously, watching him.

'William Oates is his name.'

'How do you know him?'

'My family's been here generations, you know. It would be odd if we didn't know anyone.'

'Yes, but this man was – I mean, he's not the sort of man I thought you would know.'

'Why?' Giles looked amused.

'All right. He's rough.'

'He's a common little thief who should be flogged for his thoughts, let alone his actions. What did he say?'

'After making a lot of comments about the dubious morality

of artists, he gave me a message for you. He said that he was still looking.'

'Good.'

'What is he looking for?'

'His soul perhaps. His conscience. How did he know you were an artist?' he asked sharply.

I thought for a second. 'I must have told him.'

'Mistake. Never tell Oates anything.'

'If he's so bad, why do you know him?'

'Oh, a man like that can be useful in a place like this. You should use him – if you want a life model.'

'I think I'd rather have anyone than him prying in my affairs.'

Mrs Tully removed plates.

'Were you listening, Mrs Tully? Oates is back,' Giles said carelessly, but I thought there was an edge to his voice that he had not completely disguised. If there was, it had no effect on Mrs Tully who merely inclined her head smoothly and glided over to the sideboard with the plates.

As I lay in bed later that night, I found myself turning the conversation over in my head. I was not sure why, just felt that something was amiss: that edge in Giles's voice when he spoke to his housekeeper.

Giles had asked how Oates had known I was an artist. All I had done was mention in passing that Oates had made slighting comments about painters. It seemed an odd thing for him to pick up on. But Oates had asked me an odd question about my work. He had assumed I was Giles's assistant.

Now a thought came to me that had not struck me at the time.

Assistant.

Giles's assistant in what?

I lay in bed and made steam clouds with my breath. I couldn't sleep. I wrapped myself in my blanket and sat on the old stone steps outside the studio. Above the general background hubbub of the city, the footsteps in the street, the rattle of wheels on cobbles, I heard a strong, stealthy, thudding pant.

It came and went, drifting on the breeze, sometimes quite distinct, sometimes fading almost to nothing. An engine. I felt my heart settle to its normal rhythm.

I looked at the upstairs windows of the house. A dim light faintly illuminated one on the top floor. The back rooms were in the crude modern brick extension. The light was not actually burning in the room. Though steady it was dim, as if shining down a corridor.

Sleep would not come. The longer I sat there, the more restless I felt. I sat until I heard the bells of the City strike three, and then I went to bed.

19

Mostly, however, I worked. I finished *The Vigil*, I varnished *Pandora's Box*, I reviewed all the canvases I intended to present to Gruber. In the end I decided to show him only the two finished works, some sketches, and a pencil portrait.

He saw me in an office above the gallery: a small, beautifully proportioned room full of light. He was seated at a vast desk, his back to the window. The desk was piled with papers and fine books. He stood up, a larger man than I remembered, and more impressive. Therefore his seeing me at all was made the more confusing.

He hardly glanced at my work. He has only seen me to please the Bouveries, I thought. Fighting off feelings of humiliation, I was determined to salvage as much dignity from the situation as possible. When he offered me a seat and a tiny glass of some foul firewater, I sat obediently and allowed it to wet my lips.

Gruber worked at his fingernails with a paper knife, every so often firing a question at me. Where was I from? Where did I study? Who had seen my work? The pauses after my answers suggested a complete lack of interest in both me and my work. I began answering absent-mindedly, my own mind busy with working out what would be the least humiliating means of escape.

He threw up his hands in mock horror when I told him that I intended submitting *The Vigil* for the Royal Academy Summer Exhibition. I found in him a strange mixture of familiarity and stand-offishness, humility and arrogance; even his referring to the Royal Academy's Summer Exhibition as a 'kettle shoe', in his thick German accent, suggested a yoking together of contrasts – the familiar colloquialism rendered almost unrecognisable by the accent.

'Worse than a cattle show,' he continued. 'A jumble sale organised by cretins. There is more chance, first to choose the right pictures, then to hang them properly, if you get a monkey from a zoo to wave at the paintings he likes, and then tell him to hang them in his tree. It is not art, it is wall covering. It is backward, not modern. I tell you this, young man. The modern way is to treat each work of art as an artefact, as a production of individual genius, so that when you sell, you are selling a unique expression of the only faculty of man to set him above the animals – not something just to hang on the wall to make an effect. This is my point. And there are people all over this country with the money to help me make it with them.'

'Giles said you were selling respectability,' I said, rather sharply. He laughed heartily and called Giles 'a dear boy', then asked after him.

When I said he was well, Gruber shrugged slightly, a minute, very continental gesture, I dare say, that suggested to me not disappointment that Giles was well, but disappointment in me for not having said more.

'There seems to be a frost between Giles and his parents,' I said.

'That is it,' Gruber said. 'There is a tension. Giles is a sweet boy with a good eye for good art, but his parents pull him out of orbit. That is why he persists in this matter of surgery. This slice, slice, slice. It is not good. He could have come to work with me – a while back that was on the cards. But it was considered, ultimately, too common. Imagine: to deal in art too common; to slice and hack to be considered refined. This country!'

He shrugged again.

'What?' I said.

'On this question of surgery, I think things are not quite right,' he said. 'Perhaps it is for you to get to the bottom of it, no?'

I asked: 'And what is your interest in the Bouverie family?'

Gruber laughed again. 'My dear, the more I know about this family, the better. They are clients; they keep food on my table and a fire in my grate. Art is a very personal matter; in the making of it and the selling of it and the buying of it. That is our trinity: making, selling, buying. Would you neglect one part of the Holy Trinity? No, you would not. It is one in three and three in one. Three parts separate but indivisible, yes? In short, the more I know about them, the better, no? And you would do well to keep that in mind.'

There was a pause. I could not think of anything more to say. I stood to go.

'Thank you for your time,' I said, 'and for your advice.'

My paintings were propped against the desk; the sketches scattered across it. I tidied the sketches, laid them between two sheets of card, and began to bind them.

'So, you do not want to sell?'

I just stared at him.

'You do or do not want to sell? Come now, the formalities are over.'

'I want to,' I said. 'Of course I do.'

'Show me the paintings again.' My heart whacked against my chest.

I picked up *The Vigil* and stood against the wall with it. I found Gruber was looking straight at me. So might a pig farmer look at a runt before cutting its throat. Fondly, pityingly even, but in the final analysis, finding it not worth bothering about. I hated him.

'Put it down, put it down. You are shaking too much for me to judge it properly. And the next.' He pointed to *Pandora's Box*. 'Prop them both against the wall. One, two.'

He was silent for a long while, scrutinising first one, then the other. The room was hung with a careful, eclectic collection.

Above the fireplace what might have been a Stubbs; next to it a swirling contemporary sketch by Rossetti – not Lizzie Siddal but a fierce beauty with a small, curling mouth, dark, angry eyes and a wild mane of rich dark hair: William Morris's wife, Jane. Rossetti was having her too, Giles said. Outside the window, lives clattered past. London was all movement. Only a tick-tocking clock reminded me that mine had not stopped.

'One hundred guineas the pair, and copyright,' he said.

I can't remember what I said. I had dropped into a vortex. I knew I could be carried along. I didn't have to do anything. A hundred guineas! A sale! The past was disappearing into a tiny dot above me as I was sucked further and further in. This was it; the moment. All I could hear was rushing.

And then I remembered.

'I can't,' I said.

'Can't?' He looked stunned.

'I have promised one to someone else. I only brought it here to indicate what I could do with an allegorical theme. *The Vigil* is for sale. The other . . . You do understand?'

'I most certainly do not. What do you mean by bringing it here? A painting is a painting. Every painting is different. I will not commission you to paint a picture called *The Temptation of Eve* because I have seen you could paint one called *Pandora's Box*. I do not run a salon to try and impress people. I buy and sell paintings. I offer you one hundred guineas the pair. What do you say?'

'That one is spoken for.'

'It is not sold. If it were sold it would not be here.'

'Not sold then, promised.'

'And this person has paid you a deposit?'

'No. But – '

'It is not sold. You have merely said someone could buy it. For what price?'

'No price was fixed. In truth, the party wanted to buy it, but I wanted to give it away. We are still in discussion.'

'Aha. I see. You try and bargain me up. No price was fixed. It is promised. You think that Gruber will scratch his chin and say: "Very well, another ten guineas"?'

'No, I had no intention of . . .'

'Oh, but suppose I did!'

'I cannot unsay what I said. But the other, *The Vigil*, that is for sale.'

'I will not have it.'

'But you said . . . I mean, you offered one hundred guineas the pair. So for fifty . . .'

'I did not offer you fifty for one and fifty for the other. I offered you one hundred for the pair. I cannot unsay what I said. And I do not bargain.'

'You do for copyright. You bargained with Holman Hunt.'

Gruber tilted his head. 'For copyright, maybe, I will bargain.'

I said: 'I need to think.' It was a desperate position to be in, but looking back, I wonder if I was really in any doubt. Deep down, I always knew what course of action I would take, and ride the consequences, whatever they were. We talk of turning points in our lives: I doubt if there are such things. We are preordained in our actions, not by any deity, either benign or malevolent, but by ourselves.

'One hundred guineas for the paintings,' I said. 'Thirty for the copyright.'

He insisted that copyright was calculated in pounds. I found the bargaining squalid and was beaten further and further down. I walked into New Bond Street one hundred guineas and seven pounds richer.

On the way back home I visited a tailor's and ordered a suit, a coat, and a waistcoat of silk. I bought new shoes for the first time in my life, and in each shop I visited was served by people who were better dressed than I. I did not care.

I bought champagne from a shop on the High Street and nearly took a case. The man behind the counter would not fetch the bottle from the cellar until I put the money on the counter.

I let myself into the house. It was still and quiet, as usual. I don't think I ever knew a house like it for blocking off the noise of the street.

Two paintings sold to Gruber. Realistically, it did not mean that my future was secured; far from it. But it did mean that I was rich for as long as the money lasted, and it did mean that a door was now open. For even if Gruber never took on another picture, there would be other sales now. I would have to work hard; I needed another within six months, I thought, two in the year, and if I could manage to get a portrait commissioned in the same period, it would do me no harm. It was with a sense of luxurious urgency that I now entered my studio. I wanted to look at the sketch I had dashed down in the dim light of that early morning: *The Mermaid*. There was something in the ferocity of the heavy charcoal lines that I did not want to lose, but at the same time, I knew that in transforming it to oils, the image would change. I was trying to imagine exactly how.

Giles was in the drawing room, his newspaper turned to the crime and divorce reports.

'Giles, you have done it for me!'

He looked at me and said: 'What?' in a pleasant voice.

'I have sold my first picture. Pictures, I should say. And all thanks to you.' I held up the bottle. 'I thought we might celebrate.' Still talking, I moved to the cupboard where glasses were kept. 'After you took me to the German Gallery, I wrote to Gruber and fixed a meeting with him.'

Giles was now standing up, fully alert.

'When is it?'

'When was it? It was this afternoon.' I paused a moment. 'Don't you see, Giles? I sold to Gruber. To Gruber! I now share a dealer with one of the most celebrated painters in the land. He bought two of my paintings!'

'Just like that? But he's a notorious old fiddler. He bought from you there and then?'

I smiled and nodded; in truth I was experiencing as much

pleasure from Giles's reaction as I was from my own achievement.

'Open the bottle!' he roared. 'Two paintings? We'll drink two bottles, and then another two to the future. We'll get drunk together.'

When we were drunk I told him that one of the pictures had been *Pandora's Box*. It went better than I could have hoped. He took it well. In fact, he hardly noticed.

20

A nd then Giles started taking me out and about with him. I got to know London from the inside of drawing rooms. I looked from high windows, often on the first floor, over garden squares guarded by black railings. I learned never to look at the girls with grey faces who nodded and curtseyed in cluttered hallways and took my hat and gloves, because they never looked at me, never even raised their eyes. From them I learned to value my courage and good fortune; from the young men and women who sipped tea or sherry, I learned to keep my counsel, keep silent, simply be someone who painted pictures, because that was all they wanted me to be. Usually all I wanted to be was wallpaper.

One evening I was listening to a young bore in his second term at Oxford, studying theology, telling me about Rugby football, Charles bloody Kingsley, and pointed arches, when I saw Brownlow. It was something I had anticipated and waited for, but even so I began to tremble. The events of that terrible night came back to me, but none of them so terrible as how he had stood outside the door and begged Paul to open it, while all the time Paul was lying there, half eaten by rats, and I was lying on the floor and Giles no more than two inches away from him on the other side of the door. Two inches away from being caught. Two inches. He saw me and worked his way across the room towards me, eventually standing between me and the boring undergraduate who said: 'Well, really,' and moved off.

'A word, Coffey, if you will,' he began. I hated him at that moment. He was puff-chested and looked good in the sense that he had probably never knowingly done a wrong thing in his life. He called his mother 'Mama', he called his father 'Sir'. He was manly, resolute, calm. A word, Coffey, if you will. 'I am still making investigations into Paul's disappearance, and would like – '

I knew I was staring at him, something of my thoughts in my face, because he stopped and peered at me – almost, I think, on the point of guessing that I knew exactly where Paul was. But suddenly Giles was there, shouldering his way towards us, grinning drunkenly and pulling behind him a whiskered gentleman, who looked rich.

'This is the man, Haig, this is the man.' Giles's arm was around my shoulders.

'Aha, vewwy well, vewwy well,' said Haig in a silly, piping voice. 'The painter, eh? Who did you say his dealer is?'

I let Giles carry this one. 'Gruber. The German rather likes him.'

Brownlow looked startled.

'You must come and see us, Brownlow,' I said, my voice full of false confidence and pitched so high I thought it might crack. 'One afternoon.' He nodded. 'We can talk then.'

'We will, Coffey, we will.' He looked uncomfortable, perhaps because he was having bad thoughts about me and knew that bad thoughts were wrong; perhaps because I was acting so strangely.

'Come tomorrow,' I said.

'So, you actually encouraged Brownlow to come and see us?' Giles said as we rode home along the Embankment. He had promised Haig that we would visit. Haig liked pictures of young, naked girls. The tide was rising, flowing towards us, bringing with it memories of Paul. 'You're not feeling penitent, are you?'

Was I?

'I'd rather ask him than have him come on us unannounced,' I said.

'And you didn't think to ask whether I would be there?' Giles probed.

'I didn't think I needed to.'

'So, you will be able to cope on your own?'

I thought hard. It was a trick question. 'You know I can't cope on my own,' I said.

'But you have a dealer now. There is nothing between you and fame, glory, success.'

'Thanks to you, Giles.'

'Yes. Thanks to me.' He swallowed. 'God damn it, but you're a cold, superior little thing!'

'How can I be superior to you?' I asked. 'You are my patron. I owe you everything.'

Giles gave a grunt. He twisted me round. His teeth found my lips and began to chew and tug at them. His hands pressed against my chest, then down the front of my trousers. I lay completely still. Over his heaving shoulder I saw London move past. The assault did not last long before Giles pushed me away. 'You're a dead thing, Gussie. I'm getting out here. There must be more to life than being with you.'

He tapped on the roof of the cab and walked off into Pimlico. To get drunk, I suppose.

Brownlow sat quietly by the fire. I sat opposite him, Giles to one side at a small mahogany table where he cut and recut a pack of cards. He had offered Brownlow a game. When our guest said that he did not play at cards, Giles's sneer seemed merely petulant. Mrs Tully brought us tea. After he had drunk a cup, Brownlow said: 'I expect you know why I am here?'

'To bring us news of Paul, I hope.' My voice sounded absurdly bright and false.

Giles snorted. Brownlow fixed his eyes calmly on me.

'There is no news,' he said. 'I would have thought even you

104

would know that Paul has disappeared. I was sure when I approached you last night that you had something to say.'

'No, you are mistaken,' I said. 'When I left him, or rather the night before I left him, he was in good spirits. We agreed that my coming here was best for both of us. He shook my hand. I remember there was even talk of his going back to his parents.'

Brownlow shook his head. The sound of Giles shuffling cards stopped.

'Even now you pretend. Even now you lie. It's no use protesting. A fight was heard in the rooms you shared together, a month or so before I saw you at the gallery. A fight and then nothing. No one in the building has heard or seen either of you since that time.'

I opened my mouth. Brownlow held up a broad, capable hand. 'I said: do not protest. I have heard too much from your lying mouth to gain any fresh pleasure from hearing you condemn yourself still further.'

'And did you bother to check the room?' I asked.

'Why do you ask that?' Giles asked quickly.

'I thought it might be the action of a friend,' I countered.

'It is not the action of a friend to pry,' Brownlow said. 'I would not trespass on Paul's privacy.' But he looked uncomfortable.

'But you did allow your curiosity to overcome your scruples,' I said. 'You must have done. How else would you know that we both – what was your word? – disappeared?'

Brownlow looked momentarily perplexed. Then said: 'I admit it. I did look into the rooms.'

'When?'

'The day after I saw you at the gallery. I met the landlady and she took me in. She said the rent was due. It was she who asked people in the building when they had last seen you, and one of them volunteered the information that about a month ago there had been sounds that indicated that a fight had taken place within the rooms.'

'I see. And what did you find when you went into the place?'

'Nothing.'

'So Paul had left.'

'I –'

'You looked into the rooms, and they were empty. What other conclusions could you have drawn?'

'I cannot say out loud.'

'Why?'

'Because I think it might be slander.'

'Oh, those scruples again. The magnificent scruples of Brownlow. One day I shall paint an allegory of them. But did you only go to the rooms once?'

'What do you mean?'

'You said that you went to my old rooms the day after we met you at the German Gallery. Had you been there before, recently?'

I saw Giles raise a hand in a gesture of warning.

'No.'

'Really?'

'Why do you ask?'

'Simply that if you were as concerned a friend as you now purport to be, I would have thought that perhaps you would have visited poor Paul more regularly. Let's see, between my moving here and my seeing you at the gallery, a month went by. You didn't go to our lodgings once in all that time?'

'I went there. Of course I did.'

'So you saw Paul.'

'You are the very devil. No, I did not see Paul.' His shoulders drooped. 'I only went there the once. It was the very night I saw you at the gallery and I was gripped by a terrible fear. I tried to break into the rooms. There was no light, but I felt, I felt this presence, as if Paul was willing me to find him. I failed to get in. The next day I returned and met the landlady. That was when I entered and found the place empty and desolate.'

'A whole month,' I mused.

'A month I will regret all my life. I admit it, I was angry with him for liking you. I was angry with him for putting up with you. I thought he would come to me in time, if he wanted succour. When he did not, I merely grew resentful. Even when his dear father wrote to me and said that they had not heard from Paul for three weeks, my pride prevented me from seeing him, although I was worried. Then I saw you and – '

'But you didn't see Paul. Well, well.'

Brownlow stood. His face was white. 'You sit there like a statue, so cold, asking these questions, as if you were concerned. How can you pretend? How can you?'

'I am pretending nothing,' I said.

'What happened on the night before you left him? Tell me that!'

'Why do you think anything happened?' I asked.

'Because you were heard to fight, and I think the fight took place at the time you moved here. I think something happened to Paul and you ran to your rich friend! I want the truth! I believe that you are a thief and a parasite who drained my dear friend of all life and hope and happiness. Now, what happened that night?'

I stood. I allowed my face to work itself into an angry expression. Giles looked properly concerned now and that gave me a surge of pleasure. 'I will tell you what happened when Paul and I argued. I will tell you exactly how it was.'

Brownlow looked triumphant, Giles even more wary. 'We argued, Paul and I. I told him that Giles had asked me to live with him, here. Paul wanted me to leave; I wanted to stay. He said he would be all right; I said he would not, that he could not rely on friends like you, Brownlow, to support him if he grew lonely, or if he needed encouragement in his work. I was well aware of his need for reassurance and that was why I argued so fiercely to stay, but he swore to me that in a matter of days his other friends would come to see him, friends who did not like me, and when they saw I was gone, would take my place. He knew the importance of Giles's patronage, and I knew that dear, sweet, noble soul would fret himself to sickness if he honestly believed that he had stood between me and success. So I left, having argued with Paul, but not in the circumstances you imagine, Brownlow. Quite the reverse, in fact. And I hope you can see why I tried to spare you the truth. I did not do it for you; I did it holding the memory of Paul in my mind. He would not have wanted me to reproach you, although in truth I have desired sorely to do so these last few weeks.'

Our visitor's eyes darted from one of us to the other. Giles had his head in his hands, as if overcome with emotion. I was breathing hard.

'This is madness,' Brownlow said. 'I see your game. What is, is not. How can I argue your point, when I am crippled by my own conscience?' He sat back in his seat, holding his head in his hands. Then he rose stiffly. 'I thought to appeal to your better nature. I might as well have tried to reason with – you monster. Monster!'

'I think you had better leave,' I said. 'And consider your own faults.'

I turned to the window and that was that, except for an odd thing. I had thought Giles might have hidden his face to conceal his admiration for me, or even to stifle laughter, but when he looked at me later, the expression was more like wonder, and more than that, wonder tinged with shame.

So I worked, and felt myself change. While in the past I'd thought I would like a model one day, now I felt it as a pressing need for my development as an artist. I still looked for the girl with red hair and her crippled boy, but following Giles's advice that local girls would pose for me, I started scrutinising the faces and figures of girls in the street. Perhaps it was not so surprising that those who dropped their eyes and scurried away excited me, while the ones who met my gaze frankly and asked me what I wanted unnerved me. A few even asked me if I was good-natured and I realised then that the street was an odd place with rules of its own, and a language that one had to learn like any other. I soon learned which girls would run and which girls would stay and which girls were whores. For the time being, simply learning this was enough; I could not pluck up the courage to ask any of them to pose for me.

This frustrated me. I was even contemplating following Giles's advice and seeing if I might enlist the help of William Oates when something happened to put me off. I was sitting in the first-floor bay window in the last of the light, but the room was too dark for anyone in the street to see in. From behind my paper I could see the street, and I just happened to be glancing in that direction when I saw Oates loping along in his curious, swift, sideways motion. He stopped outside the door. I reasoned he was going to knock, but if he did, he did so quietly and Mrs Tully must have been passing by the stairs at that very moment because I did not even hear the door open. I walked quietly to the top of the stairs and listened.

'Well,' she said. 'I got your message.'

I heard his voice, the words indistinct, and then the phrase: 'Tell him.'

It set off an echo in my mind.

I tiptoed down another stair, walking on the balls of my feet, testing it for creaks.

Mrs Tully said, 'Where?'

'Doesn't matter where. Just tell him I've found one. A lascar with a smashed shin. No English.'

Mrs Tully said something indistinct, then the man again: 'Yes. He'll be swimming off Margate otherwise.'

The door closed. I backed up the staircase and into the drawing room, followed by the rustle of Mrs Tully's skirts. She passed and made her way up the next flight. I went to the bottom step and listened.

I heard her feet on the stairs, creaking slightly, moving at a certain pace, then the hollow sound of her steps on floorboards, and then I swore I heard what could only be her mounting another set of steps. The penthouse. On my first day I had seen it, and marked it out as my studio. In some way now it seemed to be an element in the mystery surrounding Giles, Mrs Tully and Will Oates.

21

This impression that things unknown to me were happening sharpened my senses and pricked my curiosity.

It was a feature of my studio that the windows were high off the ground. As the hall itself stood on a half basement, it was virtually impossible for anyone to look in from the outside. But as I stood there, perhaps two days after the odd conversation I had overheard between Mrs Tully and Oates, I became aware that I was being watched. So definite was this feeling that my first reaction was one of shock. I spun round to the door, which remained fast closed, then immediately looked up at the windows, which remained clear.

I returned to my work, disturbed, the back of my neck crawling. Again, that feeling, again the same results. This time I checked that the door was closed, then opened it quickly to look in the courtyard. Nothing. I made a quick examination of the ground beneath the windows; it was undisturbed. The stones, moreover, were damp and lichen-covered, and would have showed any signs of recent disturbance. I returned to the studio and made a thorough check of it to reassure myself. It had the opposite effect. The very emptiness of a room in which there was nowhere to hide made the sense that I had shared it with a stranger all the more sinister. I returned warily to my work.

There are theories, I know, about this sixth sense. Some maintain that it is the product of a psychic faculty; others that there is a physical organ in the base of the brain which can sense a flux in the magnetic forces around us in the same way that the ear senses sound and the eye senses light. Others say that it is clear evidence of the spirit sphere around us, and we are warned by benevolent ghosts of danger.

But the theory I like is that the ear, the eye and the nose can at times each pick up signals so faint – a tiny movement, an almost inaudible sound, a fleeting scent – that each alone does not make an impression, *but taken together they do.*

And so it was that on the third time this feeling in me grew, something made me look up. I threw my hands across my face and screamed, for there above me, perched on a beam, was a monster: half bird, half man, legs tucked up to its chin, face a terrifying white blur, and dressed in black rags. I ran towards the door, turning my back on the fiend, but at the last minute, with the door safely before me, dared a look. I saw a swish of fabric, a leg, and an ungainly struggle as the thing vanished through an open window in the lantern or cupola set in the centre of the roof.

That made me think. I ran into the court to see a figure, holding one hand in a particular way, begin to shin across the angle of the roof. The dog boy, I was sure of it. Somehow he had found a way up on to the roof, and then, overcome by curiosity, had wriggled through a window in the lantern and lowered himself on to one of the cross-beams. For all I knew he had been there as I entered, and knowing that he would make a noise trying to escape, had simply squatted there, hoping to remain undetected until I departed. If I ran out of the front door and turned left, I should intercept him in the alley that ran down the side of the house.

The alley burrowed between two warehouses. From the street it looked as if it ended in a cul-de-sac, but in the end wall, set so that it was not visible unless you followed the alley to its end, was a gap. A derelict was sitting across the gap. As I ran up he half rose to try and block my path, mouthing at me, hands reaching out. I feinted one way, then the other, then pushed him against the wall. The delay, small though it was, almost lost me the chase. I saw the dog boy at the far end of the passage, whisking through another gap like a fleeing cat. I followed.

A short passage, and the alley opened up into a small square where an ancient ruined house was returning to its constituent parts: timbers mouldering to green, daub dissolving. The roof had softened and fallen in like a pie crust and an old balcony slanted from the first floor to the ground. The front door was gone and tall nettles were marching into the hall. From blind windows bobbed a hundred heads of buddleia, the woodbine of the city. Nothing was disturbed; the nettles were unbroken.

He's got somewhere to go, I thought.

There were two alleys leading from the little square. I took the left-hand one. Here, suddenly, was a crooked slum street; a face peered at me from a gap between rotten slates and jerked away. A child wailed, was slapped, shrieked, was slapped again and fell silent. The ground was like a sponge, filthy and rancid. At the end of the street a man with a goat was shouting at someone who had passed him. I ran out of that street and into another, not dissimilar, then past a factory wall that stank of chemicals and another that stank of death, past knots of incurious, apathetic men, and sullen silent women. I was following a ghost.

The street stopped abruptly where the railway viaduct had driven through it. If the dog boy had come this way, he would have been forced right or left. I stopped and looked first one way, then the other. He broke cover twenty yards away and darted down a tunnel which was a good fifty yards long. I ran, chased by the dull echoes of my footsteps, seeing the dog boy break into the light, still twenty yards ahead.

We were in the docks. A different world. Warehouses lined the far side of the street, blocking off the river, the canyons between them linked by clanging iron gantries. There were ledgermen in doorways, carters, porters, stevedores. Black and yellow faces from the ships moored so thickly they blocked the light. The dog boy, thinking he was safe, had stopped running and was stooped over a granite drinking trough. After drinking and dashing water over his face and hair, he walked off. This time I had no problem following his slight, lopsided form, even when he hopped over the river wall, skipped down a set of slick, weedy steps and began to trot along the foreshore between ranks of beached lighters.

I followed more cautiously, feet crunching on waste: smashed clay pipes, old tiles, oyster shells, a field of animal bones. The air around was thick with wheeling gulls. The wall above the high-tide mark was a rusty scab where the knackers threw their waste. I watched the dog boy climb an iron ladder pinned to the wall, and after waiting, followed him again.

There were no warehouses here, just a row of houses with a tavern attached to one end. It took me some time to realise why they were different: all the windows had glass in them. Of the dog boy there was no sign.

I looked up and down the street for any sight of him and when I turned back to the houses, the red-haired girl was staring at me. She was wearing a simple dress of grey, cut quite high across her breast. She was leaning against a door frame, hiding whatever was behind her. Her hair was more impossibly lovely than I had remembered.

'You're looking at me like a dog that doesn't dare bite,' she said.

'I was looking for the crippled boy,' I said. 'I followed him here.' It occurred to me then that he might have led me.

'And what business did you have following him?'

'He was spying on me.'

'Dog boy? Spying? And what were you doing that was so interesting?' she asked.

'I was painting.'

'Perhaps I told him that you'd drawn him. Perhaps he wanted to see.'

'You talked about me?'

She raised her eyebrows. Again I noticed how clean she was. Her face seemed a little bit sharper than the last time I'd seen her, her body a little taller. There was something very direct in her eyes, as if she were asking me a clear question I was too stupid to understand. Another girl appeared behind her in the doorway. And then I understood. The other girl was wearing a loose white shirt, unbuttoned to the waist. Her hair too was loose.

She laughed. 'Are you good-natured, darling?' It was unmalicious, quite relaxed. What she did was put men at their ease. And the question had been a parry to my curious gaze.

I felt my heart thump. I became very conscious of the shape of my body inside my clothes, defined by a prickling film of sweat.

'I would like to paint you.'

The dark-haired girl spat. 'They're worse than the Sally Army, the painters!'

The red-haired girl tilted her head forward, looking at the ground then up at me. Her hair was tied back but a soft fringe was loose over her forehead. She touched the back of her neck.

'We'll see,' she said. 'We'll see what dog boy says.'

The other girl laughed derisively then put an arm over her shoulder. Her nipple was large and diffuse, and the breast around it very clean, as if she were nursing. The red-haired girl still looked at me. It was as if she were showing off her gift for stillness; as if she knew what I wanted. Her expression changed without changing – a cat's trick.

'I don't know your name,' I said.

'She's called Pity,' the half-naked girl said quickly.

'Will you come to the house, Pity?' I stumbled over the name.

'Maybe. One afternoon.'

'When?'

'Soon.'

'How soon?'

'Going anywhere?'

I shook my head.

'Did the dog boy lead me here?' I asked.

'You'd better ask him.' She whistled, suddenly and shrilly. But the dog boy didn't come.

I walked away. The streets blurred and dissolved around me, as if melted by tears. But I was not crying – I was trembling with fear and excitement. In some ways the fact that she was a whore made everything easier. Her time was mine now that I had the money to buy it. Once I had her, or so I thought, I could do anything with her, anything I wanted within the limits of decency or imagination. And yet, and yet – that very capacity of hers which so excited me, that feeling of her availability and pliancy, terrified me as well. Somehow my ability to make her do things became a sort of power inherent in her. The power I would have over her could become the power she had over me, or at least that was the way my addled brain reasoned with it. And yet, and yet – as for the thought of having her, that was far from my mind.

I didn't want to have her; I just wanted to paint her. In my mind she was already on a dais, elevated and remote.

So I said to Giles the following afternoon as he washed blood from his hands in the downstairs sink, meeting him as if by accident, as if I hadn't had my eye pressed to a crack in the studio door for the sight of him, ghostly through the old uneven glass, going through his nightly, soapy ritual.

'By the way, I think I have my model.'

'A model? Who?'

'The red-haired girl – you remember I saw a girl, the first day I was here, and said I thought she would make a good model?'

'I remember something of the sort.'

'I've seen her again and she is prepared to sit for me.'

'I see. And what does she do, this girl?'

Something in his manner made me cautious.

'I don't know.'

'Don't you think you should find out?'

'Well, perhaps, but it hardly seems – '

'Auguste, you are bringing a strange woman to my house and you did not even bother to find out anything about her?'

'That's not how it is. I – '

'It's out of the question. For all I know she's just a common whore.' He looked at me closely. 'Auguste, is she?'

'Is she what?'

'A whore?'

'I told you,' I said. 'I don't know.'

'You're lying.'

'I am not.'

'Where did you find her?'

I said nothing.

'Come on, you found her somewhere. Where did you meet her? And remember, I can tell whether you are telling the truth or not.'

'By the river,' I said.

'By the river? By the river! The Cherry Gardens?'

'It might be.'

'The Cherry Gardens?' he said. 'Auguste, I said before that your face is transparent. That's it, isn't it?'

'Perhaps.'

'It has possibilities,' he said. 'But you'll have to wait for my decision.'

'Wait? But I need a model.'

'You want a pretty little whore to play with.'

'No. This one – '

'Is different. They're all different, of course. No. I am waiting. You can wait too.'

'Waiting for what?' Anger weakened my guard.

'You know,' he said.

'No.'

He stepped up to me. I flinched. He rubbed his cheek against mine. I felt his stubble. His breath was warm and neutral.

'How much do you want her?'

117

'How much do you want me?' I said. It wasn't anger so much as an internal pressure that quickened my wits.

'*Touché*. Come, I don't want to argue tonight. Let's get a train to Greenwich.'

22

In Greenwich Park the nannies and perambulators were being replaced by courting couples. Long shadows lay across the undulating ground. Some children had spotted a tree creeper on the thick trunk of a chestnut tree and were trying to kill it with sticks. One stick hit the little bird, but a reflex action caused its claws to grip and it hung like a little ornament from the rough, serrated bark.

Giles shouted at the children until they left, then picked the bird from the tree. It lay in his hands, trembling and panting. There was blood on its beak. One eye had been crushed by a stick and the other stared up at us, a yellow and black sequin, half veiled by a membranous lid. Its legs were little curved sticks. Giles twisted its neck and threw it away in one quick conjuror's movement.

We did not linger in the park. He marched me up the hill from the Naval College, past the observatory, down a long avenue of chestnut trees and out through a side entrance. We crossed a neck of scrubland extending from the wild expanse of Blackheath. We plunged down a muddy track, climbed a small hill, and were suddenly in a small park, set on a promontory above the valley of the Thames. Below us, stretching away in a dark and spreading volcanic pool, lay the smoking wastes of London. The sky was turning orange; the river wound like a chain of molten pewter between ranks of buildings and chimneys. Lights were beginning to glow dully in the twilight.

Giles said: 'If ever you think you amount to anything, come here and try to imagine yourself down there.'

'What are you trying to tell me?' I asked.

'I am trying to impress on you what could be. You could be nothing. Just an ant busying through corridors of brick. An ant sees a purpose for itself, but what is it? An ant.'

'I have tried to repay you by taking advantage of every opportunity that came my way. Isn't that what I was meant to do?'

'So the furtherance of your career should be reward enough for me? Very pretty. And now you want to move a whore into the house.'

'I never said she was moving in.'

'But you want it.'

'Do I? I hardly know her.'

'You've thought about it. I'll take your silence as a yes. Well, I've brought you here to meet some other whores, just to make sure you don't go rushing in too rashly. I think I want to understand why someone who finds my company so repellent could instead prefer to spend their hours in the company of some raddled hag, crawling with disease as a dog crawls with fleas.'

'It's not like that,' I began.

'Yes, it is,' Giles said. His face twisted as if there were another shape beneath the skin. He clenched his fists and then his jaw until I thought his teeth must break. Then the spasm passed.

'Under this hill,' he said, 'there's a cave. Our ancestors carved it out with their bare hands, the Romans used it as a temple, and we go there to drink.'

The cavern was deep, and high, and made up to look like a pub. Behind the bar was a large mirror which reflected a lot of darkness. Above the glasses rack was a big wooden-cased clock with Roman numerals. Above the clock the roof disappeared into a dark, irregular vault. The walls were badly panelled. The barman said: 'No action yet. Things liven up when the ladies arrive.'

But things didn't liven up when the ladies arrived. They smiled with their yellow teeth and slapped their white thighs until the flesh wobbled pinkly. One of them started to sing a bad song about a negro sailor with a huge penis. Giles's mood lifted as mine sank. He swung his beer mug and joined in the chorus, introducing me whenever he could as the world's greatest expert in womankind. I was pawed a bit and one sat on my lap, and as she was bigger than me, it made people laugh, especially when Giles put a hat with a long feather on my head.

I sat as still as I could while he taunted and teased me. When a man has nothing but his wits, his body, and his talent, and when his body counts for naught, and his talent is being stifled, then he must use his wits. For the first time I saw Giles not as my means, however inconvenient, to success and independence, but as an obstacle. It was a wise ancient who said that with a lever he could move a mountain. Giles, squatting like a sulky monolith in my path, could be moved. I just needed a lever big enough.

23

The only rooms I knew in Crucifix Lane were the kitchen on the ground floor, which was Mrs Tully's domain and so effectively barred to me, the drawing room on the first floor, and the dining room leading off it. On the floor above were the bedrooms, and the floor above that consisted of the odd penthouse built on to the top of the house. You could only get into the brick extension at the back through a locked door opposite the kitchen, and, I conjectured, from the bedrooms.

On a day when I knew that Giles was out and Mrs Tully busy, I crept past the kitchen door and ran up the two flights of stairs to the bedrooms. All the doors were unlocked but for one which opened into the back of the house. If there was a secret, I thought, it would lie here.

Of course Mrs Tully carried the household keys on a ring at her waist. She was in the habit of taking this with her when she went out shopping, but not when she made longer journeys.

The first time I saw her leave without her keys, I carefully searched her bedroom. I could not find them and was disturbed by the smell of her lingering in the air. The second time I saw her go into the kitchen with the keys around her waist, and leave a minute later without them. It took me two minutes to find them in an empty flour tin on the middle shelf of the larder. I tested them out on the door by the kitchen until one turned.

There was a short corridor, and then the room full of boilers which you could see from the yard. Stairs led off to the left, the steps turning almost immediately, passing a cobwebbed window then opening on to a landing with two doors giving off it. The first room was dingy and square, divided by a low partition with a canvas-bottomed bed to each side. The shutters were half closed; the grate cold and gritty with chimney dust. The other room was the same in every respect. On the next floor the pattern of rooms was repeated. The first one I entered was empty but for a cracked basin with two dead spiders in it. The second room was totally different. It was a little box that gleamed with cleanliness. Walls and ceiling had been painted in a white, oil-based paint. The floor was covered in stretched oil cloth, the grate had been brushed clean and there was a new, metal-sprung bed against one wall, its mattress propped against it. When I touched the mattress it folded in on itself as if it had been waiting for me, and collapsed on to the floor. I lifted it and laid it carefully against the bed. It fell again, but this time opened up and I saw that the side that had been facing inwards carried a huge water stain that spread over half the mattress.

At the end of the corridor was a door which opened into the front of the house. Halfway down this was a wall cupboard. It was instinct that made me try the door as I walked past. The stillness of the house was an entity in itself, definite enough to remain undisturbed by the jangle of keys as I inserted them one by one. It was oddly comforting – the stillness was a tangible medium and I was sure that if anyone disturbed it, I would immediately sense it, the way you know when a person sits on the edge of your bed in the stillness of the night.

The door opened with a rush of strange-smelling air. I peered inside, and saw another staircase, uncarpeted. A draught ran down the steeply sloping ladder steps like a sheet of water. It was light up there, and cold. I took a breath and climbed.

The room was huge, as deep as the house and almost as wide, diminished only by a low ceiling. Dark wooden shelves covered the long side wall, filled with books at one end and large specimen jars at the other. Pale things hung in the dark liquid: a freak piglet with two heads; a family of tiny, hairless baby cats; a vast grey walnut that I took to be a brain; a flayed

123

animal leg. More things, red organs, more things. A baby whose body tapered to a wispy root: no legs, no feet, no toes. It had large black eyes that were open and looked mildly out at the world from its glass womb with a face that was still and very wise. In the middle of the roof was a hinged skylight, propped permanently open to judge by the stained rug on the floor underneath it. Even with it open, the bottles still stank.

At one end of the room was a battered arm chair on a small, torn Turkey rug. At the other a simple, sturdy table was set under the window. Between them, stretching the length of the room, was a long work bench. There was an empty animal cage at one end. A raised shelf running along its back contained coloured, stoppered glass jars, the sort you find in an apothecary's shop. In the middle of the bench was an enamel tray with a small drainage hole fitted over a basin. Tray, bench, and basin had all been washed down and were spotlessly clean, although dusty.

In the drawer of the table, I found a loose folder tied in a red ribbon. I opened it.

14 January 1864
A cat. Adult. Female. Created compound fracture in vice. Cat bit and raked me. Ran across floor. Impossible to control. Was compelled to dispatch it. Leather helmet? Wear gloves!

Mrs T. can make full head hood

23 January 1864
Hooded and tied cat. Old male. Broke rl tibia in vice. Compound.
24 Jan
No gangrene
25 Jan
No gangrene
26 Jan
Will amputate rl and rr leg.
27 Jan
Died. Shock? Blood loss?

17 Feb
Dog. Muzzled and bound. Healthy. Will simulate abdominal tear.
Bathed wounds in phenol. Injected half fl oz.
18 Feb
Dog died. Vomit into muzzle. Choked?

22 Feb
Cat. Will amputate all legs. Front: stumps bathed in phenol. Rear: no
treatment.
23 Feb
Inflammation on both rear legs. Front legs clean.
24 Feb
Front legs clean; benign pus from sutures. Rear legs inflamed.
25 Feb
Sepsis in rear legs. Front legs clean. Intend to amputate rear stumps and
bathe in phenol
26 Feb
Cat dead. Shock? Lack of food? Water?

20 Mar
Goat. Will amputate and treat all legs in turn.
21 Mar
fl Bathed in phenol. Mrs T soaked sutures in phenol.
22 Mar
No inflammation
23 Mar
No inflammation
24 Mar
No inflammation. Signs of healing.
24 Mar
The goat's the thing! Healing.
25 Mar
No inflammation.
26 Mar
Success. Removed suture

28 March

Mrs T has soaked sutures and blade. Amputated rr leg at hip. Nicked artery. Stitched. Stitched flap. Injected half fl oz soap dil 5:1 solution. Fl healed.

29 Mar

No inflammation

30 Mar

No inflammation

31 Mar

No inflammation. Rigged harness so goat could eat, drink more easily. Success. Harness prevents goat from eating wound. Signs of healing.

1 April

No inflammation. Signs of healing. Bathing wounds in soap. Success!

2 April

If soap can prevent sepsis, can it fight? Introduce faeces into wound?

3 April

Made half-inch incision and applied approx quart oz dog faeces. Restitched.

4 April

Injected half fl oz soap sol. (as above)

5 April

Inflammation?

6 April

Inflammation

7 April

Green pus / stink

8 April

Injected half fl oz soap

9 April

Spreading inflammation. Opened wound to clean. Goat died. Shock?

I riffled through the remainder of the pages, stopped when I thought I saw something else, then had to go back and forth before I found the single entry. It was written neatly at the top of the page.

Nelly Oates
Not ready.

There were no other entries.

24

Giles was lying on my bed while I worked on *The Country Girl*. He had spent a day on the wards and had come to tell me about it. He talked and watched me. He talked in order to watch me.

'They come to us,' he said, 'to be cured. What happens? We give them Physick. Do you know what Physick is? Physick is made of iron, sulphate of magnesia, quassia and cod liver oil. It's disgusting and it does not work. When it fails to work and they are almost dead anyway, they're carried into a theatre that looks like a cock pit and stinks of death and sawdust, they're drugged, tied down by two thugs, sliced open, hacked apart, then wake up in a ward that stinks of pus, wait for an infection to strike, then die.

'Listen. There was a great Austrian doctor, Ignaz Semmelweis, who proved that post-natal fever in birthing mothers was effectively eliminated if medical students immersed their hands in chlorine before assisting at the births. Why? We know that immediately before moving on to the wards, the students had been performing post-mortem surgery in the hospital morgue. Septicaemia is a form of rot. There *is* a connection, there has to be. For him, the answer was chlorine. For me, it is soap.'

'Do you see yourself as another – what is his name? Semmelweis?'

'Me another Ignaz? I sincerely hope not. He was laughed out of the profession and died insane last year. That won't happen to me. No, after that scene in the operating theatre, I'm going to be careful. I am going to prepare and present a body of incontrovertible evidence that will shake the medical establishment to its foundations.'

'How?'

'All in good time.'

'Can I help?'

'Help with what?' He sounded wary and suspicious. I could not let him know I had any knowledge of his work in the attic. I shrugged.

'Drawing? I could immortalise you.'

'Hmm. Interesting. I'll think about it.' He looked pleased. More than that: he looked vain.

In his diary he had written an entry on Nelly Oates. *Nelly Oates. Not ready.* Did that refer to her, or to Giles?

William Oates had mistaken me for Giles's assistant. Well, he had followed me and Giles into the slums of Rotherhithe to see a dying woman so that was not so unlikely.

Oates knew Mrs Tully, or at any rate knew she would carry cryptic messages to Giles.

He thought Giles would be interested in a Lascar with a smashed shin.

The thought hit me then. Mrs Reeves, the woman dying in the slums, had had a smashed arm before it was cut off. The Lascar had a smashed shin. *Nelly Oates. Not ready.*

Giles was experimenting on people!

I glanced up. Giles had stopped talking and had gone white.

'My God,' he said.

I put down my pencil. Had he realised he was about to give away some great secret?

A moment later the door swung open. To say they came in would be to underestimate the effect. It was more of a grand entrance: first Mr and Mrs Bouverie arm in arm, then two young women, then a small, dapper man with a deferential, twittering manner, whose first reaction on seeing the hall was to throw up his hands and exclaim: 'La!'

They paused in the doorway. Again that odd radiance from Mr and Mrs Bouverie. All three women were bustled and bodiced, their torsos corked into the great spreading bell of their skirts, but apart from that it would have been hard to imagine three more different representatives of their sex. They approached, moving smoothly on invisible feet. I was reminded of mermaids.

Mrs Bouverie looked as if she had been parboiled, scraped, then buffed. One of the young women wore her blonde hair softly curled, had ingenuous, wide-set blue eyes, a short chin, and bore a strong resemblance to the father. This must be Giles's sister. The other had a strong, closed face. Her dark hair was drawn tightly down both sides of her cheeks, causing her mouth to droop. While the sister gazed about her, amazed, the other young woman stood quite still and looked at Giles.

He shot to his feet, pulling down his waistcoat and hurriedly smoothing back his hair.

'There he is, there's the man! Osgood – Giles. Giles – Osgood.' This from the father. 'Osgood, this is Auguste Coffey. Osgood's an expert. He's here to see what you can do.'

Osgood was approaching me with a curious, sideways gait, head lowered. Suddenly he darted for the easel, seemed to squeeze around it although it was in the middle of that vast empty room, and stood behind me, hand cupping chin, one eyebrow raised archly.

Giles's mother deigned to be kissed by him. He said: 'Hello, Georgie,' to his sister in a dismissive, elder brother tone, but his reaction to the other woman was strange. As she raised her cheek to him, he took her hand and bent over it, blushing. He straightened up without meeting her eye.

'We brought Fanny with us because she had not heard from you for so long,' his mother said. She had a slight lisp that I had not noticed before.

The sister said: 'Mother!' and glanced at Giles.

He stammered: 'I-I have been busy.' He spoke to Fanny, as if by way of apology. She nodded, quite unruffled.

'But not so busy today, I see,' from his father.

'Today I – there are no studies today. Professor Freeman is ill.'

'Ill. I see.'

'I'm sure if Giles says that Dr Freeman is ill – '

'Mr.'

The sister broke off and looked at her mother, who continued: 'Consultants are referred to as Mr. I would have thought you knew that.'

The sister flushed. 'Why should I have known that?'

'Hush, hush. There, there. Let's not quarrel in front of strangers,' Mr Bouverie said. Georgina answered: 'No, of course not,' and shot me an appealing glance underneath her eyelashes.

Mr Bouverie looked at Giles with mild contempt. It would have been better if he had called him a liar to his face. Mrs Bouverie stared up at a window. Fanny smiled and went to stand by Giles's side. He managed to shrink away from her without moving.

'Well, Osgood?'

'He shows promise, some talent.'

'We want somebody to paint a portrait of Georgina,' Mrs Bouverie announced. 'We have approached numerous established painters but have found that their engagements prevent their seeing us for many months.'

'Well, I would be happy – ' I began, unwilling to make assumptions.

'We want to know if you are suitable,' Mrs Bouverie said, in her high, monotonous voice. 'That is why we have brought Mr Osgood with us. He has an eye.'

Mr Osgood was squinting so furiously at my sketch by this stage that it looked as if that were quite literally the case.

'Mr Coffey perhaps has other engagements himself?' Georgina said in a low voice. She smiled at me. Now I found myself blushing. I did not know what to say.

'No,' I stammered. 'Nothing that – '

'He is busy building up his talent. He doesn't have time to waste on a frivolous society portrait,' Giles said quickly.

'We know that. We've come from Gruber,' Mr Bouverie said.

'Well then? You'll know how important it is that he – '

'I know how important it is that artists improve themselves by painting their betters in society. I am sure that Mr Coffey has no objection to my talking like this.' Mrs Bouverie's voice was like the east wind that streams off the North Sea in cold, monotonous ribbons. 'I have read it in books and my view was confirmed by the German.'

'Gruber would confirm your view that the moon was made of soap,' Giles said.

'Do not speak to your mother like that, sir,' Mr Bouverie thundered. 'Now will you paint Georgina or not?' He looked at me. To my surprise I found my eye drawn to the other young woman who had been silent up until that point.

She said, 'There can be no harm in a sketch,' in a voice that was both firm and conciliatory.

'Very well,' I said. 'If Miss Bouverie will sit for me for one hour, I shall have something that Mr Osgood will be able to judge.'

'An hour? But that is most inconvenient,' Mrs Bouverie said. 'And we have not eaten.'

'Let us eat then,' said Giles. 'I am sure – '

'We have brought food with us,' his mother announced. 'We knew you would not have enough for us all. There is a hamper in the growler.' She managed to lard even this comment with the implication that he was in some way at fault.

Osgood danced away from the canvas. Fanny levelled her cool glance at Giles, who, catching it, gave her his arm and led her from the studio. I said I would ready myself and join them later. I stood on my trunk and looked out of the window. Giles was insisting that they set up tables in the yard and eat outside. A servant brought in one hamper, then a case. Linen was spread over a rude trestle, crockery set out, then the food. Meats, pies, cheese, fruit, bread, butter. Giles and his father ate in silence; the women ate hardly at all.

★

132

Osgood was resting somewhere in the main house. Fanny sat on a straight-backed chair and watched me work. Georgina Bouverie sat well enough for me. She was nervous, timid even. I could see her hands trembling in her lap and when I told her to hold them both together, she shot me a grateful look. She had a small mole on her right cheek that I did not reproduce. When I had finished the sketch and she had come round the other side of the easel to look, she blushed.

'You have made me look far finer than I am.'

Fanny made a noise of disagreement.

'It is true. I know you think I denigrate myself to attract compliments, but I don't, Fanny, I mean it,' Georgina protested.

'I do not think that,' Fanny answered. 'I just grow impatient that you cannot recognise your beauty, and the pleasure it might bring you.'

Georgina looked uncomfortable.

'While that is true,' I said, 'some of Miss Bouverie's beauty might lie in her modesty. I have often observed how little the mere configuration of bone and flesh, the basic arrangement of features, have to do with beauty, and how much of it is due to expression. In other words, character. What you see there,' I said to Georgina, 'is what I have seen of your character, what brings your face to life.'

'Then *you* think me finer than I am,' she said, blushing.

'I draw what I see.' I held her eyes. She looked away. I thought: I am affecting her. The sensation was exciting.

Fanny clapped her hands. 'Enough,' she said, half jokingly. 'I'll have no wooing while I am cast as chaperone. Georgina was telling me that she could not believe the effect you have wrought in this room. She said it was the gloomiest place in the world previously.'

'Oh, yes.' Georgina spoke eagerly. 'The windows were filthy, the air stank of rancid fat, the floor and walls were sticky. There were great cauldrons for heating the soap – there, there, and there. It was hot too. And pipes. There were pipes laid out on the floor. I cannot believe how it's been transformed.'

'I did nothing,' I said. 'Merely moved in as I found it. Giles must have had the place prepared.'

'For you?'

'No. Before me.'

'But he must have had plans,' Georgina said.

'I do not know. He asked me to move here, I thought hard about it for all of two minutes, then leapt at the offer.'

But Fanny interrupted her. She had been looking at my sketches, propped against the wall, and now held up *The Mermaid*.

'You travel widely?' she said.

Held up by a stranger, it was as if I were looking at the picture for the first time. I was shocked by how violent it seemed.

Georgina put her hand to her mouth and said: 'Oh, I always think there is something so sad about mermaids. Was it a dream?' she said to me, eyes wide with concern.

'Of a sort,' I answered.

'A rather dark dream,' said Fanny. 'If I were a collector, it is strange fancies like this that I would collect.'

Mother, Father and therefore Mr Osgood pronounced themselves pleased with the sketch. I agreed to a price of seventy-five guineas, sittings to be arranged at our mutual convenience. Giles then insisted on giving them tea, and the family graciously agreed, before they took the train back down to their Sevenoaks home.

Georgina was silent, sitting slightly apart from the rest of the group, glancing in my direction then looking away again as soon as I caught her eye. I knew I should talk to her but could think of nothing to say. Osgood and Mr Bouverie talked about railway shares – there seemed no subject on which Osgood was not an expert – and I stood by them making a threesome, nodding at a point that one of them had made, adjusting my face according to the way the conversation was going.

Giles and Fanny were standing in the bay window and I was admiring the way she handled him; never encroaching, but presenting herself, I thought, as a haven of calm and reassurance that he could approach when and if he wanted. I had spotted no word or sign of reproach that he had been neglecting her, and I had noticed him thaw towards her as the afternoon wore on. Now he actually laughed at something she said, and whispered something back in her ear. Mrs Bouverie had told me over lunch that Giles was a good match for her. Fanny's family, the Morants, had lost money recently, although in all fairness until then there had been what she called 'a seemly parity'.

She said it loud enough for all to hear. Silence seemed to descend over the company. Glancing out of the window, Mr Bouverie said: 'I thought I'd told you to take that stack down, Giles? It's got no use and I don't like the look of it. It's been a long time since the old chimney smoked and they get damp and rot.'

'Oh, but I thought it was still used,' I said, meaning nothing, simply trying to fill the silence.

'Rot,' Mr Bouverie said. 'Absolute nonsense.'

His tone nettled me.

'But I heard – '

'The people you mingle with, Auguste, are scarcely to be trusted,' Giles said with an easy, malicious laugh. 'He does meet the most incredible types on his wanderings. Only the other day – '

'We have no interest in this,' Mrs Bouverie said, and then it was time for the family to return home. As we gathered in the hallway, Fanny murmured quietly to me: 'There is something I want to say to you alone.' Then she added in a much louder voice: 'Oh, my brooch! It must have fallen.'

There were general sympathetic noises. Giles said he would look upstairs. I suggested the studio. Fanny said: 'Of course. I took it off there. I thought the setting might be loose.'

She followed me across the courtyard. Once inside she said: 'We cannot talk for long. How has he been?'

'Giles? Very well,' I said.

'His spirits?'

'They rise and fall.'

'Giles has such a future, such potential, if only he could be reconciled with his father. There is such bad feeling there. Ever since he refused to go into the business and went his own way, it has been nothing but a battle, and Giles will always lose.'

'If they disapprove, why do they support him?' I said.

'They give him a crutch so they can pull it away, then mock him when he falls. We must go,' she said. 'But write to me if there is any serious – if anything happens that concerns you.' She took the brooch from her pocket.

'May I say something?' I asked.

'Of course.'

'And I can speak frankly?'

'I cannot stop you.'

'Giles has not mentioned you to me,' I said. 'My position here is . . . tenuous.' I had a sudden vision of myself as an Osgood, flapping and bowing around affluent families; a tutor, an expert, a failure. 'Is it possible that he has not mentioned you to me because you would have an antipathy towards me? I mean, are our respective positions with regard to him contradictory?'

She regarded me coolly, but not coldly. 'You are a strange young man,' she said. 'Too frank, perhaps, even if your sentences are slightly convoluted. I think you are asking if we are rivals in any way?'

I nodded.

'Not so far as I am concerned,' she said. 'I would never knowingly compete for status. Whether Giles feels the same way is another matter.'

I left her to hurry across the courtyard. I took my time locking the door and walking back. By the time I got to the main house, the Bouveries had gone.

25

'Why did you try and stop me painting your sister?'
'They hate my guts,' Giles said. 'And I hate theirs.'
It was eleven o'clock in the morning and he was drunk. 'God,
I hate them! God, they must hate me. I'll not have you
involved.' He was lying in bed. Morning sunlight burned white
pools on the crumpled sheets. 'Shocked? Little orphan boy
shocked? Little orphan boy's scared to let go, isn't he? Little
orphan boy's too bloody careful.'

I shook my head. 'I don't know why you're saying these
things Giles. I only wanted to help.'

'Little man Gussie thinks he can help. All right, I'll tell you
how you can help. You can take your wretched little body and
get it off my bed and leave me on my own. You're mine, do
you understand? Without me you are nothing. They're just
trying to take you away from me, spoil you like they spoil
everything.' He began to cry. 'I hate them. I hate everyone. I
hate you. Now get out!'

He waved an arm at me. There was a small blue bottle on
the table next to the bed. Giles took laudanum. It made me all
the angrier; he could try and block my career then spoon
himself into a stupor.

'So you'd show me off, take me to a gallery, parade me in
front of them. "Look at the clever little foundling. He doesn't
dribble his tea, doesn't drop his aitches, and what's more he can
draw too." Well, I can draw pictures of pretty girls and I'll
draw her!'

Giles looked at me, his eyes suddenly clear.

'By God, you've had a little daydream. I can see it in your face. It's gone all silly and hopeful. You find her attractive. That's cheered me up. Auguste and Georgina. Oh, my.'

He laughed so hard he began to cough. When he looked at me, the laughter started again. 'It'd almost be worth pushing you two together. Yes. Perhaps I'll do that. I'd like to see you together. Auguste the suitor, all bows and scrapes, and simple little Georgina, all ribbons and bows.'

By three o'clock he was sober and came to see me. He looked neat, chastened and shocked, with the face of a bad child who has had its head ducked in iced water and scrubbed with a pumice stone.

'If you ever hear me talk like that again, hit me or leave,' Giles said. 'What did I say?'

I was standing behind my easel, pretending to work, too upset by Giles's scornful behaviour to settle to anything.

'A lot of nonsense about your parents,' I said.

'Mrs Tully said I was rude to you.'

'Oh, not really.'

'I've lost too many friends by being drunk, Auguste. I don't want to lose you.' He said it calmly and simply, without the awkwardness that self-recrimination would have brought.

'Well then, you won't. If you do it again, I shall laugh gaily and jump on your head.'

'Was I awful?'

'No.'

'You mean no worse than usual?'

'I wouldn't go that far.'

'Bad, but not awful, then?'

'Exactly,' I said.

He sniffed. 'What are you doing?'

'Blocking out a canvas.'

'May I see?'

I considered then stood aside, inviting him to come round. He looked at it. I explained the story of *The Country Girl*.

138

'Why not have her angry brother pursue her?' he asked. 'No. Have a pimp eye her up.'

'I might.'

'What's this?'

He picked a charcoal drawing from the floor. It was a sketch from memory of the boy collecting dog excrement for the tanneries. I was going to include him somewhere.

'What have you done with his hand?'

'Nothing. He's deformed.'

'And it looks like this?'

'Yes,' I said.

He sighed. 'You could change this with a flick of the pen. I would have to cut with a knife. But I could, you know.'

I shrugged. 'It's for me to draw what I see. Truth.'

'And for me to want to change what I see?' He began to pace up and down. 'I was interested in art. No talent, Gruber told me. That was after my parents had told me how useless I was. Perfection. That's what they want. That's all they want. But whatever I do – it's never good enough.'

'What you were saying the other night,' I said. 'Soap. If you could bring that to your knowledge of surgery . . .'

'Don't,' he said. 'Don't try and understand me.' There was both concern and a warning in his voice. 'And don't ask why,' he continued quickly. 'Do you know what the juggernaut is?'

'No,' I said.

'It is a vast pagan statue of a Hindu deity. Big – bigger than a house. Once a year the natives bring it out to worship. They place it on great rollers and pull it through the streets, while children dance in front of it, tossing flowers in its path. By the end of the procession, the rollers are slick with the blood of the little children it has crushed. It cannot stop.'

'What are you saying?' I snorted sarcastically. 'Are you saying that you are like this?'

'No,' Giles said. 'I am saying that people are. I believe it, honestly.'

'Well, I don't.'

'Good.' He looked at me strangely, then grinned. 'See you at dinner. I've told Mrs Tully to do something special. To make up. I am sorry, Auguste.'

I'm sure he meant well, but it is an odd fact that once insulted, the victim would rather forget the slight than have the humiliation recalled by even the most sincere apology.

What was worse? No security, or a mirage of security? The mirage, I believe, because all the while it is dragging you further into the desert to kill you, you are convinced you are going to be saved.

And then, still in the spirit of making up, Giles got me drunk and we played the game again. This time I was ready: this time I wanted to play the game, to learn its ways and try and turn it to my advantage.

He smiled, and smiling asked without a pause, as if his throat had been oiled: 'What are you most frightened of?'

'Love,' I said, without even thinking.

Then it was my turn.

'Tell me, Giles, what are *you* most frightened of?'

'Death,' he said.

It was all so simple and so clear. I was frightened of love, he was frightened of death; I an artist, he a surgeon. How could we solve this problem? Could we make ourselves whole by confronting what we feared most? Was this the time to put it all behind me and start again? It was. I felt it. We are created denying what we need the most; the baby needs air and light but screams when it is born, and we go through life most frightened of that which will do us the greatest good.

And then suddenly we were both laughing, as if cares and tiredness had simply slipped away. Outside the window the sun was rising over the rooftops of Bermondsey. I threw open a window. The street was almost empty; the air almost fresh. There was gold in the clouds; there was gold in the air; there was gold glistening on the wet slates of Crucifix Lane. A child was sitting in a doorway, squinting dreamily at the light, knuckling its eyes.

26

I couldn't work. I lay on my cot, staring up at the lantern, wondering whether the dog boy would ever reappear, wondering whether Pity would come knocking at my door. I kept on turning over in my head the words of William Oates and Giles's odd reaction to my mentioning the chimney. A fat young fly, drugged by the heat of the fire, walked one way across my blanket, then another, then another. Eventually it found a crumb or something, and extended a stiff brown tongue.

I had been wondering how Giles got to know William Oates, and then suddenly I had it. Giles had said that the factory had employed forty local people. Perhaps William and Nelly Oates were employees. Perhaps there were others still in the neighbourhood.

I went out. The sky was like mercury and the air was as close as a wet woollen wrap. People carried a glaze of sweat on them like cheap crockery. I would ask at the butcher, the baker and the candlestick maker if I could find one; failing that, anywhere.

But they didn't know in the baker's, nor in the butcher's, and in the grocer's, which sold everything, they didn't know either, although the shopkeeper tried to sell me a bar of soap.

When I said I needed to know something, not to wash, he held up a bar of Bouverie's Moonlight and told me to look closely at the picture on the front. I did. In the middle stood the wizard waving his wand of cleanliness.

'No, look behind him,' the grocer said. 'That's here. These streets. You didn't know that, did you? The Borough. The

Pool of London and all. That's the docks. That's the foundry. That's the market and that's the soap factory.'

The background was quartered heraldically. Painted in miniature were scenes of activity, presumably to show people getting dirty: tiny, detailed pictures in reds and greens. The docks were represented by masts, cranes and London Bridge. The market was a maze of barrows piled high with orange and green fruit. The foundry was a furnace and chimney belching black smoke. The soap factory was the studio, as seen from the house, its chimney smoking too.

'What happened when they closed the factory down for good?'

'A lot of the soap workers moved with the factory – those that had families, and the men. They were rehoused I heard, down Croydon way. Get a bar of soap a week free, handed out on Friday with the wages. Can't say that'd be good for business. Now you'd think that my business would slacken off with the soap factory moving. Not a bit of it. Soap sales up by a factor of three. Know why? The girls were allowed to take what they wanted of the broken soap cakes, and you know what they did? Flogged it cheap. It could have been the death of me. Unfair competition, those girls.'

'What girls?' I asked.

'The factory girls.'

'Did they move too?'

'No. I suppose it would have seemed like abduction, moving single women.'

'What happened to them?'

'Try the tannery in Wilds Rents,' he said, 'by the slaughterhouse. Some of the girls from the factory moved on there.'

But there was something else I needed to know.

'Does the chimney ever smoke these days?' I asked.

'If you don't see it, you smell it.'

'So it does.'

'I wouldn't say it does, but it has.'

'After they moved the factory?'

'Must have been because we could all breathe again.'

'Why, what did they burn there?'

'They said they burned animals to make the fat. I don't know if that was what it was. All I know is one morning – maybe a year ago, I woke up and the smell was back and I said to the wife: "They've opened the factory again." And she said, "Never, they moved all the ironware out, wagon loads of it. You remember." I said: "Well, I smells it and that's that." And I did smell it, but it didn't last.'

In the yard at the tannery the women scraped meat and fat off the cow hides while the men tended the vats. A cow's head had been stuck on a spike above the gate. The stench was unbeliev-able: animal and mineral, cloying and sharp, dead and alive, all at the same time. The foreman said that Nelly Oates had been on cows' tails but couldn't take it in the cold. The cows' tails were soaked in water for a week to soften them, then rubbed down a board to get the short hairs off. It was hard in the winter and her skin had split, he said. What with the water being foul, cracks in the skin could be a nuisance, so he had to let her go but thought she might have ended up at the renderer's.

The renderer's was a long, dark, brick shed, blackened inside and out by smoke. The walls bellied, held from collapse by buttresses of undressed timbers. In the shed, the bits of cow and sheep that could not be eaten or tanned were ground down for fertiliser. It was a simple operation based around a small steam engine, a grinding unit and some sacks. The steam engine thumped and sighed, and the grinder made a variety of wet snapping noises. The women said nothing. One, planted in front of an unsteady pyramid of gore and bone, shovelled it on to a hoist then raised it with a pulley; another, planted on a platform above the grinding machine, tipped the stuff down a funnel, prodding the more stubborn bits with a long oar whose paddle looked well chewed. Two more, working in rotation, held a sack under a hopper, or controlled the flow with a lever. A final woman tied the sacks with string and swung them into brown, leaking ranks. The whole process was a back-breaking dance of death and destruction; once you started pushing the stuff in at the top, it seemed there was no way anyone could stop. They said being out of work was hell, but if so, it was only one kind of hell. The woman without an arm, she was hell; this was hell too.

A man was sitting in a small office, a wooden box with a sliding glass window at the front. He attracted my attention by banging on the glass.

'Nelly Oates?' I said. Inside the sound was slightly muffled but I still had to shout above the grinding and the thumping.

He grimaced. 'I don't want trouble. Are you trouble? An inspector?'

'No. I'm trying to find Nelly Oates.'

'Before my time.'

'Do you know the names of all the girls who worked here before your time?'

He screwed up his face and looked like he wanted to hit me.

'She did work here?' I pressed. He was still in his booth and I was still outside.

'You a reformer?' he asked, stupidly.

'No,' I said. 'Just trying to trace Nelly Oates.'

All the women had stolen glances across at me, apart from the one with the paddle. The manager seemed to be looking at her.

'Is that her?' I asked, almost disappointed. She was a plain, square woman, her sour face grey where it wasn't spattered with blood. No mystery there.

'That was her station.'

'When did she leave?'

'Mags!'

He called over to the woman with the shovel. She lifted her head, put the shovel down and slouched over to us.

'You were a friend of Nelly Oates's,' he said. 'You tell him what happened.' Ostentatiously he slid the glass across and bent his head again.

The woman was quite young under the dirt and blood. She looked at me suspiciously.

'You worked with Nelly?' I said.

She sniffed and nodded.

'At the factory?'

'Yes, sir.'

'If she was married, why didn't she move with the works? I thought that's what the girls did.'

'She came here.'

'She wanted to come here?' I asked incredulously.

'Didn't have no choice.'

'What happened to her?'

'She was up the duff, wasn't she?'

'When?'

'A year back. More now. Longer.'

'Was there some – problem?'

'There was some bump.' When I looked blank, she said: 'Her old man put her up to it.'

'What happened?'

'She lost the baby. Came out dead, she said. She got depressed. I got her work here.'

'Then what?'

'Then what what?'

'Where did she go?'

'She left. Got sick. Can't work in here with the engine if you're sick.'

She smiled. The engine noise was in my head, pumping up blood until my skull felt stretched like a blister.

'Did she kill herself?' I asked.

She shrugged.

She was right. It was rather irrelevant. I walked past the machine. Once again all the faces swung towards me, but not the woman on the top. She kept her eyes on her job and I didn't blame her.

27

A knock at the studio door. I called, 'Come in.'
Mrs Tully stood there, arms folded, looking at me
curiously.

'A person to see you.'

I looked up.

'Who?'

'I've no way of knowing.'

'Where? Who is it?'

There was a pause.

'Well?' I said.

Mrs Tully seemed to be debating whether to answer me or
not. She did so without any trace of insolence: that would have
been beneath her dignity. She knew, or implied she knew, that
if anything her position in that house was more assured, more
permanent, than mine. Insolence is disrespect from one lower
to one higher.

Mrs Tully debated whether to oblige me, found her incli-
nation matched my need, and said: 'A young person.'

'Well, show the person in,' I said. 'Please.'

Mrs Tully stood to one side.

Pity stood on the threshold of the room and looked around
her.

She was dressed for visiting. A full, sweeping dress of dark
blue, a bonnet, her hair scraped back below it, a parasol slung
over her shoulder like a poacher's gun. No, she wasn't dressed
for visiting. She was dressed *up* for visiting. There was a subtle
hint of parody in the way she carried herself. I wondered if it

were genuine or a form of defence. I eyed her from behind my canvas, my stomach turning over with excitement.

She looked at me, I looked at her. But I had the advantage. Her eyes were caught by the expanse of the hall. Her gaze wandered. She stared around her.

'Well?' I said.

'Well, what?'

'What brings you here?'

'I came to see you,' she said.

'For what?'

She couldn't stop herself from staring round the hall.

'I wouldn't have come if I'd known.'

'Known what?'

'That you had a housekeeper. That you were a gentleman. I thought you were – '

'Poor?'

'Yes.'

'I'm a painter.'

'Are you a gentleman?'

'No painter is a gentleman.'

'You're talking in circles,' she said.

'All right,' I admitted. 'I am not a gentleman. I am the guest of a gentleman. He lets me live here, while I paint.'

'Why?'

'Because he thinks it worthwhile.'

'But what do you give him in return?'

'I paint,' I said.

She snorted. 'Is that what you are doing now?'

'Sketching out a canvas, as a matter of fact.'

She fiddled with her umbrella and looked around the studio again.

'What does that mean?'

'It means that before I paint, I have to draw in an idea of what the painting will be.'

'Can I come and see?'

'Be my guest.'

Her smile was genuine this time.

'Was Mrs Tully dreadful?' I asked.

'Not as bad as she could have been.'

'What most women think doesn't bother me over much,' I said, 'as long as I can paint.'

'What's that?' she asked, pointing to the canvas.

'It's to be London Bridge. That's the river. The masts of boats in the background.'

'What's the girl doing?'

'She's getting out of her train, bewildered. I want to get across a feeling of the busyness and bustle of London, and how terrifying it looks viewed from the outside.'

'She'd never make that face,' Pity said. 'It'd draw attention.'

'I wanted it to be dramatic,' I answered. 'What sort of face do you think she would make?'

'Like this.'

Seemingly without thinking she had adopted the pose, or something like the pose, I had sketched in. In my picture the girl was going to be recoiling with horror. Pity replaced it with something more subtle. Shock, shyness, but a self-conscious bravery. She knew that the men in the background were looking at her, and she knew she could not betray her horror. She seemed to feel it and disguise it at the same time, so that both showed in her face. I looked at her in wonder. All self-consciousness had gone; or rather her sense of self had been swallowed by a greater consciousness. She was perfect. She was my model.

'Can you stay like that?' I asked.

By way of answer she did nothing. I looked at the canvas and decided it would take too long to rub out and redraw. I sketched her on paper, first her body in rough, then her face. But when I came to examine her body again in more detail, I found I could not get the correct relationship between her waist and hips and legs. In order to express both fear, and unwillingness to show fear, she had tightened her back in a curious way and that had the effect of throwing her hips into

148

an angle I could not get, and the dress made it impossible for me to render.

'Can you remember the position you are in?'

She nodded cautiously.

'Straighten up then.'

'Was that good?'

'Yes. Will you do it for me again? I mean, will you be my model?'

She laughed. 'I've always wanted to be a lady. Maybe you could paint me like one?'

'Of course,' I said. 'There's just one thing . . .'

'What?'

'Will you – ' I found it hard to ask.

'What?'

'Well,' I said. 'The girl in the picture, I know she's dressed, but – well, artists have to practise on girls without any clothes on. Why are you looking at me like that?'

She said: 'I'd best be off.'

'But you're a – '

'What?'

But she was walking towards the door.

'A girl who – ' I was prepared for anything but her laughter.

I coloured. 'Why do you scorn me?' I asked hotly. 'Is it money? If you strip, I'll pay extra.'

'Believe me, sir, you don't want me,' she said. 'Honest.'

'Why not?'

She looked beyond me. Movement in one of the windows at the back of the house. Mrs Tully must have been spying on us.

'Just believe me,' she said.

She walked across the courtyard. Mrs Tully appeared at the back door and led her away.

28

'I thought I told you not to bring your whore here?' Giles said over dinner.

Mrs Tully was hovering at the sideboard. I looked up at her; she looked back at me.

'She came. I didn't ask her.' Mrs Tully raised her eyebrows in disbelief. I wanted to kill her. 'As it is,' I continued, 'I have reconsidered.'

'What? Not right for you? Mrs Tully said she was a common-looking little scrap.'

'I did not.' The housekeeper's voice was as flat as a knife.

'Just teasing.' Giles drank wine in gulps and smacked his lips. 'So what did make you reconsider?'

'She would not pose for life studies.'

'Mrs Tully, that means the tart wouldn't strip.'

'Indeed?'

'Indeed, but not in thought, eh, Gussie? Must be the first whore who didn't in history. Do you suppose there's something the matter with her?'

I shrugged.

'Well, I can't think of any other reason.'

'Unless she doesn't want to.'

'What? Turn down a chance to be paid for sitting still? How much were you offering?'

'I was thinking of two shillings.'

'Very favourable. No, there's more to this than meets the eye.'

'There can be something very personal in the relationship

between a sitter and an artist,' I said. 'Perhaps she didn't want to – ' I was lost for words.

Giles looked at me, then over his shoulder to see if Mrs Tully were in the room. He leaned close to me. 'Auguste, there is something rather personal about having strangers' dicks shoved in you every minute of the day. You are not talking about the whore here, you are talking about yourself. I knew it from the first. I could tell. You are naive, Auguste, it's no use denying it. You saw this girl and you were smitten. It happens occasionally. Now – '

'My interest in her is as a painter.'

He repeated my words sarcastically.

'I resent your tone,' I said.

'Gussie, don't be such an ass. If ever I needed proof that I was doing the right thing in keeping this little noodle out of the house, I've got it now.'

'Why are you so anxious to make me unhappy?' I asked.

'Me? Make you unhappy? Auguste, I am trying to save you from tragedy. Look, trust me.'

We went out. We saw *The Last Disguise* at the Adelphi, the story of a chambermaid, raped (off stage with sound effects) by the master of the house, losing his child, then taking the disguise of a manservant to expose him to his colleagues in the City where he is about to commit a fraud involving a fictitious railway company. In exposing him, she unwittingly exposes herself but so impresses the wife of one of her former master's dupes that the woman takes it upon herself to educate the girl so she may become a governess. (Cue sarcastic cheering from the audience.)

The fashion of the day was to construct vast, elaborately detailed sets and cram them with every conceivable type of Londoner. A walk through the city at night could only take place in Trafalgar Square complete, as the poster promised, not only with rich and poor, fortunate and unfortunate, good and bad, young and old, but also lions, Nelson's Column, the lights of Northumberland House, the sounds of carriage wheels on cobbles – even, at one stage, a carriage driven on to the stage to pick up the villain of the piece just before our heroine could accost him. It was ludicrous and enjoyable, with half the audience gasping at the twists and turns of the plot, the other half jeering good-naturedly.

'Fiction,' said Giles. 'In reality, she would have gone on the game, picked up syphilis, consumption or pneumonia, and died within five years. Oh, do cheer up.'

'How can I? You seem intent on ruining my prospects.'

'Oh, for goodness' sake. Look, I've got an idea. Show her to me. We could go and see her.'

'When?'

'Now.'

'And if you approve?'

'If I approve?' He cuffed me gently. 'I'm not going to approve.'

'But if you saw that she was special, different, you might change your mind?'

'If I thought anything of the kind, yes, all right.'

'Thank you, Giles. You won't regret this.'

'I hope not,' he said.

29

First we went on the rip. We went to a public house in the West End. I forget its name but it had long deal tables and lots of young men with red faces and a drunk who was standing on a piano and singing something in Irish.

We drank gin there and Giles nearly had a fight with a man who had been staring at us for no very good reason. For no very good reason we found this very amusing. When we left, we found we were hungry. Giles insisted we go to an eatery back in the Borough where we sat in a wooden booth and ate chops and oysters and drank porter, and laughed at the waiter who had blacked his pate to hide his baldness.

I insisted on paying. I told Giles I loved him and it was an honour to buy him supper, and in truth it was still a tonic to be able to assert my independence a little with my new money. Giles looked amused.

When I got outside into the fresh air, the drunkenness started coming on in waves, as if it had been dammed up before.

We walked past an apothecary and Giles said that if we were going to continue like this, we would need some powders. So he banged on the door until the apothecary put his head out of the upstairs window and Giles started singing an absurd song about coca powder and arsenic, and would not give up until the man came down and sold us some, still in his nightcap and rather off-white gown. He had purple veins in his nose, white skin and a hard pad of callus on the heel of his palms, that Giles told me was the sign of an arsenic addict. He said that coca powder produced the desired effect with none of the consequences that attended taking arsenic.

In the cab the drink caught up with me again. I opened a window and stared out into the blackness, trying to fix on something to stop my head spinning. The fresh air helped. I remember the seats had ribs of cracked leather and as I fiddled, one of the cracks split and a dusty mixture of horsehair and wood shavings began to force its way out as if it were alive. It seemed very important to push it all back in but the leather was too soft and frayed and everything I did seemed to make it worse. What was inside seemed to be under pressure, and what was holding it in was too weak to succeed. Suddenly the blackness of the little swaying box nauseated me; I think I tried to climb out of the window for some fresh air. The cabman shouted at me and Giles pulled me in by the legs and both of us laughed. I felt better for the exercise, and the laughter.

The cab wouldn't go further than Jamaica Road. I paid him solemnly, surprised at how quickly money went when you were drunk.

'Well, where now?' Giles said.

I said, 'Come on, follow me!' and set off for the waterfront down an alley. It was very dark. The first whore carried a lantern. Her face white, her mouth red, her teeth piebald. We shied away like colts and only laughed when we were past her. The next whore was dying of a cough; the one after that seemed only to have one leg.

'See what I mean?' Giles said.

Stillness entered me. Even now, even drunk, Giles was pushing me, leaning on me.

'What do you mean?'

'You don't want anything to do with these creatures. They are disgusting. Loose. Diseased. Socrates thought femininity itself was a disease; that hysteria originated in the womb.' Giles cupped the back of my head with his hand and rubbed his forehead against mine.

'All right,' he said. 'I'll let up. But you'll not convince me.'

154

'Oh, yes, I will,' I said. 'She's beautiful. Wait till you see her. But I don't want you falling for her. No.' I waved my finger foolishly at him, a pale, luminous slug in the dark.

'I don't think there will be much risk of that,' he said.

'I want you to see how beautiful she is.'

At the brothel I became very solemn. It was the only lit building on the waterfront, with lanterns hanging in some of the windows and a large, ornate paraffin lamp on a curly bracket by the door. On either side hunched big black warehouses. By night, the row of houses seemed almost picturesque.

I led Giles to the river. The tide was high, casually trying to overflow the wall. The river looked immensely wide and black. Lighters were rocking in the swell and rubbing their sides together like cows in a barn, and making the oddest noises – creaking and booming almost as if they had voices. The sky was a chemical reaction: violet and orange, alive. I could see one star through the haze. My mind was clearing a little and I remember feeling very brave. A man in a coracle sculled past, almost at our level, dodging between the barges, looking for driftwood, fruit, anything that might have fallen in the river.

Still water, high tide, the Pool of London slackly full. A sense of brimming imminence, like pressure in the bowels. To resist would be to pit your strength against a force as elemental as the moon.

'Auguste?'

'Yes?'

'Have you ever lain with a woman? Any woman at all?'

'No.' My mouth dried. My head was a furnace: empty, roaring, hot.

Giles smiled. 'What were you going to show me?'

'In here,' I said.

Recently prostitutes have become very popular on the stage, where they are seen either being loud and brassy in pubs or dying pathetically in gutters, having fallen from a state of comparative grace. Harridans or martyrs, nothing in between. Of course, what is in between is all there ever is.

I knocked on a heavy panelled door. There was no answer. I knocked again. There was a simple latch. I opened the door; Giles followed me in.

I thought there would be a sudden rush of noise and heat, light and gaiety; a piano; kicking legs; a lot of laughter and horse play, and I would be reluctantly carried away by it, until suddenly, in a corner, sitting quite reserved and resisting the advances of sailors on leave and aristocrats slumming it, I would see Pity, and she would see me. Then she would stand (slowly and gracefully) and walk (slowly and gracefully) from the room, and I would follow her up the stairs (with the jealous eyes of all the men in the room burning into my back) to a simple, pretty little room with a gable end, and the smell of lavender and woodbine in the air.

And she would say: 'It is like the country home of my childhood, but you are the only man among these pigs to understand my beauty and my sadness.'

And then she would lead me to the bed and what would happen next would be sweet and piercing and joyful, and decently poignant and sad . . . but exactly what it would feel like I had not the faintest idea.

Things were not quite like that.

Instead a room like a waiting room in a small country station with brown oil cloth on the floor and a mean fire smoking greasily in the grate, yellow walls of cracked plaster, and the smell of cooking and old tobacco smoke. There were chairs around the wall. On one a sailor was asleep, his fly unbuttoned, his hand inserted into the gap. Two more chairs were occupied by men talking earnestly together who did not even look up when we walked in. Brothel etiquette, I presumed. A woman, dressed in grey underwear, sat by one of them, kneading the back of his neck and looking bored enough to hang herself, occasionally tossing her head and leering like a pirate when one of the men looked up.

Coming in we had knocked a bell above the door. An ugly youth poked his head out from behind an oil-cloth curtain, turned and shouted: 'Christ, it's two gentlemen.' He looked at us a bit longer, and added: 'Two fine gentlemen.' Then: 'Drinks, gentlemen?'

Giles said: 'Brandy.'

'I want to leave, Giles.'

'Nonsense. It'll get better.'

'You're enjoying this.'

'It's always nice to have one's suspicions confirmed.'

His eyes were darting round the room, intent and curious. A rough-looking man pushed through the curtain and scowled at us, then retreated. The girl on the chair looked at us hopefully, but one of the men slapped her on the back of the head and growled at her, and she tossed her head and leered at him like a pirate again, and the two men went back to their long conversation.

The boy came back with the madam: round-faced, beady-eyed, bustling, quite respectably dressed. She looked at us and nodded at the boy.

'What's your pleasure, sirs?'

'My friend here's a bit nervous,' Giles said. 'Do you have somewhere more private?'

'Private?' She sounded delighted. 'Private is our watchword. Boy!'

The boy said: 'Follow me, sirs,' and held the curtain back for us. I was light-headed and dry-mouthed. Quite unaware of myself. I knocked into a table as I passed it. The boy caught at me as I stumbled.

He said: 'Mind how we go, sir. That's a terrible place for a table.'

He led us down a corridor and opened a door. The room was dark.

'No gas here, sirs,' he said. We heard him fumble in the darkness for a lucifer: a flare which deepened into a spreading mellow glow as he touched the match to candles.

Against one wall a cheap rosewood piano; a rather worn carpet on the floor. Arm chairs, backs and arms worn to a shine, set on either side of a fireplace complete with battered irons. A clock on the mantelpiece. A stuffed coloured bird in a dusty glass bell. It was like a worn suburban parlour.

The boy came back with glasses and a decanter, followed by the madam. She pointed at the fire and cuffed the boy on the back of the head. He said, 'All right, all right,' and lit it, smiling good-naturedly at us. I felt despair settle on me like an autumn fog and sat in a hall chair set against the wall by a small round table.

'The gentleman's all right?' the madam asked Giles.

'Nothing that can't be made better,' he said.

'Now we have – '

'A redhead,' I said, suddenly angry that Giles was making all the running. 'A beautiful redhead with green eyes and hair – '

'That'll be . . .' The madam frowned. She looked concerned, then to my irritation whispered something to Giles.

Shock, then delight, crossed his face. He began to laugh.

'What's going on?' I asked.

'Nothing.'

'Tell me!'

'She's uncertain of your experience.'

'It's none of her business.'

The madam looked as grave as a solicitor. Giles said: 'You hear that? Now go and get it.' He turned to me. 'Do this.' He made a fist, thumb upwards. When I copied him, he tapped a little pile of finely ground white powder on to the stretched skin between the first knuckles of my thumb and forefinger.

'Coca powder,' he said. 'It will lift your spirits and clarify your mind. Close one nostril so, and inhale sharply.'

It was like inhaling powdered ice.

'And again,' he said. 'Other nostril.'

This time the cold entered my brain: it was as if a stealthy yet sharp wind had blown away veils and cobwebs, and I was not only seeing things with extraordinary freshness but as if I had been somehow renewed.

'The magic works,' Giles said.

He was right. Suddenly Pity was there. Giles caught his breath when he saw her; he might have been trying to inhale her. His eyes changed; his head came forward on his shoulders, as men's do. He opened his mouth a fraction. For a second, as she stood in the doorway, I thought she looked surprised, reluctant even. Then she gathered herself and took a step towards me.

'Well,' I said.

Giles was looking both amused and perplexed, as if Pity both confounded and confirmed something.

He took her hand and bent his head over it. She was trying to pull it away, but he must have been holding it tight. He kissed it.

'Do I know you?' she said.

'You know him.' Giles nodded towards me. 'He brought me here to look at you.'

'Why? Am I a freak?'

Giles pursed his lips and shook his head. 'I would say not. I'm leaving now.'

Panic again. He pushed me back from the door.

'You stay.'

'But you said – what do you think?' I blurted out.

'I take it all back. Special. Very special.' He kissed me on the forehead and closed the door behind him, firmly.

'Well,' she said. 'I don't know about him.' Her voice, which had struck me as low and well modulated before, grated on my ears, but at the same time it sounded expert and comforting. Her hair was up so she could let it down. When she shook it out I heard it fall.

'So,' she said. 'You come to sit for me, then?' She walked around me. 'You've got me for the evening. What do you want to do?'

I wanted the moment to be over.

She eyed me speculatively.

'Some of them want me to dance for them.'

She took a couple of steps across the floor.

'Some of them want me to sing.'

She adopted the pose of an opera singer, opened her mouth.

'But you,' she said. 'I've got to think for you. Now why did you want me to sit for you? So you could watch me. Suppose you watch me again. Would you like that?'

I nodded. I felt like an empty bucket.

She slid a hand across the front of her dress. I was rooted to the spot. I felt my being was centred in two places. My eyes and my sex.

'Want to get it over and done with and then settle down for a nice evening?'

Silence roared redly around me. I was still in the middle, empty. I thought: I could just reach out and touch her and it would be all right. The realisation that I *could* do this, that the only thing stopping me was myself, filled me with glee and terror. I stretched out my hand, expecting her to move away. But she took it between both of hers, raised it to her mouth and sucked a finger, looking at me all the while.

I nearly overbalanced and took a step towards her. Our bodies met with a tiny bump. Her free hand pressed and plucked at my trousers. I felt like a passive observer in a well-worn routine but the ritual was carrying me along. My sex was suddenly free. She knelt, pressed it along her cheek. I was on fire.

'He's almost ready to shoot,' she said conversationally. 'We'd better do something about that.'

There was a tiny bead of clear liquid at the tip and a stiffness that was so tight it was almost numbing. I was like that. All of me was like that: a spike paralysed by its own rigidity.

She stepped back, appraised me, then with her eyes lowered, as if what she were doing were slightly distasteful, turned and knelt at the sofa. She laid her head on the greasy fabric, and with her hands, worked the back of her dress up until her buttocks were bared. I couldn't move. She lifted her head and looked over her shoulder, then stood up.

'I thought you were ready for me,' she said.

I opened my mouth but my throat was a flattened tube.

Understanding spread slowly across her face. 'Oh, my lord,' she said. 'Oh, lordy, lordy.'

She stood and looked at me.

'Down here or in bed?'

All I could think was that beds were comforting, beds were warm, and bedrooms were dark.

'Bed, I think,' I said. I smiled weakly.

She took me by the hand and led me upstairs. The room we went into was dark and smelled used. There was no window. Around me I heard the house creaking and groaning. Distant laughter, muffled shouts. It was like being in a honey comb of squalor. Despair gripped me; my excitement slipped away.

'Do you want me to undress then?' she asked.

In the middle of the sheet was an oval dark area, where so many bodies had rubbed. I didn't want her skin touching it. I didn't want her bare skin anywhere near it.

I shook my head. She lay back on the bed, head and shoulders propped up by pillows.

She spread her legs. Her skirts made a sort of collapsed tent between them.

'Come here,' she said. 'Come on. Kneel there.'

She looked at me. 'It can be fun, you know. Come on. Take John Thomas out. That's right. Now. You give him to me and we'll see what Pity can do for him. That's right.' While she talked, her hands were busy, pulling her dress up, taking me in her hands, she lifted her legs, so that the back of her knees rested on my shoulders. I pulled back. It seemed so complicated.

'Look at me,' she said. 'Now push.'

She linked her hands behind my buttocks, bit her lower lip and narrowed her eyes. I felt nothing at first, just resistance, but then felt her flesh give.

'Gently, lover, gently. If this is your first time, make it last.'

I pressed again, then thrust. I had entered a place of warmth that gripped me like a fist as I pushed in. I thrust again, then slipped out. I tried to fumble my way back in but she knocked my hand away and did it herself. Then she smiled and arched her hips up to mine. A quick warm flood engulfed me. I did not know what was happening. I stopped moving.

'It's often like that the first time,' she said. 'You did better than most.'

I felt awkward, unexpectedly vulnerable. I made as if to withdraw but a muscle gripped me. She held my face between her hands.

'You've got me for the night,' she said. 'Make the most of it.'

We slept. When I woke up, dawn light was creeping round the edge of the curtain that hung over the door. She was still dressed, lying on her side with her back to me. I lifted her dress to take her again. I wanted to see her flesh and mine. I wanted to see me in her. She sleepily batted my hand away, and pressed me to her in such a way that I could not. After I had finished she got up. Moving made her wince.

'Are you all right?' I asked. I was suddenly overcome by a sense of desperate loss and nostalgia.

'I'm well.'

She did not meet my eyes. I felt a need to touch her again. I wanted her to acknowledge me mentally, as her flesh had been forced to part for me the night before.

'You will come to the studio then?'

'If you want me to.' That was not what I wanted to hear.

'You must. I want to see you again.'

'They all say that.'

'But I will paint you.'

She looked at me for the first time that morning.

'Is that a promise?'

'Yes.'

'And if I come, you will not throw me out?'

'No. Why should I do that?'

'Because you know my nature now.'

I slept again, then woke up, alone, scrunched like a rag in the corner of that bed, and overwhelmed by the sense of empty dread that entered my head at the sight that met my eyes.

Light dribbled past the dirty curtain and showed me the horrid chamber. I felt dank with shame and horror. I had been with a women and all I felt was terror, as if I had been contaminated. Suppose she had been diseased? She had bled! There was blood on the sheet, a blurred, inverted V! I fumbled my prick from my underwear. Blood had dried on it. She had bled on me! Through the thin walls I heard people stirring; sleepy voices.

I ran from the brothel, scurried through streets that were busy with honest, early-morning trade, feeling as if the mark of Cain were on my forehead. Once when a whore half fell from the door of a house and gave me an automatic smile, I almost smiled back. I felt so low that nothing could have lowered me further.

I let myself into the house, hardly daring to breathe in case Giles had risen early, ran through the yard, and locked myself in the studio. I washed in cold water, standing naked in the middle of the studio, rubbing myself with a rough cloth until my skin glowed.

At eleven Giles came to the door and knocked. He went away and came back at twelve. At one o'clock I let him in. He was in high good spirits.

'Well,' he said. 'How was it?'

I swallowed.

'She was everything I wanted.'

'She was?'

Giles looked at me disbelievingly.

'Yes.' I raised my chin and challenged him.

'And clean?'

'I think so.'

'And how would you know?'

I was silent. Inasmuch as I had gone against Giles's wishes the night before, he was now finding ways to punish me. The thought of syphilis had not entered my head.

'I am certain.'

'Good,' he said. 'So you'll be doing it again?'

163

'Damn you,' I said. 'You allowed the whole thing to happen. You have humiliated me.'

'You have humiliated yourself. Remember?'

'I will paint her.'

'Bring her here any time,' Giles said. 'I'd like to meet her again. I'll check her for pox. You too, if you want.'

'There's no need!'

'Auguste, according to Sir John Simon there are 18,000 prostitutes working in London in this year of our Lord, 1866. If one in three has venereal disease, there are six thousand prostitutes infected. Even if one in six is in hospital, then five thousand are out every night, passing their infection on to men. If each sees only one man, then each night five thousand men risk infection. Each night! If those figures are correct, over a year nearly two million visits to infected prostitutes! Auguste, that's more men than there are in London! Can't you see the risk you are running? Have you ever seen a man, his face and mind rotted by syphilis?'

I had a brush in my hand. I threw it at him but missed. I threw the palette at him, but missed again, and would have thrown the easel at him if he hadn't skipped out of the door.

30

I felt disfigured. I wept for my lost virginity, my lost strength, my lost honour. Syphilis, had I displayed any of the symptoms, would have been an apt manifestation of the state of my soul. Nostalgia for how I had been was like a worm inside me, gnawing at my vitals. I was a blasted bud, a tainted fruit, corrupted, maggot-ridden flesh.

'"Oh, rose, thou art sick",' Giles said when he saw me one afternoon, hunched over the edge of the dry fountain. I had been trying to vomit my despair away; mortification seemed my only hope, so my good friend Giles prescribed me mercury pills for the syphilis I never contracted, and for good measure dosed me with calomel which almost killed me. To bring it up, Mrs Tully fed me egg white mixed with water and a preparation of ipecacuanha. Giles held me while she tickled the back of my throat with a feather to make me sick. I was sick. And Giles slapped me on the back and said I was a lucky fellow to be cared for by two such loving friends.

But in the night I still dreamed of Pity. I was with her, I was in her, she was on me, lowering herself down on me, and I was feeling the delicious, warm tightness grip me. I would not touch myself; she came in the night and took me while I slept. Once I dreamed that she was the mermaid and to enter her I cut a slit in her scales with a knife.

That was the rhythm of my days: lust at night; mortification by day. Giles grew worried. He took me to the Cremorne Gardens to show me how little my act had been compared to the wholesale flesh market that was London. 'One little transaction, one little arrangement; a short collision of flesh – that's all it was,' he said.

In the Gardens, amidst the Chinese lanterns hanging from the trees, the sound of the orchestra, the air warm – no, more than warm, sated with this activity of love – I felt frozen.

Giles led me to the dance floor. The orchestra was sawing the night to pieces; white faces, black suits, grey shirts. The food of love offered by ghosts.

He scrutinised the dancers for a minute, then said: 'Look at them.' He was pointing to a couple dancing: he, small, round, dressed in a suit of brown check, a country clerk still wearing a hat that was knocking his partner's chin; she tall, angular, face whitened to dough, mouth like the slot in a pillar box, dressed in layers of torn silks and satins, grass stains on her arse. She whispered something to the man. He smiled beatifically, nodded his head and followed her off the stage, she holding his hand like a governess. We followed them across the park to a quiet area against a wall. In the bushes there was a minute of rustling, a gulp, a pant, then a sudden flurry of noise as the man bolted from the bushes like a jack rabbit, still arranging his trousers, to be followed a minute later in a rather more leisurely fashion by the woman, jangling some coins in her hand.

'Watching's extra.' She bared porcelain teeth at us before walking off, rolling her hips like a sailor.

Giles pointed to a pimp with rotten teeth trying to interest a gentleman with whiskers and a pock-marked face in a little girl with bad teeth. She had a grey face, grey dress, hair the colour of whey. She was sitting ten yards away and we could clearly hear her sobs.

'They still think a virgin's blood is a cure for syphilis,' Giles said. 'That's a twenty-guinea fuck, and after it they'll both have it.'

'What? You mean, he'll give it to her and not be cured?'

'I'll bet Lombard Street to a china orange she's got it already.'

'But she's a virgin. How can she? Look, she's crying.'

'That's all part of the act. And she'll scream when he gets on her and say he's tearing her very vitals, and she'll break a sachet of pig's blood on her thighs and spread it around the bed. They dry themselves out with alum before to make it tight, you know. She's good, I'll grant you that. Look at those waterworks.'

We passed a group of drunken bloods having hilarious conversations with a gang of elderly, rouged sailor-boys; we passed a drunken woman with flowers and grasses woven into her hair being furtively groped by a man with a doctor's bag; we went back to the bandstand where we saw the small round country clerk dancing with another tart and his first with another man. Round they went and round again, and the band played on, and a gay sailor danced a very gay hornpipe with a couple of the bloods, and the country clerk smiled, and Giles said: 'Do you see what I mean?'

The ground below the lanterns was dark with dead and dying insects; the bloods whooped as one of the sailor-boys fell over. One of them ran up and kicked him in the belly.

'Why have you brought me here?' I asked. 'What have you done?'

'To show you that you are not alone – that this kind of love goes on all the time. And also to show you how it can work on the soul, how it can deaden it. Look at this place: a *danse macabre* played out nightly by venal fools for venal fools.'

I shrugged. Then tears filled my eyes. They were not sentimental. Rather at that moment all the feelings in my breast resolved themselves into a clear and lucid picture.

'You don't understand,' I said. 'Ever since that night, I can't forget her. I can't get her out of my head. I've fallen in love, Giles. I love Pity. But I'm frightened. I'm scared. I want to be how I was before.'

'It's just bodies colliding, Auguste. For comfort.'

But his voice betrayed him.

'It's more than that,' I said. 'At least allow me the feelings that you so clearly have.'

'You grant them me,' he said. But then something happened

that I did not understand. Underneath his unsmiling, domineering mask I caught an expression that was the last thing I expected. Triumph. He looked triumphant, as if he had already won.

31

And then, next morning, normality. This was the game I had to play. Mrs Tully put coffee on the table and wiped toast crumbs off the sideboard. She handed Giles his letters, and as she left the room, said to me: 'You have post this morning.'

My dear Coffey
It is with great pleasure that I announce that my faith in you was not misplaced. I have sold Pandora's Box *to a wealthy collector and would like to see any other work in progress. Please advise me of a convenient time to visit your studios, and have prepared any other works you would like me to consider.*
Yours, sincerely,
Ernest Gruber

I showed it to Giles. He congratulated me but seemed preoccupied and buried himself again in his own letters. I made my excuses and retired to the studio.

I had a sheaf of sketches, some centred on a single idea, others suitable for inclusion in larger works – a pose I had noted, an expression. One sketch stood out: the mermaid I had dashed down on the very first morning I had been at the studio. The image haunted me, not least because the subject had Pity's face. But the picture would not grow. I could not see how to take it on another stage. In a sense it was complete as it lay, and yet I kept on returning to it. Giles found it one day while he was casually riffling through my work.

She was reduced to a small canvas, perhaps eighteen inches long and eight high. She was lying on a rock, facing the viewer, her breasts presented. Her tail swept round behind her, its flukes just under water pressing down on a drowning man, whose eyes, nevertheless stared up, glassy with hope and lust.

'Very powerful,' Giles said. 'The mermaid's face is the whore's. The drowning sailor's?'

'Mine.'

'Don't broadcast the fact. For Gruber?'

'Yes.'

'By the way, we have been summoned.'

'Summoned?'

'That's the beginning and the end of it. Georgina has declared that she is ready to be painted and wants a first sitting. You seem hesitant.'

'It was not me that was reluctant,' I said. 'It was you.'

'Well, I've changed my mind.' He looked at me. 'Yes?' he asked. His chin was thrust out. He looked ugly.

'Nothing,' I said.

'Good.'

It was not the time to talk. It was the time to hold my counsel and be patient.

'Auguste?'

'Yes?'

'Do I make you angry?'

'Yes.'

'There is one way in which you could have power over me.'

'I will,' I said. 'But in ways you could not dream of.'

'Oh, no you won't, Auguste. You are stitched in a sack of your own making and you can't escape.'

32

The train leapt over the slums on great viaducts. To either side a brick desert, factory chimneys like limbless, blasted trees, still smoking after some disaster. I had been invited to Wake Hall, officially, to begin the picture of Georgina. Giles had come. To make sure I did not become too friendly with his family, I think.

He leant from the window, smoking; a whiskered clergyman, our companion in the carriage, tapped me on the knee. He nodded up to my paint box in the luggage nets, the paint on my cuffs.

'A painter?'

'Yes,' I said.

'It must be wonderful,' he said. 'A God-given talent, is it not?'

'I do not know.'

'Oh, it is. I follow it. You see, I am not such an old fuddy-duddy as you might think.'

It seemed he could not stop his eyes from twinkling. Another pat on the knee.

'Truly to reflect nature is to reach a form of truth, is it not? A celebration of creation. The act of painting is indeed an act of worship.'

His face beamed with pleasure at this empty banality dropped between us like a rotten medlar falling in mud. The river flashed between warehouses, slashed by wharfside cranes, pressed by the fat ranks of nesting ships. It was the colour of coke; the sky, memorably, was viridian.

'Now, take Hunt. Holman Hunt, the artist. To paint *The Light of the World* he stayed up night after night, painting candle light – can you imagine? So that the light that falls on Our Saviour's face was a true reflection of nature, an expression of truth – '

'Did Christ ever carry a lantern?' I asked.

A beam. A waggled finger. 'Aha! And what did He look like? How can we strive for verisimilitude when we do not even know the lineaments of that dear face. But if truth is rendered in nature, then – '

Giles had positioned himself in one corner. He raised an eyebrow at me. Slid one finger across his throat.

'I have had enough of nature,' I said. 'I forswear it. From henceforth, what is not, is. What is, is not. Light shall be dark and dark shall be light. I shall reflect nothing, only transform. There is too much nature already. I am going to change it.'

'But that is putting yourself above God.'

'Try and stop me,' I said.

'But Ruskin said – '

'John Ruskin could not mount his own wife. That is how much he knows about creation,' I said. 'What colour is the sky?'

'Why, blue,' he said.

'And what colour water?'

'Blue too, I suppose.'

'If you look out of the window you will see that the sky is green and the river black. Good afternoon.'

The clergyman looked from me to Giles. Giles looked at me sadly and screwed his index finger into his temple. The clergyman left the train at Lewisham.

Giles, as soon as he was clear of the carriage, burst out laughing and said: 'Bravo! That was marvellous, priceless.'

Giles thought I was his clown, an instrument by which to vent his own spleen upon the world. He thought I was performing for him but he was wrong. I was writing my own story.

Wake Hall, the Bouveries' country house, had been built ten years previously to commemorate the heroism of Hereward the Wake and the first owner's new fortune. It bankrupted the owner and drove him to suicide.

'My parents love it,' Giles said as the carriage took us along an idiotically winding drive between bilious pillows of verge. 'It's full of stained glass. The stains make them think of washing,' he said, 'and men in coracles about to fall out and get muddy. They see themselves as the next stage of the cycle.'

Mr and Mrs Bouverie were in the grounds, supervising improvements to the south lawns. Giles went off in search of them and told me to find Georgina. I pushed open three sets of double doors that separated a dreary chain of large rooms, stuffed with chairs, paintings, sofas, books, but oddly forlorn.

She was in the south-facing breakfast room. She half rose as I entered. She was dressed in blue velvet, tightly waisted, the dress spreading loosely and generously around her feet. I bowed. Three French windows flooded the room with light and shadow. Pictures by the yard on the walls, which were as crowded as the Royal Academy's Summer Exhibition. A big stone fireplace. A coat of arms carved into it that seemed to incorporate crossed paddles above a coracle. Hereward again. The room smelled of pot pourri and carbolic.

Fanny Morant stopped plucking at an embroidery frame and said teasingly: 'You can relax now, Georgina. He has come.'

She blushed furiously, as she was meant to. 'Fanny, that is not – '

I said: 'It is never easy to think that one is going to be painted.'

'Are all your models so modest as this one?' Fanny asked.

'Less modest, but with less reason,' I said, then tried to look composed and serious. 'There is much to discuss.'

173

'Georgina has been entertaining herself with stories of villainous artists who use sittings as excuses to make love to their sitters.'

'Fanny,' Georgina wailed, and at that moment Giles and Mr and Mrs Bouverie returned, appearing through separate French windows like players in a bad opera.

'Fanny, what is the meaning of this talk?' Once again Giles's mother was wearing white around her neck and cuffs. Now her face was white; her lips constricted into a thin double bow.

'Nothing, Mother.'

'Georgina, I did not ask you. Fanny?'

Fanny Morant looked to me for support.

'She meant nothing by it. It means nothing to me,' I said. Giles strode into the middle of the room and gave his sister's hair a gentle tug. 'You can say what you like in front of Auguste. He's a monk. Head down all the time. Or is it up?'

'But to talk – '

'All over his head, eh, Gussie?'

I nodded. 'I would not know what to say,' I said.

Fanny looked gratefully at Giles and me.

'Well, if she's sitting for him, I want her chaperoned. You don't know. Someone call Osgood . . . Ah, Osgood, there you are. What is the form with young ladies and painters? A chaperone? I think so.'

'Indeed,' said Osgood, materialising like a mushroom. When he started to usher Georgina and me out of the room, she gazed imploringly at Giles and Fanny, now deep in conversation. Giles glanced up and waved her away. Fanny, still talking, followed us out.

'The dining hall,' said Osgood. He led us past a dining table the size of a field. On the panelled walls were pikes, swords and muskets arranged in sunbursts and chevrons. The black and white floor was a giant chessboard. The fireplace could have burned a small cottage.

Osgood threw open a pair of double doors. A wooden floor yawned into the distance: the ballroom.

174

'La,' he said. 'And la.' He waved an arm at the far end where a chaise-longue, a piano stool and an arm chair had been set in a corner hung with a vast swathe of dull red fabric.

'The red sets off her hair, no? Is it not perfect?' said Osgood. He took my arm and said conspiratorially: 'I have arranged it myself.'

Behind me I heard Fanny's low, attractive laugh. Georgina's eyes were flickering around the room.

'I shall find it very dull here,' I said.

Georgina looked grateful.

Watching her for a further reaction, I said: 'The light is wrong for me. I was hoping to draw inspiration from the grounds, and paint outside. I can begin it thus, and then if it needs retouching, there is light enough in the studio for that purpose.'

I was as excited as gratified by the look Georgina gave me. Osgood said sulkily: 'It was precisely to avoid such a situation that I prepared this room.'

'What does Miss Bouverie think?'

'I will follow the artist's advice,' she said, and rose. I felt Giles come up behind me.

'After lunch we have a surprise for you,' he said in a low voice. 'And pray do not forget that my sister has led a very sheltered life, up until now. She is by no means emancipated, merely rather naive.'

I nodded.

I found a spot: an old orchard where the trees were beginning to uncurl green leaves, and a wall of mellow stone was awaiting improvement, wild flowers growing in the crumbling mortar. I could begin the background, then add them as they came into season.

To assert himself, Osgood claimed the air was damp and unhealthy and insisted that Georgina go inside and find a wrap and put on stouter shoes. I set up my collapsible chair and easel, and waited.

There was human activity in the distance, about half a mile away. A small copse had been cut down and a gang of men were measuring out foundations with tapes and string and pegs. Behind the orchard, through the trees, a great horse was running up and down a field at a fierce, concentrated trot. Its mane quivered as it moved, light passing over it like wind on a wheat field. Every now and again it would stop and give a fierce bellow, then resume its hard, impatient movement. It looked to me like a stallion with the scent of a mare.

I heard the swish of crinolines behind me. I turned, rose to my feet. Fanny was approaching over the grass. She met my gaze levelly. Once again, I was struck by her composure and detachment. I wondered how that would change when she was married to Giles.

'Do you really mean to paint her outside, or was that just a ploy to bring her to London?'

'I take it that I am not meant to answer that,' I said. 'That it was intended only to assert your perspicacity.'

She tilted her chin. 'And if it did?'

'I see you are the emancipated one,' I said. She looked bemused.

'Giles told me to remember that Georgina was not emancipated, just naive. I must say,' I added, 'there was no risk of my confusing the two.' I laid slight emphasis on *my*, and saw that Fanny looked annoyed.

'Implying, or seeking to imply, that Giles has them confused?' she said.

'No. Merely that I would not.'

'You are not who I thought,' she said. 'Or else you have changed since the last time we met.'

'I think I see things more clearly now,' I said. 'We are both suitors for Giles. You want his hand, I need the security he can promise. Let us not be rivals.'

'That is the change,' she said. 'The last time we met, I would have said that you were his friend, albeit a needy one.'

'I would be his friend now, if he would let me,' I replied.

'If he would let you?' She looked astonished. 'I had gathered, from his letters, that it was you who was, how can I put it, withdrawing?'

'Not I,' I said. 'Rather a lack of confidence. You know, we plunge into things, blindly perhaps, not realising that by moving, we place ourselves to a greater or lesser degree in the hands of someone whom we do not know if we can trust. I mean, look at us now, talking. I do not know whether my comments will be reported back to Giles, and if so, reported honestly. But I trust you will not relay them.'

'You can trust me to say nothing to him that would hurt him,' she said. 'Neither would I omit anything I thought it in his interest to know. But you can trust Giles.'

'I can, I know. But always there is the matter of our respective positions. His wealth, my poverty; my dependence, his superiority.'

'Giles would never assert his status like that – '

I shrugged and looked at the ground. 'Perhaps not deliberately.'

'You mean that he has?'

'I mean that perhaps at times of stress, he . . .'

'What stress?'

'All I know is that recently . . .' I tried to dispel any impression that I might be curious, or lying. 'All I know is that recently, at certain moments, I have caught a look in his eye that is almost haunted. It is probably nothing,' I hurried on, 'but what can I do? When Giles – when these moods come over him, I must confess a certain coldness creeps into his dealings with me, and I – I admit it – find myself disinclined to involve myself further in his private life, in case I meet with or cause a deeper coldness. As well as the security,' I said, 'I value his friendship. More than that, Giles is probably the only friend I have in London. I am sorry if – '

Fanny silenced me with a gesture. She looked at the ground. She was considering what I'd said. I was anxious to make it seem as if I was making a personal confession, so that she would be less likely to report my conversation to Giles. I did not want him bringing up the subject of Pity in public.

'When you said we were both suitors for Giles,' she said, 'you hit the mark. Yes, of course, what use is my emancipation if it does not spread to all humanity, if it applies only to me and my wants? Pure selfishness. I have read of freed slaves returning voluntarily to their former owners, not because they believe they should be slaves, but because they do not know how else to behave. Worse still, I read a missionary's report of a slave who himself became a slave master. Believe it, Mr Coffey. Believe it. No, if women are to be made free, it must not be at the expense of anyone else. So, we are both dependent on him. You because of your social position, me because of my sex. Sex is the eye of the needle that we must all pass through, but then so is status. By asking you to keep an eye on Giles, and report on him to me, I was not taking into account your own vulnerable position. I apologise.'

'Please do not apologise,' I said. 'And please be assured: if I see anything wrong with Giles, I will write to you.'

'Oh, look!' The stallion had reared and now was pawing the air with his hooves. As he reared, he turned so that his belly was towards us. His part was extended and swayed hugely below him. Fanny blushed and would have looked away, but pride insisted that she did not. I felt it was a moment to say something but her expression, a mixture of fascination and revulsion, kept me silent.

Osgood was approaching us across the grass, wearing an extraordinary hat. He was beckoning vigorously and calling us.

We turned from the field. 'That,' said Fanny, 'is a sight I have never seen though have read about, through allusion, in books. It is strange how the reality is both less dramatic but more starkly impressive than anything the imagination could summon.'

I admired her for speaking when we could both have become enmired in embarrassment. She had courage and pride.

'I assume you are referring to Mr Osgood's hat,' I said.

When Fanny laughs her entire face lights up and she becomes very pretty.

We took lunch in the breakfast room because the dining room was being redesigned.

'And you saw our improvements, Coffey?' The first words that Mr Bouverie had directed at me.

'I saw building works in the distance, beyond the lake.'

'We'll visit after luncheon. My wife will tell you all about them.'

Mrs Bouverie sighed and asked if she had to.

'Go on, go on,' said Mr Bouverie. 'If it's important enough to do, it's important enough to tell our guest about.'

Mrs Bouverie fixed her eye on the curtain pelmet.

'The thing is this, Coffey,' said Mr Bouverie. 'We all recognise – I would go as far as to say that it is an instinct – that hygiene and morality are intimately connected. You only have to see the filth among the degenerate classes to see it as plain as a pikestaff. The government knows it; the Office of Works does sterling stuff with its fumigation, and who's to say what happens after it? What's clear is that things can't get worse. What we are doing, under supervision, of course, is creating a hygienic environment into which will be introduced some people,' he chewed the word, 'women and children, who through no fault of their own have been malignly influenced by their surroundings, and so been adversely affected morally. We'll scrub 'em and take 'em on from there, won't we, my dear?'

'We will make them good,' said Mrs Bouverie, the words projected from her tight lips like spitballs.

'And they'll all leave committed customers of Bouverie's Moonlight Soap, eh, Father?'

'Through God's grace,' said Mrs Bouverie. She sipped her soup as if it were biting her.

After soup, another course, and after that another and another. And after lunch, another room: the library.

'The surprise,' said Mr Bouverie. He pointed to the fireplace.

Hanging above it was my painting: *Pandora's Box*.

'Well, what do you think? Come on. We want to know.'

'You bought this from Gruber?'

'Highly recommended,' said Giles.

'I am – ' I struggled for words ' – honoured.'

'Confused' would better have described my state.

'It'll do,' said Mr Bouverie. 'Do very well.'

Giles shushed him.

I shot a questioning look at Giles. Why had he not told me? What was his part in this? I had refused to sell him the picture; he had refused to accept it from me as a gift. In so doing it had become a counter in the perpetual game of give and take between us, but this latest move showed a deviousness I was not prepared for. And yet I did not mind it as much as I thought I would. To see my picture in someone else's house filled me with pride.

'You are pleased, Mr Coffey?' Georgina asked in a hesitant voice.

'It is like seeing a child doing well in the world. It creates pride with regard to its achievements but apprehension with regard to the perils it might encounter.'

'Come now. Don't be modest. How could a picture as true, as fascinating, as that attract criticism?'

'I do not know,' I said. 'Perhaps I meant little more than that it might be ignored. That your tastes might change, that it might in time be consigned to the least frequented guest room for the least welcome guest.'

'Not while I have breath in my body,' Georgina said. 'It is too good for that, isn't it, Papa?'

'Too good for that,' he said, 'And little chance of people ignoring it.'

We returned to the orchard. Georgina seemed distracted, but it suited her, lending a gravitas to her features that would look well in a portrait. Mr Osgood flung himself down on the ground and tried to make startling conversation. I sketched. It was the first opportunity I had had to study Georgina properly. As was my wont, I spent a while just looking at her.

After a few minutes had passed, she said: 'You have not drawn for five minutes. Under your gaze I feel quite naked.'

Mr Osgood shushed her with some telling observations about truth and beauty and that it shouldn't make her feel uncomfortable, but she was not uncomfortable. I could tell from her pose that she was not tensing; instead she was working herself, almost imperceptibly, into a different position, one that somehow was more *displayed*.

And then behind her I saw the horses running. The stallion had been joined by a mare. They were moving swiftly side by side, the mare slightly ahead, the stallion seeming to nip her shoulders or tug her mane with his teeth. I turned my gaze deliberately beyond my sitter. Both Osgood and she turned, she with an expression that was both puzzled and amused.

'So beautiful!' she exclaimed.

The stallion, by pushing, turned the mare in smaller and smaller circles. Eventually she stopped running. He trotted behind her and rose, floundering slightly as his back legs thrust him up towards her, then surging with greater and greater confidence.

The mare, her back legs sturdily splayed, stood calmly while the stallion plunged above her.

'I have never seen them play like that before,' Georgina said, then gasped. We both saw at that instant what the stallion intended. I thrust myself between Georgina and the sight. Osgood, alerted by my sudden movement, said: 'What the deuce?' saw what was going on and made a faint exclamation.

'Mr Coffey, why are you standing there?' Georgina's voice was mocking.

'The sight is not suitable for young ladies.'

'Nor for young men, it seems. You have your back to it, I am facing it.'

I turned. The act was over.

'What's going on?' I heard Giles's voice from the other side of the grounds.

'Mr Coffey is being a gentleman,' Georgina called back.

'Indeed, indeed,' said Osgood. 'Thank you, sir, thank you in every possible way. With Miss Bouverie in this state – '

'I am not in any state,' she said, 'save that of vexation with my mother.'

Osgood mouthed 'hysterical' above her head in my direction.

Clearly my action had served to negate any suspicions he'd had of me, exactly as I had intended.

Osgood, to save Georgina any possible grounds for further excitement, recommended that she be taken inside, so Mr Bouverie said he would show me the improvements to the grounds while we waited for the carriage to take us to the station.

The ground chosen for the buildings was in a hollow, the natural run-off for all the surrounding land. Underfoot it was a swamp, the grass already churned to mud by the surveyors and their men. Clouds queued across the sky in ranks. Rooks circled an elm tree and shouted. Mr Bouverie asked me if I would like to shoot a few.

I said no. He said: 'The painting's satisfactory. Giles was most adamant. It's one in the eye for Mr Millais, what?'

His flattery was empty. Giles and I rode back to London with Fanny. At London Bridge we put her in a cab. While Giles was ordering a hansom for her, she said to me: 'I do not envy your position. Write to me in London and the letter will be forwarded if I am away.'

We walked home. Giles seemed pleased with himself but would not talk. I felt at a loose end, perhaps disturbed by his rapprochement with Fanny Morant and all the implications that held for me. I started to think of Georgina. At one point in the afternoon I had found myself staring at her not with a painter's eye, nor even a lustful eye, but simply because I liked looking at her. She seemed as sweet as I was sour, as fresh as I was stale. We had talked and she had smiled on me. Recalled in the emptiness of my studio, with the ceaseless din of London muttering, rising and falling in a restless tide of noise, she brought me happiness. She was manna in my desert.

And then I remembered I was only there on Giles's sufferance and suddenly tasted bitterness and rot. I had to act!

33

The half basement under the studio was where the Bouveries stored all their discarded furniture. The rough arches were covered by wooden lattices and inside the light was dim but very clear, sieved like the sun on a river passing under trees. The space was stacked with boxes and trunks, chairs, tables, wardrobes, some broken, some not so old, some new. I opened a trunk: old clothes, cold to the touch, their musty smell oddly chemical. Then boxes full of papers; I thought that they might be interesting but they weren't. There were long wooden paddles stacked in one corner, a neat pile of sawn-off lengths of pipe that must have been left when they dismantled the factory, and half a dozen large curved hooks with flattened loops for handles. I'd seen them used for shifting carcasses in the slaughterhouses; here they would have been used for dragging the soap blocks.

The end wall was divided into stalls by wooden partitions. There were metal baskets on the wall for hay, coal marks up the wall and the worn brick floor glittered with coal dust. Before the age of coal the basement would have been stables, and before that a byre, but that was an age ago when London was younger, and cattle grazed in the water meadows by a green meandering river, and fishes swam in little creeks, and the monks sat on the banks and fished, tended cows and milled – all the time watching a dark stain spread over the northern shore.

I picked my way carefully through piles of Mrs Bouverie's rejected furnishing schemes: a set of dining-room chairs upholstered in the same material as a great swag of musty curtain; a rosewood upright piano, its veneer buckling and lifting from damp; carpet rolls that were alive with mice; a vast, cracked ugly gilt mirror; a great chandelier, collapsed like a drunken duchess on her skirts; a dozen decent picture frames, empty; packing cases, mirrors, a weird pile of chaise-longues.

A sudden flurry and thump. I turned towards the noise. A big cat flattened itself on the floor, darted at me, thought better of it and bolted towards the back wall.

Pressed almost flush against the end wall was a massive piece, a cross between a dresser and a wardrobe. The cat squeezed underneath it. I heard scrabbling, then silence. I bent and hissed, then tried to shoo it out with a curtain rod. Nothing. I pressed my cheek to the floor. No sound. When I slid my hand into the space underneath, cold air moved against it. I tried to push the piece away from the wall, pressing until my muscles shook, but could not even rock it.

I picked up one of the hooks. The handle was worn and smooth, the hook surprisingly heavy. It swung from my fingers in a meaningful way. I whipped it round and brought it down on a chair. The hook sliced through fabric, tore horse hair then speared the wood frame with a dull 'whump'.

The wardrobe doors were unlocked, which was lucky for them. The inside was as big as a room; you could stand in it. Space enough to swing a cat or sling a hook. The back was cheap, slatted deal and the hook tore through it easily. Once, twice, three times, then it began to come away in thin planks. I tore a gap three feet wide and stood back. Where there should have been a wall, there was a gap. I smelled ash, dust and soap. The old furnace room. As my eyes adjusted, I could dimly see the deep black arch of the furnace, and in front of it a long table draped in a white cloth.

I lit my lantern and stepped into the furnace room. It was small and square and slightly domed, like a beehive. The chimney rose from the back. Under it was a rack from which two gutters ran into two metal cauldrons. They had been roughly cleaned but the insides still held sticky traces of fat. There was fat on the rack as well, and charred meat. Under it, in the ashes, were fragments of bone.

I turned my attention to the long, cloth-covered table. Under the cover was a wooden bench, strongly made, with a clean, bare wooden top that still smelled of soap. At one end was a sliding tray; at the other an adjustable rest. There were straps on either side at the top and bottom. An operating bench. Underneath was a tray. I reached into it without looking. A square mahogany box. I opened it carelessly and there was a shower of steel, and a thin rattling clink as the knives hit the floor. I cut myself as I picked one up without even feeling it. I only realised when I saw my own blood scurry down my wrist.

The knives fitted tightly into their velvet slots. The bone saw and longer knives were held in place by wooden stays.

I heard a sound behind me: a creak, wood falling, a sudden flurry, something crashing in the basement. I blew out the candle, then realised it was pointless. I had been seen. It could only be in my interest to find out who it had been. I clambered into the wardrobe, and listened. No sound. I picked up the hook and peered at the piles of furniture in the half light. The basement door was still open. I stood still and waited, the hook hanging from my finger, until I was sure that the room was empty.

On the courtyard wall the cat looked at me with yellow eyes. The yard stank of its piss. I didn't want to share my secret with anyone or anything. Not yet. For a day I watched the studio windows slice the clouds as they passed. I drank too much. I developed a headache and listened to the persistent drip, drip drip of the rain. Grey was crawling into the sky; barely light.

I turned over all I knew in my head. If I went to Giles with it: the disappearance of Nelly Oates, the operating table, the knives, the rack where flesh had been melted and bones burned – what would he do? Crumple? Beg for forgiveness, clemency, understanding? I thought not. He would kill me or simply go and hide the evidence so that I could not carry out any threat to expose him. And who would believe me over him anyway? No one.

No, I needed an ally. I thought of Mrs Tully but knew I could never offer her as much as she could get from Giles. I thought of William Oates. He was involved, as I saw it, but only peripherally. He was a beneficiary of Giles's crimes but not in any major sense. Together, though, we would present a formidable presence. Giles would have to take notice of us then. But I would not give Oates the chance to doubt me. He must know that I meant business and held a full hand of cards. I would lure him to the furnace room, offer him a fait accompli, then take matters on from there.

I returned to the pub where I had first met him. It was almost empty again. New sawdust lent a hint of freshness to the air. At the back of the big room a fat girl was leaning on a broom, yawning. From the basement came the gritty roar of barrels rolling. I put my head over the trap door and called down: 'Is anyone there?'

The barman I had seen before came to the ladder and peered up, a moustache of foam still on his lip.

'I'm looking for William Oates. You were talking to him. I'm anxious to make contact with him again.'

'Oh, yes.'

'He was quite keen to talk to me. I just don't know where I can find him.'

'Better not do that.'

'Why not?'

'He doesn't like it, that's why.'

'Do you know him then?'

'Why don't you piss off, friend?'

'Tell him I was looking for him, will you? I'm living in Crucifix Lane.'

I tried to sound confident.

'He knows that,' the barman said.

'Will you tell him then?'

But he was gone.

Feeling restless, I decided to paint the effect of rain on the rusticated stone blocks of London Bridge. I had a feeling I had seen damp crawl down them in a sort of veil. I wanted to see how the light worked on the wet.

At the river, I set my stool near the wall of St Olave's church, tucked my umbrella against my shoulder and began to sketch. I followed the beard of darkness as it dripped down the wall from the parapet above. Where the moisture coalesced into rivulets, it glistened on the sooty stone in precious glints.

London is at its best in the rain, when the streets are empty and the pavements are glistening, and the steam is rising off the horses and their hooves make a sharper, clearer, cleaner sound. Everything darkens: wet houses, glossy slates; dark raincoats, black umbrellas. But then, if you look, you see light everywhere. Light in the shop windows, a weird, pulsing light behind the sky; light caught in the glisten of wet on paving stones, light broken on the wet cobbles, dripping off the glossy flanks of horses. There is light in black windows, secret gleams deep in wet slates, light in every one of those myriad drops of rain . . .

I was being stared at. It is a feeling an artist gets used to. One stares at the world and as often as not the world stares back at him. But this was different. He was under the jutting eaves of a warehouse, leaning against a stack of barrels. He waited until he knew I had seen him before moving, then peeled himself away from the wall.

He walked like some sort of scarecrow towards me, the rain bouncing off his hat and drumming against his shoulders. I watched him from under my umbrella. You could see the drops hit his shoulders, glisten for a second, then dull as they were absorbed. He was narrow and he was flickering.

'Wet,' he said.

He didn't hunch, as most people do, against the rain. He simply stood there, a dark shape in the wetness.

'Painting, I see,' he observed.

'Sketching.' I saw no point in not talking to him for fear it might antagonise him. There was something poised in his stillness. But then again, I did not see the point in lying to him either.

'Is that a lucrative occupation?'

'You asked me that before.'

'I'll ask it again.'

'It can be for some.'

'The last time I saw you – the devil was in me a bit, I think. I made a comment, designed to wound.'

I looked at him closely. I was sure he wanted to talk. Getting wetter and wetter, the clothes clamping on him more tightly, he seemed an oddly pathetic figure. Like a wet dog, he seemed to be diminishing. He brushed the hair back from his forehead. His face was thinner than when I saw him last. Water dripped from his brows to his cheekbones. His eyes were as dark and glossy as plums.

'Are you ill?' I asked.

'With something,' he said. 'Can't seem to keep anything down, and the pain sometimes is like a lobster inside my stomach, pinching.'

'Do you need me to tell Giles anything? Do you want him to look at you?'

He laughed. 'I'd sooner lie with a costerman's mother!' he said. 'He'll not cut me, not if there's a lump inside me like a pumpkin. He'll not put his hands inside my gut.'

'Then why – ' I began.

He bent his head to mine. His breath was quite beyond the normal sourness of mouths. There was something deep-rooted behind the stink.

'You tell him I'm desperate, or getting that way, and if I can't help him, he'll have to help me.'

'Desperate for what?' I asked.

'Money.'

With his eyes so close to mine, I could see that his irises had squeezed to a thin halo of blue.

'Are you a resurrection man?' I asked. 'I thought they were long gone.'

I spoke on impulse and it might not have been wise. Nevertheless, I was glad I'd asked him.

He laughed. 'Me? Is that what you wanted to ask me? Rather the reverse, I'd say. And you can tell Giles I said that, my friend.' He put a hand on my shoulder. It seemed very near my neck. 'Don't try and get me to give up my meal ticket, laddie,' he said quietly, then changed his grip and patted me gently on the cheek with his palm cupped.

'Rather the reverse? What do you mean by that?'

But he had turned his back on me and was walking off into the rain. The hissing of the water half drowned my words.

I shouted: 'I've found something.'

He turned, oblivious to the water that was soaking him, only blinking more often to get the rain drops out of his eyes.

'Found . . . something? Or do you just want to watch me perish of wet and cold?'

'It changes things.'

'How so?'

'I can't tell you. I can only show you. Come to the archway into the yard tonight at, say, nine.'

He spat.

'Bring a friend if you're afraid.'

He spat again, nodded and walked towards the station. Under the bridge, the green-grey water was tugging at the piles, writhing and twisting against the ebb before racing to the sea.

The resurrection men supplied corpses for doctors to practise on. In the pubs near the hospitals, they said, the corpses were lined up in the basement next to the barrels, each one with a coloured thread around its toe. The doctors would examine the bodies at their leisure, take the coloured thread off the one they wanted, and give it to one of the men upstairs who'd tell him the price. The trade had stopped once hospitals were granted a regular supply of dead paupers. But even now it wasn't unknown for artists to buy a corpse for study and some painters affected a deep knowledge of the trade: if the belly swells too much you can get the gases out by folding the corpse in half. Always look for earth in the hair; always go for something that smells a little. Never buy a cheap one that's fresh and clean – it's probably been killed for the job. I needed to know exactly what Oates did for Giles.

It was just before nine when I slipped the bar on the big gates and unbolted one side. I tested the gate on its hinge and found it moved quietly.

My mind felt very clear and prescient. I leant against the door and listened. I didn't hear Oates arrive, but just after nine I heard someone try to muffle a cough. I waited a while longer, then opened the gate a crack. He was standing with his back to it, peering round the archway at the front door. It was satisfying to watch him jump when I hissed, and see him come to the crack in the door.

As a man passed by on the other side of the street, Oates melted back into the shadow by the wall.

'Come in,' I said. 'Quick.'

'Why must I?'

'You'll be interested in what I've found. I want to show it to you. I think you've guessed anyway.'

I could see prudence war with curiosity. He stepped into the yard. I nodded at the basement. I wished I had lit a lantern and placed it in there to make it look safely occupied.

He made his way between the stacks of furniture to the back of the basement. At the wardrobe he paused.

'Why – ' he began.

'It's stuck,' I said. 'Don't think I didn't try.'

I opened the door. I had rigged up a curtain, and placed a lantern in the furnace room to make it look occupied. What I hadn't anticipated was the speed with which he pulled the curtain back and darted into the middle of the room. I saw him glance around him, eyes taking in the table and the metal rack. He fumbled in an inside pocket then drew out a monstrous knife which he shook open and secured by sliding a ring down the handle to the blade.

'Now what's going on? Thought to catch me, did you?' he said.

He stood in the middle of the room, swinging the knife and standing on the balls of his feet, leaning forward.

'You misunderstand me,' I said.

'I think *you* misunderstand *me*. Thought to trap me here and kill me, did you?'

I was aghast. 'No. Under no circumstances.'

'So why bring me here?'

'I thought you might be more inclined to talk if you knew – if you saw for yourself what I had uncovered.'

'What, when faced with that?' He pointed at the surgeon's bench, threw back his head and laughed. 'You know I've got a little squeeze on with Giles and you thought to lift it from me, did you?'

'No. Share it.' I felt sick. I had underestimated his cynicism.

'Take my share? Steal my influence? You horrid little prawn!'

As he spoke he took two swift, dancing fencer's steps towards me and slashed down and across with the knife. I dodged the vicious arc, retreated and caught the back of my knees against the steps into the furnace room. My arm, flung out behind me, closed on the hook.

Oates stepped up to me, quite relaxed now that I was down, and as far as he knew, powerless. I lifted the hook and tried to bring it, reversed, down on his head, but again I had miscalculated. I was too near the curtain and the hook, its swing impeded by the fabric, turned in the air and caught him on the shoulder, piercing jacket and skin. His hand convulsed and the knife fell from it. He made a sort of angry grunt, and looked down at his shoulder.

I tried to free the hook but only succeeded in pulling him towards me. To stop himself falling on me, he held out an arm. This swung his body round and I was able to jerk the hook free, then push him away. He was hurt. He went down on one knee, his face twisted in bitter surprise.

'That was an accident,' I said. 'I meant only to talk.'

'To trick and trap me, you bastard sodomite!' he grunted. 'I'll rip you.' He began to scrabble across the floor for his knife.

I swung the hook wildly and it caught him on the side of the jaw. He made a bubbling sound and screamed. Tugging the hook free almost pulled his jaw off to one side.

He stood in front of me, ruined, his jaw slanting open, dripping blood. In the candlelight I could see wet glisten on his shoulder too. Something clearer, shriller and more intractable than terror rose in me like a shriek. As a child, before my parents died, I remember once breaking a prized piece of my mother's crockery, a large tureen. I had knocked into it, the lid had fallen and the handle smashed. I looked at this thing, saw the fact that the great part of it was unbroken, but realised that just this small element of it being smashed spoiled the entity. In a panic, I hid it. When the household started looking for it, I smashed it into unrecognisable fragments and buried it in the vegetable garden. Breaking it, unmaking it, was my attempt to deny the incident's reality.

It was almost a relief when Oates found his knife again and started waving it at me. He stepped back, stumbled and fell. The knife clattered from his hand. I stood astride him, reversed the hook and brought the rounded side down on his temple. He convulsed briefly, then fell forward on his face. I slid down awkwardly against the wall. The grit bit into the heel of my palm. I was panting, breathing in the bitter must of coal and damp. I could taste metal in my mouth. When I wiped sweat away from my forehead, I brushed his blood on to my lips. That made me sick. The air in the little room seemed brutally cold and obnoxiously close. I just wanted to get out. I breathed deeply until I felt more calm, rolled him over on to his back and dragged him to the surgeon's bench.

It was curiously intimate dragging him across the floor and, oddly, I found it more of a violation than when I attacked him with the hook. It was his vulnerability, his slackness, that affected me, at the same time as making it almost impossible for me actually to get him on to the table. I was not strong enough to lift him bodily, and every time I got one bit of him up, another bit of him slid off. I tried using the hook to pull him up by the collar, but the fabric was so thin that the hook tore free.

Feeling sick at what I was going to do, I placed the tip of the hook under his armpit, and pulled him up that way. The hook held on a tendon at the top of his arm. He came up like a doll, his head falling to one side. I was able to strap one arm into the leather bindings to hold him, lift his legs on, strap them, then secure his remaining arm. I was even able to work his dislocated jaw back into place. It returned to its sockets with a *tock*, like a billiard ball finding its pocket.

I must have waited an hour before he woke up. He had tried to kill me. He would never co-operate. I was trying to comprehend the enormity of what I was contemplating but it was like trying to imagine – I mean properly, deeply comprehend – the mass of a mountain, the sheer, staggering solidity of it. Cold sweat dried on me. For something to do, I pulled out the drawer under the table and took out the remaining instruments. I held them up, one by one. This a lancet, this a metal hammer with a head like a chisel, this a longer knife with a gently tapering blade, this a saw, this a sort of pliers, this like a little scythe, this like a carpet hook. There was a contraption which consisted of a rubber bulb attached to webbing, that I guessed was a tourniquet. Tweezers.

The steel was dull silver, only slightly spotted with rust. I saw a gleam under the man's eyelids, a flicker in the slit. I said: 'Open your eyes if you are awake.'

He stayed still. With the tweezers I took a little pinch of

eyelid and pulled. He tried to keep his eyes rolled up, feigning unconsciousness. I said: 'If you refuse to wake, I shall slice your eyelids off.'

I blinked, imagined him lidless, a scene like a photograph. His eyes flicked open.

'Love me, I hurt,' he groaned.

'Do you know what these are?' I said.

'It's mortal agony. You've hurt me, mister, hurt me badly. Don't hurt me more.'

'I won't if you talk.'

'Love me, Jesus, that hook went right through me! My arm's sore like it was chewed. I was born in the Borough. I never wanted to die here but all my dreams turned to dust. Help me, and I'll be your friend. Oh, I'm cold. I'm cold. The pain is like a terrible numbness.'

'You're talking nonsense. You don't normally talk like this. First tell me exactly who you are.'

He licked his lips. 'Water,' he said. 'For God's sake, water to wet my lips. I'm talking like this because I'm scared.'

'Tell me, who was Nelly Oates?'

'Nelly? Why that was my wife. My dear, departed wife.'

'Who worked for the Bouveries?'

'In the factory, girl and woman; as indeed I did, boy and man. Squire, give me water. I feel as I'm parching up.'

I checked his bonds. There was water in the studio. I stopped on the other side of the curtain, faked steps, waited, then peered through a gap. He waited, very still, then suddenly jerked into life, bringing his head round to the side, lifting his left arm and gnawing at the leather strap. By pulling the end and wriggling his wrist, he could quickly free himself. I stepped back into the furnace room. He saw me and redoubled his efforts. I saw his hand was nearly free. I picked up the long knife and plunged it through his arm. He gasped, then turned and started to try and free the other hand. I smashed the elbow with the hammer. He screamed and his head went down. In the lantern light, his face was orange and covered in sweat. I tightened his wrist bonds again then tore open his waistcoat, shirt and vest, feeling sick at what I would have to do.

'You have a choice,' I said. 'If you talk, I will spare you.'

'Oh, no you won't, you marjorie. You'll not spare me. You want my pitch, you want my hold. You won't have it.'

I took the little hammer up and swung it sideways, quite gently at his nose. There was a snap, above the sound of metal hitting the flesh. His nose was suddenly sideways and spurting blood. Sickness swooped at me like a wide-winged, stinking bird. I stepped behind him.

He bellowed. When he had stopped, he said: 'You haven't got the stomach for it, you girl bastard. I'll tell you nothing.'

It ended in a gurgle. He spat blood, then began to swallow hard.

I thought: One step at a time.

'You were married to Nelly Oates. What happened?'

He spat blood over his head at me.

'I will hurt you,' I said, 'until you tell me.'

'I can't talk and swallow at the same time. I'm drowning.'

I raised the head-rest.

'Now talk.'

'You want power over Giles,' he said.

'I want to know what happened.'

I went beside him and felt all over his stomach. In his side, quite low down, was a large, hard lump under the skin.

'This will kill you?' I asked.

'It's a tumour.'

'And you won't have Giles cut it?' I asked.

'Never. I just wanted a bit of comfort.'

'How about me?'

'What?'

'Cutting you.'

'No! Please don't. I'm begging now. Please, please, please, please, please, please . . .'

'What happened with Nelly?'

'We worked at the factory, me and her.'

'Why didn't you move when the factory moved?'

'We got into trouble. Thieving. Just soap, but there you are.'

'So Nelly went to work at the renderer's?'

'That's right. Giles, he swung it. His mother wanted us arrested. Giles persuaded her to make us wash and pray. We got off scot free, Nelly and me.'

'Then what?'

'We'd help Giles's work, finding animals and such like. We found them. He cut them.'

'What was wrong with that?'

'Nothing. Then I found this man. He was gone – a starving, tertiary syphilis, Giles said. His leg was half rotted off anyway. That was consumption. I brought him in here. Giles amputated, but when he came to treat the stump with soap, the man died.'

'And you burned him? Melted him?'

'Yes.'

'And how many more?'

'Not many.'

'So the resurrection men brought the dead up from the graves, you brought the living to the table. And what? Did Giles kill them?'

'There were not many. It was his habit of using soap. They died with clean wounds mostly. Poisoned, I'd say.'

'Where? Where did you perform the operations?'

He rolled his eyes upwards. The studio. My studio.

'The patients recovered where? Tell me everything.'

'In the small room at the back of the house. At the top. That Mrs Tully's a nurse and knows how to administer chloroform. She helped.'

'You were blackmailing him?'

'Yes. As you will. We can both play him. There's room for two.'

'No,' I said. 'You're frightened of the knife?'

'Mortally. I've seen what it can do.'

'What about Nelly?'

'What about her?'

'She was going to have a baby. What happened to her?'

'She got depressed.'

'Why?'

'It was after the fourth one.'

'Fourth what?'

'The fourth time we got rid of the thing. She was – good-natured. We never wanted to keep any of them.'

'Why did she get depressed after the fourth one?'

'Giles altered the mixture.'

'What mixture?'

'The carbolic. He shot her full of soap. By that time, she'd picked up a dose and he thought he'd cure that as well. It wasn't pretty, the way she went, but she wasn't septic.'

We were quiet for a while. All I could hear was the occasional click from the lantern casing, and the blood in his throat. Then he said: 'Can you put a cover over my face and make it quick?'

'Why?'

'Because you are going to cut me open as if you were a surgeon to make it look like Giles killed me. Everyone knows I had the screws in him. Can I ask you this?'

'Ask me.' I felt oddly like crying.

'Nick my artery, let me bleed to death. It's not a bad way. Like sleeping. But cover my face first.'

I fetched paper and wrote down what he had said, and made him sign it, and date it and swear that it was true. He had the last laugh, though. His tumour was septic and pus which smelled like pure evil leapt out at me like a cat. But he was dead by then and I cut him, laid him open, then covered him in a curtain.

34

I knew I could not return to my studio and lie on my bed above the horror in the basement. I thought of Pity and suddenly I felt alive with hope and expectation. It seemed that once I had swung at the man and damaged him, I had released the demons in my head. Almost before I knew what I was doing, I had changed my jacket and left the house. My footsteps stole through the streets. The smell of the river – weedy, rancid, rotting, alive – filled my head.

There was the brothel. The curtains were all drawn. Inside someone was playing the piano, a jangling, music-hall tune. I heard voices, cheers. I tried the door but it was locked. Instead of ringing the bell, I pressed my eye to the window to see if I could peer in but the glass was running with condensation. Someone inside was singing a coarse song in a rough treble:

> A merchant of Genoa, leaving his wife at home
> Kissed a little whore, in the town of Rome;
> 'You, my dear,' said he, 'tried full many a nation.
> Then say who had the longest tool of generation.'

There was a roar of laughter, more cheers. A figure crashed into the glass, rubbing against it with their back. I peered in through the wet smears of condensation.

> Said the merry girl, 'Oh, that's soon decided:
> You who cross the sea, are the best provided;
> What a length of tail, though the seas you roam,
> Your spouses never fail, to bear you babes at home.'

A boy dressed like a midshipman was dancing on a table. He looked familiar. The piano played faster, a sort of jig, the boy managing to make his dance both energetic and obscene. The music reached a crescendo. The boy stopped, dead, bent double, his head between his knees, then suddenly with a gesture I knew too well, whipped off his middy's cap and shook out his hair. It fell like a red-gold waterfall halfway down his back. Not a boy after all. It was Pity.

To see her like this was acid in my gut. Something in me split open. I was filled with fear, panic, envy. I tried the front door again, hoping to be able to slip in, but it was locked. The window! If I could open the bottom sash even six inches, I could slip in behind the curtain and join the throng. I did not know what I intended to do then – find Pity, have her, save her. Anything.

The window slid up an inch. Jammed. Slid another. The music had stopped. I pressed my eye to the glass. I could no longer see Pity. I forced the window up again. Again it jammed, worse this time because I'd pulled it upwards with such force. I managed to unstick it then worked it up. Between the window and curtain was a gap of perhaps a foot. On the other side of there was a row of backs. Whatever was going on in the room was holding their attention. The piano was playing more quietly now, a halting attempt at an exotic ballad.

I slid one leg over the sill, then the other. The crowd in the room suddenly roared and surged. One of the men in front of the window staggered drunkenly forwards and that gave me my chance. I slipped into his place, just as the crowd roared again.

A child, much younger than Pity, was standing on the table performing a *tableau vivant*. Her face was a blank mask as she shuffled her feet and wiggled her thin shoulders. She was swathed in layer upon layer of gauze, and as she danced, these dropped to the ground.

On a chair at the other end of the table sat a young boy, dressed in a toga and a crown. Salome dancing for Herodias.

Under the table lay a plate with a plaster head of John the Baptist on it.

I saw Pity. She was on the opposite side of the room sitting on a swell's lap, legs thrown over his, one arm round his neck, the other fiddling with the buttons of his waistcoat. He was fat, whiskered, with splayed yellow teeth and thin hair ringleted with grease. As I watched she tilted his hat playfully and ran her hand all the way down his front. He looked down on her blurrily then nodded at something she said. She stood. My heart stopped, She led him upstairs.

I could not let Pity go with that man! I inched my way round the back of the room, but every time I pushed into someone, they pushed back at me and swore. The piano meanwhile was tinkling on, the crowd growing more restive, and still more layers came off the dancer. The music speeded up; the child's shuffle became slightly more animated. Some of the crowd had begun to sway in time to the music and this made it easier to move, but even so two minutes must have passed before I was halfway round the room. Still I pushed past. Now the child was naked, pulling a scarf between her legs. Now Herod was standing, pointing to his crotch. People were straining, forcing their way forward. Suddenly I was free from the crowd, dashing for the stairs, trying to remember how the cubicles were arranged.

I ran up the stairs. At the top was a small landing, then a narrow corridor lined with the curtained cubicles. I began by peering round the edge of curtains, but empty cubicle followed empty cubicle. The corridor turned a corner. Cubicles now to left and right. I grew more hasty, running past the rooms, pulling the curtains back until I heard movement, the sound of springs creaking. I flattened myself against the wall; found myself panting and sweating. Lifting my hand, I dragged the curtain back across the doorway.

Pity was sitting on the edge of the bed, still dressed like a midshipman. The man with splayed teeth was adjusting his trousers. He looked up, unconcerned.

'Wait your fucking turn, matey,' he said before pushing past me. 'Bastards can wait.'

Pity bent over a pot on the floor and spat into it. Her eyes looked red.

'You're crying,' I said.

'He nearly gagged me.' A heartbeat. Ten. 'Well?'

She was looking at me curiously.

Madness was on me. 'I've come to take you away,' I said.

She stared at me blankly. 'What?'

'I've come for you.'

'You're lying,' she said.

'I mean it.'

'What about your friend?'

'He does what I say now,' I said. 'He can't refuse me anything.'

'If you say so.' For the first time, a hint of archness.

'I want you.' Watching her closely, I saw a brief, galvanic jolt, followed by a look of poised wariness.

'All to yourself?'

'Yes.'

Her eyes flickered over me. She said: 'Suppose they want me back?'

'I'll hide you.'

'And your friend? What will he do when he's finished examining me? We get a doctor a month come knocking on the door asking to check us. Some are fake, some real.'

'He's a surgeon,' I said.

'Ah.' She went into herself for a second.

'Are you clean?'

'As far as I know.'

'Can you come to me again?' I asked.

'I can walk out any time. What will a girl like me do except come back? The workhouse? The street? They know I'm better off here. It's all I know. I do it well, I can make you happy. I can make you believe – '

'What?'

'Whatever you want.'

'You'll come?' I asked.

'I'll come and see you,' she said. She paused. 'You really think you'll look after me?'

'Yes,' I said. My mouth was suddenly dry.

'And you'll paint me?'

'Yes.'

'Now give me a shilling. No, better make it more. They'll be wondering what's going on and I'll need to tell them I've just been with a madman who climbs in through windows.'

'You saw me?'

'Yes, I saw you.'

'And yet you stayed with the other man.'

'I had to.'

'I want to get you out of here.'

She looked at me levelly.

I turned to go.

'Can I ask you one more question?' she said.

'Yes.'

'Do you know who I am?'

'What do you mean?'

'Do you know who I am?'

'You're a girl with an odd name,' I said.

'And you'll paint me?'

'You can be my model.'

'I can be more than that,' she said.

35

So I returned to the studio. I slept like a dead man but awoke in my bed, cold and alone. I shivered. For a minute I had forgotten the horror of the night before but that shiver seemed to shake my thoughts into order. They fell into my mind like crows off a branch and started circling. I had killed a man. I had emptied him of life. The deed seemed enormous now, but I needed to put it behind me. It was conquered territory. I must move on.

I held William Oates's testimony. I placed it in an envelope and lodged it with a solicitor on Borough High Street, leaving strict instructions that it was to be opened and published if I died. I then returned to the studio, stripped off my sour clothes, wrapped myself in a robe and strode across the courtyard to bathe. It was a fine morning. Rain, falling at some point in the night, had washed the air clean and the chimneys of London had not had enough time to choke the sky. There was an underlying warmth to the day. It was going to be the first warm one of the summer. I felt like celebrating. The omens were good.

I was so elated that I pushed into the bathroom without checking to see if it were occupied. I found Giles, stretched out in the tub, looking curiously at me.

'Well,' he said. 'You're looking pleased with yourself.'

'Am I?' I said. 'Perhaps I am then.'

'What have you done? Been down to the brothel again?'

He was half submerged, soapy water lifting his parts which were tumescent. His skin was grey, unlike Pity's. Unlike Pity he seemed vast and indelicate. I was surprised at how the hair on Giles's chest looked against the skin when it was wet. Surprised too at the heaviness of his musculature in the breast and upper arms.

'You're strong,' I observed.

'Yes.'

'How come?'

'A surgeon must work for his bread and butter. It's hard, sawing and cutting. People don't know.'

'I do,' I said.

He ignored that. 'Have you been back to the brothel?'

He swirled water casually around his prick. I thought of bladderwrack in a rock pool.

'Yes,' I said. 'I saw her again. Asked her to come here.'

'Did you indeed?' He considered. 'Have you worked out how she is going to live here when you are pushed out into the street?'

'You wouldn't do that. Not while I'm to paint your sister.'

'You like the idea of that, don't you? Oh, yes. You like the idea of getting your grubby little hands on Georgina too.'

'I'll move Pity in *and* I'll see your sister. And then we'll see where my grubby hands end up. You seem to think you're clever, but any fool could see that you're just jealous of any liaison I have with another person. I will have my whore and your sister, if I so desire.'

'Auguste, have you gone mad?'

'I'll not stand for your superiority any longer. Things will change here, Giles, from today. From this minute, from this second. You have lorded it over me, flaunted your superiority and insulted me with your foul approaches once too often. Well, events will take a different turn now.'

He laughed. 'Auguste, superiority is knowledge and you know so little. So little. All the time I have merely been trying to save you from yourself. I might as well let things take their course now.'

'No longer. The course is mine.'

Giles opened his eyes wide. 'Auguste. Knock. Knock. Is there anyone in there? You're a poor, second-rate artist. I can throw you out on to the street any time I want. Do you think that your precious Mr Gruber will be so happy to come and see you then, you simpleton?' He spoke in a sort of mocking chant. 'And you were beginning to bore me anyway,' he added.

He slid further into the bath. I leant over and pressed down his head. It was not a decision. It was a reaction. His arms swept up and tried to find purchase on the sides of the bath. I smashed my forearm down on to one, then the other. Very quickly, his feet began to thrash; he had not drawn breath before submerging. He hit the side of the bath with his fist.

The door slammed open. Mrs Tully rushed in and screamed. I let go of Giles and stood back against the window. He hauled himself up from the water, leant forwards and began to retch water and cough. He would have done better if he had not been trying to shout at me at the same time.

Eventually he managed to say: 'You tried to kill me.' In a tone of disbelief more than anger.

Mrs Tully looked at me. Worry and frank curiosity warred in her face.

'You get out of here,' Giles said. 'You pack your bags and get out. I'll see you finished. I'll have you broken . . .'

I was still breathing heavily from the effort of keeping him down.

I said: 'Get dressed. Wait until you see what I have found.'

'What have you found?'

'In the old furnace room.'

Giles and Mrs Tully stared at me, then at each other. He rose from the bath.

'For God's sake, will somebody get me a towel?'

When I pulled back the curtain in the furnace room the stench rushed out like darkness. Giles winced and put his hand in front of his face, then bravely started taking little sips of air.

206

'Pus,' he said. 'Definitely malign. Auguste, what little secret have you got hidden away for us down here?'

'Here,' I said. 'Take the lantern. You first, then Mrs Tully.'

Before he stepped into the room, Mrs Tully said: 'Ask him how he found out.'

'Well?' Giles said.

'Mrs Tully means to have it on record that she did not tell me,' I said.

She was looking curiously at me again.

'Do you mean to spread suspicion?' she asked. 'You are quite effective. But this room holds no fears for me.'

She made as if to go in first, but Giles pushed her back. Once he was inside, she said to me: 'Now you. I want one of us to be outside while you are in.'

I stepped in and she followed.

I had covered him with a red velvet curtain, aware of the effect it would have. Giles gave a sharp intake of breath when he raised the lantern and saw the shrouded bench. Very few details were discernible; just the red shroud, the smell of pus, and now the smell of blood.

Giles turned questioningly to Mrs Tully, who shrugged.

'You'll need to see who it is,' I said.

Giles's face was very strained. The way the skin stretched made him look younger. He marched up to the bench and snatched back the shroud. He swore. Unable to contain her curiosity, Mrs Tully pressed past me. I could hear the blood on the floor kiss her little slippers as she lifted her feet.

'It's William Oates,' she said.

Giles was examining the arms and frowning. He squeezed the man's nose between finger and thumb and waggled it.

'Quite detached,' he said. He pulled the shroud down past the corpse's arms. 'At least he died peacefully,' he said. The slit in the wrist was deeper and darker than I had thought, or perhaps it just contrasted with the whiteness of the drained body.

He pulled the shroud off completely and said: 'Oh, sweet Jesus!'

Not really knowing what I was doing, I had laid him open like a flower, endeavouring to be neat in my work. I felt a need to explain.

'Actually, he gave me the idea. I wanted to know the truth. It was he who said that everyone knew he was putting the squeeze on you, Giles. He probably boasted about it in the pub. If I cut him like a surgeon, it would look as if you did it.'

'You think you cut like a surgeon?'

'The public will buy it, or the police will, which is more to the point. He was blackmailing you. What simpler thing than for you and Nurse Tully here to lure him back to the furnace room and finish him off?'

'What do you want?' Mrs Tully asked. Again, that look of curiosity in her face.

'Only to live in peace here,' I said. 'And a measure of ascendancy.'

Giles laughed. 'Every worm will turn.'

'You forced me to it, Giles,' I said.

'If you believe that,' he said, 'there is no telling what lies you will believe about yourself.'

'We must get rid of him,' said Mrs Tully. 'Oh God, we must get rid of him.'

The calmness of her voice belied the horror in her eyes. I suddenly saw the woman I had seen at the window my first night here.

'Light the fire, Mrs Tully. The chimney must smoke again.'

I found I was trembling. I saw Giles look at me, as if he were trying to comprehend the change in our relationship.

'"See saw, marjorie daw, Johnny shall have a new master",' he sang.

'I did it because I had to.'

'Hush,' said Giles. 'You did it from desire. Your desire to dominate me overrode your scruples. The juggernaut, remember? Crushing all before it as it rolls down the road. The first day you were here I helped deliver a baby. I didn't realise I would be delivering a monster at the same time.'

'You are hardly an innocent yourself.'

'Oh, I know, but I always think one murderer is enough for any household, don't you? Of course, I could justify what I did in terms of medical research: the greater good, the march of science, the benefits it will bring to humanity at large. How will you justify your act, Auguste, when your conscience really begins to gnaw you?'

36

So my relationship with Giles changed, but not so much as might have been expected. I was anxious not to place him in the position to which he had reduced me. But I was helped by his curiosity regarding the odder corners of life, and this curiosity was now extended to his own existence. The situation he found himself in fascinated as much as it appalled him; indeed, fascinated him *because* it appalled him.

One night, after supper, I said: 'She is coming.'

Giles nodded. 'Have you been with her since?' he asked.

I shook my head.

'Will you do one thing for me?' I asked.

'What?'

'Examine her for me.'

Giles held my eye. I could see the glitter of candle light in it, and movement, almost as if it were communicating fast and active thought.

'If you force me, I will,' he said. 'But a forced diagnosis can be wrong.'

'You refuse?'

'On the contrary. I just refuse to do it voluntarily.'

'But before you were so keen.'

'Things have changed.'

'What, exactly?'

'Just remember this: from now on, everything you do is your own responsibility.'

And he laughed.

★

I had arranged a time for Pity to come, but as the day approached, a feeling of reluctance grew in me. Giles was pressing me to tell him when she was due to arrive, something I found odious in the light of his previous reluctance. I did not want to tell him or talk about it at all.

I was working on a canvas when she arrived. Gruber had written to me, asking me if he could visit the studio and see what I had to offer, and I wanted *The Country Girl* to be sufficiently advanced for him to put down a deposit on it. I worked on it obsessively – Pity had posed for it. The girl in the centre of the picture had her face, her body, her secrets. And then one afternoon I looked up from the canvas to see her standing in the doorway.

Why is it that these moments are never easy, that the more one anticipates, the less an event lives up to expectation? One minute she is not there and I am trembling in expectation; the next she is there and all expectation is gone, to be replaced by what? Fulfilment? A sense of completeness? Satisfaction? None of these. With the vacuum of expectation punctured, doubt, confusion, and oddly a sense of panic, were sucked in to fill the gap.

She was at her most demure; a plain dress, her hair scraped back. She made a mock curtsey.

'Well, here I am.'

'Yes,' I said. I felt a very long way away from her. 'You're here.'

I added a highlight to the country girl's hair. I couldn't get it right. Everything I did looked hackneyed, but at that moment it seemed nothing could be more important than to get it right.

She laughed nervously.

'Sit down,' I said. 'Please.'

She walked across the floor to the table and chair and sat down. I watched her out of the corner of my eye.

'I'll be with you in a minute,' I said. 'You could help me if you took off that absurd bonnet and shook out your hair. Like that. No, in the light. Head up. Up, for God's sake!'

When I next looked at Pity she was crying. Confusion swamped me. I reached out a hand to touch her but she knocked it away. I threw down my palette and ran to find Giles.

He was peeling an apple with a scalpel in one long, continuous strip. The strip was so thin that it was already trailing on the floor. His movements, as he turned the apple in one hand and held the blade steady with the other, were very steady and very smooth. It looked as if he were skinning rather than peeling it.

He stood and measured the strip against me.

'About five foot six. One of my best.'

'She's come.'

'I know. I saw her.'

'I don't know what to do. I was painting. I asked her to take her bonnet off and stand for me. It made her cry.'

'Well, of course it did, you pitiful wretch,' Giles said. 'I'm surprised you didn't drive her straight back to the brothel. You have to be nice to them.'

'I don't know how,' I said. 'I've nothing to – I've no experience.'

He looked at me as if he had just seen me for the first time and said, or rather breathed: 'My God.'

'So what should I do? This is not what I expected. This is not how I expected to feel at all. I thought my emotions would sweep me along, but it's the opposite. I don't know what to do. Help me, Giles.'

'What can I do?'

It was a risk, in my position, to admit to any sort of vulnerability, but I felt desperate.

He smiled. 'Oh, I'll help you, and would even if I had no choice in the matter. I wouldn't miss this for the world. Wait.' He sniffed his hands, then wrinkled his nose. 'Can you smell that?' He waved his hands at me. I smelled that smell you feel in your stomach. It is sweet and foul at the same time. Old meat. 'The consultant today, a well-respected gynaecologist, calls that hospital odour. He thinks it is a good thing. It is the smell of a three-week-old body that I was dissecting to ascertain the cause of death.' He sniffed again, then grimaced. 'Mere soap is not enough. Bouverie's Moonlight for me.' He waved an imaginary wand. 'And then, I shall be at your service, master.'

As I waited, I watched the peeled, contaminated apple turn brown. Its spoiling was so stealthy and so gradual that it tricked the eye into seeing nothing. Only if you looked away could you mark the change.

Pity was curled up in a far corner of the room, looking like a shadow.

'Auguste, she is not just taken nervous, she is terrified,' Giles said.

'But surely this is better than her brothel?' I replied.

'Her brothel was familiar to her,' he said. 'This is not. Try and remember your feelings on leaving the orphanage.'

I tried but could not.

'What can you do?' I asked.

'It's you she wants. Go on. Approach.'

I went and kneeled before her. She turned away from me. I put my hand on her shoulder. She shrank back.

'What is the matter?' I said. Then, as if inspired: 'Do you want a doctor?'

She looked up, green eyes red-rimmed.

'A doctor?' Her voice was hoarse.

'I just thought – '

She shook her head.

'I won't see the doctor.'

'But you must. If there is anything wrong with you . . .'

'If there is anything wrong with me, I will tell you. I know what there is to know.'

I returned to Giles. 'She will not talk to you,' I said. I had caught a glimmer of triumph on his face, the same expression I had seen back in the Cremorne Gardens. He was craning over my shoulder to look at her. I suddenly wanted him away from me.

'Perhaps if you would let me approach . . .' he said.

'No,' I said, with unexpected force. He was hiding something from me. Perhaps my freely admitted confusion had rearmed him.

'You bring me here, now you tell me to go. Really, Auguste, it is as if you do not know your own mind. Very well, I'll go.' But his eyes were narrowed on Pity, and I could see that his curiosity was aroused.

When Giles had gone, she said: 'Close the shutters.'

I looked at her questioningly.

'You will not want your friend to see what I am going to show you. We're overlooked.'

She jerked her chin at the back windows of the house. I glanced up, thought I saw a shape move behind the glass. Giles was spying on us.

I closed the shutters. The numbness I had been feeling was gone, replaced by nervous excitement. It was dark in the studio. Pity lit a candle. She stood immobile. I could hear blood pound in my ears.

'What is it?' I asked. I was filled with an overpowering sense of nostalgia for something I had never had. 'What is wrong?'

By way of answer she walked towards me. She took one of my hands and placed it on her breast. I felt desire for her. She stepped up to me, twisting my other hand behind her, so it rested in the small of her back. She raised her mouth to mine and kissed me. Her tongue was slick and hot, a darting salamander in my mouth. I pressed her to me. Her body gave and came alive. I wanted her badly. She broke away.

'Tell me this,' she said. 'When you lost your virginity to me, had you ever been with a woman before?'

'No.'

'I mean in any sense – kissing, touching, playing?'

'No.'

214

'Have you seen a woman naked, touched her, felt her skin, learnt its contours, its textures?'

I swallowed. 'No.'

'When you lay with me, was I naked?'

'No.'

'And that didn't strike you as peculiar.'

'I don't know . . . I didn't know.'

'Haven't you guessed?' She looked at me wonderingly. I think for the first time there was real tenderness in her expression. I felt increasingly baffled and upset by her interrogation. It must have showed. I tried to regain the initiative.

'Oh God, you *are* diseased.'

She shook her head. 'Hush,' she said.

'You are with child?'

She laid a finger across her lips.

I was suddenly taken by a great shuddering wave of feeling, nothing I can describe exactly but pure, molten emotion that seemed to dissolve all barriers between me, the world, and Pity, so that for a moment we were bathed in some white-hot, singing magma. I wanted the feeling to go on, but knew it was a preparation for something else. What could I do? I wanted just to stand there and shudder and not decide, but it was not to be. Everything leads to something.

'You know I could have had you earlier,' she said, 'when we kissed. Remember that. Do you want me to go?'

I shook my head.

'And you will have me as I am?'

'Yes.'

'I have given you your freedom. Remember that.'

'What are you going to do?' I asked.

'Undress.'

The dress fell stiffly from her shoulders. Under it she wore a simple shift. She shrugged it off her left shoulder, then her right, and let it fall to the ground.

Her breast was white and flat, her stomach taut and muscled, her waist slim. The shift fell past her sex to the ground. The shock was swift and total. Pity was a boy.

Time froze around me. I felt panic, not as something that grew and grasped but as a state of being. The walls of the studio dissolved. Around me was a still, collapsed world, a desert where everything had worn to dust and time had died. I could not move. I was a pillar, paralysed, and it was a relief to be so still for that meant that nothing could change. The panic could not become worse.

Pity saw my shock; I think he had been expecting it. He smiled, a sphinx's smile, all in the corners of the mouth. I tried to speak but my throat had closed. From feeling that my stillness was that of a pillar, I now felt too weak to move, too weak even to collapse. I was held by what I saw, my eyes travelling up and down his body. Darkness swooped in on me, and his body began to flicker before me like a thin, pale flame.

I looked at his face, expecting to be terrified and humiliated, but I didn't see a boy: I saw the Pity I had known and accepted as a girl. A girl's face. A girl's hair. A girl's eyes.

My confusion now was total. Everything I had thought had been overturned. My eyes slid desperately from the child's sex to its face and back again, hoping to see something that could confirm an impression either way. But I was not to be spared.

I finally managed to get out a word.

'No.'

'Some of them are sick,' Pity said. 'When they see me. But I'm usually pretty careful. Make sure that they want me.'

'No.'

'Don't you want me?'

I could move then. I moved away.

'Does none of them know?' I asked.

'Oh, some of them do.'

'But you're so – '

'I know. Would you rather I dressed?'

'Is that all you do?' I said. 'Shock?'

'No. Like I said, some of them know.'

'And still – '

'And still. Some of them want me like a woman. Some of them never know I am anything *but* a woman. Some of them know that I am not, but pretend to me and to everyone that they think I am.'

He paused. 'I could have fooled you a while longer, until you lay with a real woman. I could have played you along.'

'Why didn't you? For Pity's sake – I mean, for God's sake – it would have saved me from this.'

'It was you who wanted me. You came after the dog boy to the brothel, told me to leave the place and come here. You would have found out in the end. That is, if you kept seeing me. I didn't want that. I wanted you to know either now or not at all. I played my hand badly the first time I came here. I wanted you to paint me like a lady so I dressed like one. When you asked me to strip, I thought you'd just throw me out.'

'I don't know,' I said. 'I just don't know.'

'But you would have thrown me out?'

'Probably. What do you want?'

'I want you to paint me. It's the only way I'll be a lady.'

'That's all you want?'

'That's all I've got. My ability. My skill. That's what we were taught at the Cherry Garden: "Find out what they want. Find out what you've got. Use it."'

'What do we do now?' I asked.

'I get dressed,' she said. 'Unless you want me? I'm bloody freezing.'

He, she, wrapped pale arms around that slim body. I could see the skin dulling with goose bumps. I thought that by the fire that skin would loosen and begin to glow – and recoiled from the idea. I needed to lie down.

I watched furtively as Pity dressed, bending over gracefully to pick up his shift. He lifted his arms, his skin stretched over his ribs, and as he let it fall over his body, I could not look away. The slide of the skin over the bones, the fleet, unfussy movement of the muscles in his belly . . . I was aroused by the simple understated beauty of it, as anyone would be.

I tore my eyes away and hurt myself in doing so.

Pity went and sat at the table. Now I could see him more clearly in the candle light, his hair seemed to coil like snakes. I do not know how long I lay there. I could not take my eyes away from him. I stared at the slanting green eyes, the face that narrowed to a small pointed chin. I saw now that he had an Adam's apple; I saw now, in the candle glow, that light caught in the small hairs above his mouth. And yet his beauty now was a repellent thing.

'How do you live?' I asked eventually. 'How can you bear the obscenity of being a man and living as a woman?'

'Like I said, I learned it. It was what I could do that the others couldn't. I would go with men. I look the way I do. I let my hair grow. Some of them like it.'

'And the clothes?'

'They feel all right.'

I smiled bitterly.

'Have you ever worn the right clothing?'

'The right clothing?'

'Men's – boy's clothes?'

'Sometimes. For dressing up. At first it was a sort of disguise, I think, dressing like a girl. Now it's funny for me to wear anything else.'

'Did they make you?'

'Who?'

'The people in the brothel. Your keepers.'

'No one makes me. I like it. My father did at first, before I ran away, but like I said, I didn't even mind much then.'

'Your father did this to you?'

He approached me, and squatted down by the bed. He touched my forehead. His hand felt cool. 'Shh,' he said. 'I can be a companion to you. Some of my gentlemen talk a lot about the creative process, and the woman within the man.'

'I cannot,' I said. 'I cannot.'

'What spoke to you, what you saw, was the woman in me,' he said. 'You saw it like no one has seen it. That is why – '

'You thought I could paint you as a woman?'

'Yes.'

'I paint the truth. To paint you as a woman would be an obscenity! It would be a lie. I could not do it.'

'But you saw me as a woman,' he said. 'You still do.'

'How dare you? I – '

But his face was very close. He placed his mouth over mine. I wrenched myself away from him, but he held me down.

'No one will ever know,' he said. 'It can be our secret. It will have to be a secret.'

His hand moved down to my waist. I tried to move away but could not. I lacked the moral force. His fingers, slipping inside my trousers, touched my sex.

I closed my eyes. He said: 'Open them.' I obeyed.

'Call me by my name.'

I said: 'Pity.'

He smiled. 'Remember that,' he said. His fingers pulled my shirt free. He bent his head and kissed my belly.

37

It was Pity's desire to be seen as a woman, and so I did. I was not deceiving myself – I was believing in her. Was I doing wrong? I asked the question a thousand times and every time I answered: No. The very fact that I was able to paint her as a woman proved to me that I was submitting to a greater truth than that of mere bodily attributes. And it seemed that Giles somehow saw this too. He could have made our life together impossible. Instead it was as if he perceived the essential rightness of it and so submitted too.

Once he asked me: 'Is this what you want?' And when I answered yes, he simply nodded, allowing himself only a small wry smile, as if he were acknowledging defeat.

Time passed. I was satisfied with the progress of *The Country Girl* – with Pity as my model I was able to work in a sort of enlightened frenzy with none of the exhaustion I normally experienced afterwards. Then I painted her very much in the style of Rossetti, as a face and a body in a robe, more a presence than a portrait.

I worked. She watched. We made love. We ate. We slept. I worked. She watched.

One day I returned from an excursion to find her seated at an easel. She looked embarrassed, and tried to hide what she had been doing.

On a piece of prepared board, she had sketched in her face. While the technique was undeniably flawed, the face was recognisably hers. And the neck. Below her neck, she had sketched in a dress with a plunging neckline. She had given herself breasts.

'Is this what you want?' I asked.

Her face was red and already swelling with tears.

'Of course.' She had cupped her hands in front of her chest, as if her bosom were really there. I felt such tenderness for her that sympathetic tears came to my eyes.

'I will give you the body you want,' I said, placing my hand against her cheek. She tilted her head into it. 'Meanwhile,' I said, 'you are trying to walk before you can run.'

And so I set her exercises. Lacking any plaster casts, I suggested she first draw those parts of her she could see: a hand, an arm. Later, we would try and see if we could not arrange for someone to sit for her. Pity said she was happy just to follow in my footsteps. In the meantime, she would draw whatever came to hand: fruit, flowers, a plate set on a table. They would be memorials to her happiness, she said. She had talent, real talent. I found it flattering that she drew and painted in a style that resembled mine, but then of course she was a fine mimic. She could be a woman if she wanted, and when she wanted could put on a manner that was positively ladylike. Her voice lost its customary archness, the whore's slightly hoarse insinuating tone. Instead, she took its natural low pitch and turned it into a well-modulated, quieter version of Giles's voice, just from listening to him talk.

We are lying side by side in the studio on a vast bed that I have placed facing the fireplace. The bed has a high headboard that can sound like a drum. When the weather is cold I light the fire and we lie naked in front of it. I like it in the dark when the only light and the only heat come from in front of it. I like the way the red light plays on Pity's skin. I would like to paint it but I don't think the way of doing so has yet been discovered. Nothing I do works. I had the idea of breaking the colours down into their constituent parts, but then did not know how to apply them separately to a canvas, so that they could all come together. The eye does not see colours separately so the melding must take place at some point yet undiscovered. Perhaps the currents of the air twist the individual threads of colour into thick hanks. A prism then would be like a comb, untangling them. Or are they mixed by some process we do not understand inside the eye or brain? I do not know. Giles does not either. Pity does not know but does not need to. Perhaps I am thinking more about fathoming the mystery of her sex.

Her skin is different from other women's. It is clearer, for one thing, and thinner. When I look at other skin I see a coarseness in it, a sort of fatty, milky opacity, a thickness like a cheap glaze. Pity's skin is like a membrane. It is thin, translucent. It carries colours within it. Looking at the fire, I can see how her blood responds to the heat and rushes in a million veins to the surface, suffusing it with a warm, imitative glow. In the day, when she sits for me, bathed in this strange, artificial London light, her skin tautens and stretches, thins. I can see the veins across her breast, her arms, her face. She seems delicately blue-green then. I can always see her heart beating under the skin; sometimes I can imagine I see it, red and pulsing, deep within her.

She sits, legs tightly crossed as I have taught her, trapping her sex. She can stand like that as well. She likes it. I have plans for her. She will be the making of me, I know it. She is drawing the best out of me, making me alive.

I realise something else. When I am with Pity, I am away from Giles and that dreadful need of his. Which is a relief.

The bed is Pity's empire. She is playful; she is vulnerable. When she screams, and cries sometimes, it rends my heart. She never tells me to stop when I enter her, and if she did, I could not. It is the price she pays, her choice. Sometimes she closes my eyes and lies on her back and lifts her legs so high that they are resting on my shoulders. When I enter her I feel I am slipping in so far it is only the tightness of muscle that stops me. She can hold me in that soft ring forever, she says. I want to ask her how she knows, but any question of that nature, any question that touches on her past, is too painful for me to bear. And yet pain can be like a spur, and when I think of what she used to be, it makes me love her fiercely but in a way that sometimes makes her cry out. I tell her that it is just a different way of loving. I could never share her with anyone else, but sometimes she needs to scream to know it is I who am with her.

The mood can take me suddenly; it comes on like a storm. I was once with her, she on all fours, her head against the headboard of the bed. I was holding her head up by the hair. I can twist it round her throat and across her mouth and pull it back like reins. She was like that and I was on her when the door opened and I saw Mrs Tully standing there. I stopped moving. She would have seen only me. She couldn't have seen Pity. She took my order for lunch, and as she talked I began to move in Pity, a fraction of a fraction of an inch. To Mrs Tully it must have looked as if I were simply kneeling on the bed. When Pity made a noise, I pulled the gag of hair more tightly across her mouth and moved again. The pleasure I took from this episode was immense. If it was wrong to hurt her, she should say. I have never taken pleasure from hurting anything else in my life. It is her; it is something in her talking to something in me. It is a silent conversation. It is between us both. It is a way of coming to complete, silent, total understanding.

But it had to end, this honeymoon. Gruber's visit opened the door and the cold wind chilled the bud, and blighted it. I had champagne for him, and quail's eggs, and some German sausage that he did not touch. I showed him *The Country Girl*.

He nodded sagely, commented on the composition; said that he could see nothing of me in it, as if that signified approval. Then he said: 'And what else have you to show me?'

I had placed *Pity* on a covered easel under one of the windows. I did not want to build up too great an expectation, but at the same time wanted Gruber to take it all in, in one eyeful, so to speak.

I said: 'Oh, yes, there was something else. Now where . . .?'

And as I was turning around, as if accidentally pulled the covering off the canvas.

I watched him carefully. He hardly blinked, but at the same time his gaze became harder and brighter.

'I call it *Pity*,' I said.

He nodded, then turned back to the other canvas. I made as if to hang the sheet over *Pity* again, but he shook his head and said: 'Leave it,' as if it were of minor importance. I walked to the other end of the studio. All the time he pretended to be scrutinising *The Country Girl*, he was sneaking glances at *Pity*.

'Two hundred for the railway station scene,' he said. Then, almost as an afterthought: 'And fifty for the girl.'

'Three hundred for *The Country Girl*,' I said. 'And four hundred for *Pity*.'

He looked straight at me. 'You are out of your senses,' he said. 'I said fifty.'

That told me he was thinking only of *Pity*. I said: 'Three hundred for one. Four hundred for the other. Guineas.'

'Preposterous. I — you are quite mad. Why did I ever leave my country and come to this land of savages? Four hundred pounds — '

'Guineas,' I said.

'It makes little difference because it is all fantasy. Four hundred anythings for an unknown face by an unknown artist? I have never — '

'You sold the last one. You sold *Pandora's Box* to the family of my benefactor. You could buy an apple from a grocer and then sell it back for double.'

'You have seen it?'

'Yes. In their mansion in Kent. When you bought it off me, you did not say that you were purchasing on behalf of another party.'

'And who is to say that I was?'

'It seems clear. Giles wanted to buy it.'

'Then why didn't you sell to him?'

'I could not accept his money as well as all this.' I gestured to the hall.

'Scruples, scruples. Well, you do not have his money. You have mine, and the painting hangs in the Bouveries' pretentious country house.'

'And if that was not what I wanted?'

He flapped a hand dismissively. 'Once you have finished a picture, it stops being yours. It is finished, complete, private no longer. It belongs to the world and your only control over it is to get as good a price for it as possible. I am serious here. Never forget this, and once you have painted a picture, say goodbye to it and that is that. Now, I must be off.'

'One minute,' I said. 'I want you to meet someone.'

The door at the end of the studio opened and Pity walked in. She had let down her hair and wore a dress of deep blue. She moved towards us, gliding on invisible feet. Gruber looked from her, to the paintings, back to her. Pity held out her hand and curtseyed, her eyes modestly lowered.

I said: 'This is my model.'

'My God,' he said. '*Mein Gott.*' He examined her, took a turn around her. His face split into a broad grin.

'And she is beautiful,' he said. 'Quite exquisite. My dear, tip your head, so.'

He tilted his own head towards the light. Pity followed his movement. The light caught the moulding of her face, the pose hollowed her cheekbones. She was wearing powder. It caught in the soft down that covered her cheeks and held the light in a soft nimbus.

'She is quite new,' he said. 'This is very interesting.'

'Yes.'

'And no one else has painted her?'

'As far as I know, no.'

He spoke as if thinking aloud. 'A mystery model, here in the heart of the slums. Your history, madam? Your past?'

'I have none,' Pity answered.

'Everyone has a history,' Gruber said.

'And it's private.'

I looked at Pity in some surprise. I had not heard her so tart before.

'And have you any classical poses?' he asked me. 'Of the girl?'

'Not classical,' I said. 'But imaginative.'

His eyes widened as I showed him *The Mermaid*. 'I see,' he said. 'I will tell you this: do not try and copy Millais. He is worried all the time that he is not respectable, and tries to pander to respectability in his work. I do not want to see her welcoming her soldier husband back from the wars, or sheltering a sparrow from the cold, or saving a beggar girl or what have you. But I tell you this: there is now enormous interest in things bad, mysterious. This I saw in *Pandora's Box*, this I see in this picture. Find the right tone, the right level, and we will both become rich men.'

'And her?' I said.

'I said: we will become rich men. What happens to your model is your concern. Now I take these.'

I held out my hand to stop him.

'Seven hundred guineas.'

'Preposterous, as I said. A messenger will come tomorrow. And it is pounds.' He nodded at me. I nodded back. At the door he stopped. From where he stood, Pity was behind me and slightly to one side. I could see the point of focus in his eyes slipping from me to her.

'Extraordinary,' he said. 'She is quite like you, and you like her. I have heard of old married couples growing alike as they age; never an artist and his model.'

I shrugged, pretending nonchalance. Gruber had come closer to the truth than he suspected. He gazed once more from Pity to me as I moved forward to usher him out.

Afterwards I embraced Pity. She was like a board.

'He knows something,' she said.

'What?'

'I do not know. I do not trust him.'

'Dearest, he is our reality as much as that table, that chair. My painting. He can be trusted. He will send the money.'

'If he brings it, I am not at home,' she said. 'I do not trust him.'

38

Pity took to walking in the courtyard. She was devoid of
self-consciousness, both awkward and elegant. From my
window I could see her hold conversations in her head as if
acting in an imaginary play. Sometimes her face lit up in smiles,
sometimes it fell into a heavy frown. Sometimes she looked
sad. These were the times when she allowed her feelings to
show. In the normal run of things, her face was unusually
inexpressive.

But I was not the only one who saw her. Soon after she took
up this habit, the old fountain was cleared of leaves, a workman
patched it up and set it running. Then a flowering cherry tree
in a large tub arrived, and then a bench.

'You know Giles is doing this?' I said.

'Who else? You wouldn't.'

It is another unwelcome introduction to my life: this
pertness. Winter has passed into spring and spring is passing into
summer. Summer, it seems, brings freedom with it: freedom to
explore, to roam. Freedom to change. Except I do not feel I
can change. I do not know how to. The frost has bitten too
deep.

'Is he bothering you?'

'He never talks to me except to say good morning, or ask
after you.'

'That's a lie. I saw you deep in conversation with him
yesterday.'

'Yesterday? Let me think . . . Oh, yes, he was asking after
you. Said he never sees you any more.'

'There's a good reason for that.'

'What is that then?'

'He tried to press his desires on me. I worry he's doing the same to you.'

'What? Are you jealous?'

'Am I jealous?' I mimicked her voice.

'You suspect us of dark dealings? Dirty work at the crossroads?'

'I live with a whore and a degenerate, and I'm not supposed to be suspicious?'

'Giles – a degenerate? Who says?'

'Giles is – Giles is not interested in girls.'

'Oh, really? He's looked at me so he must be.'

'But you – ' I could not say that she was not a girl. 'You're different,' I said.

'He thinks I am.'

'What? A girl? Or something different.'

'He treats me differently. He treats me well. Not like some I could mention.'

'Me, I suppose?' My anger mounted.

'No. Mrs Tully. Anyway, either Giles likes the look of me or he doesn't. If he does, he's not a degenerate. If he doesn't, no danger to you or my honour, sir.'

She dropped me a curtsey.

'Unless he's guessed,' I insisted.

'What?'

'You know what I mean.'

'In that case he's the one living with a whore and degenerate, and he's got as much reason to worry about it as you.'

She turned and tried to leave.

I grabbed her, held her face in one hand, my fingers biting into her cheeks.

'Why do you talk to me like this?' I asked, choking with anger.

'Because you're so cold. You're like a puppet. The lust is going. Soon there'll be nothing left. Not even a glow.'

'You dare to complain about the way I treat you?'

She closed her eyes. 'No, I do not complain. I can't, can I? I saw you come for me. You asked me to leave that place with you. You have somehow, I don't know how, made it possible for me to stay here. But I must know – ' Her eyes were closed. A thin crescent of tears appeared on her eyelashes.

'Know what?'

'If you are to keep me as a slave, I must know so I can prepare myself. If I can expect anything else – '

'Like what?' I interrupted.

'Like affection. Like pleasure in my company, the sort even one of my gentlemen at the brothel might occasionally display. If I can expect that, then I will adjust my expectations accordingly.'

Her voice shook with emotion. I was affected by a powerful rush of sympathy. I felt a warmth in my solar plexus, a sort of rushing lightness in my head. I took her and kissed her. Her lips were tense at first, but then I felt them yield and she allowed me to fill her mouth with my tongue. I took her down to the floor. For a while, for a passionate tangle of time, we made proper love and I was abandoned with her. When I awoke it was dark and she had covered my body with her hair. She was looking down at me from inside the tent of her hair, and whispering to me. Her eyes were tender and suddenly I was embarrassed and ashamed.

I had been stung by her words: I could not take pleasure in her company. It was true; so simple a thing but I could not do it, however hard I tried. Yet Giles could. I saw them talking easily, not a hint of anything between them that could be thought of as out of place, but oh! the black jealousy I tasted at the sight of them taking these simple pleasures together. I watched, I was determined to copy, I tried. And it worked. I mean insofar as I could see the gratitude on Pity's face as she responded to my pathetic attempts to talk, to be lighthearted. But I felt ever more like her puppet, jerked by alien fingers, and sometimes the strain grew too much for me.

One day – it was about a week later – Pity was sitting for me. A wealthy collector from Birmingham had written to Gruber, saying that he wanted something for his study: a picture that celebrated beauty of the Grecian kind, if the dealer knew what he meant.

Gruber had written to me, enclosing the letter, and adding a note: 'To say *Grecian* is not necessarily to say *Classical*. Let us not be too restrained.'

I roughly blocked out a picture of the rape of some Greek women by centaurs, but on considering the rather amorphous confusion of bodies and horse's legs, decided to concentrate on the event itself – a Grecian maiden chased into a grove by a centaur, the creature pinning her against a tree while she looks over her shoulder, terrified at what is about to transpire. I had set myself the task of painting it within four months. The price, were the sketches accepted, had been set at five hundred guineas.

I had placed a hat stand to simulate the tree, and Pity was clasping it with both hands, leaning forward at the waist while looking over her shoulder. I paced around the tableau, trying to ascertain the best angle from which to paint it.

Pity was wearing a work frock, a simple high-necked thing of cotton, with a faintly spreading waist. I found what I thought might be a good position from which to sketch, trying to imagine how it would appear with the centaur rearing behind. I made a couple of quick charcoal sketches to fix Pity's pose in my memory, then a third, on which I tried to superimpose a centaur, but something was wrong. I was not understanding the flow from the back, through the buttocks to the legs.

'Not disturbing you, am I?'

It was Giles. I didn't answer. Pity glanced at me. She had held the position for a good half hour, supporting herself on the shaft of the coat stand, bent at the waist, her back arched and rump thrust out. At the same time, she had to look over her shoulder, away from the door, towards me.

Giles came to stand behind me.

'What's this?' he asked.

'A rape,' I said.

'Of a woman by a horse?' He squinted at the sketched swirl of charcoal, a smudge of finger marks.

'A centaur.'

'And where are you going to find such a thing as a centaur to draw?'

'Really, Giles, this insistence you have that I claim to draw everything from life is wearing.'

'I forgot. You changed.' I heard him scratch his shadowed jaw. 'Centaurs, of course, did not exist, even in the minds of the Greeks,' he said. 'They were figments, symbols, designed to draw attention to the dual nature of man: reason above, beast below. They are either presented as demonically lustful or paragons of wisdom and virtue, suggesting the inability of man to reconcile his two sides.'

'Very interesting,' I said. 'This is being painted for an old man in Solihull who has probably grown rich making corsets. Pity, do not move! I need your head just so. Bend your neck back! Back! Yes. The hair – do not move your hair yourself, you little idiot – the hair must fall more behind you. I cannot obscure your breast.'

Pity strained her head back. Giles said: 'She is in pain.'

'Nonsense. Can you mend her hair? Take a hank of it and let it fall over her shoulders. There, now another and bring it over her back.'

Giles moved to do as I said.

'Now she has tensed. She is too wooden.'

'My back,' Pity said. 'It hurts.'

Giles said: 'She is in real pain.'

'I have not finished,' I said. 'Hunt made his first wife miscarry through posing. We are still some way from that.'

Pity's face was twisting.

'It's cramp,' Giles said.

'It's you,' I said. 'She just thinks she can win some sympathy. Hang on, I can use that expression.'

I sketched a while longer.

'Auguste, I must insist . . .'

'I wish you wouldn't,' I said, not lifting my eyes. 'I'd hate to disappoint you.' I sensed them exchange a quick look, no more than a glance. I looked up. Giles stared stonily at the wall. Pity was squeezing out a tear. She cried as much as a woman, at any rate.

'If you want to help her and me, Giles, stand behind her. That's right. Now pretend you are a centaur. You can support her by the waist, can you not? That will relieve her slightly.'

'I cannot.'

Pity was looking desperately over her shoulder, first at me, then at Giles.

'Do it!' I shouted. I put down the sketch, giving up all pretence of working.

Giles stood behind her. He took her by the waist. I saw his hand close gently on her, then grip harder, as she relaxed to try and take some of the pain from her back. He staggered slightly to try and adjust his balance. In so doing he moved more closely against her, gripped her more tightly. By bending her legs, she rested against his crotch. Giles's face was stony. For half a minute he stood there, legs trembling with the effort, and the only sound was from Pity, sobs rasping from her heaving breast. At last Giles looked at me and said: 'Damn you, Auguste,' and pulled away. And Pity collapsed. Giles left the room, not looking at me or Pity.

'Why did you do that?' she asked.

'To see whether Giles felt for you at all,' I said. 'Now I know that he does.'

'And are you jealous?'

I was, but could not admit it. 'Have I anything to be jealous of?' I asked.

'No. But I wish you were. It might mean that you cared.'

'The way you behave, and you expect me to say that?'

'Say anything.'

I could not say I loved her, I could not say I cared.

'You ask for too much,' I told her. 'You want my emotions to behave like animals in a ring, ready to jump through hoops at your request.'

'No,' she said. 'I want them to be free, but to respond to me willingly.'

'The more you want, the less free they feel,' I said. 'I was always taught to be grateful for what I received.'

39

The first postal delivery arrived before breakfast and letters were placed on the table in two piles, one for Giles and one for me. He was generally the first down to breakfast, and if the post had not arrived late that morning, I am sure I would never have received the letter from Georgina. He would have hidden and then destroyed it. As it was, out of the corner of my eye I saw him slip one of the letters to the bottom of the pile, go down it again, as if to check, and hand the top three on to me: bills from my tailor and artist's supplier, a letter from my bank.

Giles left his unopened by his side while he picked at his toast.

'Not opening them, Giles?' I said.

'Not this morning, no. I know what they will be.'

'Oh, really? Let's see. What's that top one?'

'A letter from my mother exhorting me to wash.'

'And the one below?'

'A bill from the medical school, I suspect, for dining expenses.'

'And below that?'

'Oh, just a letter from a friend.'

'Really? If ever I received a letter from a friend, I expect I would open it immediately.'

'Perhaps I prefer to open it in private.'

'Aha. A letter from a lady friend? I thought I detected a feminine hand on the envelope. A close lady friend?' I asked.

'Yes.'

'Miss Morant? She has written before and that does not look like her hand to me.'

'Another.'

'Another fiancée?' I asked.

Giles stared at me dully, then slid the envelope from the bottom of the pile and flicked it across the polished table. It was addressed to me. I read the letter aloud:

Dear Mr Coffey

It would give me the greatest pleasure if we could continue with the sittings as previously discussed. Naturally, I am anxious to make whatever haste is possible. I gather that you are now having some success and while we understand that this will create added pressures on your time, we are confident that you will find the opportunity to complete the portrait, as discussed.

Yours sincerely,

Georgina Bouverie

'Two interesting facts emerge,' I said. 'One, your sister's enthusiasm for seeing me is matched only by your reluctance to allow it. It seems strange that she wrote direct to me. I would have thought it would have been more normal to write to you, enclosing a note to me, or even just a comment for you to pass on.

'But no. A letter. Rather formal, but then that is to be expected from a well brought up young lady. A letter addressed directly to me. And you tried to intercept it. Could it possibly be that at some stage, unknown to me, you have told her she should not continue with the commission? And could it be that she refuses unless you tell her why? And could it be that you are strangely reluctant to do so?'

Giles looked blackly at me. He said in a thick voice: 'And why should I be reluctant to do so?'

'Because anyone intelligent – and I am sure your charming, graceful sister is intelligent – would be inclined to ask why you permitted me to stay here if I was so unsuitable?'

'And?'

'And the last thing you would want to do is tell anyone why I am still here.'

'Why don't you leave?' he said. 'Why do you delight so in torturing me?'

I thought. 'Because I can. Because it does not seem to me as if I am torturing you: merely that for the first time in my life, I am getting my own way. And I like it.'

'Oh, yes. You and your creature comforts.'

'That you seem to covet yourself. I've seen the look in your eye. I've seen the way you behave around her. I would have thought she was rather outside the normal range of your tastes.'

'What do you know of her, or of me for that matter?' he said.

'Only that you were after me like a sniffing dog. That you sought to exploit your position by blackmailing me, by forcing me – '

'I never forced you. I never blackmailed you. Your willingness to accept my hospitality when you knew my nature and my feelings, or lusts, for you, led me to believe that perhaps there was hope. That you might find it possible to respond to me. You are the hypocrite! You are the blackmailer! You are the murderer!'

'And so are you,' I said. 'But I have the upper hand and the means to fulfil my desires, while you are forced to satisfy your appetite on crumbs.'

He rose to his feet and stood at the end of the table, knuckles resting on the surface, head thrust forward, eyes popping slightly.

'And what is more,' I continued, 'I will see your sister. I will enjoy it. And just as I get my own way with you, I will get my own way there as well, if I feel the urge.'

Giles threw a knife at me. He threw it wildly and the handle hit me in the corner of my eye. I was so shocked that I let him leave.

★

One day, I came back from an outing and Pity was not there. I waited, thinking she might have gone into the main house. After ten minutes or so I went to look. The house was empty but for Mrs Tully.

'Have you seen Pity?' I asked.

She was sitting at the kitchen table, peeling potatoes. When she moved, all of her rustled. Her dress was always something with a faint shine, like a carapace. You could not quite trust commonsense and experience to tell you what went on underneath. She regarded me calmly.

'Yes,' she said.

'Where?'

'In the hall.'

'Was she going out?'

'Yes.'

'Where?'

'I have no idea.'

With Mrs Tully, there was often a pause between question and answer, a pause that was minute, frosty and insulting. I felt more and more angry. To talk, she had put down the potato parer, a short, stubby little knife with a sharp tip. She had put it down to emphasise the fact that answering my questions was an imposition and a disturbance, although there was nothing to have stopped her from talking to me while she worked. As long as I was in the room, she would not move.

I picked up the knife. I was not threatening her with it, merely trying to find a way to vent my pent-up feelings. The knife was level with her face, no more than six inches from her cheek. Mrs Tully looked very obviously at it, then she closed her hand around mine. Her eyes darkened. Her hand was cool and I felt it very distinctly. She did not seek to push my hand away, either, merely encircle it, in as far she could, and hold. Then she relaxed her arm, still holding. I felt the weight of her arm, her shoulder, her, on my hand. A passive weight, but heavy.

I was confused. In some way the gesture was very intimate. I let my hand fall.

'Perhaps she went out with Mr Giles,' Mrs Tully said.

'The devil she did!'

I checked each room then ran from the house. Pity with Giles? I was not thinking straight. All I knew was that the idea was insupportable to me. It was simple pride that stopped me from shouting: 'Pity! Pity!' I ran up side streets, peered down alleys. The streets were stark and empty. I was anonymous, a speck in a void. The horrid tumult inside me amounted to nothing against smoky brick, hard cobbles, steaming slate. They would last; I was crushed. Those few faces that jumped out at me from windows or shops, stared at me pitilessly. I suddenly saw everything as a threat. I knew I could not bear to lose her. I could not bear not knowing where she was.

My steps clanked in the narrow alleys, rattled on cobbles, slipped on mud. I ran between warehouses, terraced houses, factories; every step seemed further to awaken my doubt. My journey took me little by little to the river, and thence to the brothel. Had she returned? I could not believe it. The door was closed; lights shone from behind closed curtains. Doubt and certainty warred in me. I could not open the door; I could not look inside.

I ran back home. The house was silent. I ran across the yard and flung open the door to the studio. Pity was in bed, lying on her back. Moonlight, gaseous London moonlight, made her skin like marble.

She sat up as I stood by the bed. Her face was alive and excited. She started to say something. I put my hand over her mouth.

'Don't ever do that again,' I said.

She lay quite still, eyes huge and scared, light reflected from their wetness. I took my hand away.

'Do what?'

'Leave me.'

'I didn't leave you.'

'Where did you go?'

'I cannot say.'

'Tell me.'

'But it was nothing. You can trust me.'

'Were you with Giles?'

'You must trust me.'

'How can I trust you when I know where you came from?'

'It is not what you think,' she said.

Mistrust is a spur. I made cruel love to her, pinning her down under me and spearing her, forcing her to open wider and wider for me, threatening to go on forever. She started defiant but her face softened in the end, before I did. Yet even this did not allay my doubts.

The next day I found Giles in the sitting room. He was reading the paper, feet on an ottoman. He did not look up as I approached.

'Giles,' I said.

He rustled the paper in acknowledgement.

'Giles, I need to talk.'

He dropped the paper and looked at me.

'About?'

'Mrs Tully said you were out with Pity last night.'

'Mrs Tully said: I was out and Pity was out. She did not say that we were out together.'

'You discussed it with her?'

'With whom?'

'With Mrs Tully!'

'No, she discussed it with me. She said that on receipt of this information, you ran from the house like a madman. She was concerned. She told me.'

'So you deny that you were with Pity?'

'I deny nothing.'

'You *were* with Pity!'

'I confirm nothing.'

'You must tell me!'

'Auguste, I once saw a little cock robin lose its temper. It shrieked and stamped its little feet and achieved nothing. I must confess that you put me in mind of it.'

'But – '

'But everybody in this house must do exactly as you order, every minute of every day?'

'No. Only when I ask.'

'Whenever you ask. Auguste, you must learn to distinguish between power and authority. You have one, but not the other. I leave it up to you to decide which you have. Now, leave me in peace and save your tantrums for something really important. You forget, you can only break me once, Auguste. You forget too that in killing Will Oates, you killed rather an important corroborative witness. It is all down to Mrs Tully now. She is a curious, complex woman. At the moment, I think, the balance of power rather interestingly favours you. I have not quite worked out how to proceed with my life. However, if you continue to act like a raving madman, she will undoubtedly adhere to me, and you, my friend, will be skewered. Now you do not want to lose all this, do you?' he said.

I was silent.

'My advice, dear Gussie, is to learn to enjoy what you have and not to risk it.'

An old Thames wherry had moored at a wharf on the north bank of the river in front of an old sherry warehouse. Above it and half a mile beyond, the grey of St Paul's Cathedral seemed to float, shimmering in the heat. The wherry's hull was bitumen black; its sail a dull red. As the warehouse crane swung over it, the wherryman directed a docker with the stem of his clay pipe. In the bows sat his wife on a barrel, suckling a baby. The barrels were being rolled into a net, lifted by the crane, and swung into the fourth floor where a gang of warehouse workers were waiting. The warehouse's name had faded almost to nothing on the brickwork – huge ghost letters, maybe a G, maybe an H. Separating it from the next building was the Fleet ditch, pouring sewage into the Thames. I had stared at that building for six months, and smelled the stink, and for what?

Now I was selling my work to the best dealer in London, I had a solid commission, I had a lover and a home. Six months ago, as I sat in that garret in the Blackfriars factory, I could never have believed how great my good fortune would become. And yet what did it mean to me? Had I as much as that wherryman and his family? The crane swung, the barrels rolled, the wherryman pointed with his pipe, the wife dandled the baby on her knee, lifted its little hand and made it wave at its father. The porters and dockers shouted good-naturedly at each other. What did they care of fame and fortune? Would they have killed to secure it?

A train panted across Blackfriars Bridge, leaving the dark arch encased in steam and smoke. As it gathered speed, gouts of vapour erupted from the funnel and rose in the air, each separate, each distinct, each linked. They did not last. Even in the still air they faded suddenly to nothing.

Paul had died by accident; I had never intended to kill Oates. The question forming in my mind was this: Would I have killed them deliberately to be where I was now?

I could find no answer. The past was a pit and Oates and Paul had fallen into it, along with everything else that had ever been in the world since time began. I saw it now. Behind me was a great boiling abyss. As time moved forward, and I moved forward in time, the world crumbled behind my heels, devoured by the great molten mass of all that had been.

Would I have killed last winter for what I had now? Yes! No! What matter? The past consumed itself, and with it all regret, all remorse. What was done, was done. I could not change a thing. All I could do was move forward, run to avoid the cliff crumbling behind me. If I had set myself a course, I would follow it to the end. I could do nothing else. And if Giles and Pity were to be my life, I would take them with me.

I hurried home and wrote to Georgina Bouverie, receiving her answer the next day. Yes, she understood the necessity of coming up to London to sit in my studio for preliminary studies. She would pretend she was visiting friends who would have arranged to meet her at the station. She would take a cab to the studio and be there by four o'clock on Friday.

I had two days to prepare myself.

'If you are bored, you should go out.'

'I'm not bored.'

She was sitting on my lap and I was guiding her hand, showing her how to shade the side of a flask to give its outline substance. I was surprised at her progress. She had an eye, but more than that, she had concentration.

When we look at a thing, we do not really see it. As an example, ask most people to draw a head, and they will draw a face. But a face is in fact only a small part of a head; it is just that part which we need to see. The key to any head is the relation of the parts. Pity, in her first study of me, had the proportions perfectly. She lacked the skill to draw a nose, or an ear, but each related to the other. Out of interest I asked her to draw an eye. I sat opposite her across a small table. She laid paper down in front of her, took up a pencil, glanced at me, made a mark, stopped and then stared. Ninety-nine people out of a hundred would not have done that. They would have drawn what they thought an eye was. Pity stared at my eye for a good two minutes before she began to draw.

But now she was bored. She had glanced at the clock, surreptitiously, at least three times in the last half hour. I had prepared the ground by telling her I would be out that evening.

'Would you like to go out?'

She yawned and stretched.

'No,' she said.

'Well, what?'

She looked at me. I could still lose myself in those eyes. 'I can be bored, you know. It means nothing.'

Sometimes, when she speaks, I can hear London in her voice. It makes me think of grey rain on grey roofs, something clear but bitter. She doesn't talk about her past. She's too busy living in the present and planning her future. When she talks, she takes on the voice of whoever she is talking to, if she thinks it sounds better than her own accent, so that you hear in her inflection snatches of me, Giles, Mrs Tully and others. If you could interpret every voice, you would have her secrets. Sometimes I can't help torturing myself by hearing every man she has ever been with in her mouth and throat.

'I don't want you to be bored. I am frightened that if you get bored, you will leave.'

'Leave this?' she asked. 'Leave you? I couldn't.'

'Why not?'

'Why not? Because I love you.'

I flinched.

'What? Have I said something wrong?' she asked.

'No.' But a ghost had just splashed through me. I was disturbed.

'Am I not allowed to say that?' she asked.

'Of course you are.'

'Then what?'

'I don't know,' I said. I felt sick.

'Come here.'

She took me in her arms. Her mouth pressed against mine but my lips felt dry and resistant. She pressed her tongue into my mouth. I could not unclench my teeth. She rolled it around the inside of my lips. I felt my neck begin to lock as she pressed her head against mine. Her hands had dropped to my waist and began to feel through my trousers for me. Then it was as if she were falling; her head was buried in my crotch and my hands were in her hair, clutching it. I felt dizzy.

'I need to go out,' I said.

'Tell me what I've done?'

The words surprised me. 'You haven't understood me,' I said.

'Will you be gone long?'

'Why do you ask?'

She shrugged. 'I don't know.'

Once outside the door I turned into the alley by the side of the house and waited. It did not take long for Pity to leave. On the step she paused and I pressed myself back against the wall, turning away my head as she passed. She was so close I could almost smell her as she hurried to the river.

I followed her through the railway tunnels and past the warehouses. She never looked back; she never suspected. I followed her to the brothel. The bitterness was just beginning to well up inside me and a black, murderous rage overwhelm me when I saw that she was not heading for the brothel but just past it. I was too far away to see exactly what happened. One minute she was there, the next she was gone.

I ran forward. There was a gap between the brothel and the building next to it, and in the gap was a ruin. The top two storeys had fallen in; the ground floor was on the point of collapse. Someone had wedged props into the holes where the windows had been to slow the decline. Someone else had lit a fire against the front door, half burning it. The waterfront was empty; the tide was out. The beached lighters were like heavy things sleeping on mud. I listened. I heard the roaring susurration of London punctuated by the odd cry from the river. No other noise, no footsteps. Pity had gone into the ruin.

I approached it as silently as I could. The door gave to a finger's touch. Inside I smelled damp, charred wood, piss. Heard nothing. Ahead of me the staircase had collapsed, blocking the corridor. Doors opened on to empty rooms to left and right. Above me I saw only stars.

Gingerly I tested the floor. It gave slightly and something changed. I could not tell what it was until it started again. Very dim, very quiet, the sound of crying.

I slid forwards as silently as I could. The house was suddenly full of little sounds, but always that sobbing that stopped and started and stopped again, as if a child were being comforted before being overcome with grief again.

The sound had grown minutely clearer since I entered. All I could suppose was that there was a way through the mess of collapsed floorboards and plaster that blocked off the back of the house, but as I drew nearer it seemed clear to me that no one could have disturbed it. In the side rooms then? No; crying in there would have been heard more clearly. Anyway, now the crying had stopped, I thought I could hear voices. To my right, under the broken stairs, was a cupboard. I leaned against it. The door swung open. Suddenly I could hear the voices more clearly, and although I could not distinguish individual words, I thought I could hear Pity's voice.

I looked into the cupboard. There was the smell of earth, a faint whiff of candles and something else. I had matches in my pocket. I struck one. Below me, stretching down into the darkness, were the cellar stairs. I memorised where they started, shook out the match and inched towards them in the darkness. I kept my right hand against the cold wall, my left ahead of me. When that hand touched the wall, I knew I must be near the bottom of the steps, and they turned to the left to bring them under the rest of the house.

At the bottom of the steps I extended my hand and touched something that yielded: a heavy curtain, sticky with damp. There was no gap in the middle of it but one side was looser than the other. As I pulled it, a little light spilled through. I inched it back until there was a gap and peered round.

Two things struck me. One was the sight of Pity, sitting against the wall, cradling a head in her lap and crooning. I adjusted my footing to get a better look. My foot knocked into something. It fell with a hollow clang through the curtain and on to the floor – a filthy, battered tin bucket. A shape detached itself from the wall and a figure ran towards me through the darkness. The head on Pity's lap looked up. Something struck my head and I fell. Dog boy began to cry again, the darkness exploded into a starry night sky, then the stars went out.

40

I woke up in the same room feeling sick and damp. I was staring at a brick wall that was running with damp. Shining green weed covered the bricks and mortar. The beams of the floor were picked out by gentle phosphorescence. I rolled over.

Pity was sitting on a stool by my head. The bed was a pile of bitter-smelling rags bunched beneath me uncomfortably. She was staring abstractedly at me. For a second, and it was only a second, I saw through the veils of artifice to something private at the core. I saw a child, but one tempered by life into something more than adult. I saw a boy, but I also saw a girl; the face seemed to flicker between the two states by the light of the candle.

'What happened?' I asked, more to break the silence than anything.

There was a glimmer of panic on the face before it settled into the familiar configuration.

'Giles hit you,' she said.

'Giles?'

'He was frightened of you and panicked. He didn't want you to know that he was here. I said you'd already seen him.'

'I'd guessed,' I said. 'What were you all doing here?' I continued.

'The child was sick. I wanted help for him.'

'Dog boy?'

'He's called Simon.'

'Why didn't you just ask?'

'I thought you might say no.'

I fought back waves of nausea. Would I have said no? It was true I wouldn't have cared overmuch about the dog boy. I might have said no in case Pity's involvement with him inconvenienced me.

'Where is this place?' I asked.

Pity looked around her. 'It's where I lived for a time. It's a while ago now. Dog boy stayed on.'

'It's next to the brothel.'

'Afterwards I moved in there.'

'Where's Giles?'

'He's taken Simon home with him.'

'He'd do that for you?'

Pity shrugged. 'He's doing it, isn't he? Who cares who it's for? It's funny, Giles asked him so many questions.'

'Like what?'

'Like had he ever seen him before? Like did he know who Giles was?'

'What did the dog boy say?'

'Just burst into tears.'

'And he still went with Giles?'

'I told him to. He'd do anything I say,' Pity said proudly. I missed the point of what she was telling me.

41

The dog boy had a fever – Giles seemed to think it was pneumonia – and would not last another two days in the unwholesome air of his den. By bringing him back to Crucifix Lane and allowing him to sleep in the recovery rooms, at the very least he would not die alone. But I still felt that something was wrong. My head felt horribly like a coconut: brittle on the outside, pulpy and sloppy inside, but I was able to walk. I draped my arm over Pity's shoulder; she held me round the waist and gripped my wrist with her free hand.

Then I remembered the afternoon only a few short months ago when I had seen the dog boy hiding on my roof. By following him I had found Pity. With my head so scrambled and confused, it was as if memories and reality, past and present, had coalesced so I was confused as to whether we had come from Crucifix Lane, and were going to the brothel, or vice versa. And suddenly the thought came to me, as it had come to me on the waterfront, that I had been meant to follow the dog boy to Pity; in other words, that he had presented himself as a lure.

At the time it had meant nothing. I had merely been pleased that she had wanted to see me again. Now things had changed. Subsequent events had stacked up behind that first one but now their weight had crushed the meaning out of it. If that event had been planned, was it not possible that everything which followed had been also? Could it be so?

The ramifications were infinite, incomprehensible, twisting endlessly out of sight. Cobbles flickered past my eyes. The world was shifting in and out of focus, blurring to greyness then leaping at me with flashing brilliance. The street sounds, so familiar they were generally inaudible, now encroached on me brassily. An organ grinder was competing with a group of Ethiopian serenaders, the dizzying hoots of the instrument weaving in and out of the wailing barbarian voices in a nauseating amalgam of sound. A match seller bellowed in my ear; a crippled flower girl, her face stitched into a pathetic smile, cried 'Come buy, come buy' as if her heart would break. Pies, muffins, matches, shoe laces, ginger beer, medicines, pictures, daughters, children, sex – the whole world just a confederacy of whoredom. I wanted to get out, I wanted to get away.

I looked down at Pity. Her face was flushed with the effort of supporting me. I deliberately let more weight fall on her shoulder, and she immediately braced and took the strain. Under me I could feel her muscles, her bones, the organised movement of them. All directed at what? Me? No. Escape. She just wanted to escape too. I was the ticket from Sodom to Suburbia, just as Giles was mine. I almost laughed to think of it. The world, which I thought I had managed to escape following the murder of William Oates, now seemed to press in on me again. Somehow I had to wrest back control.

By the time we got back, dog boy had been settled and I felt too tired and weak to confront Giles. Pity undressed me and made up a camp bed for herself. Giles gave me some sleeping powders. As I drifted off, I saw through the great hall's windows a light shining from the back of the main house. The sick room. And Pity had opened a shutter and was lying with her head turned so she could see the room where the dog boy lay.

Giles came in to see me that evening. My head was still throbbing and I felt sick. He took my head in his hands and felt it. His hands were cool and strong.

'Well,' he said, 'that was a narrow shave.' He smiled at me uncomfortably.

'What?'

'I panicked. I'm sorry. I was down there and felt compromised. I was worried in case I was found by someone who might be unfriendly.'

'Blackmailed you?'

'What, for helping a sick child? I thought you might be a footpad, a robber, a degenerate member of the criminal fraternity. Please don't be angry, Auguste.'

'Then don't joke. And I feel too ill to be angry,' I said. 'Why? That's what I want to know!'

'Why what?'

'Why go behind my back?'

'You'd better ask Pity,' Giles said. 'She told me she needed my help. Naturally I was reluctant at first, but after all, I am a doctor.'

'And dog boy's a patient. Why not just admit him to hospital?'

'And watch him die? He's better off here.'

'The House of Healing.'

'That's right,' Giles said, ignoring my sarcasm. 'Now,' he continued. 'Tell me how you feel?'

'My head hurts and I feel cold and sweaty at the same time. How on earth was I able to walk home afterwards? I couldn't do it now.'

'The after effects of concussion are serious and rather unpredictable. We know little about them. My own belief is that the longer the patient can rest under proper medical supervision, the better. A man came into the hospital the other day, complaining of a headache. When Mr French examined him, he found that the patient had a four-inch nail buried in his skull, almost all the way. The brain's a funny thing. We took the nail out, the man went home, and fell over dead three days later while going about his daily business. We never did find out who put the nail in his head.'

He shook his head. 'Now, I want you to sleep and I want you to sleep a lot. That's the best medicine for you. I've

251

prepared a sleeping draught for you and I'd like you to take it.'

Something had changed in his tone, something had closed down. He was hiding something.

'You know what happens if I die?' I said.

'Oh, yes. We all want you to stay alive.'

I swallowed. 'Good.'

Giles stood up, knee joints clicking, and stretched.

'We've got ourselves into a pretty pickle, haven't we?'

I grimaced.

'Now are you going to take your medicine?' he asked. He held up a glass, half an inch of chalky liquid in the bottom. 'Just laudanum.'

I drank it, grimacing at the taste, then lay back on my pillow. I was overtaken by a pleasant spinning sensation. The fog in my brain cleared temporarily.

'Giles?'

'Hmm?'

He was standing under one of the windows looking up at the sick room.

'You wouldn't be thinking of operating on the boy?'

'Operate? Operate on what?'

'His hand.'

'Why should I do that?' he asked.

'I don't know.'

I didn't know. All I knew was that I had asked the wrong question, or that Giles had given the wrong answer.

Why should I do that?

That was missing the point, surely? *Why shouldn't I do that?* That was what Giles should have said.

He had every right to operate on the dog boy and had no reason that I could think of for hiding it. I lifted my own hand. It seemed a very long way away.

Why should I do that? He was asking me to find out. With the clarity of intoxication I saw that this was a deep truth. Giles wanted me to ask questions, wanted me to find out.

I tried to speak but my tongue was too heavy. I saw his face in quarter profile: a tiny smile was dimpling the corners of his mouth. The pain lifted from my head. The room began to rise and spin, and it was as if I was flying. Then everything was flying. I turned my head. Near the door I saw Giles and Pity talking. I knew they shouldn't be, but there was nothing I could do about it. I noticed something strange. They weren't talking about me. Giles said something and jerked his head behind him. Then Pity looked up. It wasn't me they were talking about, it was the dog boy. I tried to rise, horribly aware that I had been tricked in some way, that I was being drugged because they wanted to do something. Just as the pair of them had met at dog boy's room, so now they were making me unconscious for another reason. Then I was back in that dreadful basement. Then I heard dog boy crying again. Faces loomed over me. Giles. Pity. Mrs Tully. For a while dog boy was lying next to me. When I looked at his hand, it was no more than a red, bleeding stump.

42

I woke up in the morning feeling no more than slightly sick. Pity was sitting by me.

'Awake?'

I nodded. I could do so without hurting my head. 'What happened?'

'Giles gave you a sleeping draught.'

'I dreamed of dog boy,' I said.

Pity swung her head away. Her face tightened.

'What's wrong?' I asked.

'He died in the night,' she said.

I waited a moment, then said: 'Sorry.'

'He never had much of a life,' she said. 'I wanted to share some of it with him.'

'Pneumonia,' I said. 'Nothing they could do, I suppose?'

She bowed her head and began to cry.

'Do you miss him?' I asked.

'Yes. Badly. He was what I had.'

She didn't say: He was all I had. She didn't have enough for that to mean anything. He was what she had. I was distantly jealous and it hurt like cat gut tightening around a cold finger.

'What is it?' I asked. 'Just sad?'

She nodded but there was more to it than that.

'It's all my fault.'

'What is?'

'He was happy the way . . . the way . . .'

'The way he was? He was happy with pneumonia?' It was an odd thing to say. She shook her head.

'Did you betray him by coming here?'

'No. Yes. I don't know.'

'If it's any consolation,' I said, 'I had to leave someone behind to come here too.'

'So?'

'So we're in the same boat.'

She began to cry again.

I asked her to prepare a bath for me. When she was gone I stood up. The room danced a bit and the floor tried to rise up at my face. I staggered and stumbled forwards, falling on my hands and knees. I was weaker than I'd thought but at the same time my head felt better than I felt it should. When I touched it, I was sure that the swelling had gone down in the night – but then it was two nights ago that I had been struck.

Two nights!

As the thought hit me, my stomach rumbled. I was starving. I was about to rise when I slid a hand across the floor. I stopped. The floor was colder there. Damp. I lowered my head and sniffed. Coal tar. By walking on all fours, I managed to discover what seemed to be a wide, faint circle of dampness, although much of it was drying out. I was on my hands and knees when Pity came back.

She saw me and stopped dead in the doorway.

'What are you doing, my love?' she asked.

'What has been going on in here?'

'Why, nothing.'

'The floor is wet.'

'I – '

Her mouth opened and closed. I tried to stand but got only halfway. A hot black weakness rose up from the floor and engulfed me.

She ran to me and caught me just as I was on the point of fainting.

'Don't excite yourself,' she said. 'It it too early for that.'

I pushed her away, weakly, but the action gave me strength.

'What happened in here?' I asked.

'What do you mean?'

'Why were you talking about dog boy?'

'When?'

'Before Giles knocked me out. What happened in here?'

'I don't know what you're talking about. He died. He was ill. We were probably just trying to – I was probably asking if there was anything anyone could do.'

'So why – what – ' Thoughts danced in my head. 'What happened then?'

'I will tell you what happened in here.' Mrs Tully appeared in the doorway then moved smoothly to the middle of the room. 'Excuse me. I was asked to tell you when your bath was ready. The young lady felt that you might be in need of her and ran back.'

'Worried I might find out something, more like,' I said. My words were oddly slurred, as if my mouth had changed shape.

'You were sick in the night,' Mrs Tully said, 'and then collapsed in it. I dare say she was just trying to spare your feelings by not informing you of it. You also needed a change of clothes.'

I was wearing a pair of Giles's pyjamas. I had not noticed that before. 'Which night?' I asked.

'Last night,' Mrs Tully answered. But she had not answered quickly enough to mask Pity's sharp intake of breath.

I looked at her.

'Stand in front of me,' I said. 'I need to lean on you.'

I placed both hands on her shoulders and made her walk in front of me, so I could lean on her without her seeming to support me. I squeezed her until she cried out. I think I thought I might feel the truth inside her.

It was frustrating. Once I had moved into Crucifix Lane, almost from the first I had been aware of a mystery. I had uncovered that mystery: Giles, to feed his ambition, had been performing operations on people. I had been moved in merely to cover up the traces, and give him something else to think about. By uncovering the secret, I had found a lever with which to dominate him, but now I felt the balance had shifted again. Almost since Pity had come to live with me, in fact, but I was not ready as yet to find out why. Since the dog boy's death I had been reluctant to leave them alone together, but in the end had decided I would find out nothing by keeping things as they were. I decided to take up an invitation from Gruber to get out of the house and try and clear my head. Giles would not come, although he was always welcome at Gruber's parties, and I was not comfortable being out with Pity. It was not jealousy as such, the feeling I had when men looked at her; it was more the uncertainty that was engendered in me. For while I knew what they were thinking, I had had no idea of Pity's thoughts, and Pity's thoughts, now I had her body, obsessed me. One night, when she had me in her mouth, I found myself thinking that my prick was a pearl fisher's spike, her mouth the lips of an oyster, and I wanted to prod my tool into the meat of her brain to find the hard, milky ball of truth inside it.

The gallery was as usual packed tight. The pictures, from what I could see, were rather murky landscapes of somewhere hot. I saw pyramids and deserts, which meant Egypt; olive groves and mountains, which meant the Holy Land; and an assortment of beggar children, water carriers, nubile maidens and doe-eyed bedouin bed-fodder, which meant desperation. I recognised a few other artists there and found myself comparing my clothes to theirs; mine were better. I assessed their manner. Mine was more elegant.

I sipped chilled wine. Here, away from my home, strangely enough I felt more secure. A man pushed his way towards me – Morton Shrike, a mediocre landscape painter and general hanger on. We shook hands.

'Well, Coffey, I hear you are to be congratulated?'

'On anything specific?'

'Who's a confident fellow? You'll have to watch it or I'll start visiting! No, no. Word is that you've got yourself a stunner.'

I affected coolness.

'Word from where?'

'Word everywhere. Eyes that could melt the Antarctic or freeze a volcano; hair like spun gold, and lots of it. Shall we see her? You're so damn' secretive these days.'

Shrike put his chin on his chest and affected regret. His last comment was absolutely empty; he had never sought out my company before and was in no position to know whether I was more or less secretive now than before.

We were joined by two other men whom Shrike introduced as Smith and Lewis.

'This is Coffey,' he said. 'Got himself a stunner.'

'So we've heard. Got her a place to live?'

This from Lewis. He was a young man with a pleasant, open face. He was sweating profusely and kept on feeling around his mouth with a grubby forefinger.

'She lives with me,' I said. I had grown unused to the ways of men. Their reaction was extreme: a sort of ritualised popping of the eyes, followed by spluttering guffaws. Shrike banged me on the back: 'My God, but you're a cool one, Coffey.'

'Did you hear me?' said Smith. 'You can't just – '

'"Lives with me"! Cool as ice!'

'It's a lie anyway,' Shrike said, eyes twinkling. 'She's still in her old employ, so I've heard tell.'

'Oh, ho. What's that? Snail seller?'

'Cod slapper?'

'Bag snatcher?'

'She – ' I began angrily, but was quickly as angry with myself for falling into the clumsy trap they had set. I tried to begin again but my mouth had gone dry. Staring at me from the other side of the room was Brownlow.

I was isolated in my panic. Casually, Shrike, Lewis and Smith followed the direction of my gaze. I saw Shrike's face light up with curiosity and delight, and he nudged Lewis then beckoned Brownlow to come over with exaggerated friendliness. He looked to me like Nemesis as he walked over to join our group.

'Timothy, this is Coffey,' said Shrike.

'We know each other,' Brownlow said easily, and held out his hand. His seemed to have grown, mine to have shrunk.

'Yes,' I said.

'Why, Coffey, is anything the matter?' Brownlow said. 'You look ill.'

'A trifle hot, perhaps.'

'Coffey's got himself a little red-headed stunner,' Smith said. 'What's her name, Coffey?'

'Pity,' I said.

'Pretty?'

'Pity.'

'Pretty Pity. That's no name at all. What's her real name?'

'I have no idea.'

'He's going weird on us, look. Didn't you say he went weird on your friend, Timothy? You know, the man who disappeared – Paul Frederic?' asked Shrike.

'Weird? No, I don't remember saying anything of the kind.'

'Any news of him?'

'No,' said Brownlow.

'Still nursing his broken heart,' said Smith, with mock gravity.

'That's a foul allegation!'

'No offence. Expect he's having a high old time of it then, somewhere.' His ugly face split into a gleeful grin.

'Careful,' said Shrike. 'Or he'll revoke his invitation.'

'What invitation was this?' Brownlow asked levelly.

Lewis put his arm around my shoulder.

'Why, to tea, of course. To meet his missis. Madam Pity, Queen of the crumpets. Tuesday would suit us all, I think.'

'I wouldn't miss it for the world,' said Brownlow.

43

'You are now drinking brandy at breakfast?' Pity asked me. I was still working on the nymph and the centaur, Pity modelling for me patiently. We were waiting for the fire to warm the hall. While I liked the colour of Pity's skin in the cold – it went a sort of translucent blue – Giles pointed out that ancient Greece was generally considered to have been warmer than London in spring. If I were to be realistic, I should try and recreate the conditions and paint Pity in the warm.

'I am,' I said. 'It helps.'

'It helps what?'

'It helps me to see.'

I pulled the cover off the canvas. Three foot by two of empty carnality to satisfy some impotent old lecher in the Midlands. I had changed the pose. Pity was now backed against a cliff, arms outstretched, while the slavering centaur picked its way towards her. I did not yet know whose face I was going to give the beast but was enjoying deciding between Giles and myself.

I had begun with Pity, as she was to be the focus of attention. I was experimenting with bases – the landscape, out of which the centaur would emerge, was to be on Academy sepia, while Pity's outline was sketched on ground white. She was going to glow.

I had her pose worked out and had begun to build up her form. Something caught my eye. I bent to the canvas and studied it. Her body had changed, slightly and subtly. I looked. The more I looked, the more I was certain but the less I could see.

'Have you – ?' I began. Then, 'No, no.' The thought was inconceivable.

'What?'

Pity began to undress, slipping the muslin dress from one shoulder and letting it fall.

'It seems that something has changed. Or I thought that something had changed here.' I peered again at the canvas. The Grecian girl, arms thrown wide, head held back, her pose a combination of invitation and terror, glowed with inner light; the centaur loomed vastly, a thing of shadows.

I peered at the girl's breast. For all that Pity was a natural model, it was hard to place the breasts correctly on her chest, especially as the tension across her rib cage and the position of the shoulders would have the effect of lifting them, giving them a shape I did not think I knew. So I had decided to make her a young girl, barely ripe, but even so had run into difficulties. Perhaps it was the fact that I had worked so long at that area that was confusing me.

Pity was naked now, standing on the dais and adopting the pose. For the cliff I had hung a large dust sheet dyed black. To help hold the pose, Pity had sewn loops into the material to support her wrists. She placed one wrist through, then the other, laid back her head, then crossed her legs to hide her sex.

I prepared my palette. Later today the vultures I had met at the gallery would be coming; on Friday, Georgina. I stared at Pity's breast, at the flat nipples, at the skin that strained across the ribs. My mind skidded off again. What would I do with Shrike and his cronies? More to the point, what would I do with Brownlow?

'You haven't touched the canvas,' Pity said.

She had come out of the pose, and her sex, warmed by her thighs, swung free, slightly tumescent. She was so much a boy.

'Get dressed,' I said, disgusted. I thought I could discern a slight fuzz of hair growing darker around its base.

'You look preoccupied.'

'There are some visitors coming to tea,' I said. 'Gruber must

261

have told them about you. Why my personal life should be of such interest, though, I cannot imagine.'

'I didn't trust him.' She shuddered. 'He's after something.'

'Oh, really. What?'

'Everybody does everything for a reason, don't they? What does he do, this Gruber?'

'Sells paintings.'

'No. More than that.'

'He represents a lot of artists. We sit in our studios, painting for all we're worth. He swans around the parlours of the rich and newly rich, convincing them that they have not achieved respectability unless they buy one of his pictures.'

'And what makes them?'

'Preference, I suppose.'

'And? These people, if they're so worried about what others think, aren't going to waste their money on anyone's paintings, are they?'

'Maybe he wants to make me talked about.'

'People talk about you already, you're famous. But there's talked about and tattled about, famous and infamous. Heard of Miss Walters, the biggest tart in the West End? She was so famous she stopped the traffic when she went riding down Rotten Row. She could pick and choose who she went with and now she's got three houses and her own carriage. But has she still got a good name?'

'Thank you,' I said sarcastically.

Pity shrugged. 'You see if I'm not right. Anyway, what do you want me to do with these people?'

'Be silent and mysterious,' I said. 'I'll parade you like a trophy. I'll have put up all the studies of you I've done and they can compare you to your ideal. Then they can scurry back to their sitting rooms and salons and cafés and publics and say what they like.'

Pity stretched, a singularly lewd gesture, sticking out her stomach, slightly crooking one leg. She swung her hair over her shoulder and tied it into a bun.

262

'It might help if they saw Venus rather than Ganymede.'

'One of my callers called me that.'

'And I suppose he called himself Zeus?'

'Clever! Yes, as a matter of fact. He laid me on a couch and fed me grapes, and I had to eat them like this.'

She bent back her head, opened her mouth in a lascivious pout and fished with her tongue.

'Do you even know who Zeus was?'

'A Greek god who could have anyone he fancied. He once turned himself into a bull to have this girl.'

While talking, her hand had drifted to her sex and started to play with it.

'Stop it!' I shouted.

She snatched her hand away. I do not think she had even been aware of what she was doing.

'You revolt me,' I told her.

'I'm sorry, it's just habit. My callers, they liked – '

'How can I see you as a woman if you – ' The words were grit in my throat and would not emerge.

'I forgot myself.'

'You forgot your act,' I said. 'That was yourself.'

'No! That wasn't. It was just – sometimes I forget what you like.'

'What I *like*?' I could have howled. 'What do you think I like? Do you think I like being with you, like this?'

I stood over her. She caught the back of her leg on the edge of the dais and scrambled away, pulling her clothes behind her. She began to pull on a shift then stood, hair falling about her strained, white face.

'If only you could accept – '

She stopped.

'What? You as a boy?'

'No – the fact that you like me as a boy! It's what you want . . . it must be! Otherwise – '

I struck out at her. She fell on to all fours. I fell on top of her, raining blows on the body that had betrayed me.

263

Eventually, spent, I lay still. She had curled up. I lay behind her, cradling her curved shape against my body. I the old moon; she the new. She in my arms; I in her spell.

'On Friday,' I whispered, 'I have a woman coming here and I want you away from me then. Lock yourself in the attic.'

She had been silent all through the beating. It was only when I said that that I felt her body begin to shake.

44

I t was odd to see Brownlow again and not to feel nervous. I made no pretence that I took any social pleasure from the visit, and betrayed no sign of nervousness or worry, relying on the effect of the studio, and Pity. To my satisfaction, while Brownlow tried to contain his curiosity, he could not. As I led my visitors through the house and out into the courtyard, I could see his eyes darting from side to side. Shrike, Smith and Lewis behaved in their usual way, like jackals, but I sensed they knew there was history between Brownlow and me, and were watching closely to see how I behaved.

In the courtyard I stopped the group, and invited them to admire the studio from the outside. It was a warm, early-summer's afternoon and the sun, orange through London's pall, lit the stone of the old hall and made it glow.

'Well, Coffey, you've found yourself a decent gaff, at any road,' said Smith. 'What's your hold over Bouverie?'

'None,' I said simply. 'Merely his generosity.'

'Auguste has this effect on people,' Brownlow said.

Shrike raised his eyebrows.

'And where are you living now?' I asked Brownlow.

'Chelsea,' he said.

'He's quite the darling of the new set,' commented Shrike. 'What's that American called? All muddy daubings.' The description chimed rather uncomfortably with my description of Paul's work.

'Whistler,' he answered.

I shrugged. 'Who's he?'

'If you don't know, it's not worth going into.'

'I didn't know you painted?' I said.

'River views. But I keep myself by journalism.'

'Radical stuff. You should hear him bang on about it. Wants to start a new gallery.'

I raised my eyebrows.

'We want to set up a large new gallery in London to challenge the stranglehold of the Royal Academy,' Brownlow continued smoothly. 'When I say we, I hardly mean that I am a prime mover, but they do need their friends in the press.'

'I thought the Brotherhood had succeeded in doing that,' I said. 'You mean to follow them?'

Brownlow waved away the suggestion. 'That's old hat, along with Ruskin and all the rest. No, no, a modern movement for the modern age. Some of the things they are already doing in France – paintings dashed down as quick as the eye can see. Light . . . light is everything. Paul was getting there,' he added. 'If only he had stuck at it.'

I shrugged, smiled. I could see he had lost Shrike and his friends.

'Well, if you say so,' I said. 'And he always did have a slight problem with form. Have you see him?'

'Have you?' Brownlow said.

'No, but then you're his friend.'

My heart was thumping. It felt good to talk like this. Brownlow shrugged. I could see the others exchange looks. A point to Coffey.

'Come inside. See my work,' I said grandly.

They came, they saw, they were conquered.

All except Brownlow.

First they saw the hall which I explained had been the monks' refectory, then they saw the pictures, and then they saw Pity. She was seated at the back of the room, a book on her lap, but obviously not reading. She was sitting very upright, wreathed in green velvet, her eyes abstracted.

Smith said: 'I'd not be a monk for long with that around.' Pity raised her eyes, looked at him, then lowered them. I wanted to applaud.

We made polite conversation, Shrike's eyes darting from Pity to the naked girl in the picture, and back again; Smith looked openly adoring; Lewis silent and awkward. Only Brownlow maintained his composure, standing apart from the group, looking detached and grave. I saw Pity's eyes dwell on him the most, but then women are drawn to silence, seeing in it a void to be filled.

Brownlow had his revenge, of course; gentle, painful revenge. The first barb came as they were leaving. He stopped by the door where Pity's first attempts at painting were stacked, knelt and began turning through them, the wooden frames clicking softly against one another. He picked one out and ran a practised eye over it. I think it was a still life.

'These are not yours, Coffey.'

'They are Pity's.'

Shrike and Smith trotted oafishly over, hoping I think to see something sensational.

Brownlow looked at her. 'These are very fresh,' he said. 'I hope you continue.'

'You used to admire what I did,' I said, rather piqued. 'But obviously can't think of anything to say about it now.'

'Oh, but I can,' he said, and smiled, and walked from the room.

The second gentle swipe came a week later. As well as reviews, Brownlow had a regular diary piece in the *Onlooker*, a fortnightly art journal. Giles read it out to me over breakfast, a week later.

> To darkest Bermondsey where Auguste Coffey, yet another young painter whom people insist on comparing to the young Millais, consults his muse in an old monks' refectory, under the watchful eye of soap heir Giles Bouverie. I look in the stars, I

consult the oracle: I see a fruitful connexion between the two men. As for the muse: another stunner who floats quite silently through the darkened halls, long-necked, long-haired, long-faced. So stunning was she, she reduced two of my party to gibbering wrecks, while this writer, while not exactly loquacious, found evidence of a precocious artistic talent there. A Galatea come to life in her paintings? What will poor Pyggy do?

Whatever Brownlow had intended, it made me famous. Shrike had spread the word around London; Gruber, through friends in the press, had given a statement, à propos of nothing, that he would never sell my first picture of Pity. He announced he was going to hang it in the window of the gallery but had requested a constable to keep the crowds from pressing in on it. The headline the next day ran:

Mysterious Beauty Sparks
Bond Street Disturbance
Constable called on request: 'I could never sell this picture,' gallery owner claims. 'It would be like selling my daughter.'

Within hours, the press was knocking on the door of the house in Crucifix Lane.

'Well, what are you going to do about it?' Giles asked. 'Keep her locked away?'

We were standing in the living room, well back from the window, peering down into the street. A small crowd had gathered there early in the day after noticing the handful of reporters who had started banging on the front door at eight in the morning. I made the mistake of taking them into the studio – Pity had hidden from them in the main part of the house – and they had obviously gone back to their papers and told other reporters. Throughout the day there had been sporadic bursts of knocking, after which the reporters either repaired to the public house or stayed on the street, obviously canvassing passersby for stories about us.

'I've got to show her,' I said. 'This sort of thing could be the making of me. The only question is, how?'

A further burst of banging at the door, and a voice calling through the letter box.

'They can't always be this persistent,' I said. 'You'd think they'd show a bit of respect.'

Giles laughed. 'I suspect this is your old friend Brownlow's doing.'

'What do you mean?'

'You know there are already rumours abroad about you?'

'Me?'

'As I say, rumours only, probably started by Brownlow. They won't print anything, not unless they can talk to you first.'

'What about Pity? Don't they want to know about her?'

'The less said about her, the better. For all of us,' he warned.

'But I can't let a chance like this pass me by,' I said. 'It's got to be the theatre, or opera, and afterwards the Café Royal. Something to make a headline.'

'Perhaps you should find out what Pity wants?'

'She doesn't know.'

'Pity?'

'I can't go out. I can't face them,' she said.

I snorted in disgust, not just at Pity's answer but at Giles's soliciting it. The expression on his face startled me. His face was open in a way I had never seen before. It looked as if something was dawning on him.

When I looked at the work that I had to deliver, my heart failed me. Gruber's ploy of pretending to be unable to sell the portrait of Pity had worked. Not only did it sell after all for six hundred guineas but he had now received firm commissions for at least two more paintings. Meanwhile I had the *Rape of the Grecian Maid* to complete as well as Georgina's portrait, which the Bouveries were clamouring to see. The fee agreed seemed ludicrously low now, but I realised that if I did not complete the picture soon the prospect would hang over me forever. My interest in it had revived. Without either party knowing, I intended to paint Georgina and Pity as a sort of pair – a dark twin and a light twin.

The idea had come to me when I had seen a Rossetti drawing showing a man and a woman, walking through the woods, suddenly confronted by their doubles. I thought too of *The Awakening Conscience*, and the expression of horror originally worn on the mistress's face as she rises from the lap of her lover.

I envisaged a pair of portraits that could hang together in the gallery. The first showing Georgina, calm, placid, fair ringlets floating softly around her face; the second showing Pity, her red hair writhing, her expression a subtly twisted blend of envy and remorse as she looks across, out of the frame, at her beautiful counterpart.

And the more I thought of Georgina, the more eagerly I anticipated having her to myself, still and silent under my penetrating gaze. It was an exciting thought, made all the more so by my irritation with Pity.

The Country Girl was almost ready for varnishing. I was resting Pity while I touched up the background. She was developing a pretty style of her own and was working on a portrait of me. For the first time she was bashful and reserved, and would not let me see it until she was further advanced. I took this as a sign of progress. Just so an adult is more embarrassed of its body than an infant. In so many cases, shame is the goad that gives the higher being the energy to bestir itself.

At three, I requested she should leave the studio and find somewhere in the house to wait while I conducted my business with Georgina. Pity left me without a murmur. I tidied up the studio, erasing all the traces of her I could, then began to work again. At four o'clock promptly Mrs Tully announced Miss Bouverie's arrival.

She entered the studio looking strangely elated. I waited for someone else to follow her, then remembered that she was unchaperoned.

She burst out laughing. 'It's all right, Mrs Tully, you can leave us,' she called over her shoulder. 'You can leave us,' she repeated more firmly. 'I am here by subterfuge,' she said to me, after Mrs Tully had retreated, drawing the door closed after her. 'My companion for the day, a neighbour called Mrs Willoughby, accompanied me to London and is at present convinced that I am visiting the Museum of Natural History with a party of independent young ladies, intent on elevating themselves through high-minded pursuits such as discussing Mr Darwin's theories and methods of bringing hygiene and birth control to the working classes. I have quite enough of that at home, thank you.'

She barely stumbled over the words 'birth control'.

'You are a remarkable young woman,' I said.

'It is Fanny's influence. She seems keener on the young women than I – '

Her voice tailed off. She pulled a handkerchief from a sleeve and began to tug at it.

I searched for words. 'You seem somehow more liberated today?'

'Oh, do I?' Her face lit up and her eyes sparkled. 'Truly?'

'Truly,' I answered. 'I never lie,' I lied.

'It's just that with Fanny . . . she is so . . . She is far cleverer than me and yet thinks I am cleverer than I am. So that means she can't be all that clever, doesn't it?'

'But to notice that means that you must be cleverer than you think,' I told her.

She frowned, very prettily. Two little lines of exactly equal length and depth appeared suddenly between her eyebrows, and then as suddenly faded. Like everything about Georgina, the effect seemed to have been studied but was in no way offensive. She reminded me of a child playing at being an adult.

'How does that leave us now?' she asked.

'Where we started,' I replied.

She closed her eyes. 'Alas,' she said. 'That can never be, for we have learned from we have said, and moved on from it.'

'Bravo,' I said. 'More intelligence.'

'Oh, no, I'm just imitating Fanny. She's always saying things like that. You know, I think she likes being the intended – I mean, being Giles's intended, and not his wife.'

'That may be because she'll lose her independence when she marries him. She has a little money of her own?'

'A little.'

'She will lose that too.'

'It is not so much that it will hurt, and the security that Giles offers will make up for that – but it is also her sticking point. As she says, a prison is secure; chains are secure. I don't know. Sometimes I find her ability to find ironies everywhere rather tiring, for is it not the case that all of life is to do with balancing one thing against the other? What are your views, Mr Coffey?'

'On irony?'

'On marriage.'

'I think that for a man it must be most wonderful to gain authority over his wife. I think for a woman it must be miserable.'

'But not necessarily. There *are* happy marriages.' I inclined my head. 'And in your marriage, would you insist on dominance?'

'I would not marry unless I felt there was a measure of natural respect. But that respect must be mutual.'

'A balance.'

'You are very perceptive,' I said.

'I am trying to be.'

'For what reason?'

'For – no, I must not say. I have not come here to test myself against just anyone, but against one who is not hidebound and stifled by convention. An artist.'

I was taken aback by this. It was the sort of thing bad painters said to each other when they were drunk and trying to impress themselves. Coming from someone as fresh and naive as Georgina, the words took on new significance.

'Where did you develop such ideas of artists?' I asked.

'From Giles. He always wanted to be one but has no talent. Painting and medicine were always his passions. Until a few years ago, we would talk together − such talk − of how he would have a salon, and I would be his hostess, and how all the great artists and writers in the land would come and take tea with us, and talk, and how sparkling and bright and gay it would be. And now it has come to this.' She looked around the studio. 'Oh, I did not mean that there is anything amiss with − it is just so different from what we planned. A year ago, things went wrong. Giles withdrew, from me and from Fanny.'

'Have you also come here to find out why?' I asked.

'I would never ask his friend to betray a confidence.'

I pretended to think.

'No,' I said. 'I did not think you would. Believe me, if I could tell you . . .'

I broke off, as if suddenly overcome.

'Then you *do* know! I knew you would. And you are helping Giles overcome it?'

'I am trying to.'

'I knew you were a true friend. I insisted to Fanny it was so. Tell me,' her voice dropped and she looked at me earnestly with her blue eyes open very wide, 'is there anything I can do to help?'

I smiled reassuringly. 'For the time being, nothing. I am sure that Giles is on the mend. But rest assured if there is anything that you, as his sister, would be better at than me, I shall not fail to ask you.'

'Any time,' she said softly. I smelled her breath and it was sweet.

'For Giles,' I said.

It seemed natural for her to take my hand then. And it was an instinct of mine, while in the studio, always to glance up at the house.

In a window at the back I saw Pity. She was looking straight down at us. Her face was tight and pinched. I turned my eyes back to Georgina, then raised her hand to my lips. She did not resist when my lips lingered on it. The scent of it was different from Pity's. I let her hand fall. I looked into her eyes. Everything about her was different! The texture of the skin! The set of her jaw. I touched her cheek, she did not step back. I touched her throat, and then the bodice of her dress, just above the swell of her breasts. She gave a little intake of breath. Her eyes were moist, lustrous, wondering. My courage failed. I said: 'The portrait will turn out well,' and turned away. She left without saying a word. All I could think of was the utterly unknown territory of her body beneath those rustling layers of clothing.

45

As a result of Gruber's efforts, I was now living the life of a successful artist. I had visitors to the studio, and at times would paint while they watched – displaying the same restless energy as a madman in Bedlam, as one remarked. Not only could I do this, but my painting did not suffer as a result. (Even if it had, I would have continued with the practice for the reputation it gave me.)

For a month or two of that summer, while Parliament was in recess and there were no riots in Trafalgar Square and no one was massacring anyone else in the empire and the queen wasn't ill or unamused and not too many headless corpses had turned up in the sewers (although apparently black, nocturnal swine were breeding under Holborn), in short, because people were bored, it became almost fashionable to slum it with the painter and his pretty whore model in Crucifix Lane. Sometimes I made sure that Pity was sitting for me when they came. We made a *tableau vivant* for them. You see, they had all heard of artists living with their mistresses, but very few of them had actually seen it. There was even a cartoon in *Punch* about us.

Bohemian couple lounging in garret: easel etc. in background. Bottles, opium pipes around. Both smoking cigarettes. Both in deshabille.
    He to she: 'Adjust the curtains a bit.'
    She to he: 'Why, my love, they are quite tightly drawn.'
    He to she: 'You misunderstand me, my dear. Open them a crack so our public can see us.'

You would have thought that disapproval would have killed off interest in me, but not a bit of it. When did disapproval ever lead to less interest?

One warm afternoon, Pity and I went to the West End. We ate, then went to a play. It was the story of a married man who visits a prostitute and, driven mad by guilt, kills himself. His wife, made destitute by his death, is turned out on the street where she saves the life of a dying woman, who it comes as no surprise to discover is the very prostitute who seduced her husband. To reward such devotion, the doctor on whom the destitute woman has spent her last pennies to save the whore, falls in love with her and marries her.

Pity joined in the applause. Outside, walking down Shaftesbury Avenue in the rich twilight, just one of the crowd, she asked me: 'Did you ever feel guilty for going with me?'

'Guilty? Whatever for?'

Pity looked at me as if I should have known.

'Nothing,' she said. 'Nothing. Did you feel guilty for kissing Georgina's hand?'

'That,' I said, 'was work. Did you feel guilty for spying on us?'

'No,' she said. 'Just sad.'

I managed to begin another study of Pity, this time as the *Sleeping Beauty*, asleep on a bed of soft moss while the knight who has hacked his way towards her stands stunned, both by her beauty and by the bleached bones of other knights suspended in the thicket around her. Gruber fretted about the composition of the piece, which I had based on a photograph, cutting Pity's body off crudely just below the breast, and showing the stricken knights, bones, briars and all, as if seen through gauze – or *out of focus* as the photographers say. But unlike photographers, I could dwell on certain details: Beauty's little white teeth peeping from the red, slightly parted lips; the delicate green network of veins marbling her eyelids; her hand, pressed to her breast, dimpling it.

276

When Pity was not sitting for me, I banished her. Her constant fretting and fidgeting wore me down. She set up the little easel I had bought her, her canvases, oils and brushes in the recovery room in the back of the house from where she could look down on the studio.

I painted, and I slept, and I painted and I slept. And in between I travelled to Wake Hall to paint Georgina, and then I would return, and then I would receive another letter and another possible commission. There was no question now of my staying with Giles out of necessity. I was a long way off that. If things continued at this rate, soon I would not only be able to move out, but set up a respectable establishment.

Then one morning I was disturbed by loud voices in the yard. Pity ran to a window, pulled over a chair and peered out.

'They're here,' she said.

'Who?' I muttered sleepily.

'The workmen. Giles is decorating the house.'

I blinked against sunlight. 'Why are you so excited about it?'

I saw her shoulders tense. 'Oh, no reason. Just something to do,' she said. 'Something to watch.'

I began to enjoy my visits to the country. I took the train from London Bridge to Sevenoaks and there the ridiculous Bouverie carriage would be waiting for me at the station. I would sit in it and tap on the roof when I was ready, and off we would trot down winding country lanes, between dusty verges frothing with wild flowers to the nonsense of Wake Hall. Why was that day different? Why did the rocking of the carriage agitate instead of soothe me? Why did thoughts that normally lay dormant or barely stirring, awaken and begin their noisy clamour?

It started as a daydream, such as any young man on the brink of success might have. He does not see himself alone – he sees himself with a wife on his arm, and as far as a wife for me was concerned only one candidate was eligible: Georgina.

To court her I would have to impress her parents without

seeming to be out to impress them. I would have to seduce the girl without her knowing she was being seduced. After that, once I was nestled in their bosom, presented as a firm, ambitious, honest, adventurous, responsible, sensitive, manly type, marriage might not be unthinkable. An established painter could bring in a very handsome income – there was the example of Millais. And then an artist was granted social licence, more so than almost any other profession. The work did not brand you: Hunt's father had been a clerk, Leighton's a lord, and yet they were now more or less on an equal footing. An artist could come from anywhere and go anywhere. We were the angels of the modern world, flitting hither and thither, bringing joy where'er we landed. Just look at Hunt. He'd had two bites of the cherry. After marrying Fanny Waugh, he was now, rumour had it, set on marrying her younger sister – even though the law forbade it. It has always amused me, that law. A man may not marry his late wife's sister – just in case all the frumps and wallflowers of England knock off their sisters so they can snaffle their brothers-in-law.

But what of Pity? And what of Giles? Were I to court Georgina, how would they fit into the picture? Giles I could deal with. His secret made him my slave. But Pity? All I had over her was the security I offered her. If that went, as go it must were I to marry, I would lose her and any influence over her. I could set her up as a mistress: not unthinkable. I could attempt to compromise her: impossible. She had been compromised since the day she was born. What then?

Wake Hall. Georgina is tired. I am happy to let her break. It gives me a chance to walk with her in the grounds. Osgood is with us, talking as usual. Nothing so calculated to keep us apart has ever brought together two people so close.

Osgood's continual inane chattering has been our opportunity for shared looks, secret smiles. By his presence he has created a need for intimacy. And here we are, walking past the greenhouse, and the furnace, hidden behind the kitchen garden wall, is blowing smoke up into the air. The windows are dripping with condensation, and from a vent drifts the thrilling, musky scent of hot, wet earth.

'A peach, a peach, do I spy a peach?' Osgood cries.

A peach tree is trained against a wall in the temperate room, visible through a window. Although it has been a dull summer and the poor crucified tree has been tricked into producing sparse clusters of small, pale peaches. Osgood darts inside and picks one. It is not ripe and the whole tree shakes as he tugs at it. Georgina and I wait outside, patient and silent, not looking at each other.

'Who was it, remind me, Coffey, who said there was no way of describing with mere words the colour of a fair young maiden's skin?' Osgood's questions do not need answering. I stare at Georgina, pleadingly but proudly, until she blushes. She has very fine skin.

'But I trump the fellow. There is a perfectly good word for it. Peach. See here, see! This colour. Is this not the colour of Georgina's cheek?'

The dense, downy skin is flesh-coloured. He points to where it is pulled tightly into the dip and the rough, brown stalk rises. I think of my finger touching skin, pressing in. The peach *is* the colour of Georgina's cheek.

I take the fruit from Osgood, and looking at Georgina over it, bite it. She blushes again with tremendous, rewarding suddenness.

Osgood says nervously: 'Not ripe, I'll warrant.'

I make a show of moving my jaw, and wipe imaginary juice from my chin. The fruit is acrid and musty. It is like eating a dusty ornament.

'It tastes of – '

'Oh, no,' Osgood says, suddenly aware of where he has led us.

'Heaven,' I say.

Georgina's breast is heaving. She seems so helpless, so pliable. I want to tear her clothes off and devour her. Osgood never moved more than five feet away from me the whole of the rest of the day.

In Crucifix Lane, Pity says: 'You come back from Wake Hall in a dream sometimes. What's going on down there?'

She asks it mockingly, teasingly, but behind the banter there is fear.

'Going on? What could you mean by that?'

'I mean – oh, nothing. You look tired. Can I draw you a bath?'

'I am not tired.'

'Are you feeling – good-natured?'

An old joke. Today it simply makes me angry, reminding me of her depravity and my contagion.

'Don't look at me so!'

'How is that?'

'As if you hate me.'

'And if I do?'

'I could not stand it. I could not – '

Where some might embrace, and some fall at my feet, Pity falls on her knees, works my prick free, then pleasures me.

When I am done, she looks up at me and asks: 'Do you know anyone else who would do that?' Her lips are very red from the work, her voice slightly thickened.

'No,' I say. 'But I could buy one anywhere.'

And push her away.

And Georgina, talking about her childhood while Mr Osgood picks the lint from his waistcoat. The light that trickles through the dense leaves of the apple tree is green.

'Giles and I were so close as children, such good friends. I told you of our dream of our life together in London. He was to be an artist – another Turner, he thought – and live in a grand house in Mayfair and have all the most famous in the land to visit him. I would be his hostess, gracious, witty, adored, and would move like a swan between the chattering men, swaying my fan, bestowing a look here, a comment there, a laugh, a frown. It's odd how – when Giles discovered that he had no talent, it was rather a blow.'

'As it would be.'

'And you?'

'From the outset, drawing was to be how I would make my way in the world. First drawing, then painting.'

'And that is all?'

'Would you have me ambitious so my hopes may be dashed?'

'No, I – '

'You see, for Giles it was only a lack of talent that stopped him drawing. Apart from that, he has the connections and the wealth to achieve what he wants. Without those – '

'But you are a painter. And successful.'

'But were my ambition to lead me on, beyond painting . . .'

'Towards?'

'Happiness. Security. Respectability. There are rocks that have smashed many a hopeful aspirant.'

'You talk in riddles,' she said.

'Without family, without connections, without wealth, there is an area of life where the dearest, fondest hopes must wither and die.'

This time she understood.

Her skin tightened; minute goose pimples appeared on her upper arms, lifting the fine down.

At Crucifix Lane, back from a day in the country . . . No time alone with Georgina, who nonetheless seems troubled by something. Osgood looks at me furtively. Mr and Mrs Bouverie their old, magnificent selves. Mr, magnificently bland. Mrs, magnificently spiteful. But even so, I notice a reticence about them. A watchfulness. Almost as if sentence has been pronounced on me but what, or for what reason, I do not know. I return to Crucifix Lane earlier than is usual.

Walking through the hall I notice for the first time that new paper lines the walls and the house stinks of paint and glue. The upstairs drawing room is closed off by a sheet hanging over the doorway. Inside I can hear the sounds of hammering and splintering wood. I peer round the sheet. Dust is thick in the air. The fine panelling is being ripped from the walls and the rather elegant fireplace lying face down on the hearth. The dining room is full of furniture. I walk upstairs; the sounds die away. There is no disturbance on the landing; the doors are closed. The landing smells of bedrooms: of laundry, of lavender, and of bodies. I open the door that leads to the old servants' quarters at the back of the house and hear voices.

'And so the heavier pattern for the smaller room?'

'I think so. I like it.'

'Very well. And the woodwork?'

'White.'

'Hmmm. Off white.'

'Yes.'

'And the basin in that corner.'

Giles and Pity, talking. I push open the door. They are standing together, heads bent over a large volume of wallpaper patterns. Both look up with surprise, but no guilt, as they see me in the doorway. There is a pencil sketch of Giles on the easel. Pity's work. It is good enough, I can see that, technically proficient and showing something not only of the sitter's expression, but his character.

'Auguste, my dear fellow. Just choosing some papers for Pity's rooms. How was the country?'

'Rooms?' I ask. Giles checks himself, then nods in stagey understanding.

'One to be her studio, the other her reading room.'

'Pity does not read.'

'That may change. How was my family?'

'Well.' I toss the word to him over my shoulder, so to speak, while I stare at Pity. She is wearing her Brontë dress. Is it my imagination or does she look more boyish? Changes here as well. What else have I not been noticing?

'I want my tea,' I say to her.

No protest. Eyes lowered. Out of the door and down the stairs. I glance at Giles to see if he is watching her leave. No. He is watching me watching her. His portrait, radiating a sort of inner happiness, is watching him approvingly.

Wake Hall. My last journey in the Bouverie carriage. The road, dried white in the clear, yellow summer sunshine, winds between impenetrable hedgerows. A hare, barely disturbed by the carriage, lollops down an aisle between tight ranks of hop poles. In the distance a train is vainly chased by its scarf of steam and smoke, and the landscape, divided by the soft scars of ancient hedgerows and dotted with dark green spinneys, rolls easily to the horizon. Somewhere to the north London sprawls in its own pall of stinking effluvium; out here the world is free to breathe.

And yet I feel apprehensive.

At the gates the carriage stopped, unusually. I waited, then the door swung open and Georgina climbed in. Her face was drawn, quite grey, and she was perspiring. I took both her hands in mine. I wondered if this was my moment.

'Tell the driver to go quite slowly, not to stop at the front door but to go round to the stables,' she said.

I did this, then asked: 'What is it? Something is amiss.'

'I do not know. I am not sure . . . All I know is that they have taken your painting, *Pandora's Box* – '

'What? Thieves? Stolen it?'

'No. It is still there. I am not explaining myself clearly. They are using it in some way. I heard Father talking about it with Mama.'

'Using it? How could they use a picture?'

'I don't know. They said Beddoes wasn't up to doing the job, a thorough job.'

'Who is Beddoes?'

'Again, I don't know. Quick, we are passing the house! There is Mama. She has seen us. I must escape!'

'You are hysterical,' I said. 'You must calm yourself. There is nothing more natural than your walking in the grounds, and my seeing you and asking the carriage to stop.'

'No, no. You don't understand – I must not be seen with you. Osgood has talked.'

'Osgood? But what has he seen?'

'It is not what he has seen, it is how he has described it.'

'This is monstrous!' I said. 'But my painting . . . What of that?'

The carriage was now passing down the side of the house. The entrance to the stables lay beyond.

'I do not know. I have told you all I can.'

I thought furiously. Now had to be the time to act, but there were only seconds left to me. Already the rumble of wheels on flagstones told me that we were entering the stable courtyard. I took both her hands in mine and leaned towards her. 'Georgina, I must be honest with you. Your portrait is finished. It is only the thought of you that has kept me returning. If you are now telling me – '

'It is too late,' she said. 'If you had said this earlier – '

The carriage stopped. A lad opened the door to reveal Osgood standing there, something pertly sinister about him. It was not so much that his mask had slipped, more that he had removed it.

Georgina was sobbing and trembling. He took her hand. She tried to snatch it away but he held on firmly.

'Take your hands off her,' I said.

He looked at me. 'Do not try to seduce her. That will do your reputation no good at all.'

'What is this about Beddoes?' I asked.

'Oh, she told you? All's well that ends well. We have a picture, a portrait, and now an advertisement.'

'What are you talking about?' I bellowed.

'I think you had better return to London and find out.'

★

As we approached Sevenoaks I asked the driver whether he knew Mr Beddoes. The driver nodded, and said he had driven the family to his shop. I told him to take me there, then settled back in the seat to think.

Someone once told me that railway engines are not kept on the tracks by the outer flanges of their wheels, but rather by some scientific principle that the public is too stupid to understand. All they know is that if the wheel did not have these flanges, the trains would look too dangerous and be prevented from running. Principle or not, I have always thought that the flange is our way of telling the powers behind the universe that we do not take things too much for granted. One has to earn privileges with caution. I had not been cautious enough. The gods were about to take their revenge. But how?

The carriage stopped near the parish church. The driver pointed me to a little alley that first squeezed between the crooked walls of a haberdasher's and an ironmonger's, then opened into a small yard overlooked by a bay window. The contents of the window, a meagre display of prints, were protected from the sun by a half covering of yellowing paper, though I could not see how the sun would ever reach them. Above the window the shop name. Beddoes: Engravings, Prints. On a scrap of card by the door the legend: Commissions undertaken.

Inside, bunches of picture frames hung like bats from the ceiling and engravings of local scenes, well enough executed, lined the panelled walls in crooked rows. There were copies too, much finer than mine, of art works and local sights. The church; a viaduct; grand houses: one of them a modern house. Wake Hall.

The shopkeeper was a tall man, now bent, with white hair, tired eyes and a dripping nose. I felt superstitiously sick to think that this could have been my lot: growing old and bent and mild in Sevenoaks, Kent. I asked him if he stocked paints; he looked at me sadly.

'All people want is photographs. I calls it cheating. Photographs for this, photographs for that. There'll never be an end of it.'

'I suppose it's cut into your trade?' I said.

'Of course. People don't want engravings no more. Why bother when you can take a photograph? But where's the skill in it? That's what I want to know.'

'I used to engrave,' I said. 'Cards mostly, taken from paintings. Some of my own work.'

The old man looked at me more brightly. 'That's my work,' he said. 'On the walls. The banks of the Darent; St Nicholas's church. There's some of Canterbury Cathedral. *Beddoes' Views of Kent*. Used to sell quite well.'

'I see you've done Wake Hall?'

'That was when it was first built.'

'When was that?'

'Ten years ago now, or thereabouts.'

'I hear the Bouverie family lives there. I suppose it was they who built it?'

'Lord, no, sir. They simply bought it. Not that they couldn't have built it, mind, but then they that've got an eye for money, know how to make it grow. Understand its ways, so to speak, like some gardeners understand plants.'

'You speak as if you know them. You've had dealings with them?'

'Nothing so direct as that. They've honoured me in my shop, and I've been happy to advise them.'

'Whatever on?' I tried to sound hearty and amused.

'Well, it was the strangest thing, and captures exactly the point I was making before. They bought in a painting to be copied.'

'A painting? I didn't know they were artistic.'

'Well, judging from what I've seen of their taste, they're not, and as I say it was only money they seemed to be talking about – apart from the young lady who appeared distressed.'

He paused, shaking his head at the wonder of the thing.

'Go on,' I prompted.

'Well, they brought a painting in – a garish, modern job, horrid to look at. A girl opening a box. All very fanciful and bright. Three of them there were: the old man, the son and the daughter, I'd guess. The old man, the father, he puts this picture down on the table and asks what sort of a job I'd have to do if they wanted it copied. I said that I'd need to think about it, never having done such a thing, and the young man, whom I didn't take to, said that he knew that they were wasting their time and he should take it up to town and hand it over to a man who could do a proper job of it.

'I said there was no doubting my ability to do a proper job, but the young man, very overbearing he was, says that they want it big anyway. I said I could do it as big as they pleased, I've got the equipment, but then he started talking about printing and colours and I said I was sure I would expand very prettily but colour was beyond me. Then the girl breaks in and says it was all wrong because it wasn't their picture anyway, not to do what they wanted with just like that, and the young man said it was because they'd taken the trouble to get the copyright and they could turn it in ha'penny cards if they wanted and sell them on street corners. Which is why, as I said earlier, the Bouveries had a knack for making money, for who else would think of such a thing? Well, the old man, more to smooth things over than anything else, picks up the picture and says that they may well be back, just to see what it looks like in a print, which as every tradesman knows is a fine way of saying: I'll never see you again. And that was that. I never did see them again either.'

My heart was pounding and my head felt unpleasantly light. 'When was this?' I asked.

'Four, five months ago.'

'And the picture. Can you remember its title?'

'It was mentioned but – '

'Was it *Pandora's Box*?'

'Yes. Yes, it was. But how . . .'

287

But I never heard the rest of his question. I was running for the station, more to try and still my howling brain than anything else. The thought hit me like a navvy's fist: Gruber had bought the painting on Giles's instructions. Giles and his father wanted to take a print of it. Both of them had referred to me in the same breath as Millais but it had never been in the sense that I'd thought.

I boarded the next train to London, thoughts twisting into nooses. The hop rows flashed past, each aisle opening, turning, shifting to the vanishing point, closing, to be replaced by the next in the blink of an eye as the train hurtled on.

And the outcome of all this? I awake one morning and all of London knows my work. I am popular, perhaps the most looked at painter in the country. Thousands, hundreds of thousands, perhaps millions look at one of my finest pictures, not every month, not every week, but daily. Perhaps twice daily. From the duchess at her toilet to the shopkeeper at his counter; from the housemaid in the scullery to the soldier at his ablutions; from the toiling worthies passing over London Bridge each morning and each evening to the filthiest dosser in the gutter: all, all of them, know my work.

46

Upstairs the decorators had finished Pity's room. The walls were papered and hung with a miscellany of pictures and prints. There was a small desk under the window, an armchair to one side of the fireplace, a chaise-longue to the other. Giles was lying there, smoking.

'Where's Pity?' I asked.

'Having a bath.'

'She's having a bath and you're lying – ' The words thickened in my throat and choked me.

'She invited me. Decent of her, don't you think?'

'Invited you to do what?' I asked.

'Now don't be like that. With the rest of the house turned upside down, what else do you expect her to do?'

'Why is the rest of the house being decorated?'

'We thought it would be fun.'

'You thought – '

'Well, you're not here any more. All work and no play. You know the sort of thing.'

'Some of us have to work.'

'And some of us don't,' Giles said.

'What are you trying to do to me? Don't you know I could break you?'

'What have I done to you, exactly?'

'Taken a print of one of my paintings.'

'Aha. So you've found that out? I wondered if you would.'

'Why?'

'Because I could. Because the copyright is mine. Because you sold it to Gruber and I bought it off him.'

'*You* bought it?'

'Yes, as a matter of fact. At the time I thought I might give it back to you as a present. Then things changed. And then I had an idea.'

'To copy it? Popularise it? I've spoken to Beddoes.'

'Good. What else?'

'I don't know. But you're going to tell me.'

'Am I? Why?'

'Because if you don't, I will expose you.'

Giles laughed.

'Poor old Gussie. You were ahead for a while, I admit, but you're so – so stupid. I mean, time and time again you commit the most perfectly awful blunders.'

'I will,' I said. 'I'll see you ruined.'

Giles took a step across the room. Before I could react he put a hand behind my neck, grabbed my hair, pulled back my head and kissed me on the lips. I felt his tongue press against my tightly clenched teeth, squeeze around them on to my gums. I staggered backwards. With his free hand he blocked my nose. I gasped. He pressed his tongue full into my mouth, then pushed me away. His eyes were wet and glittering. He was flushed and breathing heavily.

'You fool, you sore, you blow fly!' he said. 'You think I'd lie back while you strutted around, planning to lay waste to me and my family? Nothing to say? I had a very interesting conversation with your friend Brownlow. It seems I rather underestimated him. I thought he was a weak sort of fellow, but on the contrary: his will is rather steely in one regard. He would like to see you broken but cannot quite see how to do it.'

'Brownlow? You and him?' I stammered.

'Idiot. Idiot. Idiot. Sit down.' When I remained standing Giles pushed me back into a chair. It was too much: more than I could bear. I sprang up from it and grappled with him. He toppled us sideways on to the chaise-longue. I felt madness come over me then. I managed to free my hands and put them round his throat, but he knocked them away. He was much bigger than me, and heavier. We rolled on to the floor. He landed on top of me, knocking the breath from my body, then straddled me, his knees on my shoulders. His buttocks pressing down on to my belly. I tried to reach up to rake his face with my nails, but he swatted my hands away and slapped me twice on the face, once with the front of his hand, then with the back. Frustration weakened me. I felt impotent.

I said: 'I'll expose you. And I have papers with a solicitor which will be released when I die.'

Giles just said: 'Wrong.'

'What do you mean?'

For answer he called: 'Pity!'

'Pity? What has she to do with it?'

'Pity!'

'Leave her alone.'

'Oh, Auguste, I could kill you but it would be too awful to let you die in a state of ignorance . . .

'Pity – there you are.'

There she was, her hair tied up, a towel tied round her waist, naked above it.

'Cover yourself,' I said.

'Boys can walk around like that, Auguste. Boys are allowed to.'

When I didn't react, Giles slapped me softly on the cheek.

'You found out?' I asked.

'I knew from the outset,' he said. 'The moment I set eyes on him. In the brothel, Auguste.'

'She is a woman,' I said desperately.

'In your mind, you self-deluding popinjay! See yourself as I see you. Strutting around with your whore boy on your arm, calling him a her, calling a boy a girl. Look at yourself!' He punctuated his words with blows on my chest. 'You think you have succeeded on your own, when it was *my* word that brought you Gruber, when it was *my* money that bought your pictures, when it was . . . I even asked you. I even tried to warn you. "Is this what you want?" I asked. "Yes," you said. You wanted a boy, but you never wanted me. You never wanted me! You never wanted me!'

To my astonishment Giles was crying: huge tears falling from his twisted face as the blows rolled on like breakers.

'And now – Pity! – you must pay the price!'

I was frightened. He seemed to be in a trance.

'Giles.' Pity's voice, raised but calm.

I craned my neck. 'For God's sake, help me.'

But she just stared at Giles, as if she were waiting for a cue. I looked from one to the other, the realisation dawning that they had reached an understanding.

'What have you done to him?' she said to Giles. 'You haven't hurt him, I hope?'

'Nothing serious.' Giles lifted himself off me. I was too hurt and bruised to move. 'Tell him,' he said. Pity shook her head.

'I can't.'

'You must.'

'Can't.'

'Tell me what?' I asked.

There was silence from both of them.

'TELL ME WHAT?'

'Very well,' Giles said. 'My conditions. You will stop seeing my sister. You will refrain from going out. You will stay here until further notice, unless . . .'

'Unless what?'

'Unless you want the world to know that you are living with a boy, that he is your catamite.'

'But Pity is – the world thinks – '

'The world thinks one thing but I know another.'

'But if we deny – '

'You and Pity, you mean?'

'That is right. If Pity and I – '

292

'Pity will back me up,' Giles said. For a second I was too stunned to answer.

'Is this true?'

'Pity will tell the truth.'

I looked at Pity. She was white in the face. Her eyes very dark. She did not have the courage to look at me.

'So you will tell Brownlow, she will confirm it, and he will write the story?'

'That is right. Your very celebrity has undone you. It will be the biggest scandal of the year.'

'And to prevent this happening, I must do as you ask?'

'Yes,' Giles said.

'Then you both have me,' I said. Bitterness, black, liquid and overpowering, threatened to engulf me. All along, Giles had been duping me. He had had the upper hand but until I pushed had been happy to play along with my fantasy of power simply to keep me in the house. Now I had pushed too hard and he had destroyed me.

I looked away. I thought I had been so close to freedom, but I had not moved at all. Outside the window was the blind gable end of a warehouse. Once bare, it was now covered by a monstrous advertisement. For a second I stared at it in disbelief and then I started to laugh. When Pandora opened her box, she did not let evil into the world: she found a bar of Bouverie's Moonlight Soap. There she was, looking at the soap in wonder. And as the final humiliation, Giles had substituted Pity's face for mine.

47

'Once upon a time there was a poor fisherman who lived in a hut by the sea. He was so poor that his hut did not even have a door, but he was strong and he was loved by the people around him for he was kind and helpful and very strong, and he never said no to anyone.

'In spite of his health, and his great strength, he did not have a wife, for who would marry a poor fisherman who could not even afford a door to his hut? At night, and sometimes during the day, when the seas were too rough for his little boat, he would sit on the cliffs above the water, and look at the sea smashing itself to white spray on the terrible black rocks, and wonder if he would ever find a woman to love him.

'One moonlit night he woke up. He thought he could hear someone crying.

'"Help! Somebody help me, please!"

'Pausing only to put on his shoes, he ran from his hut. He looked up and down the shingly strand but could see nothing. A fierce wind was beginning to whip white streamers from the spines of the great, green rolling waves. He ran to the clifftop and looked out to sea.

'"Help . . . help me!"

'Narrowing his eyes against the wind and the flying spray, he saw the most beautiful woman he had ever seen. She was trapped by her waist in a cleft in the rock, and waving her arms in a piteous manner. Her hair, long and red, hung down over her shoulders. Because of her waving, he could see that they were bare.

'Without thinking, the poor fisherman dived off the cliff into the water. The wind tore him, the waves tried to suck him under, the black rocks threatened to pierce him cruelly, but so great was his strength that he was able to swim to the rock where the woman was trapped, even though the seas were as high as great mountains. He lifted her from the cleft, tucked her under his mighty arm and swam back to shore.

'Only when he had reached the shore and laid the woman on the shingle strand did he see whom he had rescued. She had almond eyes of green, flowing hair of red, a long, graceful neck, milk-white breasts, a slender waist and gently rounded belly. But below her waist she was a fish.

'He had rescued a mermaid.

'The mermaid looked at him and loved him. She said: "For rescuing me, fisherman, I can grant you one wish. Will it be love, will it be riches, what will it be?"

'And the fisherman, looking down at her, loved her, and said: "Neither, or none. Just to live with you under the waves."

'And he picked her up and carried her to the water, and she gave him her hand, and they swam beneath the waves, and for a year and a day they were happy.

'And yet, when a year and a day had passed, the fisherman began to grow restless. He said: "I am neither one thing nor the other here, under the waves. I am unhappy."

'He was filled with a deep yearning, and he left the ocean and the mermaid, and returned to his hut, and lived there for a year and a day. But all through the year his longing for the mermaid grew, and he knew that while he was neither one thing nor the other under the sea, on dry land he missed her, and anything was better than that.

'So he went to ask the witch what to do. The witch was very ugly. She had teeth of wood and an eye of stone, and she ate earth and fire came from her breasts where it was drunk by a little pet dragon.

'"Witch, what shall I do?" asked the poor fisherman.

'"Would you become a fish for her?" the witch asked.

'"I would," said the fisherman.

'"Then rub your head and spit into that bowl," the witch said, "and go to the high place above the sea, and jump in, and when you touch the water, you will be a merman."

'Meanwhile the mermaid had gone to the great Lord Poseidon, who lives in his coral caves under the southern oceans. And he has the mouth of a shark and the tail of a whale and is slow and lazy.

'"Great Lord Poseidon, what shall I do?" asked the mermaid.

'"Would you become a woman for him?" Poseidon asked, yawning.

'"I would," said the mermaid.

'"Then spit on this wand," Poseidon said, "and leave the ocean and go to his hut and sleep there, and when you wake up, you will be a woman, and a wife for him."

'Meanwhile, the fisherman reached the ocean and jumped in and became a merman, and swam the oceans, looking for his love.

'And the mermaid reached the shingle strand and crawled to the little doorless hut and slept on the floor. And when she woke up she was a woman, and day after day she walked the strand, looking for her love.

'And one day, when she was gazing out to sea, she saw her lover's head rise up from the waves and understood what had happened and didn't know whether to laugh or cry. And when the merman, returning to his old haunts, saw the beautiful fisherwoman mourning by the shore, he wept, for both had changed when only one needed to.

'And when Poseidon saw what had happened, he laughed, and then took pity on them, and was touched by their love. And he let it be that for half of every year they were both fish, and for half of every year they were both human, and for half of every year they looked at the rocks, and for half of every year they swam around them, being careful never to be caught.

'And so they both lived happily ever after.'

★

I was cold again. The earth had stored the heat of summer like an apple holds sweetness but I was always cold. I had a fire burning in the great fireplace and kept it heaped with wood. I sat in front of it, its heat almost burning my skin, but the heat could not melt the ice which enclosed me with Arctic cold. I was lost in northern waters, where the weight of the ice on the shrouds can tip a ship over and the cold makes the water as thick as grease.

I could not work. When I lifted a brush my arm grew weak, and the brush would become too heavy to lift, and the weakness would spread through my body and I would crawl to the couch where Pity would minister to me. She could not read but she could tell stories. She told me stories that she had heard from the other tarts. (She'd heard about the mermaid from an eleven-year-old boy whose mother had come from Brittany.) She told me how when Mrs Turner, the brothel keeper, found out that it was one of the children's birthday she would provide a cake and organise games, and for an hour or two the cubicles upstairs would be filled with joyous screams as children played tag, or hide and seek, or sardines. She told me that such moments were the happiest she had ever known. Afterwards, of course, the children would weep because the happiness had brought back memories of another place and another time, and Mrs Turner would go among them, blubbering herself like as not, and dose the most seriously sad with her special medicine, which was laudanum mixed with fruit cordial. Mrs Turner was very particular about her children not taking to tobacco or alcohol, but thought that a little opium did wonders for the soul. She had a dog called Poppy.

Pity told me about her life; how she was a foundling adopted by gypsies, and lived with them and travelled mostly between Manchester and Kent, and how they wintered in Bangor Street in Notting Dale or the Mint in Southwark with all the other travellers. Her father first took her to bed when she was six and the first time he set her to work was at Epsom Downs when she was nine. She got more trade as a girl and worked with her mouth so no one knew, and it always seemed right for her, so what started out as a disguise, soon took over. Her father was quite gentle compared to the gentlemen who watched the races, she said. When she was nine she overheard him talking of selling her to a brothel keeper in Belgium. Then she decided she had had enough and ran away from the lodging house in Notting Dale and was alone in London for the first time. She told me of the soup kitchens of Ham Yard and Whitechapel and Drury Lane and Fleet Street, and how the best places to get lost were Kent Street in the Borough, not far from where we were, and Whitechapel, but it was harder for a child to get lost in the rookeries, because like as not you'd be caught and sold.

She said that the railway arches of Rotherhithe were rather damper than the arches of London Bridge, but it was hard to beat the tunnels under the Adelphi for a good fire and a bit of a sing-song. She said that in the winter they put straw down on the steps of the Foundling Hospital every night so the babbies left there would not freeze to death, and she never stole the straw, being a foundling herself, but others did in desperation. She told me of the Christian missionaries who every night would be out looking for children to save, and how she did not think being saved should involve such boredom. She told me that you never went into a workhouse because they would break your spirit worse than prison, and if you were cold you slept next to the brick kilns in Willesden, and if you wanted to earn a shilling you worked the penny gaffs where men would pay a penny for a bed and tuppence to be tossed off, some of them.

After two years of living like this, she had fallen ill. Dog boy had found her, and had taken her into his den. Then the whores next door had seen her, and taken her in, and given her pills and such, and she found laudanum helped her keep up the work rate, but at least she wasn't like many of the other children there, she having been broken in early. There was a nine-year-old girl they called Cabbage because she was kept so drugged, and that was the way some of the gentlemen liked it. Some of them liked it to hurt, and some of them didn't, but the whores mostly took laudanum to kill the pain and when they were screaming it was to keep the men happy. Mrs Turner could often charge more when the children were hurt and she used to say, 'Loud as you can, my darlings. The gentlemen like a chicken that squawks.'

I wasn't the first man who had been gentle with her, but I was the first who looked at her in a way she called loving.

I was dependent on her through the long months of my collapse, but did not love her. The very weakness that made her so attentive, made me writhe in helpless frustration. I felt like a baby being licked by a spaniel: trapped, and smothered, by love.

'You'll drive her away,' Giles said. He visited often, sometimes to talk with Pity, sometimes to sit with me.

Summer passed. The sky was torn by broken clouds which screamed by overhead. The wind carried life, litter, even the odd leaf. I was drawing again, a series of pictures called *Work in Progress* in which Pity was transformed progressively from boy to woman. I cannot say what bit of me it satisfied but please me it did to see those thin stretched ribs swell with a young girl's breasts; to pinch that flat waist into a tiny taper then flare it out into softer, womanly flanks; to erase that terrible, rearing sex and replace it with − what? I had never seen; I did not know.

But I couldn't talk to her. Not any more. The only pleasure I took was in the way those drawings changed her, and how afterwards she would be aware of her real body; the shoulders broadening, the sex thickening, the smell changing.

'You'll drive him away.' Giles picked up one of the sketches and examined it critically under the window, turning it this way and that way in the light.

'She'll never leave,' I said. 'She'll stay here forever; you've seen to that.'

'I didn't mean that,' he said. He put down the sketch and

leant against the wall under the window. 'You miss a lot, you know. Pity loves you, you see.'

'How can you say that? She conspired against me with you! She has tried to destroy me and I am left like a cripple, forced to accept succour from the very source that crippled me.'

'You only see half the story. You – '

'Oh, I know. That is a failing. I was only ever asked to paint your sister in order to blind me to what you really wanted. Gruber only ever took me up to please your precious family. You used him to buy the copyright of *Pandora's Box*,' I said bitterly. 'You planned to ruin me from the outset.'

'Not from the outset, and I haven't ruined you – just clipped your wings. I used Gruber. Gruber used me. You haven't done too badly from the relationship. And if he did only take you up at first because I asked him to, your talent has since convinced him of your true value.'

'To paint pornography for lechers!'

'But compare yourself now to your state a year ago. Why, I hear you can turn commissions away.'

'Until you made me the laughing stock of London.'

'That will pass. It's only a few articles in the press and we all know where they come from. Brownlow is merely cashing in on your past relationship. Even he admits your reputation was growing before this. And who reads those articles, except for a few people like him? With your pictures all over London, your reputation is assured – among those who really matter. Your clients.'

'Why did you do it?' I asked. 'Why? All I had is my talent. Now it is owned by you.'

'I had to contain you somehow, Auguste. I like to think that now we are back where we stared: two friends on an equal footing. Can we not try?'

He looked at me, so open and manly that I warmed to him again and felt the tears running down my cheek quite unexpectedly, almost as if my heart had been opened by a knife so sharp I did not feel its entry.

We shook hands. He embraced me. As we held the embrace, it was as if all my regret for what had passed was turned to tears, and the tears softened and sweetened me so that I felt human and remorseful. We were like that when Pity found us, and suddenly she was embracing us both so that the three of us were locked together. She kissed me, I kissed her and Giles, and Giles kissed me. But when he turned to kiss her, she turned her head away from him and frowned.

It was like the chill that a little cloud casts when it moves across the sun, a chill so quickly past you hardly credit it, but which has an effect quite disproportionate to its size. It reminds you that you can be cold, that you will be cold, that the golden warmth cannot live forever.

The moment passed for all of us. Giles sat back. We were all possessed by the same sweet sadness. He wiped tears away from his face, then from mine.

'The three of us,' he said. 'The three of us.'

We began to go out, the three of us. I was so apathetic, so limp, that I merely followed in their wake. Pity, made up to look older, sometimes on Giles's arm and sometimes on mine, kept silent, although the joy in her eyes was plain to see. She was growing, and was forced to buy new clothes. Her evenings were spent poring over patterns, or adjusting the stitching of garments she had already bought. We went out to theatres, concerts, music halls and recitals. On more than one occasion I saw Giles cut a former friend dead. It seemed that this strange, silent party we made up – surgeon, artist, whore – was all the company he needed.

And gradually I recovered. Strength returned to my arms and legs. I found the period of enforced rest, of lying fallow, enabled me to return to my painting with renewed diligence and a different sort of energy. After a period of darkness it seemed as if a new painter had emerged, blinking, into the light. The fury had lessened. In its place was a focus born of a new awareness of my own frailty and fallibility.

Curiously, too, my strength returned after I had finished the series of drawings. As they progressed and as Pity became more female, my own strength seemed to increase. In the last picture she lies on the chaise-longue, an old woman with a young girl's face, her flesh crinkling, her figure corpulent, breasts wide and flat.

'You'll drive her away,' Giles said, when he saw it.

My confidence returned with my mounting strength.

'No, I won't,' I said. I knew her better than that. She was too weak to leave me. She was like the mermaid: beached. She might once have had the strength to leave her world and crawl to my home, but she could never drag herself out again. And anyway, the colder I became, the more submissive she was, and the increased pleasure this gave me compensated for much that I had lost.

One day, I was standing in one of the old servants' rooms in the back of the house. From them, one could look down through the high windows into the studio itself. I had moved Pity's easel and chair under the window so I could watch her work. It gave me pleasure to see her; she was marvellously quick in her pencil strokes and I thought, if she persevered, she would be a fine painter. But today she was worried. I could tell by the way she doodled aimlessly on the paper; by the way she would stop frequently and rub her hands together.

After a while she rose. A minute later I saw her cross the courtyard. She seemed to be carrying a packet in her hand. From my vantage point I heard her enter the house and open the kitchen door. There was the clatter of a saucepan.

I wondered what she could be cooking, and tiptoed down the stairs.

The kitchen door was ajar. I opened it a crack. Pity was standing over the stove. I thought she was humming in a high voice as she waited for a frying pan to heat. She reached for a jug which I had not noticed and poured thick red liquid from it into the frying pan. There was a quick, violent hiss. She gave a little cry and jumped back. Steam billowed up.

She stepped back to the frying pan. I heard her saying something; it sounded like a rhyme, or a chant, repeated over and over again. The smell was horrid, like burning flour, and eventually she took the pan off the heat, plunged it under a tap, scraped it clean, soaped it, then hung it up again. She washed the jug. I moved back from the door. She left the kitchen. Her head was bent and she had been crying again.

In the kitchen I sniffed the pan but apart from a lingering, burning smell, there was nothing to tell me what she had been doing. I looked at the jug. It was clean but in the sink, droplets of pink water clustered by the drain.

She had walked across the yard carrying a packet. It wasn't on the draining board or any of the table tops. I pulled the slops bucket from under the sink. There, scrumpled on a bed of peelings, was a ball of shiny paper, covered in writing.

I laid it on the table and smoothed it with my hand. A bad picture of a dragon. The words: *Dried Dragon's Blood.*

On the back in tiny letters were instructions:

To reconstitute the Dragon's Blood, simply stir the contents of the packet into a gill of cold, fresh water.

To make your spell for love, follow these simple instructions.

Pour contents on to heated pan, hot enough to make liquid turn to droplets. While pouring, and while Dragon's Blood is boiling, chant these words:

'It is not this dragon's blood I wish to burn
It is my lover's heart I wish to turn
May he never eat or sleep until he returns to me.'

Humbled by this secret protestation of love but at the same time buoyed up by it, I went to see a prospective client, a wealthy Greek who lived in a Gothic-style castle in Hampstead with his silent, unresponsive wife and gorgeous, dark-eyed daughter, who needed painting quickly before she went off.

He saw me in his study, a fine, light, square room at the back of the house overlooking a generous garden of hedges and shrubs. It was a wet afternoon. The light in the study was green and clear. It made me feel happy – I was glad to be out picking up my career. Not only that, the price I had mentioned in my letter to him was acceptable. Then he asked me whether I would be able to start work on Monday.

I said it was out of the question. What with my other commitments, it was unlikely I would be able to begin for three months, and then I would like another four to complete the portrait, the time to include half a dozen sittings. This, I knew from experience, would stretch into six months, once I had made my excuses a couple of times, and the daughter had inevitably made hers, and I thought this would be a more realistic timetable to follow, although I would never have dreamed of telling him so outright.

He huffed and he puffed a bit, and said that the schedule was quite absurd and if he wanted a portrait painted of his daughter, he wanted it started now, and he wanted it done like that. At which point he snapped his fingers theatrically, because that was the sort of man he was and he wanted me to be quite clear about it too.

I pointed out that the only reason for the delay was the fact that I was so busy. From his point of view, couldn't he see that the busier I was, the more this proved how right he was to choose me to paint his daughter, and that only a bad painter would be free immediately? The main thing, I concluded, was that the portrait should be painted.

This seemed to sink in, but not in the way I'd expected. His face was suddenly illuminated by understanding. He smiled, and nodded, took a cheque book out of his desk and began to write. After blotting it carefully with a blotter carved like a Boucher nymph, he slid the cheque across the desk to me, his short fingers barely touching the paper, as if it would contaminate him. The hair on the backs of his fingers was so thick it looked like fur. His nails were fine, very pale, lightly ridged and curved.

He smiled. 'Now you start on Monday.'

The cheque was for half as much again as I had asked. I

stammered that he had missed the point, and that it was not the money which caused me to place him at the back of the queue but the pressure of time, my professional needs, etc., etc. Halfway through my explanation he held his hand up and began to write again. I remained silent. Again he slid a cheque across the desk, this time pushing it with a single fingernail. The cheque was for the same amount, thus doubling the price. The total, I reflected, was ten times my earnings for my first year in London, and reflected only a part of my earnings for this year.

This time I was less vehement in my protestations. I was reviewing in my mind exactly why I was so certain I could not see his daughter before December.

I was about to push the cheques back, when I realised that if he then presented me with another, I would accept.

I looked him full in the eye and saw him reading me.

Somehow, my new state of mind had communicated itself to him. I do not know how, but I did know that my reasons for not painting his daughter before December were no longer so important as they had seemed at first.

Whereas originally I had genuinely thought I could not fit her into my schedule, now I had admitted to myself that I could, *if only the price were right*. In other words, I was already dishonest in his eyes, and would only confirm this by holding out for more money.

At this point one of two things would happen: either he would tear the cheques from my hands and kick me out of the house denouncing me as a blaggard, or he would be my master. He would have corrupted me, and know that I would do anything for a price.

My hand, caught halfway between us, hovering over the desk, stopped.

'This is most generous,' I said. 'And you think this a fair price for your daughter's portrait?'

'For the great Auguste Coffey, of course.'

He sat back in his chair, and having spread his hands

expansively, folded them over his belly which was tightly encased in a waistcoat of emerald silk.

'Then I must thank you for your high opinion of me,' I said, 'an opinion I feel would only be compromised were I to pretend I could paint your daughter at any date earlier than December. All that has changed is your valuation of me. My timetable remains the same.'

His face froze in a mask of surprise mingled with curiosity. Cautiously I folded the cheques and placed them in my jacket pocket. Then, after slightly inclining my head to show that, for all my trumping of him, he still had my respect, I walked from the room. I swear that as I crossed the hall I heard laughter peal out from behind his closed study door, and for a month afterwards, apparently, he regaled London with the story. As a result, I received several invitations to consider new commissions. I was now in a position to turn down work.

It had been my plan to lunch with Gruber, but I found that the meeting had excited me strangely. I was all soft tumult inside, butterflies bouncing off my ribs. I needed to share my excitement with people. I considered Gruber's reaction should I tell him the story, but the thought of his missing the point, seeing only the result and not the daring, convinced me it would be better to return to Crucifix Lane and whirl Pity and Giles away with me for a glorious celebration.

How quickly one's whole arrangement of mood and personality changes. I had begun that morning feeling relaxed, almost passive. Now circumstances had so altered my state that I was almost unrecognisable. I was invulnerable, happy, and so generous that I could put anything and everything behind me and begin again. I wanted to share my luck with the world.

I laughed as I passed one poster of Bouverie's Moonlight Soap after another. I felt like shouting out of the cab's window that I had painted it. But the thought that truly inspired me was that I had played the game better than the man who had initiated it, and carried it off with such style that he had conceded there and then. A bit of dash – that was all that was needed. Dash and the courage of youth.

The cab dropped me; I burst through the front door. I opened my mouth to announce my arrival when the sight of Mrs Tully pulled me up short. She was standing on the bottom stair, having just descended, and was staring at me in shock.

'Where's – ?' I began.

Almost as if she were surprising herself, she laid a finger to her lips.

I said: 'What?'

She made the gesture again, only more insistently this time, started for the back of the house and, looking over her shoulder, bade me follow her.

I did. Instead of going to the kitchen, she turned left and opened the door to the back stairs.

'What the hell is going on?' I asked.

She shook her head.

'Is there something I should see? What is the reason for this mystery?'

'There is something you should know,' she said.

'What?'

I took her by the shoulders. They were unexpectedly solid.

'What?'

A blank stare only.

'I insist.'

She considered me. It is something I have noticed: that when one person is really looking at another, their glance tends to flicker from side to side as they focus on first one eye, then the other. Mrs Tully was looking beyond me. Her stare was fixed and glassy.

'I cannot say. Go up. Go up the stairs. I heard something. It frightened me. Excuse me, I am not used to shocks.'

'You think it is a burglar? How would they get in?'

'Over the wall. Through Mr Giles's skylight. All I know is that I heard noises.'

'And Pity?'

'As far as I know she is out, and so is Mr Giles.'

'Probably an old cat sneaked in,' I said. 'It would be a foolish burglar who tried his luck in broad daylight, and what he could cart off through that skylight wouldn't be worth carrying.'

'Mr Giles sometimes leaves money in his room.'

'And which one is that?'

'At the front of the house, there are two doors facing you. His is the right-hand door.'

'Get me a poker,' I said.

She hesitated a moment. 'Very well. Wait here.'

She was back quickly.

'I could not find a poker,' she said, and handed me a large cleaver. 'If he means you any harm, you can threaten him with this.'

I was sure that she was hiding something from me, even to the extent of making up the entire incident. But the sight of the cleaver filled me with alarm and brought home to me the risk attached to what I was being asked to do.

But when I hesitated, she hissed: 'Would you rather *I* did it? Give me the weapon!'

I shook my head.

'Then go.'

It was a peculiarity of the house that the back stairs opened only on to the ground and second floors. As I approached the second floor, where Pity's rooms were, I slowed and became more cautious. The sitting room was empty; the fire had not been lit. Outside the window the sky heaved. In the studio her painting stood on the easel, but her brushes had been laid down dirty. The coal fire had burned to a glowing shell which was frosted with ash, but the guard which should have been left in front of it was lying on its back.

I stared at it, suddenly gripped by fear. That something so small should seem so out of place! It looked like a dead turtle lying there, an omen of death. The quiet was broken when coal settled suddenly in the grate. Panic flowed through me as the silence rolled on. Thoughts raced through my mind. Pity had been about to leave when she had been surprised by a villain, attacked, and in the struggle the fireguard knocked over.

Where was she? Mrs Tully would have heard if she had been taken downstairs. She was here, somewhere in the ominous silence. I walked down the corridor, rolling on the balls of my feet, trying to be as silent as the air. My heart was knocking at my mouth and my throat was dry. My hands were slipping with sweat and the cleaver felt very heavy. The door to the front of the house stood ajar. I paused, listened, then pushed it open with my finger.

There was a muffled sound and a cry. It was repeated. When I swallowed, I seemed to imitate the cry. I continued down the corridor.

The noise was coming from Giles's room.

I was encased in panic. I felt oddly detached but enormously frightened. My head felt swollen from the pounding of my blood.

I took another step to the door of the room and pushed it.

It was closed.

I turned the handle, raised the cleaver and pushed the door open.

My mind did not at first accept the pattern that I saw of snow-white sheets, intermingled flesh, entangled limbs, and hair.

Their eyes were closed. They were moving in a sort of trance, together, he on his side, turned away from me, she pressed into him. Sun had sliced a gap between the curtains and the white sheets glared. As she moved in him, she bent her head and kissed him on the back, on the shoulder blades, on the neck. Then, with great tenderness, she bared her teeth and took a tiny nip of flesh between them.

He moaned.

In response she kissed him on the cheek. His arm came round and just touched her.

The way they moved was together. I can think of no other word. Together. Together. Together.

I raised the cleaver. They did not know I was there.

Togethertogethertogether.

I wanted them to hear me; wanted them to see me in my grief.

Togethertogethertogether.

I raised the cleaver again. Pity was murmuring, Giles crooning.

Togethertogethertogether.

I could not kill them together, not now. It would be like drowning gods in ambrosia.

So I left in case my sobs disturbed them, and met Mrs Tully on the stairs. She saw my tears, and closed her eyes, and shook her head, and gently took the cleaver from me and led me to my bed. I was cold again.

'You sent me to them!' I cried. 'You made me see. That was no burglar.'

But Mrs Tully only raised her eyebrows and said: 'Oh, yes it was.' Then added: 'I will wait, but I will not wait long.'

'What do you mean?'

'You idiot! You treat him like a nothing. It is no wonder he looks for comfort with that – thing.'

'Why would my treatment of him make him do that?' I asked.

'Because he loves you.'

I laughed out loud. 'Giles does not love me! It is only because of my manoeuvrings that he has not thrown me out of the house!'

'It is your manoeuvrings that have nearly brought us all down!'

'But Giles – what about the picture? Why did he do that to me?'

'Spite. Jealousy. He thought that when you came here, you and he would be like brothers. If he brought you low, it would increase your dependence on him.'

'That was his plan from the outset?'

'Of course not. Not from the outset. Initially you were his pretty little plaything. Yes, you. A pet artist to pen pretty pictures. And then something happened. When you turned into a monster, instead of frightening Giles off, he came in some strange way to look up to you. He'd been so wrong – I think it shocked him.'

'But had I stayed as a pretty little artist,' I said, 'he would have tired of me then.'

She looked at me, her eyes rather sad. 'He could have accepted anything but your ignoring him.'

'So he sleeps with my – He steals my – '

'If a coin jumps into a pickpocket's pocket, do you call that stealing? That foul creature will be the end of both of us. She came to you for comfort – she'll take it from Giles if she has to. And then what of us?'

'What of you? I believe I already have a career. I was thinking of moving out as it was.'

'Little fool!' she snapped. 'Move out with the threat of Giles's exposing you for the rest of your life? Could you survive with that hanging over you?'

'*I* could expose *him*. The scandal would ruin him.'

'And who has more to lose? A penniless artist reliant on his commissions, or the heir to a fortune? On top of that, the creature is yours. She is your model. She is your fortune and your millstone. Exposing Giles will not achieve anything. He'll just turn the tables.'

I thought for a minute. She was waiting for my reply. Then I saw why. Something Giles had said so long ago that it seemed like another lifetime: how we would have to wait to see which way Mrs Tully would jump.

'You would join me?' I asked.

'As things stand, it is my only hope of survival. I can hardly bear to live with Giles and that creature, but without them I cannot live at all.'

'And you would trust me?'

'No more than you trust me.'

'But together, if we reach a level of understanding, we can present a single face to Giles. For example, if he thought we would both denounce him as a pederast, while backing each other up . . .'

'Quite so.'

A late wasp bounced off the window and fell to the floor, buzzing its wings but without sufficient power to fly.

'But if we can bind Giles in yet tighter, for good, so that he never, ever threatens to tell, then there would be security forever, whether I moved out or stayed here, and regardless of your situation.'

Mrs Tully smiled at me.

'Do you have such a plan?' I asked.

'It will come,' she said. She looked at me almost tenderly and stretched out her hand to stroke my forehead. Her brow was so white and her face so calm that I expected the touch to be smooth and cool. It was strange to be touched by a housekeeper's hands: rough and capable. Strange, but in the manner of strange experiences, not unpleasant after the first shock. But she was saying something to me. I looked up at her.

'You said something?' I could have lain there forever, and wondered why I had never thought of it before. 'Did you never enquire what became of dog boy?' she asked.

'He died.'

'How?'

'Of pneumonia.'

'Then where is he buried?'

That made me think. Of course, if he had died of pneumonia, there would have been a proper burial. As far as I knew, there had been none.

'Where *is* he buried?' I asked.

'Why don't you ask your benefactor?' Mrs Tully said.

'Why don't you just tell me?'

'No,' she said. 'I want you to find this out for yourself.'

48

A quick pencil sketch I did at that time was called *Arthur and Lancelot*. In the foreground, two heads look at each other from opposite sides of the canvas. I am Arthur, Giles is Lancelot. Both faces are stubborn, angry, enigmatic. In the background, burning to death on her pyre, is Guinevere. The heat has caused her hair to rise in a red fan above her head.

The fact that I knew, and they did not know I knew, gave me an odd sort of power. I could see now how anxious the two of them were not to antagonise me, while at the same time they could not seem to be appeasing me: ostensibly they had no reason.

To cause Pity pain, I dreamed up a picture called *The Holy Ghost*. I showed her the sketches and she shuddered.

I imagined a tomb, a great, domed, marble structure, and on the dome I was faintly to stain the continents of the world. The mouth of the tomb was cracked, and from it tumbled a frozen stream of bones and corpses, very white. This was to be done very small, for above it, hovering with wings outstretched, was the Holy Ghost, arms raised to heaven in supplication. I took particular pains to show the hovering figure to be under enormous strain; the toes pointing downwards were not dangling but straining like a dancer's, the muscles in the legs were flexed, the skin stretched over the ribs, the tendons all down the arm as taut as wires – so that while superficially the picture might give a sense that the figure was floating, after contemplation it would be clear that it was hanging.

'How will you do it?' asked Pity.

'I'll rig a harness and hang it from the cross-beam,' I said. 'It shouldn't be hard. You'll do it for me, won't you?'

She bowed her head and said she would.

I saw the harness as a canvas sling that fitted under the crotch, but attached to this would be two wrist bands, leather manacles really. Once Pity was hanging over the beam, I could adjust the tension on her body by shortening or lengthening the straps. For greater tension, I could lengthen the body strap so that more weight would be taken by the arms. When she needed to rest, I could shorten the body strap, to take the strain away from the arms. In this way, I thought, I would be able to see how the skin and muscle would stretch over the ribs.

Giles came through to see me and picked up the sketch. His face looked younger, his skin clearer.

'Hello, what's this?' he said.

I was blinded to what he was by the memory of what I had seen. Giles in ecstasy. Transported to a place I had never been. How? How? Was it love?

He snapped his fingers.

'This looks interesting.'

'Oh, yes. An idea. Pity's complaining about it, of course. I don't know. She's getting to be more trouble than she's worth. I think I might ditch her.'

'Ditch her?'

'Ditch the little bitch. Kick her out. To be honest, I'm bored with her.'

I looked at Giles without looking at him. Was that shock on his face? No. It was hope! He wanted me to kick her out so that he could have her, so he could set her up in a little love nest in Pimlico and visit her whenever he wanted. Kicking her out would be the last thing I'd do.

Giles, as I said, looked younger these days. Pity, I thought, looked strained. There was a strange tautness in her, a sort of desperation. And while she treated me differently, it was not in the way you might expect. She looked at me desperately. She followed me round pathetically. There seemed nothing she would not do for me, and the colder I was to her, the more obedient she seemed to become.

That night, as Pity slept beside me, I saw what I had to do. I did not concoct the plan. Providence shone a light on me and I saw the way. I embraced her; inhaling her night smell, feeling the sleeping looseness of her body, holding it against me, pressing my groin into her curves. I felt her move, slowly, as if her body had awakened while her mind still slumbered. I inched her nightdress up and over her thighs, pressed her legs apart, raised her hips and knelt between her legs. Sleepily she pulled me down on to her. Now it was her hands on my night clothes. She laid me on my side and suddenly I felt her sex pressing up against me, questing at me bluntly. I lay still, immobilised by curiosity. Her breathing grew harsher and louder. I looked over my shoulder at her face in the moonlight. It was hard and wooden with desire. For the first time I saw how her jaw was thickening, how her Adam's apple was growing. I was suddenly beset by regret and horror, and that odd destructiveness that follows in the wake of beauty spoiled.

I twisted. My hands rose to her neck and I started to strangle her. At first it seemed to stimulate her more but when she started to choke, and realised what I was doing, she stiffened, stopped moving and went limp. Her eyes, beginning to start, rolled open and stared at me. Huge eyes, green eyes, going red. She didn't struggle but I could not kill her.

I let her go and she rolled away, coughing so that the tears came and the breath roared through her body in great whoops. The red fell away quite quickly from her face, as did the swelling. She was trying to speak. I bent my ear to her mouth. At first all I could hear was the hoarse breath in her throat. Then came the words, very faint and pinched-sounding: 'You bastard. Why don't you just finish it?'

315

49

The dog boy's hand was in a glass jar in Giles's attic, hanging in fluid, peeled like fruit.

It was already difficult, looking at the whitened flesh at the cuff, to remember that it had once been connected to an arm. I saw the crescent amputation blade slicing the flesh, then the saw grinding briskly at the bone . . . No. It was a hand in a jar now, something quite different from what it had been, in the same way that lovers' posies are different from growing plants.

There had been a hand under the tight bag of pink skin. Giles had peeled this back so that it hung like a bladder below the wrist, still joined. The fingers had bones, little knuckles, and there were five of them, although they looked weak and useless.

I heard the stairs creak behind me.

'You killed him,' I said.

'No.' It was Giles but it could have been any of them. 'Not me. We all did.' I heard him inhale, as if weary. 'Pity suggested it; I persuaded him; Mrs Tully administered too much chloroform.'

'So she did it?'

'It happens.'

'Dog boy spied on all your operations, I think. You had to have him killed.'

'Dog boy spied all right, but he died for a different reason.'

'Oh, yes?'

In the last few weeks Giles had somehow turned sideways on the world. His face had twisted slightly into a permanent, lop-sided grin. He looked like someone expecting the worst, but determined to meet it with an ironic smile.

'Mrs Tully thought I was wooing Pity. She believed that if the operation succeeded, I might have a chance of winning her from you. She couldn't let that happen; couldn't risk it. So the dog boy died.'

'So you're saying she *did* kill him?'

'No. It was as much my pride. I wanted to show that I could do more than hack. I wanted to show I could mend flesh and mould it, like an artist, a real artist. When I saw what you had done with the dog boy's hand, just by a few slashes of the pencil – here a finger, there a finger. Deformity gone! When I saw that, I was jealous of you. I shouldn't have performed the operation. He was too weak.'

'And Pity? What part did she play?'

'Why don't you ask him yourself?'

But I couldn't. The thought that Pity had played a part, rather than merely observing, rather frightened me.

I had thought that the battle had been between Giles and myself, but if Pity had had a hand in the dog boy's death, I was beginning to think she had been the queen all along, and we two mere pawns.

'You must do exactly as I say.'

We were standing in the graveyard at the bottom of Bermondsey Street, Mrs Tully and I. It was a rotten place, stones leaning drunkenly on weedy soil. Body was buried on body here, and from the smell of the place, some of them not too deep. A lot of dogs lived nearby. There were folded sausages of dog shit everywhere. The dog boy could have lived like a king off the accumulation. The earth had been paddled to mud by the paws of dogs, and the claws of rats and birds. At the entrance stood a small watch house, empty now; the resurrection men being dead themselves.

Mrs Tully looked around her. 'You didn't think that meeting here would in some way intimidate me?'

317

I shook my head; the idea was as ridiculous to me as it was to her. There was an old brick wall around three sides of the graveyard, the blackened bricks of the church made up the fourth. The glass in its lancet window was frosted with soot.

'I feel overlooked anywhere in that house,' I said. 'There's this atmosphere . . .'

'I wonder whose fault that is?' She raised an eyebrow into a perfect arc. I kicked at a mound of earth, then stopped when I realised what I might be exposing. Standing in this place, the earth was like a thin skin over a sore, and the skin was wearing away.

'It's private here,' I said.

'"The grave's a fine and private place."'

'That sounds like a quotation?'

'I've no idea. My mother used to say it. Her father was a vicar.' Her voice tailed off. Her eyes grew haunted. I had a sudden picture of Mrs Tully as a young girl. A house in Holloway. Her mother marrying into trade, respectable and with prospects. Mrs Tully, mute and pliant but always watching. Maybe. Or maybe Crucifix Lane did it for her.

'Who was Mr Tully?' I asked. I had never even considered him before. It was odd how this atmosphere of conspiracy had forced into me a desire for intimacy.

'He died,' she said shortly. 'I had to work. I became a nurse.'

'An odd choice for a respectable woman. Could you not have gone back to your parents?'

'No.' She hunched over, suddenly defensive. 'No.' The word whispered to nothing. Next she would be confessional. And suddenly I saw in her the possibility of that ghastly, haunted face I had seen at the window. The last thing I wanted was to release her demons. Mrs Tully's mysteries would have to remain her own. I was not going to peel away the layers.

'Well,' I said, 'be that as it may.'

She stood upright and blinked, as if I had slapped her on the face. I did not look at her while I gathered my thoughts. Words between us ceased for a minute. All of life is wheels within

318

wheels, cog biting cog, but sometimes you know you are giving the machine a push and these moments need savouring. At that minute, I could hear a barrel organ in the distance, the creak of wheels on cobbles, the thump of the engine in the rendering house. A drunken costermonger shouted: 'Pineapples from Arabee! Come eat the fruit of kings! Come on, you fucking bastards, buy my fucking fruit!'

'Did the dog boy die because he had seen the operations?' I asked. 'Is that why you gave him an overdose? Or was it to nip the growing friendship between Giles and Pity in the bud?'

'It was both. Two birds; one stone. So what do we do?' she asked.

It was a shock hearing her say 'we'. It seemed to take for granted a relationship I had not considered. To have Mrs Tully stroke my head with her rough, competent hands was one thing. To have her translate that contact into recurring intimacy made me feel nervous.

'What you must do is this,' I said. I emphasised the 'you', and Mrs Tully looked as if she had been slapped. 'You must threaten Giles with complete exposure, as crudely and roughly as you know how.'

She was silent. I sensed the tiniest hint of apprehension.

'Me?'

'Yes.'

'Why not you?'

'My work will be harder. It'll be my turn next.'

'What will you do?'

'I will have to go to work on him,' I said. 'Persuade him.'

'To do what?'

'I cannot tell you that now. Only this: it will bind him so tightly to us that I do not think he will able to breathe, and it will nullify any threat from Pity.'

'And I must threaten him, just like that? He will ask me why. And I do not have a reason.'

'You must say that what he does horrifies you.'

'He will laugh in my face.' She looked at me vengefully, still smarting from the snub I had delivered. 'The truth is that what you do horrifies me more. Compared with your evasion, your pretence that the boy whore is a woman to make you feel less of a damned pervert — compared to that, Giles's behaviour is honest, manly and upright!'

I struck out at her but missed and overbalanced. I reached out and grabbed a tombstone but it was loose in the earth and began a slack, unresisting topple, prising the earth open as its base pivoted. I smelt death. Mrs Tully grabbed me by the collar to stop me from falling with it.

'This is my point,' I said. 'You must pretend to him that your revulsion for what he is doing is such that almost nothing can stop you denouncing him to the police. There will come a point where he will ask you what you want. You will confess that you are frightened that Pity will squeeze you out of the house, and out of your only livelihood, because who else would employ a nurse like you? Giles will then swear blind he will never desert you, if only you will keep quiet about his secret. And you will say that while you believe him, you require proof of his good faith. Do you follow?'

'So far, yes.'

'When he asks you what proof, you will say that you are not certain but will tell him soon. You will also insist on this: that in principle he agrees to your conditions. If he looks like wavering, threaten him again. Do so until you have an undertaking that he will meet your conditions. Are you clear about that?'

Mrs Tully licked her lips. The air had suddenly turned wintry dry. Acrid cold that tasted of dirt.

'I am clear that you have set me an impossible task. If Giles agrees to meet my terms, he is even more desperate than I suspected.'

Her eyes suddenly narrowed as she levelled them over my shoulder. I turned quickly, flinching, arm thrown up, half expecting my last sight on earth to be the head of Giles's walking stick plunging down on me.

No one. Nothing. I followed her stare.

At the foot of the church wall was a mound of earth. A brown dog with a distended belly was scraping at the earth. It had uncovered a head. The head was swollen, the skin of dirty yellow tightly inflated. It was a sight beyond horror, inspiring only pity: pity that someone or other had been so desperate to get the corpse on to consecrated ground they had decided to forego the convention of a grave; pity that having got the body here they had been too weak to dig it even a foot into the earth, merely leaving it on top and scraping dirt over it. Pity, too, not that we had witnessed it, but that it, while resting, had seen two, poor blasted souls plotting the destruction of a third.

Mrs Tully picked up her skirts and rushed from the little graveyard.

I came into the studio looking cold and pinched.

When Pity offered to build up the fire, I just looked at her with wild eyes and shook my head. I paced up and down the room, staring at her when she was not looking at me; then looking away, hurriedly and furtively, when she lifted her eyes from her sketching.

'Something is worrying you?' she asked.

'Nothing.'

'There is something.'

'No, no.' More wild-eyed staring, fingernail-gnawing.

'You must tell me or how can I help you?' she pressed me.

'It's beyond that,' I said. 'I – no.'

And I continued my pacing. I drank. After I had taken two tumblers of brandy Pity put down her pencil and said in some distress: 'You must stop this and tell me. I cannot bear to see you like this.'

'Very well,' I said. 'If what Giles has said is true . . .' I searched her face with my eyes, shook my head, muttered, 'No.'

'What?' She came towards me. She reached out a hand and touched me on the wrist. I resisted the temptation to pull my

321

hand away. Instead I grabbed hers and clutched it before letting it drop.

'I feel ashamed.'

'Of what?'

'I heard something. It made me – it brought a great many feelings together.'

'What did you hear?' she asked softly.

'It is too painful.'

'There is no need to explain,' she said. 'Only . . .'

'Yes?'

'Nothing.'

'Why do you say there is no need to explain?'

'If it gives you pain – '

'It is not the explanation that hurts. It is the information.'

'Please – '

'No. I must say. It concerns you and Giles.'

I deliberately looked evasive.

Her cheek was suddenly wet.

'Oh, no,' she breathed.

'You see, I saw Giles. Or rather – I mean, I did see him but he did not see me. He was bragging with a group of friends, standing in a circle, boasting of this little red-haired tart he could have whenever he wanted. They all laughed. All of them in that cocksure, cock-of-the-walk way. One of them said he should be sharing his good fortune, and Giles said that all they had to do was ask. That he just had to snap his fingers. I think he was drunk. If I thought – if I thought he . . . you . . . I probably deserve it,' I said. 'I have no right to insist. It was not until I felt sick, physically sick out there by the hospital, that I realised how badly I'd been treating you.'

She gave a sort of gasp and buried her face in her hands.

'The other night, when you strangled me, I didn't know what to do,' she whispered.

'I didn't know what I was doing. I saw you, in the kitchen, burning the Dragon's Blood. I thought it was for me. If I knew it was for anyone else, I would go mad with jealousy. And then today, it was as if I went beyond jealousy. But it can't be true that you have been with Giles? I could not bear the thought.'

'I was burning the Dragon's Blood for you,' Pity said. 'I just wanted hope. I just wanted comfort.'

'Tell me it isn't true?' I said. 'I beg you. I know it is no more than I deserve, but tell me it isn't true?'

Her face was white, red where her hands pressed into it.

'I love you,' she said.

'Tell me it isn't true?' I said.

'I love you.'

'Tell me it isn't true,' I said.

She looked at me.

'It isn't true,' she said.

50

Two days later Mrs Tully told Giles that if he did not throw Pity out on to the streets, she would denounce him to the police. The trap was closing in on him. He could not tell me what Mrs Tully had threatened, and was too emotionally incontinent to manage his despair on his own.

The one remaining avenue which could have brought him comfort – Pity – I had cut off by my story of seeing him boast of his power over her. The way I had brought it off elated me. Under normal circumstances she would have been suspicious. Had she talked it through with anyone else, they would have been suspicious. The coincidence of my being there at the precise moment Giles chose to boast of his sexual prowess was far-fetched, as was the idea that he would offer a whore of Pity's nature to his friends. But she was too horrified by the thought that I might unwittingly have stumbled on a truth to think straight. Her own guilt and fear had so concentrated her mind on betrayal and exposure that she was incapable of dissecting the story, and was forced, in short, to swallow it whole.

For my part, while I accepted that my behaviour had driven them together, I could not dull the gnawing ache of jealousy inside me.

The pain was almost physical, constant, faithful. It drew me into obsessive contemplation of its nature; I could not simply forget the reason for the pain. It was in me, and part of me, every hour of every day and most nights. I drank to help me sleep, but for an hour or so when the drink had excited me, and before oblivion took me down, I was like a madman. Drink does not dull jealousy; it sharpens its teeth. At times my head was empty but for a swirling blackness, and in the blackness, the teeth.

Pity tried to comfort me, but did not know what the matter was. It was not right for her to understand that I had seen her and Giles together. The pain of seeing them joined as one, and moving as one, was so intense that if I described it, the words would have destroyed my composure.

I took pleasure only in contemplating Giles's misery, and Pity's future.

Of course he made every effort to see her, but as his free hours were limited and my time my own, I managed easily never to let her alone with him. And yet, even so, he nearly gave himself away so many times.

On the first occasion I heard his feet pound up the stone steps to the studio. The heavy door swung open without his knocking. His breath, ragged, uneven and hoarse, was clearly audible as he looked at the sight in front of him.

I was starting my painting of the Holy Ghost and Pity was hanging in the leather harness, naked but for a loin cloth, stretched between floor and ceiling like a child Christ.

'My God, what have you done?'

I said to Pity: 'Don't move.' Then to Giles: 'This actually isn't a good time.'

'What are you doing to him? Are you all right?'

Poor Giles, to stumble out of one nightmare and into another; to run from a terror of the mind towards this strange, straining flesh.

'She's fine,' I said testily. 'Now what do you want?'

'To talk.'

I knew very well he meant talk to Pity, but consulted my watch and said: 'I'll be free in about ten minutes. Shall I come and find you?'

Giles didn't answer. I went looking for him but he had gone out. It was not me he'd wanted to see.

Another time he came in while Pity was cutting my hair. I was sitting on the dais, robed in a sheet like an emperor, while she moved around, cutting here, cutting there, smoothing my scalp with a touch that made my flesh crawl.

Giles's face was like a mask when he saw the casually intimate little scene, which I made more casual and more intimate by holding Pity around the waist, pulling her towards me and kissing her on the lips.

'I'm glad to see the two of you have made up your quarrel,' he said in a pinched voice. His back was so straight and his head so rigid, he might have been wearing a corset.

He was looking at her, and she was looking at me, or rather through me, a false smile stretching her lips.

I looked from one to the other. 'What's going on between you two?' I asked. 'Not a smile for Giles?'

Pity glanced at him. I thought I saw him mouth the word 'please', then turn away suddenly.

'Well,' I said. 'Giving him the cold shoulder seems to have done the trick. Anyone would think he was in love with you.' She tensed in my arms and kissed me.

So I never left Pity alone when Giles was in the house. I watched him circle us like a dog, waiting for a moment when he could slip in and take Pity. But my story had done the trick, and anyway the extra attention she was getting from me delighted her so that there was no need for her to seek comfort from Giles.

51

After a week or so, I decided it was time to move. I dressed carefully and Pity helped me. She dropped the newly laundered shirt over my head. It enfolded me with a delicious, light roughness. She fiddled the collar studs into the neck and I was like a chid being dressed. She knotted my tie with quick, nimble fingers. She held my trousers for me to step into, cradled my shoes between her hands as I inserted my feet between the stiff rims of new leather. She handed me my new watch, brushed the collar of my new jacket. Thus prepared, the knight blessed his page and left to do battle.

Giles was drunk. He was standing in the window of his living room, staring at the twilit street. The lights in the sitting room were down low. He twisted as I entered, and his face lit up with hope. He turned quickly away when he saw that it was me.

'Come and see this,' he said.

A few yards down the street three workmen were standing near a hole they had dug. The freshly turned earth was the colour of brown sugar; near it the lifted cobbles lay in a heap like a nest of dead puppies.

'You see the tall one, the one with a bowler? Look what he's doing.'

The man was reaching into his heavy jacket, plunging his hand here and there as if pursuing an elusive itch. He pulled out his hand with something alive in it.

'What's that?'

The thing was twisting and turning. His hands were moving around it in a sort of caress.

'A ferret.'

Under the influence of the man's hands the ferret grew calmer. It lay like a long tube of fur, seeming to lengthen as he stroked. While it lay still, one of the other men looped a piece of string around one of its back legs and tied it in a knot.

The ferret handler kissed the animal, then knelt by the hole. He took the ball of string from the other man and held it, then let the ferret go. He paid the string out, maintaining a gentle tension. After a while the string stopped running through his hands.

'What are they doing?'

'I imagine there has been a fall in one of the sewers. The ferret will run along the pipe until it gets to the fall. You measure the distance by the length of string you have paid off, then dig. Look.'

The ferret handler, having now marked the string, was pulling it back, arm's length by arm's length. The ferret came free. For a second it hung in the air, twisting and splayed, before it was gathered to its owner's bosom.

'There's a message there somewhere,' Giles said. He looked at me for the first time. 'My God, what are you wearing?'

'New clothes,' I said. 'I find my clients prefer me to look prosperous.'

'I can't decide if you look more like a strutting bantam cock or the cat that got the cream.'

I looked out of the window. The men had let the ferret down the sewer again. They were gathered by the hole, kneeling on the dirt. The ferret handler was pulling the string back again, slowly. I could see that there was no tension in it. He held it up. No ferret.

'I came to see you because I wanted to find out what was going on between you and Pity.'

'Oh, yes.'

He sounded bitter.

'She says you tried to rape her.'

A moment's silence. I could see him struggling with his

reactions. Shock. Hurt. Fear. They flickered across the face like cards in a magsman's shuffle. Then he gave a bitter laugh.

'And you believe her?'

I said nothing.

'Pity accuses me of raping her. Mrs Tully threatens me with exposure . . .'

'For what?'

'Mrs Tully says she saw me lying with Pity. Don't pretend you don't know.'

'And did she?'

Giles shrugged.

'Which is true?' I asked.

'It makes no difference,' he said. 'The only truth that matters is that you are going to ruin me, and I doubt I have the strength to resist.'

'Come now,' I said. 'I'm only interested in the truth. Do you remember how interested you were in my true nature so long ago?'

'Yes. And trying to uncover it has released pure evil. A true Pandora's Box. You have suborned Mrs Tully somehow. I saw the possibility the night you killed Oates. She's come down against me because you and she are in this together.'

'In what?'

'This conspiracy to ruin me!'

He moved from dim shadow to dim gaslight. The room hissed calmly around us.

'Why?' he asked.

'Perhaps you had better tell me what Mrs Tully said? Exactly.'

'She told me she knew I was sleeping with Pity, that she was frightened in case it meant she would be pushed out – with you, of course – and he and I would live together then.' Giles sniffed. I think the words were conjuring the possibility to life.

'And?' I said.

'I denied it, of course. Then Mrs Tully said she had evidence. Said she could back it up. Said that whatever I said, the word of two people against me would carry the day. I could only think of two people who would do such a thing: you and Mrs Tully.'

'Or Pity.'

'He would never do such a thing.' Giles said it too quickly.

'How do you know?'

He shrugged, attempting to look casual. 'Too stupid.'

'And is she?' I asked.

'Is she what?'

'Is Mrs Tully going to expose you?'

'Are you her accomplice?'

I shrugged.

'You know, until you came to live here,' Giles said, 'I was more or less happy. Now my life is in ruins.'

'You brought me here,' I said. 'Is Mrs Tully going to expose you?'

'She said she would bring me her terms.' He raised his chin and tried to look brave. 'Terms. To live in my own house. Terms.' His face suddenly sharpened. 'No! It's you that has come to bring me terms,' he said. 'You!'

'And what if I have?'

'You have driven a wedge between me and Pity. I understand that now. Oh, I'm not going to ask you how – spreading foul stories about me most like. Was that it? I think it was. Now why would you do that?'

'Perhaps to stop you and she from forming an alliance,' I said.

'We formed the alliance out of love for you. Both of us poor miserable creatures, only happy when we were being kicked. We were like orphans in the workhouse, hugging each other for warmth!'

'Don't talk to me about the workhouse!' I did not realise I had shouted but when the words stopped, I heard a quick, flat echo, and Giles had my spittle on his face. 'Can you not see that Pity planned this from the start? That it is *she* who is standing on the middle of the see-saw, tilting first this way, then the other, as the fancy takes her?'

330

He wiped his face and looked at me in wonder. 'I never knew what it was about you that so attracted me, but now I see. I was always aware that you were different, but now I see that you are mad.'

'Insulting me will get you nowhere,' I said. 'I am above it. We have started an engine rolling and we must do what we can to keep it on the tracks.' I gathered my thoughts. 'Truth,' I said. 'We must have truth. You said that you and Pity only developed a relationship out of love for me?'

'You are a monster!'

'Are *you* saying that?'

'Yes!'

'Then you must join me on this journey. Now we have started, we must carry on until we stop.'

'But this is nonsense.' Giles spread his hands. 'You can stop at any time. You can call off Mrs Tully, you can stop torturing me. You can treat Pity with some respect. You can move out, go far from here. Yes. Why don't you do that? You're rich enough now, or will be soon. Why don't you rent a house in Chelsea, or move to Holland Park? Why don't you paint the daughters of rich men until you marry one of them? Why do you persist in staying here, arranging your life to cause as much pain for others as it is possible to imagine? Why?'

'Because of what you know about me,' I said. 'Once the game is started, it has to be played to the end.'

'People aren't like that, Auguste. People like to live, people just want to get on with it. That you know a secret about me, and that I know a secret about you, this is merely the stuff of life. Go away from here. I will never try to ruin you so long as you don't do it to me.'

I shook my head. He didn't know. He didn't know of the illusion of security. He didn't know that houses, homes, cities, streets, work, play, love and hate were just the songs of fools, dreamed into existence by desperate men and desperate women. All you had to do was narrow your eyes and peer through the crack in the door and you would see the featureless plain spreading forever around us. Could I explain that to him? Could anyone? What was I doing? I was showing him the truth, and better that he be shown it than told it.

'What then? What do you want?'

When I said nothing, Giles exhaled heavily. 'Oh, for God's sake. Have a drink.'

We both drank. The men in the street had dispersed. Only the ferret handler remained, kneeling by the sewer, pursing his lips, whistling down an empty hole.

After a while Giles said: 'Well? What are your terms?'

I said: 'The terms are simple. Do you remember a long time ago we played a game – Truth or Dare?'

'I remember.'

'We play it again, only this time it is absolutely binding.'

'Those are your terms?'

'Those are my terms.'

'Very well.' There was almost no hesitation on his part. He leaned forwards in his chair, looking amused. 'Who goes first?'

'You do.'

He smiled. 'All right. Here goes. Truth. What do you really want from me?' he asked.

'I want you to prove that you love me,' I replied. 'That is the truth.'

Giles jerked back as if he had been hit. He shuddered, then blinked.

'Don't look so surprised. It's only what you've been saying all along. Now it's my turn.' I pretended to think. 'Are you ready?'

'Ask me,' he said. His voice was as light as a wafer.

'To show that you love me,' I said, 'I dare you to change Pity.'

'Change her?' he said dully, and slowly came back to life. 'Change her? What on earth do you mean?'

'Do you remember a long time ago, when we were walking along the river, and you said that surgeons are artists?'

'Did I? I can't remember.'

332

'You did.'

'Well?'

'I dare you to use your art to match mine. It failed on the dog boy, use it on Pity.'

'My art? To *change* Pity?'

'Just as I have changed her countless times with the paintbrush and pencil, so you must change her with the knife.'

'No! You cannot mean it, not seriously?'

I ignored him.

'That is the challenge,' I said. 'Your honour rests on it. And your ascendancy. Do it, and I am your slave, and she is your creature and creation. Fail to do it, and you risk losing everything. From the outset, when she came here, she needed to oust one of us. Don't you see? Just as you knew that she was a boy, she knew what you had done. The dog boy saw those operations: do you think he would not have told her? From then on, she just wanted to come inside so she could use her knowledge against us. This is your chance to use yours against hers.'

Giles seemed to shrivel up. It was like watching a dog die at my feet.

52

I n the midst of these developments, Gruber paid me a visit.
'We were worried, my dear chap. We thought you had
become a recluse.'

'I have not been out,' I said. 'I have been feeling rather – '

'Yes, yes. I quite understand. And how is the beautiful Pity?'

'Well,' I said shortly. She was at the other end of the room.
Gruber looked at her appraisingly.

'She looks more stately than I remembered,' he observed.

Pity was causing me some anxiety. She seemed happy, and
happiness was bringing with it a measure of coarseness to her
features, or perhaps that was just her growing older. Already I
fancied she was almost as tall as me, and she was filling out.
Good food, rest, absence of worry, all these were combining to
disastrous effect on her body. It had quite lost that fine
luminescence I had loved at first. I sought but could not find
the shadows of green marbling under her skin. In short, she was
growing up.

'Anyway,' Gruber said. 'What of the *Rape of the Nymph by
the Satyr?*'

'Centaur,' I corrected him.

He waved a hand.

'Almost ready for varnishing,' I said.

'May I see?'

I had it on an easel, apart from my other work. I was letting
it lie for a while, so I could look at it afresh.

'Your brushwork is getting heavier,' Gruber said. 'You must
watch that.' He bent and peered more closely. 'Also, this

nymph looks rather like a boy. First wrong in one way; now wrong in another. You have not been observing nature.' And he chuckled good-naturedly.

I bent to look.

'It has the body of a boy,' he said. 'Surely you can see that?'

'This is the body of a young girl,' I said. 'Pity.'

'I can see breasts, it is true. But − no.' He stood back and looked at it again, turning his head from side to side. 'Maybe.' He shrugged. 'Only a comment,' he said. 'It will not displease our patron, I am sure. Such ambiguity is exciting, at any rate.'

His gaze flickered from me to Pity and back again.

'You know, you two really are growing more and more alike. Mirrors in flesh. Pity, my dear.'

She raised her head again and smiled at him.

'Pull your wonderful hair back. Now make a face like Auguste's.'

Pity gathered her hair, pulling it back across her forehead. Holding it loosely behind her head, she scowled ferociously.

Gruber clapped his hands.

'Wonderful,' he said. 'Beautiful. Come here, my dear.'

She approached him. He held out his hand. She extended hers which he took and kissed. She curtsied. 'I was almost forgetting,' he said, slapping his forehead. 'I am on the strictest instructions to look at your work, my dear.'

'Instructions from whom?' I asked.

'Your good friend Timothy Brownlow.'

She frowned and looked at me. Gruber caught the look.

'A friend at any rate. He was most insistent.'

'Friend? Is that what he calls himself? He was rather more impressed with Pity's work than mine,' I said.

'He has an eye,' Gruber said, 'that looks to the future, while you and I, my friend, look to the present. Now show me.'

'No,' I said.

'What is this?' Gruber looked at me, his coarse features forming themselves into a perfect amalgam of condescension and surprise.

'You will not see Pity's work.'

'And why not?'

'It is not ready; she is not ready. She is too young.'

'Nonsense,' Gruber said. 'Show me, come on.'

I found something so powerfully overbearing in his clipped German tone that I took a step towards him, a fog of anger closing in around me.

'Stop it!'

Pity's voice was like a whiplash. To my astonishment I saw that Gruber had backed away from me, eyes wide with fright. He stumbled; I held out my hand. He flinched.

'It would be better if you did not see Pity's work quite yet,' I said.

'I'm ready,' Giles said a week later. 'But I want to do it soon.' His face was clear; it was as if he had seen a way *through*.

I nodded. 'The sooner the better.' The odd jingling phrase, so familiar, made me laugh. Giles smiled sadly.

'Will Pity know?'

'Soon enough,' I said.

This time he shivered. I thought he would have baulked at that, but he just shivered.

'I do not know which is crueller,' I said. 'To tell her before or afterwards. What do you think?'

'If I thought one way less cruel than the other, I would never let you know,' said Giles.

'Why not?'

'Because, of the two ways, I think you would choose the crueller.'

'It hurts me to hear you say that,' I said.

He looked at me with such concentrated loathing that I found myself once again giving a surprised, and rather foolish, laugh.

And he was wrong: I had no real motive for causing Pity pain. I felt the pain was purely incidental. In the end, I decided to drug her so she would be unconscious when Mrs Tully applied the chloroform. The pain would be all mine.

The arrangements were complex. Mrs Tully feared that to drug Pity with laudanum in sufficient quantities to make her sleep would interfere with the action of the chloroform, and slow her heartbeat dangerously. But we had somehow to make her unconscious during the period of actual preparation. This would take a long time. The surgeon's bench had to be brought up from the old furnace room and properly washed; that area of the studio had to be washed too. Pity would have to be washed; and the hair she had down there shaved.

In the end I was forced to buy powders from a chemist who insisted on asking me questions for which I was barely prepared. In the end I told him I was a frustrated bridegroom whose attentions caused his wife such acute embarrassment that I felt she should be rendered unconscious for her own good, as much as mine.

'The Good Lord has seen fit only to bless marriage with his authority if it is consummated,' the chemist remarked.

'Indeed,' I said.

'I feel it is my Christian duty to assist in such a matter. You never know,' and here he gave me a salacious leer, 'the young gentleman might find that this extreme degree of passivity is a desirable end in itself.'

He began to weigh powder on a small set of scales, pouring the contents into squares of thin waxed paper which he twisted into screws.

'Five doses, sir. One or two should be sufficient. Double them up if you will. And do come back if you require any further assistance in this or any other matter.'

I said: 'Amen,' and left.

They say a dog will know when his master is leaving; so Pity knew that something was up. For a day she went about with a

337

long face. By evening she looked ready to lay her down and die.

'What on earth is the matter?' I asked.

She was seated by the big roaring fire, her face a barbaric mask of flaring lights and silky shadows.

'My father said anyone could see the future when they looked into the flames,' she said. 'He claimed that what was in their hearts was in the fire. I've often wondered what he meant. I think he must have been saying that what was in your heart determined your future and your heart would force its pattern on to the flames. They never stop moving, do they?'

'And neither do we,' I said. 'What do you see in the flames?'

'You want to know what is in my heart?'

'Yes, dearest.'

'I see terror and a new beginning,' she said.

The fear her words brought upon me was like a little breeze from a cold, cold wind.

'In your heart, you want terror?'

'Not want. But it may be my destiny. Perhaps I am not doing enough to avoid it. Today, while I was hanging in that harness, I hardly dared look at you.'

'Why?'

'Your eyes were like stones. They were hiding something. They hurt me.'

'Then the terror is not in your heart, it is coming from me.'

'But I do not do enough to fight it,' she said. 'That is what I am saying. Every morning I climb into that harness, am hoisted to the ceiling. I hang there, torn between the air and the earth, every fibre in me wanting to float, but every ounce of flesh and gill of blood drawn downwards so I seem to be tearing myself in half. My life is like that. All I have ever done is step into the way of pain.'

'Perhaps pain is truth.'

'Then I must have had a bellyful of it,' she said. 'I am sick of it.

'Come here,' I said.

338

She sat at my feet. I buried my face in her hair and breathed its thick, oily smell. I rubbed my face in it. I lay on the floor. She let her hair fall on my face as she crouched over me, and when she turned and lowered herself on to me, she leaned back on her elbows and let her hair fall into my mouth. It was thick and living. I gathered it and let it grow warm in my mouth.

The following morning I gave her a triple dose of the sleeping potion in her coffee. She fell asleep looking terrified.

We set to work. Mrs Tully scrubbed the floor, and after Giles and I had brought the surgeon's bench up from the furnace room, that too. Giles prepared a bowl and filled it with liquefied coal tar soap. He washed his instruments in it, poured it away, then filled it again and left them to soak.

By midday we were ready. I cleared the end of the studio and lit a fire. Giles felt that warmth helped relax the patient's muscles. We manoeuvred the bench underneath the lantern.

Giles was calm and clear in all his orders, seemingly without nerves. The sky was empty of clouds that day. The cold made sounds carry farther. Every noise was a cry in an empty room. Smoke from a thousand chimneys trickled greasily into the air which hung like a great grey china bowl above us.

I watched Giles in the courtyard before he came in for the operation. He breathed in air deeply and appreciatively, like a man on his way to the scaffold and resigned to his fate. He took the steps two at a time as if a weight had been taken off his shoulders.

Pity slept still, her face ugly and heavy with drugs. Mrs Tully slipped an anaesthetic mask over nose and mouth: a frame of wire and pad of gauze. Orange rubber tubes led from a metal bottle with plunger on top into the mask.

Giles frowned and held Pity's wrist. 'What do you think?' he asked.

Mrs Tully felt the pulse. 'Regular enough.'

'Should we wait?'

She shrugged.

'If we wait,' Giles said, 'it will be safer. However we will miss this glorious light. There's nothing like it. I think we go ahead. Perhaps not too much chloroform at first. If the patient starts to stir, increase the dose.'

Mrs Tully nodded.

'Now,' Giles said, 'for preparation. Have you cleansed yourself?'

'I have.' I had washed my hands for five minutes in Giles's prescribed mixture of water and carbolic soap.

'Semmelweis recommended chlorine and they broke him,' Giles said. 'We'll paint the patient in carbolic – that's in the jar there. But first, we must shave him. Could you do that?'

I nodded.

'Let's get the patient on to the table then. Mrs Tully, could you make a note of the time?'

I took Pity under the arms, Giles took her by the legs. When she was laid on the table to Giles's satisfaction he lifted up her nightdress to above the waist, exposing her. I wet soap and worked up a lather with a brush. Working it into the darkening shadow above Pity's groin was an unexpectedly emotional moment. I felt very tender towards her, and almost fell into a trance as I brushed the lather on to the flat skin of her belly and lower, making it foam. 'That's enough,' Giles said. 'Ready?'

I nodded.

He handed me a razor and flipped open the blade. It was odd. I felt quite calm but breathing seemed only to make me more breathless, and when I took the razor, my hand started to shake violently.

'That'll stop as soon as you start,' Giles said. But it didn't. As the blade approached Pity's groin, it shook so badly I was frightened I might cut her.

'Very well. You hold, I'll scrape,' Giles said. I pulled the penis away from the blade by taking a tiny pinch of skin halfway up it. It was warm, alive between my fingers. It went beyond reason and imagination to think that in a matter of minutes, perhaps, it would be gone.

When Giles was finished, he put down the razor, carefully, some distance away from the bench. 'We don't want that getting mixed up with the real blades. How's the breathing and pulse?'

'Fine,' said Mrs Tully. 'Both strengthened when you were preparing.'

'Possible mechanical arousal,' Giles said. 'Well, here goes. Auguste, are you clear as to your duties?'

'I am to wipe the sweat from your face, to mop the blood from the incision, replace the cotton pads underneath the patient when they get sodden and assist both you and Mrs Tully.'

'Quite right. I would prefer someone to hand me my tools but in the circumstances, I'm afraid you might drop them. If I shout "Suture", you will have to move in close and do whatever I ask while I stitch. Is that clear?'

'Yes.'

'Now I am going to paint the entire area in a solution of coal tar.'

He poured the liquid into a dish and began dabbing it on Pity's penis and scrotum. He put the brush down to roll back the foreskin and paint the head, then rolled back the skin and painted the outside too. He wet an area much greater than I had imagined, all down the inside of Pity's thighs and into the crack of the buttocks. I had to lift her legs while this was going on, resting them on my shoulders. They were dead weights, very heavy.

'Christ. What's that?' Giles asked. 'Mrs Tully? Didn't he move?'

'I don't think so.'

'Heartbeat?'

'The same.'

'That's surprising. Perhaps the pain's getting through. I wouldn't fancy dabbing this on my family jewels. Look at that.' He lifted Pity's penis and pointed to the scrotum with the haft of the brush. The skin was crawling. 'You're sure there's no change?'

'Quite sure.'

'The first thing I am going to do is remove the scrotum and expose the testicles.'

And he made a long, circular, sawing cut that was quick and deep. I felt sick and crawled away to sit with my back to the wall. I was covered in cold sweat and trembling. Unlike Giles and Mrs Tully, I had no resources to fall back on; no training, no experience. I watched Giles hunched over the bench, the way his shoulders and elbows worked, and was reminded of a man carving a roast at the head of the table.

Giles shouted: 'Bucket.' He held out a hand. I crawled over and hooked the bucket in his direction with my foot. What dropped in it looked like a scrap of bloody rag.

'I'd appreciate it if you helped,' he said. 'There's too much blood for me to see.' He grabbed a rag and dabbed between Pity's legs.

His exclamation and Mrs Tully's shout of alarm were instantaneous.

'Patient's awake!'

'Use the straps!'

'What happened?'

Giles was lying across Pity's chest. Her legs were thrashing and she was mumbling incomprehensibly.

'I dabbed the wound with coal-tar solution.' Giles's voice was muffled. 'Make a note, Mrs Tully.' Pity was beginning to scream and wail. 'For God's sake, Coffey, stop crawling around and get up here and help!'

I hauled myself up by the bench and held on to Pity's legs. She began to buck. Her groin thumped at the bench. It was red and wet, and carried a fresh circular wound between the legs.

Mrs Tully wrestled Pity's arms into the restraining straps. As I continued to press down on her legs, Giles tied her ankles.

She was screaming now.

'The mask's come off.'

'Hold her head while Mrs Tully gets it back on,' Giles ordered.

I did. Her back was arching galvanically, head tossing from side to side. She kept on repeating, 'What . . . what . . . what . . .' She saw me. Her eyes locked on to mine. They were wide and dark and desperate. Mrs Tully slipped the mask back over her mouth.

'Hold her head.'

She had the eyes of a person drowning, unreachable behind ice. I put my weight on her chest and held her head between my hands. Mrs Tully began to pump at the chloroform bottle. I turned my head away. After a minute Pity was still.

'Shall we continue?' said Giles.

I watched him cut in a dream of blood. Blood is very bloodlike and flesh is very fleshy, but in between, in disguise, the apparatus or deep structure of the flesh seems to be full of mysteries: tubes, differently textured muscle, fatty tissue, bloody tissue which is different from skin. He showed me the urinary tract, the connective tubes to carry the seed.

Halfway through he muttered something. I asked him what. He said that he'd thought he would be amputating but knew another way, one that would allow Pity to retain her organ in adapted form.

I thought for a second and then agreed, but realised he was far removed from me and had not been asking, simply telling. Time passed. I watched his quick hands do things slowly, or rather do an immense amount of complex, close things in a way that seemed compressed, so that every action pressed the seconds apart. Apart from the sounds of metal on flesh, all I could hear was the heavy breathing of Pity and the calm rustle when Mrs Tully shifted on her stool at Pity's head.

When at last Giles said: 'Suture,' I thought he must have cut an artery and panicked. He said calmly, 'It is all right, Gussie. I'm sewing her back together now.'

'At last you call her she,' I said.

'Did I? I think I swore to myself that I would not.'

At last I dabbed the last of the blood away. She was lying on white cloth. Before Giles put on the bandage, she could have been a young girl, the flesh disappearing into a smooth slide between her closed thighs.

'Well,' Giles said. 'You have your mermaid now.'

The operation took four hours and outside the clear day was slipping into night.

After the operation I wanted to be alone, but after a while I had had enough of that. Giles, washed and changed, was at his usual place, staring out of the drawing-room window, the room he had redecorated for Pity.

'Well done,' I said.

'What would you know?'

'I know you did your best.'

'I did it for Pity, not you. Look after her, won't you?'

'Why? You shall be her doctor.'

'I am leaving. Tomorrow.'

I was struck dumb by shock.

'You cannot!'

'I can.'

'But all I said to you . . . about what I could do?'

'It means nothing to me. I am empty. I have done this thing for you – I would have moved out before, if I'd had the courage. But I didn't. I throw myself on your mercy. If I stay a moment longer in this house, I think I will probably die.'

'No,' I said.

'I am moving out,' Giles insisted. 'You can do what you want. But for your sake, and for Pity's, and even Mrs Tully's too, do not bring the whole house down. Accept the change. I am going. That is that.'

'Do not bring the whole house down sounds more like a threat.'

'It was not meant to be. I beg you to leave me alone, as I will promise to leave you.'

It was like listening to a polite corpse explain to its murderer that there really wasn't any call to go on kicking him because he was already dead.

53

And so Giles is gone.

The house is rather empty now, a place full of winter cold and winter calm, apart from the random thrashings of a sick child who is lying in the recovery room on the second floor. I am surprised by Mrs Tully. She is the most assiduous nurse, hardly leaving Pity's side, and only then to rustle down to the kitchen to prepare beef tea, vegetable soup or gruel for the patient, or fill a pitcher with cold water and wring out a cloth, or to carry down the sweat-stained, blood-spotted sheets to soak in the copper, waiting to be boiled to whiteness again. I have rigged up lines across the courtyard and every day I hang up sheets and bandages to dry. I have washed them to glowing whiteness with Bouverie's Moonlight Soap. My face stares down at me from a board overlooking the courtyard, my face sweats above the coppers as I plunge my hands into the milky suds and scrub, and scrub, and scrub. My life has achieved circularity.

I watch the sheets dry from a back window, the room below Pity's. I hear the bed creak as she tosses; I hear Mrs Tully move the chair across the room, its legs scraping softly on the linoleum. As I watch, the sheets turn from white to grey as they are stroked by London's sooty breezes.

I have been into the studio once. It smelled of chemicals. The surgeon's bench, the knives and saws still soaking in carbolic, the bucket which I would not look into, the piles of bloody gauze, Giles's cutting coat which he dropped as he walked from the room, knowing he would never return, the ashes of the fire — all there as we left them as we carried Pity out on a stretcher.

I took my clothes from the studio, my pictures and my kit, closed the shutters, barred them, then locked the door behind me. It was not meant to be a final gesture but it felt significant, elegiac in its way, the sound of a lock turning on my past. Above me, in bed, the future is close to death, or so Mrs Tully says.

I have seen the wound, and on Mrs Tully's insistence have even touched it. Where the scrotum was, Pity's filleted penis has been spread and sewn across the wound. The place looks like a face without a mouth; smooth and featureless as the sex of a Greek statue.

My mermaid.

When she urinates it probably causes some stinging, but Mrs Tully says that is inevitable and soon it will stop and control will develop. Pity will then be perfect.

So what of this sickness? It is not infection. Even I can see that. A certain redness about the stitches, but the blood has dried to a crusty black crackle glaze and there is none of the taut, plum-skinned ripeness of infection. Yet Pity is burning up and Mrs Tully fears such heat in the head will cook her brain and turn her into an idiot. She has seen it before, she says, a fit young man turned to a twisted, leaking fool. That is why she bathes Pity's head and fans her continually. The fever, she says, is a fever of the brain, engendered by the shock of waking up in the middle of the operation. She thinks perhaps the brain is trying to burn out the memory.

I have nothing to say to that, or to any other medical matter.

She woke me one morning at three.

It is the dead time, when the cold in the air matches that in the grey hearts of the dead.

'The fever has risen again,' Mrs Tully said. She was dabbing away tears of exhaustion. 'It had dropped, I thought it had broken, but then it suddenly returned. Her head is hot under

346

the hand; her body too. Hot like – something in the kitchen. I have bathed her body and done what I could but I'm frightened. Oh God, I am frightened.'

I rose from Giles's bed and followed her down the corridor.

At first I thought that Pity was actually shimmering in a heat haze. She was lying stark naked on the bed. The sheets were greyed with damp. Her body was the sort of sugar pink that some people think is healthy. Her head seemed to have detached itself and floated free from the pillow.

I could not understand at first, then saw.

'You have cut off her hair,' I said.

A scream began to rise inside me.

'I had to. She was so hot. It's immediate relief. The hair was so heavy it was as if her poor head was wrapped in a blanket.'

Her hair was lying all around her, still part of her, I thought, splayed out in a massive fan, dripping over the edge of the bed like something fiery and molten.

I touched it; hair caught hair caught strand caught hank until it slithered from the sheets and lay on the floor around her. It looked like a big dead dog curled on the oil cloth.

Pity's head was so small and grey, covered in an uneven, blotchy stubble of red . . .

She looked ordinary, and so pathetic. I couldn't touch her.

'Gather up the hair,' I said to Mrs Tully, 'and put it in a pillow case. Do not leave a single strand.'

When she was finished she stood, stooped with exhaustion, eyes flickering open and shut. I thought she was going to faint. The pillow case swung in her hand. I took it from her. It actually had weight. Pity was still. Mrs Tully came out of her trance and instinctively reached out to touch her forehead.

I saw her start, then look at the still body. I reached across. Pity's forehead was cool to the touch.

Mrs Tully's mouth started to tremble.

'She's dead,' I said harshly. 'For Christ's sake, don't cry.'

'No . . . no.'

'She's dead!'

But Mrs Tully shook her head. 'No. Look – there. There! It's the heart. The fever has broken. She's asleep! Asleep!'

I sat up and looked. In a hollow between the ribs the tight skin was fluttering. Pity slept. I stared at his head, his tight features, his grey skin. I did not know what to think except that he looked like a sick boy.

He was a sick boy. That was all.

And Mrs Tully died that night. She took the sleeping powders I had used to drug Pity, took the two remaining packets together, and a bottle of laudanum, and that did for her. I found her at teatime the next day, in her room, in bed, in her night things. She was curled up in a little ball, stiff as a stuffed cat, folded around a Bible that I hoped saved her soul. So she lived a mystery and died a mystery and I burned her in the furnace room and the chimney made black smoke for the last time. Her ashes I scattered in the little churchyard, close to a wall, where a cherry tree from the vicarage garden could stretch its dry black branches and drop dirty little blossoms on her come the spring.

One of the first things Pity said to me was: 'Where's Giles?'

'Gone,' I said.

'And Mrs Tully?'

'Gone as well.'

He was quiet for two months. He made no effort to leave the house. All he wanted to do was sit in the little sitting room that Giles had made for him at the back of the house and stare down at the shuttered windows of the studio. For my part, I found I was listless, as if Pity's stillness communicated itself to me. I would draw my chair into the drawing-room window and watch the street below. At first people looked up and stared, but soon I became as familiar a sight as the knife sharpener outside The Wheatsheaf, or the match girl twins scampering up and down the street like water fleas, offering mad, made-up services for a penny in an alley to pay for

Mother's next baby. Each one of them a pity. And so time passed. I bought food, cooked it, but more often called to the urchins outside The Wheatsheaf for plates from the Hygienic Working Man's Dining Rooms. And so we lived, back to back if not side by side, and more time passed.

'What's your name?' I asked.

He looked at me. He was coming back to health. His face was filling out. After it had been flushed with fever, his skin turned slightly yellow, then went grey. It had now regained its delicate, mother-of-pearl translucency, all the more striking in a boy's face. His hair was now close and dense. You could no longer see scalp beneath and it lay, angled but flat, like an animal's pelt.

'Peter,' he said.

Another day I found him standing in front of the fire, looking at himself in the mirror. He was cutting his hair again with a big pair of scissors. He saw me in the glass. I nodded and left him.

That afternoon I took the pillow case of his hair to a wig maker. The man declared he had never see hair like it. He said it would take six months to knot it all. I gave him three and said I would pay him double if he did it in two.

But mostly I was bored. I had moved my stuff up to Giles's penthouse room with the clapboard sides and wide glass front, and froze, high above the streets, like the winter before. Circularity.

I looked at my pictures and saw that they were nothing, or perhaps, in their new context, they were nothing. Context is all. Gruber said that forgeries always stood out a century later because the forger's art was not to reproduce the painter's style, but reproduce whatever people of that age saw in the painter. Because that was always changing, so the forgeries had to change.

I was a forger, trying to hide behind the camouflage of my contemporaries' taste. My paintings had been fine one month before. Now that was over.

I finished them off easily, copying my own style, and sent them in a hansom cab to Gruber.

I started to teach Peter to read and write. He was frighteningly fast and concentrated. He memorised the *shapes* of words as he saw them, not bothering to decipher the letters. He had to relearn each word every time he saw it in a new hand or style.

I taught him to see the meaning in each letter, and break down the words like that, so that this meaning, rather than their shape, gave them substance.

It was a difficult concept for the lad to grasp. He was enamoured of words for their own sake and thought that once they were divided into letters, they were broken, like vases or plates.

So I taught him to write.

The first word he made gave him such an exultant rush of pleasure that he laughed like a sultan. When I saw him laugh like that, my heart contracted.

We were sitting in the drawing room to either side of the fire. Peter had finished his sketching and was poring over *The Times*, frowning at the mystery of its dense print. Sometimes when I read bits of it to him aloud he would scowl because he did not believe that the eye and mouth could be nimble enough to piece that grid of curves and dots into anything intelligible.

'What's that word?' That was usually a sign that he had come across something he thought he recognised. He did not like to venture anything unless he knew he was right.

I bent beside him at the table, aware of the shape of his back, the contraction of muscles under his eye; the way that his hair, now kept short, had darkened to a dull, deep copper.

'Bouverie,' I said.

'Read it for me.'

When I hesitated, he said: 'Go on.'

I read: '"George and Martha Bouverie are happy to announce the engagement of their son, Giles, to Frances

Margeret Morant, daughter of the late Colonel and Mrs Morant, of Glasgow and London."'

'What's all that about?' he asked.

'It means Giles is getting married.'

'Did he love me?'

'He liked you.'

'Does he love this Frances Margeret Morant?'

'Out of necessity, yes.'

'He'll come back. He won't stay. He can't keep away from the boys, that one.'

I thought: Was that all I had been? Was that all I was? Just one of Giles's boys?

I thought, and it surprised me, that I felt betrayed. I realised then that while the game with Peter might be starting, the game with Giles still had some distance to run.

In the morning I wrote to Fanny at her London home:

My dear Miss Morant

How happy I was to hear of your official engagement to Giles. It fills me with great pleasure to know that in you he will at last find someone who can give him the necessary protection and support from life's travails, to allow him to discover his true genius in the field of medicine. Believe me when I wish you a long, happy and prosperous life together, blessed with all the fruits of sanctified union.

At this time, however, there is one small matter that has come to my mind, and do what I may, I find I am unable to ignore it. Clearly I do not want to alarm or even worry you, but do you remember talking to me once in the old monks' hall here, and saying that if there was anything amiss with Giles, you would want me to tell you?

As I say, there is one small matter I feel I must discuss and would be grateful if you could write to me, arranging a time for us to meet. Naturally you must tell Giles if you feel you must. But as this is a relatively small matter, I wonder if you could not balance the concern this might cause him, were he to catch wind of our assignation, against the obligations of a fiancée? In other words, I think it would be better if Giles did not know that we are meeting, but I would quite understand if you felt you must tell him.

Life here in Crucifix Lane seems rather dull without the stimulus of his company. Mrs Tully left us, I am afraid to say, and all I have is a sort of pot boy, very much a jack-of-all-trades, alas master of none. Still Peter, as he is called, is willing and has changed enormously since he first arrived and I have become quite fond of him. Giles recommended him and I am sure will be glad to discover that he is working out satisfactorily.

Believe me when I say, I am,

Yours sincerely,

Auguste Coffey

Peter asked me what I was doing.

'Keeping an eye on Giles. That's all.'

'How?'

'I have an understanding with his fiancée – the woman to whom he is engaged.'

'What understanding?'

'I am not sure yet.'

'Can I – can I sleep with you tonight?'

Peter was so direct. He was having to relearn the proper way to live. This was the biggest change since the operation. The very thought turned my insides to water.

'No.'

'You ruined me and now you've turning yourself again me! When I had a prick, all you wanted to do was forget about it. Now it's gone, you don't want to know.'

'It's not that.'

'Then what is it?'

I found it hard to put into words for him, but I was terribly confused. He should have hated me but didn't. I wanted to feel guilty but his behaviour seemed to detract from that. In fact, since the operation he had become, in a sense, simpler and more dependent, as if undressing, shaving his head and slicing him, had pared away the complexities of behaviour he had demonstrated as a woman.

He wanted to read, he learned to read. He wanted to write, so he learned to write. He needed security, and so enfolded himself in me so deeply that my very being had grown around him. If I had cast him out, I would have had to have torn myself to do so, and done myself terrible harm. When he wanted comfort, he asked for sex but I found it too animal. I'd liked the complexities that had previously defined our relationship. I could rub against them. They created a charge, a crackle. It hurt him, I know, but I simply could not allow myself to fuck him now.

And deep down, under all that, I was terrified of him. Mostly this was a deep under water, deep under mud, dark, barely realised, never glimpsed, terror. Two things served to bring it to my attention, and gave me a sense of something vast and ominous – like looking at an iceberg in a calm, moonlit sea, and seeing it move, and then seeing the sea around it heave, and realising that the ice mountain, itself so vast, was only the peak of something huger, and that huge underwater thing from which it grew was only a frozen speck on the spreading, surging back of the great kraken.

Peter's face never looked unguarded. Even in repose there was a stiffness to it. In fact, it was in repose that the mask was most apparent. In the normal course of the day, it was glossed by the shimmer of human feeling. It did not make me suspect him of anything, it merely made it hard to relax with him. It was only when he was disguised, only when he took on the character of a woman, that he could relax because it was only then that he felt protected.

The other was an idea that arrived fully formed one day when I was watching him paint. He placed a single apple next to an old pewter coffee jug, and arranged them under the window in his studio on an old table cloth. He sketched the shapes on to a painted board, as was his habit, and stood poised, brush in hand, ready to make the first stroke. Just as he began to paint, a shaft of sunlight broke through the uniform cloud and speared the little arrangement on the table. I watched him work, fiercely concentrated, as colour built up form and defined shape. But at the same time it did more. The colours seemed to take on the quality of light itself, so that instead of highlight and shadow expressing the solidity of a shape, they were expressions of light itself. It was crude, it didn't come off and he knew that, but he was possessed by the need to explore this world of light and colour and make something come of it. Make something come of nothing. The sun went in. The shaft of light receded. Peter looked at what he had done, absentmindedly scraped it off the board, and began to paint as I had taught him.

I thought then: I have never seen anyone who learns so fast, but at the same time cares so little.

'Where's my jacket?'
  'Which jacket?'
'And my waistcoat?'
  'Which waistcoat?'
'My best jacket and my best waistcoat.'
  'Maybe you sent them to the laundry.'
'I need them.'
  'I'll go and ask.'
There were drawbacks to not having Mrs Tully in the place.

People had accepted easily enough that she and Giles had left – after all, what could be keeping them in Bermondsey? More people asked after the 'red-haired girl'. I said she had gone away but would be back and this seemed to satisfy them. That her disappearance coincided with the arrival of a pale, crop-headed boy excited no comment, as far as I could see.

I looked at him. He blushed. 'I'm sorry,' he said. 'I forgot that you wanted them. What are they for, anyway?'

'Fanny Morant is coming to see us.'
'Giles's girl?'
'Woman. Lady. Fiancée.'
'What do I do?'

354

'Stay hidden – no, I mentioned you in the letter. Better show yourself once, briefly. Don't hang around.'

I was annoyed with myself for what seemed like needless bravado. My intention had been to remind Giles of where he had come from, but at the same time I had given a hostage to fortune, and fortune does not lightly release her prizes. Fanny had suggested a meeting at the house and I had to agree to it.

I waited for Peter to come back with my clothes. For some absurd reason I wanted to impress Fanny. When he didn't return, and the time she was expected drew closer, I dressed in my painter's smock and waited. A filthy painter's smock was more respectable than a not very respectable jacket.

Fanny arrived.

She had changed since our previous encounters. There she had been reserved, quite tart but basically approachable. This time she swept into the hallway, brushing me with her crinoline, and preceded me up the stairs.

Her face, when she turned to me in the living room, was white and pinched around the mouth and nose.

I stammered out a greeting. She looked at me scornfully. I was unprepared for this. Outside I could see a carriage in the street. It surprised me, I cannot say why, but I realised it was a sign of status, a signal that for the time being at least, she was asserting her superiority.

The interview was awful. She said she had never read so low, so base an attempt at insinuation; that Giles had told her I had attempted to debase him; that the pressure I had put him under due to my corrupt behaviour had finally driven him from his own home, and she assumed I had summoned her in order to try and poison her against the man she was going to marry. This she considered, regardless of what I was going to say, a sin blacker than any I had previously committed. As for what I had done to Georgina – it went beyond mere sinfulness. She had suffered a breakdown. Ovariomania had been diagnosed and the offending organs removed. She had then been taken to the seaside to recover, but showed no signs of improvement. If anything, her condition, which presented itself as an obsession with the picture *Pandora's Box*, had worsened.

They say that the best form of defence is attack but attack takes preparation. I tried to buy time.

'You accuse me of a great deal,' I said. 'At least tell me what it is that has turned you against me? I cannot believe that my innocent letter, written with both your own and Giles's interests at heart, could excite this frenzy in you.'

'Frenzy?' Normally she had a sallow skin. Now it flushed. No, blazed. 'Do not mistake rage for frenzy. Giles took you in. He took you in and offered you shelter. He offered you status; he gave you status. Where do you think you would be without him? Starving in the gutter! Which is where you rightly belong. I come to bring you terms. Giles will allow you to live in this house another month. After that you will leave.'

'Leave here?'

'Yes. You'll leave here. Can you really be surprised? My God, you are. He said you were mad. I did not think I would find such easy confirmation.'

'And what is it he accuses me of?'

'Do I have to spell it out? Not only that you lived under the same roof as your whore, but that you – offered her to him in an attempt to bind him to you forever.'

'Is that what I did?' I asked. 'And what of it, for heaven's sake? All London knew she lived here. You cannot honestly believe that two young gentlemen would not get up to tricks?'

'You are disgusting. I am not blind to what young men get up to. It is a failing of my sex that sometimes we rely on hiding from the truth to give us strength. It is a failing of yours that you believe its true nature needs hiding. I am not a woman such as that. I do not connive. I cannot. It is not in my nature. I can take the truth. I can accept it. I know that there are prostitutes in London and that they are poor helpless creatures for the most part, driven to satisfy the needs of men by poverty

356

and desperation. That is not the issue. Giles is no saint, but neither is he a devil. You, I think, are.'

'Did you show him my letter?' I asked.

'Of course.'

'And?'

There was a check, a moment's hesitation. 'What was his reaction?' I pressed.

'Something has been wrong ever since he left here. He has been a shadow. I have seen him depressed before but nothing like this. When I read him the letter, he cried. Just cried as if he did not have the strength to do anything else. After I insisted, he told me.'

'I see,' I said. I walked to the window, then turned back. 'And did he say how many times he had lain with the whore?' I asked. 'And did he tell you what he did to it?'

The first question breached the dyke; the sea punched through with the second like a mighty, irresistible force.

Fanny staggered.

Her breath started coming in shallow gasps, each seeming to negate the effect of the one before, so it seemed as if she were actually suffocating on air. Her eyes glowed, panicking behind their fluttering lids. I went to help her. She beat me off and fell. I looked at her, lying at my feet. It was a moment of great exultation for me, a single, irresponsible second of joy, and I knew that if anything had been to hand, I would have capped the moment by striking her, and would have loved striking her. I have read of a cult in India, worshippers of the goddess Kali, who hold that destruction is in itself an act of creation; indeed that creation and destruction are bound together and equally holy. I felt holiness rush through me like the beating of a great bat's wings. On the floor, Fanny Morant watched me like a sick cat. I think she had read my thoughts. It was enough until I had had time to plan.

I stepped away. Slowly her breathing returned to normal. She tried to rise but was still too weak. It was then that I heard the front door slam. I called to Peter.

He looked at me, and at the woman on the floor. His face was blank.

'Miss Morant has taken a turn,' I said. 'Be so good as to help her to her feet, then walk her down the stairs and into her carriage. Peter is my new servant,' I added, but she was in no position to refuse. In fact, I think she would have taken help from a leper to get away from me.

Peter stooped and raised her gently, an arm across her back, the other under her elbow. He did it in a practised way, as if helping a drunk from the brothel floor, and walked her to the door. She glanced up at him and frowned but there was no sign of recognition. Just a question.

I said to her: 'All is not as it seems.'

It didn't seem a bad way to part. She merely closed her eyes in exhaustion.

54

'Are we going to leave?' Peter asked me the next day. After Fanny's visit I had prowled through the house. In Giles's and Mrs Tully's absence it had degenerated. The dining-room table was scattered with dirty plates and dishes. There were empty bottles, half full bottles, bottles with cigars stuffed in the neck. There were ring marks on the French polish. In the drawing room the windows were grimy. Cold ash heaped in the grate spilled over on to the hearth. Chairs were pulled at odd angles; the carpets were rucked; the boards dull.

'Are we going to leave?' Peter repeated.

We cleaned the house; it didn't take long to make it homely and the work was satisfying, awakening an odd sort of nostalgia in me, for it felt as if I were making a home again, when of course I had never made one in the first place. A cuckoo might feel like this, I thought, but cuckoos always sound so lonely. I lit a fire.

'We'll stay,' I said.

We ate simply off cold meats and bread and drank wine from clean glasses. We sat on either side of the fire, in silence.

'What do we do now?' asked Peter.

'How are your letters?' I asked.

'Bad. Still bad.'

'It doesn't matter. Does Giles know you can't read?'

'He never asked.'

'You are going to write him a letter,' I said.

'I can't.'

'We'll take our time over it. You can copy, can't you? I'll write, you'll copy down the shapes of the letters.'

'What will it say?'

'It will ask him to meet you. That's all.'

'Suppose he refuses?'

'He can't.'

'Why?'

'Because you are going to show yourself to him as a boy. He won't be able to resist. And you are going to meet him somewhere very private and it is all going to be your idea.'

He looked at the fire. It had burned down undisturbed and a coating of white ash had formed on the dome of glowing embers.

Something occurred to me.

'Why did you ask whether we were going to leave or not?'

He paused. 'I heard you and Miss Morant talking.'

'I won't let them throw us out,' I said. 'Trust me.'

'Thank you,' he said, then added politely: 'I love you.'

Giles was not at his parents' house. I wrote to his mother at Wake Hall, posing as an old medical school friend, and asked for his address. I got a stiff letter back giving me the address of a small private hotel in Kensington, near Fanny's lodgings, but not too close, for decorum's sake. It made my job a great deal easier.

Posing once again as an old friend, I found out from the landlady that Giles's hours were irregular but he could generally be found in up until ten o'clock every morning. There was no guaranteeing when he would be in during the afternoon and evening, although he was generally back by eleven. She clearly did not want me calling that late, so I said that I would be sure to surprise him in the morning.

Anticipation sits in the stomach like a sleeping animal: it is there all the time like a presence, occasionally awakening and turning, creating the oddest fluttering sensations around the abdomen. It has a psychic effect as well. It blurs past and future.

360

I was aware only of the present. I had my goals, my aims, but I moved towards them like a bull's eye lantern in a London fog: a glimpse of clarity where the mist is burned away; beyond that, the void.

The letter Peter wrote, or copied, was short and to the point. It just said: 'Dear Mr Giles, I must see you. With deepest respect, yours, Pity.'

I thought it simple and affecting. Giles's rooms, I had ascertained, were on the first floor overlooking the street.

We arrived at the house at half-past nine in the morning and waited on the corner. I was wearing a long coat with its collar turned up, and a hat. Peter was wearing his simple brown dress and a woollen shawl over his head against the cold. With his rough, shaggy crop covered, I tried to convince myself he looked every inch the young girl again, but it was not true. I had noticed it before, but the dress allowed me to compare him properly to the Pity that once was. He no longer looked like a young girl, full of life. Now he looked like a young woman who had seen too much and lived too long. I remembered the first time I had seen him while I waited outside Giles's house in Crucifix Lane. I remembered the confident, calculated coquetry as he'd let loose that heavy fall of hair.

My heart contracted.

At that moment I saw movement in Giles's room. I kissed Peter tenderly on the forehead and sent him on his way. He had grown since he had last worn that skirt. His feet, crammed into tiny stained pumps, showed below the hem. They left dark, evanescent prints on the wet flags of the pavement.

He walked up the tiled steps to the front door and knocked. He clutched the letter in one hand and the black iron spear of the area railing in the other. When the door opened, he curtseyed, stammered something and held out the letter, then curtseyed again. The landlady looked curiously at him, frowned at the letter, and without looking up again, closed the door.

Peter crossed the road and stood with bowed head in full view of the house.

Behind the dark upstairs window I saw a quick gleam of white as a door at the back of the room opened. That would be the landlady delivering the letter to Giles.

I closed my eyes and watched him take the crudely lettered envelope. I heard his questions to the landlady, and her reply. *She said she was one of your charity patients. A funny-looking creature.* The landlady's face softening; Giles's blood beginning to ice. The door closing. The envelope ripping open. The words hitting him like blows. A sickening lurch in the stomach. He runs to the window.

Peter looked up at that moment from under his shawl, a lone, pathetic figure on the other side of the street.

Giles loomed in the window, hands pressed against the glass, face white and twisted.

Peter drew off the shawl and stood revealed for an instant, as what he always was: a simple, pale-faced creature with a narrow chin and great green eyes, dressed in clothes that did not quite fit.

Giles's face clenched.

I whistled.

Enough.

Peter covered his head and ran to me.

Behind us we heard the thin crack of glass under pressure.

I waited three days, then had Peter write again. I wrote the letters out in disguised block capitals. He stared at them.

'What's it say?' he asked.

'Never mind. It's pitifully brave,' I said. 'But it's also rather gracious. Advance, or seem to make any advances towards Giles, hint at any need for him, and he will run. Retreat and he'll follow. It's human nature.'

It was not writing, it was forgery, and I intended the pun to stick. The words were forged as wrought iron is forged, in the furnace of skill and effort. It was forged because it looked like writing but was not writing. After we had blotted it, and I had erased the faint pencil lines, Peter was grey with exhaustion.

He said he was sorry to have disturbed Giles. He just wanted to see him. He ran because he was scared of his own feelings. He was sorry. He had been weak. He would try and be strong. He would not bother Giles again. He was also well, and growing stronger, and thinking of making a new start in Australia or New Zealand or Canada where there were plenty of opportunities in the mining communities for work of any kind. Auguste left him alone, which was a mercy. He was hardly ever here and spent all hours locked in the studio, working.

I am yours, Pity.

That was how it ended.

We had to wait a week. When the letter came I hardly recognised the hand as Giles's, it was so weak. The letters were large and badly formed, so that he only had room for a half a dozen lines or so on each page.

Dear Pity,

This is the first day I have been well enough to write. Your first letter, my seeing you, your second letter, shocked me and I had to rest. I need to see you. There are such demons in me. I must have been mad, or was it that devil Coffey? I need to see you, if only to explain.

How could I have done such a thing? If I can atone, I will try in the best way possible. I must be honest. I have done a terrible wrong – to use and exploit someone as vulnerable as you and then leave you alone without proper care . . . It is too late to act now. The die is cast and my destiny decided.

I think I can see a way to providing you with a measure of security and have made conditional provision for you. If you want to meet, we can. Write to me and state a time and place.

I remain your friend,

Giles Bouverie

I looked at the second page. It ran from 'How could I have done such a thing?' An idea was growing in my head.

55

On either side of Blackfriars Bridge, deep bays are set into the parapet, each supplied with a wide stone bench, each bench supplied with a tramp or traveller, or family of tramps or travellers, huddled against the cold, hunched around mean fires burning on the flagstones, drinking, eating, shivering, staring at the river where the traffic never stops and lighters surge up and down on the tide and the moored barges roll and boom in the swell. The river makes no sound. All you hear is the noise of men and machines; the rhythmic thud of the steam crane's engine, the scream of the winch, the hoot of a whistle, a shout. Odd shouts. There is a rowing boat poised in the eddies that swirl around the bridge's piles; two men, one rowing, one peering into the wet blackness: *Whoa, here's one. Slowly, you bastard, slowly . . . and left and on! Now back – back, you bastard, and hand me that gaff. This is the one. Just gone in.*

Or the lookout on a steam tug, or a docker on the shore, or a drunk in an alley, or a madman on the foreshore, howling at the moon. Or all of them together.

'Why meet here?' Giles said. 'For God's sake, Pity. It's freezing.' He moved towards me along the bench.

I kept my face muffled. A wide scarf was pulled over my head and wrapped around my face so that only my eyes showed. I kept my voice hoarse.

'No, no. Keep your distance. I do not trust – I am frightened still.'

'What of?'

I looked at him. What was he feeling? Bafflement, guilt,

impatience? He made a chopping gesture with his hand, then rubbed his face.

'No need to say. I understand.'

'If you'd been through – '

'Yes, yes, I know. That's why I came. That's why I wrote.'

'I woke up. I felt the knife in my – '

'What do you want me to do?' He was desperate, suddenly.

'I don't know.' I shrugged. 'I can't say. I'm so frightened.'

'Is Coffey – ?'

'What?'

'Is he mistreating you in any way?'

'It was you performed the operation. It was you who ruined me.'

'And it was Coffey who ruined me! Don't you see? We have both been ruined by that man, we have both been emasculated by him. And my sister . . . my poor, poor sister. But he can't see it. He can't even *see* it. The last time he talked to me, he was saying that you were the one we had to watch.'

Was now the time? I thought. I touched my hair, so thick, so long: so miraculously long and heavy. I felt my body, thin and tight within the·frock. It was like living in a tube, pressing in on the ribs and abdomen but leaving me free below. I hugged the cloak around me. Layers like this could keep the cold out. And layers of lies. In the next bay, a child looked across at me. Its parents were drinking and singing. Across the road a pitiful family of country people, wrapped in hessian, were propped like sacks of grain against the parapet.

'I suppose so,' I said. 'Only it hurt so much.'

'Did it heal properly?' Giles sounded almost eager.

'Yes, Mr Surgeon. I should be grateful for small mercies, eh?'

'That didn't sound like you.'

'What?'

'You sounded for a minute like – you're spending too much time with him.'

'Probably.'

'But it's good to see you.'

'We see what we want to see.'

He smiled wistfully, then said in a more businesslike manner: 'So. What do you want from me? Are you laughing? I used to love to hear you laugh. God, it's cold.'

'You know, I thought I just wanted to see you again, and maybe have the promise of seeing you some time after that. Now, I don't know.'

'Don't know what?' Giles sounded – how did he sound? Tickled? Flattered? Men!

'I don't know if that is all I want.'

Giles's next question sounded guarded. 'What else?'

'I want you to want to see me.' When Giles didn't answer, I went on. 'I know that it's not something I can insist on. I know that it's wrong and silly, and I know that I probably shouldn't say it. But I can't help it! It's what I want.'

He said: 'I wish you had said anything but that.'

'Why?'

He looked out over the wide river, then up at the sky where a sickle moon was slicing free of a silver cloud.

'God, it's cold. Auguste was always saying he was cold.'

'Can I ask you a question?'

Giles nodded.

'What did you ever see in him?'

Giles shrugged. 'I can't say. When I'm feeling melodramatic, I think I saw in him my destiny, my doom, something like that. If I hadn't embraced him, it would have been like running away.'

'But was there anything you liked?'

'I liked his – he was such a dirty little thing, and yet so cocksure. That was the first thing I thought. He was very pretty, of course, and cleaned up I expected to see him blossom into someone . . . Then I caught a sense of something else: that inside him there was something hard and precious that you couldn't touch. It was like a buried diamond. It wasn't that he wouldn't let you close to it; he didn't even know that was what

366

you let people do. But as soon as I sensed it, I wanted it. Then there was his talent. That was exciting. And the fact that he never seemed to know what he was doing, or grasp the implications. He was like a terrible, monstrous child. Children have an uncomfortable habit of telling the truth at times. Auguste could tell the truth, see the essential nature of anyone other than himself. I think he's as big a mystery to himself as he is to everyone else. Perhaps – no.'

'Go on.'

'Perhaps I was waiting for someone to come and find out the truth about me. My life was ruined, you see. All my patients had died. Someone, a ruffian, was blackmailing me – quite respectfully, as it happened. Perhaps I thought that if I were not to be discovered as a genius, then I might be discovered as a criminal and a fool.'

'And what did you see in me?' I said.

'I don't know what I see in you.'

'Do you want me?'

'Yes.'

'Where will I live?' I asked.

Giles swallowed. 'Get rid of Coffey and you can have the house in Crucifix Lane.'

'That's the provision you have made?'

'That's the provision I have made. Will make. A place for you. A clean place where you can paint and perhaps, if you ever forgive me, I can visit. Perhaps one day we will even laugh together.'

I coughed. It was a hoarse rasping sound. Giles reached across, a sentimental expression on his face.

'You really should let me listen to that chest of yours. It doesn't sound good.'

He first knew that something was wrong as soon as he grasped my wrist. He looked like a man who has absent-mindedly put on the wrong coat. At first he is simply confused because, for the time being at least, he is certain he has picked up the right coat, and has shrugged it over his shoulders and run his fingers down the front looking for the buttons. Then he is aware of nothing except perhaps a certain feeling of discomfort. I should be feeling this way, wrapped up in my nice warm coat. Instead I feel that way, as if something subtly alien has touched me.

Giles looked puzzled. He stared rather dully at his hand, then raised his eyes to mine. He saw the truth in them and mouthed, rather than said: Oh, no.

He rose. He staggered back and banged the back of his knees on the stone bench. He continued to back away, climbing on to the bench, his hand on the parapet. Once on the bench, he climbed on to the parapet. Once on the parapet, he fell backwards. There was only a small splash; the tide was just coming in and the water only a few inches deep. Giles fell head first and broke his neck when he hit the mud, but by the time the rowers found him, the tide had come up and he was beginning to float.

I returned home, closed the front door carefully behind me. The silence of the house engulfed me like ice. Then I realised that the unnatural silence was due in part to the extraordinary weight of the hair covering my ears.

I brushed it back, taking a hank and rubbing it between my fingers. I pulled it in front of my nose, and inhaled deeply. It smelled different: of powder, of strange people's fingers. The thought both excited and disgusted me. I walked upstairs, lifting the skirt carefully above my ankles, feeling my shins brush against the cotton. In the bedroom I lit two candles and placed them in holders on either side of the full-length mirror. I tilted my head to one side and smiled.

Reaching behind me to unhook the fastenings was difficult and my fingers felt fat and awkward, but I persevered because I wanted to be able to slip the dress down; lifting it over my head would disturb the hair.

I succeeded at last, and wriggled my shoulders free. The dress fell. The shift underneath it suddenly felt very thin. I rubbed my hand across my breast, then between my legs. I wriggled myself free from the shift.

Standing there naked, the hair falling front and back, reaching almost to my groin, I was overcome by my beauty almost to the point of fainting. When I moved my head, I felt my hair brush my body, connecting with every part of it. That my hair was disconnected was a source of concern, and I tried to devise a way to make the artificiality exciting.

I failed.

I wanted that hair. I wanted it to be mine. The feeling was like a flame creeping over a lamp wick, faint at first, then harder, brighter, lighter. It flared. It illuminated. It simplified. While it burned it obliterated all other thoughts and needs. Worldly success. Art. Friendship. Power. All were consumed by this new desire.

I began to feel sexually aroused by the wanting.

Behind me a voice asked: 'What do you really want?'

I looked deeper into the mirror, into the dark light behind the glass. I saw a figure, slight but trim. He was smartly dressed, wearing my fine waistcoat and best jacket. The darkness of the back of the glass was in him; he was a thing of darkness and candlelight. It was me, but not me. I was Pity, and therefore could not be me.

Suddenly I began to feel very frightened.

'What do you really want?' the voice asked.

'I want to be Pity.'

'Why?'

'Because Giles has made provision for her. She will be safe. She'll be able to live here.'

Silence again. I heard myself swallow. Was it really that simple? Did it really come down just to that?

The figure in the glass was both me, and not me. The figure in the room – the not-me in the glass – was both me, and not me. I suddenly became aware of the danger I was in. In neither place did I have an identity. I was two halves in two different places, the one negating the other.

I panicked and struck out. The glass fell and broke, and the figure in it disappeared. I tore the wig off my head and threw it on the ground. Sobbing and ashamed, I went to bed.

56

Giles's death was reported in the papers. His wealth, his grieving parents, the nocturnal rendezvous on Blackfriars Bridge, the first-hand account by the bankrupt smallholder from Kent, gave the story a stature lacking in your common or garden tale of watery doom.

According to the evidence, the mystery girl whom Giles met had no weapon and never touched him. All she did was pull the scarf from around her face and smile, and that seemed enough to send the gentleman over the edge.

It was noted that Giles had shown generous patronage to the young and prodigiously talented Auguste Coffey. (Examples of his work were presently held by Mr Gruber of the German Gallery in Bond Street.) When interviewed, Mr Coffey said that he believed that Mr Bouverie had committed suicide, but this was a personal matter, and unless the police thought the facts germane to the public interest, the contents of a letter he had in his possession would remain a secret between the police, him and Miss Frances Morant of Holland Park, West London.

The letter was the one he had sent Pity. I had it in my possession, although I had destroyed its first page.

'I am still not sure what it was that Giles did to this creature.'

Fanny had arrived at Crucifix Lane, unannounced. I still couldn't paint and was glad of the chance to talk. She said she wanted the truth. She looked old; I looked embarrassed.

'There was evidence of a growing feeling between – I mean, demonstrated by Giles towards the young person. I blame myself,' I said. 'If I hadn't been so wrapped up in work, if I had kept my eyes open, this whole tragic episode might never have taken place. It is not as if there weren't warning enough yet . . . What I mean, Miss Morant, is that you should not blame the child for what was, after all, a role in which she had been brought up. I attempted to elevate her. Perhaps it was arrogance on my part to suppose that I'd succeeded. So that when she and Giles found themselves together, it – '

'She slept here?' Fanny asked sharply.

'In the servants' quarters,' I said. 'Overseen by the estimable Mrs Tully.'

'I see.'

'You see what?' I asked, precisely.

She acted as if I had slapped her. She turned on me, tears flashing in her dark eyes, her mouth a tight line.

She said in a small voice: 'At my last visit, I accused you, wrongly, of all manner of things, so it is no surprise that you feel aggrieved. But I beg you, put yourself in my position. I felt I was having to balance the word of a man whom I had known for many years, the man I was going to marry, against that of a near stranger. However bad my behaviour, can you blame me utterly for behaving in such a way?'

I lowered my head contritely. 'I cannot,' I said. 'My own behaviour was excessive. I was surprised at how hurt I was by your coldness to me. Your good opinion of me was, and is, a precious thing.'

She blushed. I noticed a smear of dirt on her forehead where she must have brushed it with her glove. It was that kind of weather; the city was wrapped in fog made up of one part dirt to one part wet to one part cold.

'Now I reconsider, as I have to reconsider, all I can see is your loyalty to Giles. That prevented you from describing his full depravity, but you had the courage to try and warn me. That, considering your dependence on him, was estimable. I take it very kindly.'

I bowed.

'But there is one other thing.'

'Yes?' I said.

'I would like to ... I feel I must ... see this creature. I realise that I have been judging her. That is something I will continue to do, however much my higher nature tries to stop me. But I am so weak, I hate her, and I feel guilty for hating her, but know that I cannot stop.'

'Why are you asking to see her then?'

'I am asking to see her so that I have at least something physical on which to focus my emotions. And perhaps, when I see her, my mind will be changed. It will be a relief.'

'Would you pity her?' I asked.

'If there is anything to pity, yes. One day I might. But first I must ask her.'

'Ask her what? You said you merely wanted to see her.'

She looked at me in some surprise. 'But I must ask what Giles did to her. He referred to it in his letter. I must hear.'

My head felt crowded. 'But surely ... how can ... It is hardly delicate.'

'Women have a capacity for honesty that no man can know,' Fanny said.

'And courage too,' I answered with a stilted bow. 'I will find ... her.'

He was in his room at the back of the house, looking down at the shuttered windows of the hall. He was sitting very still, legs together at the knees, his hands cradled in his lap. As I entered he rose. I often found him like this, withdrawn into himself, eyes as dull as scoured glass. I think in his mind he was back in the brothel.

I explained that Fanny was here and wanted to see him. He looked unsurprised.

'What do you want me to do?'

'Look brave and pathetic,' I said. I scrutinised him. He looked too solid. 'Wear the blue velvet. And the wig.'

'And do what?'

'I want her to be in no doubt that you are a boy. I want her to be disgusted with Giles and full of pity for you. Not pity,' I added hastily. 'Guilt will do. Go. Quick.'

I went back to Fanny. After a pause, the door opened and Peter walked in. He was dressed in blue velvet, the wig tied back in a plait as thick as my arm. Fanny drew in her breath sharply. Not in disgust, nor disapproval. Something quite other.

She bowed her head. Pity made an awkward curtsey.

'Well, young lady,' Fanny said. 'You may know who I am?'

'Yes.'

'It seems my fiancé did you some wrong.'

'Yes, he did.'

'It seems the lot of the fairer sex is to suffer at the hands of the stronger. You have my sympathies.' Her eyes suddenly softened. 'What did he do to you, my dear? Tell me.'

'Are you prepared?' I asked.

'Yes.'

Pity's dress was fastened at the back by a few hooks. I walked behind her and unfastened them. Pity stepped out of the dress.

Fanny blinked.

She looked at me in surprise. Pity was dressed in a man's undergarments.

'Show her.'

Pity took off her wig.

Fanny's eyes strayed from face to breast, and then, helplessly, to crotch.

Her mouth opened and closed. Each time she started to say something she was stopped by a contrary impulse, as if faced with such a contradiction, she could not find the words to express her emotions. And yet, wonderful to behold, I saw her gather herself, and as she did an expression crossed her face that was close to comprehension.

'This is a boy,' she said eventually. One of her hands strayed upwards to her neck and touched the vulnerable triangle at the base of her throat.

'Yes,' I said. 'I myself only learned when Giles – '

'He had – relations with – '

'Yes,' I said. 'I am sorry. And he would have seduced me with – '

'Enough. I do not want to know any more. This then is the thing that Giles wanted to make provision for?'

'Yes,' I said.

'What utter, damned vileness,' she said. 'No, no. I cannot say that. My mind has been . . . tossed, hither and thither. For as long as I knew Giles, I have sensed – I am, I hope, a woman of the world. Not for me the vacillations of my sex. At all times I have been prepared to face the truth, however impalatable that truth might be. I thought you,' she turned to me, 'were to be the one. I misunderstood the situation. I tried to talk, to find a language that would somehow express the inexpressible. I am putting this badly. There are marriages, you see, where for the sake of respectability, an accommodation – yes, that is the word, an accommodation – that is mutually satisfactory can be reached. I thought that he and I and whoever else, might find a way. Now I have seen, I must go.'

'Wait.'

Peter's voice was pleading.

Fanny swallowed, looked at me and said: 'There is only so much I can take. Unuttered, these truths can be borne. I find that confronted by them, my strength – '

Her arms were suddenly as rigid as pistons. Grief and revulsion made her face unfamiliar.

I looked at Peter and jerked my head at the door.

'That's enough, boy,' I said.

'It isn't,' he said.

'Get out.'

'No.'

I raised my arm to cuff him; Fanny flinched.

'Look,' Peter said. Before I realised what he was doing he had slipped off his underwear and stepped out of it in a quick movement.

Fanny's eyes rolled to the ceiling. She looked as if she were being martyred.

Peter said: 'Look. You'll understand. There's nothing to fear.'

'Don't,' I said. 'There's no need.' I gabbled. I sounded frightened more than worried. I should have held my tongue.

Fanny stole a glance at Peter's groin. Looked away, looked back. Every move I made came too late. I grabbed Peter by the arm.

'Leave him . . .' Fanny's voice trailed away, wonder finally swamping her disgust.

Peter had managed to force tears into his eye. His flesh tightened into goosebumps; his hands hovered indecisively over the blank terrain of his sex. He looked like an awkward, obscene doll.

'How?' Fanny asked. Her eyes were glistening now.

'They cut me,' Peter said simply.

'Who?' She darted a look at me. 'Who?'

I spoke on a note of defeat. 'It was Giles,' I said. 'And Mrs Tully. I'd hoped I might spare you this. But perhaps you see now why I feel there is a debt to be paid to the poor creature? It's all right, child, you can get dressed now. You have done enough.'

57

As I walked down the street I felt a gentle breeze play on my face. The bodice held my back erect, pinching the skin at my waist slightly, but it was a discomfort I was happy to bear. I held my chin high; I had to, the collar, slightly too tight, stopped me from lowering it. My eyes behind the veil were bold, I felt, and the looks men gave me were admiring. Under the hat, my hair was secure. I had spent long hours the night before brushing it, plaiting it into a thick, writhing coil which I then twisted around itself and pinned in place. I had held it; it felt very entire, very dense, quite unlike a disguise. It was rather an extension of the self that one could take off and take on at will. I think that was why I had plaited it. I wanted it compressed. When I had been with Pity, I had had no desire to dress like her; now she was gone, I felt nostalgia for that time. In dressing like her, in being her, I felt the pang both sharpen in intensity even as it diminished in scale. It had come to a point. I was the point. I had reclaimed her. In me she was reborn.

I left the narrow confines of Crucifix Lane, passed the abattoirs, picked my way daintily through puddles of blood (my skirts hitched up, my feet delicately arched), passed the hospital and dived into the bustle and life of Borough High Street.

The excitement I felt was manifold. There was the excitement of acting, of stepping outside myself. There was the excitement of knowing something that no one else in the world knew. There was the sense of danger, but I do not know if that was caused by the fear of discovery, or the threat lying behind the eyes of men as they looked me up and down. More than once I felt them willing me to meet their eyes so that they might have a chance to force an opening on me. There was the knowledge that I was in every sense the opposite of what other people thought. In short, they thought I was a woman; I knew that I was a man. This knowledge, clear-cut and decisive, gave me a very distinct sense of superiority.

Perhaps there was something else. I have heard said that an electrical current can be generated when a field of magnetism crosses another field. This I understand almost intuitively. I see huge flat planes of colour, like sheets of stained glass, floating dangerously through the air. Where one crosses another, there is a spark, a melding, a forcing, an almost audible crackle as a new colour, the progeny of that chance meeting, is created. In taking on Pity's character, and passing from the sphere of man to the sphere of woman, I have created an electric tingle in my body. As I walk I feel the brush of petticoats on my sex, and feel the charge rise.

I saw a fancy bakery, one where we had kept an account, and seeing a particularly tempting pastry in the window, decided to enter the shop to see what their reaction would be. It was foolhardy – as soon as my foot crossed the threshold I recognised it as such. In the street, even if I excited interest in someone, what could they do?

But in a shop . . . I could not allow the smallest matter to go even slightly wrong. Either I was a woman, or I was a man dressed as a woman, trying to buy a tart at eleven of the morning in the centre of London. It would make the newspapers; I would be disgraced. I was about to retreat but the bell on the spring above the door clanged and the fat man behind the counter raised his head.

He said: 'Hallo, miss. Haven't seen you for too long.'

He was small, round, with a ridiculous moustache and waxy cheeks as pink as dyed icing. His manner was affable but just a little bit too sweet for my liking. I had never seen him before;

there was no one else in the shop. My heart started to thump. He was talking to me as if I were Pity.

'Been away, have you?'

'Yes.' I had spoken too deeply. I hid it in a cough. 'Back now, though.' I tried to imitate the delicate intimacy of Pity's husky voice.

'Lovely.' He really wasn't that interested. 'And what can I do for you? Another one of them?'

He gestured at the tray I had noticed in the window. That surprised me, as did the comment: another one. But I let it pass, thinking he had made a mistake. Then, as he reached over, his thick waist threatening to snap the thin apron string, the trousers straining against his vast buttocks, he half turned his head and said: 'Can't get enough of what he fancies, can he?'

I said: 'Who?'

'Come on, your bloke. Him indoors, my missis calls him, on account of never having seen him. But then I tell a lie, because of the fact of his being in here not three days ago to buy his favourite cakes.'

'That's impossible,' I said.

'Impossible?' The shopkeeper didn't like being contradicted by a girl. 'You telling me I'm blind, girl?'

No, I'm simply telling you that you're wrong. On account of him being me, I thought, and me knowing things like that.

'But he never shops,' I said.

'Oh, ho. Does he not? Mrs Prosser?' he called over his shoulder into the back of the shop. 'Does he not?' he repeated. There was something in his sly confidence that should have warned me to retreat, concede dutifully that he, as a shopkeeper, knew all there was to know about shopping, and I, as a girl, should yield before the pressure of his swelling, plump certainty. 'Never shops, eh? Ah, there you are, Mrs Prosser. The young lady, the young *model* from the Bouverie house in Crucifix Lane, claims that the gentleman of the house, the *painter*, never shops and never has shopped here. Is she right, Mrs Prosser?'

'When I say he never shops, I was simply surprised that he came in here because I thought he would have mentioned it.'

Why was I making an issue of this? It was simply a question of defending myself against further falsehood. I was ready to agree to anything to get away from these people when the woman said: 'Oh, yes, it was him all right.'

I pressed my forehead and said: 'Of course. Of course he was in here. He'd just finished one of his canvases and went out to get something special.'

'Doing all right, is he?'

'Oh, yes.'

The baker sniffed. 'He was a bit peakier than what I imagined.' My heart tripped, then quickened. 'What?' I said.

'Peakier. Thinner round the face. Of course, he was wearing a hat and was muffled – '

'How did you know him?' I asked.

'Why, he's very distinctive, what with that red waistcoat, and him being on the slight side for a gentleman.'

'What did he buy?' I asked.

'He bought half a dozen fancies.'

'That was all?'

I had spoken too harshly but needed to know.

'I think so,' the baker said stiffly. His wife looked at me closely. I could see her eyes straining to focus behind my veil, then she brushed her hands on her apron and moved off to the back of the shop. 'Of course,' I said weakly. 'Well, I'd best be off.'

'Haven't you forgotten something?'

'What? Have I?'

All of a sudden I was frightened again. I felt strength draining from me, sucked away by this dry vampire phantom self that visited shops and ate what I ate.

He held out his hand. 'Threepence-ha'penny,' he said. 'Dearie me, left our brain in bed this morning.'

I fumbled in my purse and brought out a sixpence. He gave me change, folding it in my hand and giving me a wink.

'Don't be a stranger now,' he said. The bell jangled fretfully. I looked at him from the street. He was wiping down the counter, his expression blank.

Out in the street the world was tilting and Borough High Street was sliding off the edge. My thoughts would not steady. For a few terrible seconds I had been Pity, and Auguste had been someone else. I was lost; the world behind me was trackless. I looked at the sky but it was throbbing white. Then I felt a hand under my elbow. It was a gentle, reassuring touch. It steadied me; the pavement felt solid beneath my feet, and that was a relief. The crowds on the busy street, the creak and grind of wheels, the clop of hooves, the cries of seagulls, the shouts of children, all felt good for a while until I looked at my helper.

It was myself.

Panic was like a vacuum. I looked at *me*; *me* regarded I with less charity. I sucked in air to try and fill the void but only filled my head with blackness. I tried to speak but was packed in black gauze. The world came at me dimly. I saw my back receding. My hand reached out to steady myself; I felt it squeak down the glass. I couldn't breathe; the tight tube of the costume held me in a vice. I collapsed.

The fit did not last for long. I never lost consciousness and so was able to brush away the hands, too many hands, that came down like birds, plucking at my throat to loosen the high-buttoned collar, to carry me back into the bakery. I lay on the floor. The private freedom of my legs in the wide skirt mocked the terrible constriction of my body. People kept on telling me to breathe but I could not, not properly. Someone fanned my face; I think it was the baker. Someone else waved smelling salts beneath my nose. The fantastic shock of ammonia opened my head so that the front of it was a roaring tunnel. I gasped a bit and turned away to get clear of it and my hair began to loosen and I grew terrified that my wig was going to work its way crooked, or someone would insist on getting a doctor.

I pushed myself to a sitting position. Expressions hardened. My pose, legs akimbo, arms straight out behind me, was disagreeably masculine. I tucked my legs under me and straightened my veil. The baker's wife brought me water.

Kneeling beside me, she put a supporting arm around my shoulders; I felt her flinch as she squeezed. My back was too broad. I thanked her and got to my feet on my own, looking clumsy and unladylike but reluctant now for her to feel my weight on her arm or become aware of the size of my hands, for even though I am small, still my extremities are large. I backed out of the shop, murmuring thanks. They watched me go as if I were something faintly disgusting.

I hurried home, down the High Street, through puddles of blood. My hair was loose and wild. A young man, respectable-looking, quite needlessly spat at my feet as I passed him. I felt tears coming. Once home I ran upstairs and threw myself into a chair in the drawing room. There Peter found me, hunched over a glass of brandy, ten minutes later. He took the wig off my head like a bishop removing a crown, and laid it on the sofa. Then he hit me across the side of the face, once, twice, three times.

His face was impassive.

'Why did you do that?' I managed to ask him through my tears.

'For reminding me what I had,' he said. 'For making me look like a fat drunken floozy in the street.'

'You followed me?'

'In everything you do,' he said.

He was still wearing my clothes.

'Stand up,' he said.

I stood.

He approached me and we stood, faces only inches apart. He lifted my skirt, hauling it up like a sail. His hand cupped my groin and felt me. I felt my penis swell out of his hand.

'Hold your skirt up,' he said. His voice was like cold oil. A terrible smile twisted the corners of his mouth.

He slipped his jacket off, and his braces, then let his trousers fall. He turned to the fireplace and gripped the mantelpiece with both hands. Looking at me in the mirror hung above it, he said: 'Do it.'

There, in the daylight, with my skirt rustling against the backs of my legs, sweat stiffening and drying on my bodice, I did the unmentionable act. Our eyes met in the dark silvered neverland behind the mirror. His smile never wavered. My loins unloosed me. I gave a helpless cry and fell to my knees and stayed there when he left.

58

He paints; I wait. I wait on him and for him, and more generally I just wait. What for I do not know, I just have this sense of imminence, the feeling that things must come to a head, and if they do not, I will force them. For the first time I live with emotion, a quiet, powerful sea that rocks me to nauseated insensibility. In moments of calmness I walk around the house in Crucifix Lane, as if I am saying goodbye to it. My leavetaking is oddly painless. I am a water-wet scab, ready to drop from the body, leaving only a small area of redness that in time will fade to nothing.

I am still waiting. There must be a conclusion to all this, but there are so many routes leading to a multiplicity of outcomes that I quail in the face of my potential to be wrong.

59

And then it happened one day that I saw a maid looking at house numbers stop at our door and knock.

I was moving when I heard footsteps on the back stairs. I stayed still until Peter opened the front door. I saw the maid put a note into his hand, and the door closed.

I waited, heard Peter on the back stairs, then moved up to the next floor and passed to the back of the house. When he returned to his studio I counted to ten then pushed my way in without knocking.

He held the note in his hand and was frowning at it, his face wrinkled in concentration and frustration. As I pushed into the room, his face lightened – almost the only thing he asked me to do for him these days was to help with his reading – but as quickly he composed it, and closed his fist over the note.

'Hello,' he said.

He could barely stop himself from wincing at the sight of me. He had worn this expression ever since he had seen me in the baker's shop.

'I heard the door,' I said. 'I was in the kitchen. You moved fast.'

'You moved slow. It was just a note from an artist's supplier. I was ordering something.'

'What are you working on?'

He stood back from the canvas. 'It's all right,' he said. 'You can look.'

I felt my face burn with shame. It was a self-portrait, or portrait, of Pity. It was painted in a modern, exaggerated style

– none of the fussy gloss of the new Academy, or the stark simplicities of the Pre-Raphaelites. The brush strokes were bold and energetic, the figure elongated and elegant, looking over her shoulder at the viewer, arm resting on a mantelpiece. Yet there was no languour in the pose; Pity looked at the world directly, openly, without fear, deference, or weight of history. The whites in her long dress glowed; the moulding of her features was daringly sketched in blue and green tones. The features were hers, or mine, or his. It didn't matter. Pity was a fiction, a creation, a work of art, and available for the world to enjoy.

'Very good,' I said shortly.

I was expecting a tart rejoinder from him; instead I saw him look at me with something like tenderness.

'It's for you,' he said. 'I want you to have it. I don't want you being Pity again.'

I hung my head. Tears started into my eyes. 'I missed her,' I said.

'She's gone. Come here,' he said.

I approached him. He embraced me. I sank my head on to his shoulder. The fire crackled. The paint dried. I saw the note on the table behind him where he had pushed it.

I put my mouth against Peter's and kissed him on the lips, pressing him back with my tongue. He retreated, backing to the table. I reached round, and behind, hugged him until his ribs began to creak, then reached down while he laughingly tried to push me back and unfolded the note.

It was from Fanny. She had news of great importance that she wanted to tell Peter, and also wanted him to meet some people who, she thought, might help him. But it was vital, she said, to come alone. She suggested a rendezvous in a respectable women's hotel in Pimlico, where we could talk in private, at three o'clock in two days' time. If she did not hear from Peter, she would go ahead as planned.

It would be beyond Peter to write. I replied in his name, saying that I was certain that Coffey had read the note and the chances were he would turn up at the rendezvous himself. Could we not meet at Crucifix Lane, at the same agreed time, by which time Coffey would be at the hotel in Pimlico? I added that she need not reply to the note, but I would be here, at three o'clock, on the day appointed.

60

On the day, Peter left the house at two o'clock, neatly dressed in his own clothes. I dressed as Pity and was brushing my hair when the bell rang and I ran down the stairs to greet them. My reasoning was this: it would be difficult enough to pass myself off as Pity to Fanny unless I had control of the situation. In a strange hotel room, following a stressful and potentially hazardous trip across London, the advantage would be hers, whether she knew it or not. Here, in my own home, I could be me, and could flow through the familiar space in a way I knew would impress them. I could make sure that the light was sufficiently muted and my dress properly arranged. But, most importantly, I could have my hair the way I wanted it. I knew that the trick of deception is not imitation, but flattery. In order to flatter the eye of the onlooker into seeing what it wants to, first you must give it something to look at. All morning, in the privacy of my room, I practised putting my hair up and letting it fall. I wanted them to see me in my glory.

The doorbell rang; I trotted downstairs. When Fanny saw me, her eyes widened. I touched my hair self-consciously.

She said: 'I hardly know how to – ' Then tucked her chin in and said determinedly: 'Mr Osgood, this is Pity, the young man I was talking about. Mr Brownlow.'

I turned away from them hurriedly and led the way upstairs. I had not been prepared for the two men. Osgood. The last time I had seen him – I stopped. No, of course, Pity had never seen him. Pity did not know who he was. I was Pity. I did not know who he was. On the other hand Brownlow had come to the studio and had admired my work at the expense of Coffey's, so I could acknowledge him.

I sat them on the opposite side of the room from me. They were in light – I had half opened the shutters on that side of the room. I sat in relative gloom. I could see Osgood sitting forward on his seat, straining to see me more clearly.

'Mr Osgood is a friend of Mr and Mrs Bouverie,' Fanny began.

I nodded.

'He has news that he had every reason to keep to himself, but now feels honour bound to divulge what he knows.'

I nodded.

'I am concerned,' he said, 'about your relationship with this man, Auguste Coffey.'

'In what sense?' I asked.

'He is an exploiter, an adventurer. He does not know his station, nor even the rules of station or status. Did you know that he made love to the sister of his benefactor, defiling the sanctity of the family seat, insulting the generosity of Mr and Mrs Bouverie, and quite overturning the rules of normal, decent human behaviour – to the extent that he caused Georgina Bouverie, his subject, to betray her family, or attempt to betray her family?'

'All Georgina's madness lay in her feelings for Coffey,' Fanny said. 'The cause of all this was Coffey, and it is him that we have come to talk to you about.'

She looked at me in a sisterly way.

'Frankly, my dear, we are worried. I have heard things . . . They worry me.'

I was sure she only spoke so warmly to me because Osgood was there.

'Why so?' I dared to speak.

'I have been making investigations into Auguste Coffey, into his past.' Now Brownlow spoke. After Fanny's rather harsh monotone and Osgood's twittering, his voice was forthright and manly. I orientated myself towards him accordingly.

'His past?' I asked.

'He lived for a while with a friend of mine, Paul Frederic.' I nodded. 'He told you?' Brownlow asked quickly.

'He did,' I said. 'He talked about him.'

'Warmly?'

'Nothing about that man is warm,' I replied.

'He treated Paul shamelessly. That is by the by. It was Paul's choice. What worries me is that Paul has since completely disappeared. His parents are distraught, I might add. It is not even as if he had nothing to fall back on if his artistic career did not flourish. He could easily have entered his father's business.'

'But many people disappear,' I said.

'Indeed. But not many like Paul. He was a conscientious man, thoughtful and kind. Listen, perhaps on its own this would not seem suspicious but there are other . . . events. Giles Bouverie is dead. There was a housekeeper here, a Mrs Tully. She has not been seen for a number of months.'

'There was a child too,' I said. 'A friend of mine. An orphan, deformed, little more than a freak but I loved and tended him. He too disappeared.'

'This man is a monster,' Fanny said. 'Your safety cannot be taken for granted.'

'And this is what you have come to tell me?' I asked.

'Yes, and to plead with you to share any information you have about this man with us and the police. If possible, we will have him arrested.'

'I see.'

'Do we have your support?' she asked.

'He has been good to me,' I said.

'He seems good to everyone, at first.'

'Very well,' I said. 'I do not promise to help, but I will hear you.'

'In the first place,' said Fanny, 'will you promise us that you will be careful? He will be returning soon.'

'Believe me,' I said, 'I will.'

'The law will help.' Brownlow again. 'If half, if a tenth, of what we suspect about Coffey is true, he will be put away, tried and hanged. Good riddance so far as I am concerned.'

I felt a cold worm move in my breast, near the base of my throat.

'I am not sure if that would be such a good idea,' I said.

'But whyever not?' Fanny's voice thrummed pleasantly with concern, but it was not towards her that I addressed my answer, but to Osgood.

'Scandal,' I said simply.

Osgood looked flustered. 'What do you mean?'

'Coffey's arrest would mean a trial, and a trial takes place in public.' I paused. Fanny said in a low voice to Brownlow, 'What did I tell you? The child is remarkable, whatever her, his . . . Whatever the details of the past.'

'Go on.' Osgood rose to his feet and began to pace the room.

'You forget how well I know Coffey. He is like a desperate animal seeking warmth. He will do anything. I know about desperation. I have seen the poor lay sackcloth on the offal of slaughtered beasts and lie there for the warmth. Coffey would do anything to preserve himself, even crawl inside another's skin.' I allowed myself a shudder. 'He ingratiated himself with Giles. He destroyed Paul Frederic. He tried to worm himself into the Bouverie family. Why, madam, I would be surprised if he had not reached out to you in some way. Tell me, have you at no time extended a warm hand to this man?'

Fanny blushed. 'I felt gratitude to him, it is true, when he told me . . . when he revealed to me something of the goings on in this house.'

'That is my point,' I said. 'He could do anything. He would do anything to survive. He destroyed your fiancé and then attempted to usurp the remnants of your warmth towards Giles. Given time he would have tried to fan those sparks to a glow, and then a fire.' I sighed. 'You would have kept him warm, I know it. I, even I, loved him.'

'Let me get this clear. You are saying that in a trial he might . . . what?' Brownlow looked intent.

'He would tell a tale of a poor orphan lad, cast out in the world, struggling to survive without patronage or support. He would tell how he was seduced by Giles Bouverie, a lazy, irresponsible, vain man who flew in the face of the finest medical minds of his day to try and prove his own disreputable theories. He would describe how Giles would stop at nothing to get his own way, even to the extent of trying to seduce this poor innocent by the foulest means imaginable: by taking him drunk one night to a brothel, introducing him not to a decent woman, or even a girl, but to a foul catamite whore, who tricked him into love. How Giles then brought this creature to the house to bind poor Auguste Coffey to him in the chains of blackmail. Coffey would then tell how he tried to lift this creature up from the depravity into which it had sunk, and how Giles, in a fit of jealous rage, did something so awful that I cannot bring myself to describe it.'

'We know what he did,' Brownlow said. 'He castrated the child. Miss Morant has told us.'

'No,' I said. 'You are wrong. He did not castrate the whore. If he had done so, I would be the eunuch but I am whole.' I started to cry.

'But I saw.' Fanny's voice was sharp. 'In this very room. He showed me.'

I cried still harder. 'You do not know what you saw,' I said.

'I saw with my own eyes, the poor child's . . .'

She stopped.

'Who am I?' I asked suddenly.

'The whore . . . Pity. . . whatever you're called.'

'And in the room that day, you saw Pity walk in, disrobe and show you his scar?'

'Yes.'

'That was not Pity. That was Auguste Coffey. He forced me to do it.'

'Ridiculous,' Fanny said.

'Hear the poor fellow out,' said Brownlow. 'Do what?'

'Pretend to be him. At the time he did not want you to know that Giles did not castrate Pity. Giles castrated Coffey. That afternoon he forced me to take his part.'

Three heads were facing me. I saw Fanny begin to register doubt, then lose confidence entirely, for at that moment the door opened. Auguste Coffey stood there. I had almost been expecting him. He looked at me calmly, raised an eyebrow, and smiled.

One by one the faces turned to him. Osgood narrowed his eyes. Coffey quickly walked to the darker part of the room and stood by me. I felt him like a force. Fanny closed her eyes. Brownlow stood, eyes flicking from Pity to Coffey and back again.

'If what you say is true,' he said, 'the man is Coffey and does not have his parts, and you are Pity the whore and have yours.'

It was Coffey who nodded. He said: 'But if what he said is true, I am the victim of a vile conspiracy between this whore and her dead master, Giles Bouverie.' His voice was as level as a plain of ice. 'I heard everything.'

'Justice,' Fanny said. 'What of justice?'

Brownlow worried a nail. He threw open the shutters and let the afternoon light flood into the room.

'We must decide between the evidence of our ears or the evidence of our eyes. Either everything we have just heard in this room is a lie or it is the truth.'

'Do we force them to strip?' Osgood asked.

I felt an arm descend on my shoulder. In the mirror, dark and silvered, I saw Pity and Coffey side by side, balanced by deception but alive to the infinite possibilities of truth.

'There is no truth left,' Pity said.

'Only what we see and how it is seen,' Coffey said.

'What would you have us do?' Fanny's voice was quiet and came from the other side of the glass.

'Only leave us,' we said. 'Leave us and we will survive together.'

'But what should we do?'

'Pity them,' Brownlow said hoarsely. 'Pity them.'

And we smiled. For the first time in my life, Pity was the last thing I wanted. They left. We embraced. Naked we became one, so that when we explored each other, we each explored ourself. And the contours of our skins became one co-joined landscape and the great game began in joy and in earnest.